THE *Story* WE WROTE

M. HARTLEY

Page & Vine
An Imprint of Meredith Wild LLC

Paperback ISBN: 978-1-964264-50-9

To all the people out there who needed
a cozy cowboy romance as bad as I did,
this one is for you!

CHAPTER 1

"I'm sorry, Aspen." Mrs. Wilder's slender hand rested gently on my shoulder. Her voice trembled, and tears glistened in her eyes before she brushed them away with a quick swipe. "You've done so much for us over the years. But it's time for Gus and me to move on, and closing up shop is the first step."

Her words hit me like a tidal wave, each one pulling me under. Memories flooded in, every shift, every late night, every ounce of blood, sweat, and tears I'd poured into this place. The Coffee Cup wasn't just a job. It was a piece of me.

"I know this is short notice," Gus added, stepping out from behind her. His voice carried the same soft regret. "But with the grandkids growing up, we want to set aside time and money for them. Selling is the best option for us."

I swallowed the lump forming in my throat. I'd been working at The Coffee Cup since I was fifteen. Back then, I'd dreamed that by twenty-five, I'd be the one to take over the shop, buy it from the Wilders, and send them off into a well-earned retirement. But here I was, paycheck to paycheck, with nothing close to the funds I'd need to make that happen.

"I get it. Family is important," I replied, voice tight. "But I have one question." I inhaled deeply, the comforting aroma of freshly brewed coffee filling my lungs. It wasn't just a job I was losing. The sale of the building meant my tiny apartment upstairs would go, too. "How long do I have before I need to move out?"

Gus and Mrs. Wilder exchanged a glance—one that spoke volumes. My stomach twisted.

"We were hoping you could be out by the end of the month," Gus said gently.

The end of the month. It was already the second week of May. That gave me just three weeks to pack up my life and figure out what was next. My savings, a small nest egg I'd worked hard to scrape together, would barely cover a month of expenses.

Panic bubbled up, threatening to spill over. Where would I go? Could I really move back in with my parents? How would I pack, find a place, and start over in just three weeks?

Tears stung my eyes, but they weren't from sadness. They were born of frustration, of anger. I'd poured my heart into making this business thrive, and now I was on my own. I understood their reasons, I truly did. But understanding didn't make it hurt any less.

I blinked back the tears, squared my shoulders, and forced a steady breath. Somehow, I'd figure this out. I had to.

AFTER DISCUSSING THE timeline with the Wilders, we decided I'd work through the next week, and then they'd officially close shop. The optimistic part of me tried to see this as a fresh start, a chance to go after what I'd always wanted. But uncertainty lingered, casting a shadow over my thoughts. The Coffee Cup was all I knew.

This cute, vintage café wasn't just a business; it was a cornerstone of the town. A space where people came to mingle, to relax, to feel at home. Every inch of it told a story. The mismatched furniture—tables, chairs, even the cozy couches—had all been gathered from locals. One wall was lined with rustic bookshelves stuffed with donated books, their worn spines creating an array of colors. Nothing matched, yet somehow it all fit together perfectly. Even the coffee cups were a collection of second-hand finds, each one unique and full of charm. That's what I loved most about this place: everything and everyone was welcome.

I started working here as a barista at fifteen. My grandma had mentioned to Mrs. Wilder that she had a granddaughter who loved books, coffee, and, let's face it, didn't have much of a social life. Mrs. Wilder must have thought I was a perfect fit because she hired me on the spot. After high school, I began managing the shop while the Wilders slowly stepped back. Fast-forward seven years, and now it was time for them to move on completely.

With a final wipe of the counter, I headed to the door, flipping the sign from "Closed" to "Open." I paused, gazing out at the quiet town coming to life.

It was seven a.m., and the streets were just starting to stir. Locals were jogging, walking their dogs, or heading to work. The stone-paved streets were lined with red oak trees, their branches forming a canopy over the sidewalks. Tall, black lampposts dotted the roads, and Faircloud Community Park—with its lush greenery and winding paths—ran alongside the main street in Faircloud.

This small town was everything to me. I'd stayed here, forgoing college, because Faircloud felt like home. It was safe, comforting, familiar. If there was one thing about me, it was that I didn't like to leave my comfy cozy.

And if I had to define comfy cozy, it would be a romance novel, a porch swing, and a glass of red wine. There was a kind of magic in a good book, the way it could transport you to another small town, introduce you to breathtaking romances, and make your heart ache in the best way. I wanted that. One day, I hoped to live my own small-town romance, the kind of love story so vivid and beautiful it deserved to be written down and shared.

I sighed, smoothing my floral-printed sundress and tucking a stray hair back into place as I caught my reflection in the glass door. Then I headed back to the counter. I'd finished all my morning prep before the Wilders came in and dropped their bombshell. Now I just needed an escape.

Sliding onto the wooden stool, I opened my book—a cowboy-inspired romance, the second in a series I'd fallen in love with. Meadowlark, Wyoming. If that place were real, I'd buy a ticket today and hop on the first flight.

THE MORNING FLEW by in a blur of friendly faces and bittersweet conversations. With each customer, I had to break the news about the shop's closing. Everyone had the same reaction—the town wouldn't be the same without The Coffee Cup. I kept my smile plastered on, even as the nagging knot of uncertainty tightened in my stomach.

I was pouring coffee for one of our regulars when the familiar chime of the doorbell rang.

"Welcome in! I'll be right with you!" I called, not looking up from the coffeepot. As I handed off the steaming mug, I wiped my hands on my apron and turned to greet the newcomer at the register.

"What can I get—" The words died on my lips as my gaze locked onto a pair of striking blue eyes. No, not just blue. They were green too, flecked with gold, and framed by a shadow cast from a khaki-colored cowboy hat.

Boone Cassidy.

He stood at the counter in a plain white T-shirt, light-wash Wrangler jeans, and well-worn cowboy boots—the epitome of rugged charm. Boone had a reputation that preceded him: a little wild, a little reckless, and every bit the life of the party. He had an energy that made every girl nervous, including me. And I'd be lying if I said he didn't make my heart race just standing there.

"In all the years I've lived in this town, I've barely stepped foot in here." Boone's voice was deep and laced with amusement as he took in the mismatched furniture and the handwritten menu board. When his eyes met mine again, they were full of mischief, and I melted. My brain turned to mush.

We'd never really spoken before. Sure, we went to the same

school, but our worlds couldn't have been more different. While I spent my time reading books and hanging out at the park with my two closest friends, Boone was throwing parties and causing chaos wherever he went. We were opposites in every way.

I opened my mouth to say something, anything, but the sound of a cup shattering behind me jolted me back to reality. Shaking my head, I gathered every ounce of composure I had, determined not to look like a total idiot.

"So, what brings you in today?" I asked, attempting what I hoped was a flirty smile. It probably came off awkward instead. They made it sound so effortless in romance novels.

"I had to come see what the fuss was about," Boone said with a crooked grin that could charm the paint right off the walls. News spread fast in a small town, nothing stayed secret for long.

"Well, now's as good a time as any," I replied, leaning casually against the counter. "Are you a coffee drinker? We've got the best coffee in town. Oh, and the blueberry muffins are baked fresh every morning."

Boone glanced up at the menu, giving me the perfect opportunity to take him in. His toned arms strained against the soft cotton of his T-shirt, and his light brown mustache, a perfect match for the messy hair beneath his cowboy hat, made my pulse quicken. I didn't know what it was, but I had a serious weakness for a good mustache.

"I'll take a coffee," he said after a moment, "extra cream, extra sugar. And one of those muffins."

He handed me a twenty, and as I reached to take it, our fingers brushed. His hands were calloused, worn from hard work, and my brain went rogue.

I bet he's good with his hands.

Aspen, stop! Get your mind out of the gutter.

My cheeks burned as I quickly made change. My hands trembled as I prepared his order, placing it neatly in a to-go bag.

"Here you go." I slid the bag across the counter with what I hoped was a confident smile. "Have a great day. I hope it's worth all the fuss."

Boone didn't take the bag right away. Instead, he lingered, his gaze fixed on me in a way that sent a shiver down my spine. Finally, he reached for the bag, tipping his hat in a slow, deliberate gesture.

"I think I'll be back, regardless." Boone's smirk deepened.

As he walked out, I watched him go, knowing in my heart that this wasn't the last I'd see of Boone Cassidy. And judging by the way he'd looked at me, I had a feeling he knew it too.

CHAPTER 2

Boone

Sweat trickled down my face as the Texas sun beat down relentlessly. Working a cattle ranch meant long, unpredictable days and backbreaking labor. I'd been raised on this land, watching my dad pour his heart and soul into running the family ranch.

As a kid, I admired his dedication and vowed to follow in his footsteps. Now, a couple of ranch hands and I tackled the physical work while Dad managed the paperwork and logistics. My younger sister, Ellie, had taken charge of our farm stand—a leap of faith that had started to pay off. She'd turned it into a thriving business, selling everything from fresh meats and eggs to wildflower bouquets she picked herself.

That was, until she decided to leave.

Ellie had announced at Sunday dinner a few weeks ago that she was traveling the world to "find herself" after her breakup with Buck, her longtime boyfriend. We were blindsided. Her decision came with more questions than answers.

"How long will you be gone?"

"I'm not sure."

"Are you sure this is what you want to do?"

"I don't know."

I loved my baby sister fiercely. Seeing her heartbroken over Buck made me want to kick his sorry ass all the way to the next county. At first, the farm stand wasn't even on my radar, I was more concerned about Ellie's well-being. But now, a few weeks later, the reality had sunk in. We were struggling to keep the stand open.

Mom was busy teaching school in town, and Dad already had his plate full. If I left the ranch work to oversee the stand, the ranch hands would slack off, and nothing would get done.

We were barely managing to open the stand a couple of times a week, and that wasn't sustainable. The momentum Ellie had built was slipping away, and so was the income. We needed a plan, fast.

Ellie and I had always been close. I'd taken my role as the protective older brother seriously, especially when we were kids. If someone messed with her, they'd have me waiting for them after school. That's why, when Buck stuck around despite my best efforts to scare him off, I grudgingly accepted him. He made Ellie happy, at least until he didn't.

Now, with Ellie halfway around the world and the farm stand in limbo, I'd finally come up with a solution. It involved The Coffee Cup and the blonde behind the counter.

Aspen Westgrove.

Even now, I couldn't get the image of her out of my head. Her bright blue eyes had a way of staring right into you, and her soft blond hair framed her face perfectly. I'd looked at plenty of women in my time, but looking at Aspen was something else entirely.

Growing up, I'd pretended not to notice her, but I always had. Her beaming smile, her sweet laugh, and those rosy pink cheeks made her impossible to ignore. She was gentle and kind, everything I wasn't as a teenager.

News about The Coffee Cup closing after decades of business had spread fast, and when I heard, I found myself walking into the café for the first time in years. The last time I'd been there was in high school, buying a latte to impress some girl. Coffee shops weren't really my thing. I was up before sunrise most days, long before any place like that opened.

But fate had other plans that day.

Aspen had grown into a stunning woman, her curves enough

to make any real man lose his damn mind. I couldn't take my eyes off her.

FOR A SMALL town, we stuck to our circles pretty well. From what I'd heard, Aspen had done an incredible job keeping The Coffee Cup alive and buzzing for the locals.

Four days had passed since I last saw her, and every day since, I'd made it a point to swing by the shop. Watching Aspen manage the place, effortlessly juggling customers and brewing coffee, was mesmerizing. She had this natural grace, and I couldn't help but think she'd be the perfect fit for Cassidy Ranch.

The stand had the potential to have decent traffic, especially on Saturdays when tourists came looking for "farm-fresh" goods. After tasting her blueberry muffins and that killer cup of coffee, the idea was cemented. I had to pitch it to my parents. Sure, part of me wanted her around for selfish reasons, but why couldn't it be both? Helping her and helping my family made perfect sense.

I pulled my shirt off over my head, using it to wipe away the lingering sweat as the sun dipped lower in the sky. My body was sore, but there was a satisfying rhythm to the work. Walking through the front door of the farmhouse where Ellie and I had grown up, I called out, "Ma!"

I made my way to the fridge, pouring myself a tall glass of water just as I heard my mom getting up from the couch. She appeared in the kitchen, Kindle in hand. Her long brown hair cascaded down her back—a look that hadn't changed much over the years.

"Where's Dad?" I asked after giving her a quick kiss on the cheek. "I've got something to talk to you both about."

She raised an eyebrow, suspicious. "He's in his office. What's going on? Is everything all right?"

"Everything's fine." I chuckled lightly, trying to keep the conversation casual. "It's about the farm stand. I think I've got an idea."

Taking her hand, I led her upstairs to my dad's office. Knocking lightly, I pushed the door open. My dad's office was every bit as rugged and practical as he was—dark wood everywhere, a solid desk, bookshelves, and a black leather couch that rarely saw use.

Dad sat in his high-backed chair, reading glasses perched on his nose, a stack of papers in front of him. His graying hair framed his sharp blue eyes, the same eyes I'd inherited.

"Dan," my mom said, turning to my dad with mock seriousness, "apparently our son has 'something to talk to us about.'" She added air quotes, a smirk tugging at her lips.

I laughed, though it sounded more like an exasperated sigh. "Ma—"

"Don't 'Ma' me," she cut in. "Every time you want to *talk*, it starts with an apology. Should I list examples?"

Before I could protest, Dad joined in, ticking off memories on his fingers. "The car you crashed, the old barn you set on fire, that time with the officer—"

"Okay, okay, I get it!" I interrupted, grinning despite myself. "But this is different. This is a good thing."

They exchanged a skeptical look, waiting.

"With Ellie gone, we need someone to run the stand. Someone who manages inventory, who can keep the store running like it deserves. And I think I know just the person."

I paused, letting the idea settle before continuing. "The girl from The Coffee Cup. Aspen Westgrove. She can bake one hell of a muffin and make a mean cup of coffee. With the shop closing, why don't we bring her here? Add some of that charm to the ranch."

I stopped, gauging their reactions.

Mom's eyes lit up first. "Aspen Westgrove," she said thoughtfully. "She's been at The Coffee Cup for years. It's a shame to see it close. That's a great idea, honey. Why don't you invite her over so we can talk? If she's interested, I'm sure we can make it work."

Dad nodded slowly, considering. “We’ll look at the finances and figure out what we can manage. It’s worth exploring. Thinking like a real businessman.”

Pride flickered in his eyes, and my chest swelled at the rare praise. I’d made my share of mistakes growing up, but I’d been working hard to prove I could handle the responsibility of running this place one day.

As I left the room, the plan felt more real than ever. Now, all I had to do was convince Aspen Westgrove to take a chance on Cassidy Ranch.

THE MOMENT MY parents gave me the green light, I couldn’t wait to pitch the idea to Aspen. Excitement had been building ever since I first thought of it, and now, with their blessing, I needed to see if the last piece of the puzzle would fall into place.

I pulled up to The Coffee Cup just minutes before closing. Throwing my Chevy into park, I jogged to the door.

Aspen was perched on a wooden stool behind the counter, her nose buried in a book. As I walked toward her, I forced myself to slow down. I must’ve looked a mess—dirty shirt, hole-ridden jeans, and boots still caked with a day’s worth of work. I hadn’t even bothered to shower or change; my excitement got the best of me.

“Boone?” Aspen’s voice broke through my thoughts. She looked up from her book, her brows furrowed in curiosity. Those blue eyes locked on mine, and just like that, I forgot how to breathe.

“We close in a few minutes,” she said apologetically. “I already turned off the coffeepot, and the muffins sold out hours ago.” Setting her book down, she added, “But I can check if I have something else for you.”

She started to head for the kitchen, the swinging door already half-open before I found my voice.

“Wait, no. I’m good. I don’t need anything.”

Her book was still on the counter, its colorful cover catching my eye. A cartoon couple adorned the front: a cowboy and a tattooed woman. Aspen noticed me staring and quickly swiped the book, pressing it to her chest.

"What do you want?" she asked, her cheeks turning pink. Realizing how that sounded, she flustered, "I mean, what brings you in? If it's not coffee or food?"

She was nervous, fidgeting with the book and avoiding eye contact. It was adorable.

"I have an opportunity for you," I said, trying to keep my tone even. "Just hear me out."

Aspen took a cautious step back toward the counter. Her short blond hair was curled perfectly, and the soft green sundress she wore hugged her curves in all the right places. She tilted her head, her skeptical gaze meeting mine.

"The Coffee Cup is closing down," I started. "Do you have something else lined up?"

Her hand went to her hip, drawing my attention to her hourglass figure. She leaned slightly, her posture both confident and cautious.

"If not," I continued, "I've got a job for you. My family has a farm stand at the ranch—well, my sister does. She's off traveling, and we need someone to take over. You'd be perfect. You know inventory, you're great with customers, and you bake the best damn muffins I've ever had."

I paused, letting her take it in. "If you're interested, you could come by tomorrow after you close up here and check it out."

Her wide eyes softened as she sat back on the stool, her shoulders sagging. She exhaled deeply, and for a moment, I swore I saw relief flicker across her face.

"Are you serious?" she asked, looking up at me.

I crossed my arms and smirked, towering over her. "Completely."

Aspen stood, pacing in short, quick steps. Her brows knit together as she worked through something in her mind. I gave her space to think, though the silence was almost too much to bear.

Finally, she stopped and whispered, "Okay."

"Okay?" I asked, unable to hide my grin. "Like *yes,* okay? Or *I-need-to-think-about-it* okay?"

She turned to me, her lips curling into a soft smile. "Yes, okay. I don't need to think about it. I haven't had any luck finding something else. The fact that you came here like a knight in shining armor feels like a sign."

"Do you need the address?" I teased, unable to resist.

She laughed, a sound so light and pretty it made my chest tighten. "Boone, your family owns the only cattle ranch in Faircloud. I think I can find it."

"Fair enough," I replied with a chuckle. "Tomorrow, after the shop closes. My mom's making dinner, so come hungry."

"I'll be there," she replied, her smile shy as she looked down, but not before I caught it.

Tipping my hat, I headed to the door. Once I was in my truck, I lingered just long enough to see her lock the door and flip the "Open" sign to "Closed." She glanced back, catching me watching, and I raised a hand in a small wave.

As I drove off, I couldn't help but grin. Tomorrow couldn't come soon enough.

CHAPTER 3

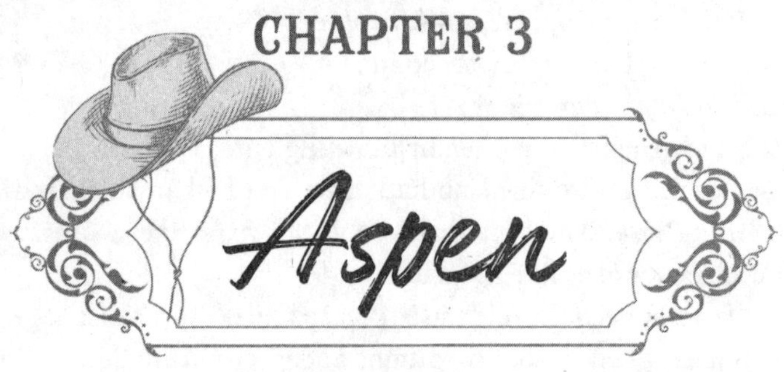

Closing the shop was my favorite way to unwind after a chaotic day. I didn't rush the cleaning or prep for the morning, it was all part of a ritual. I'd put on music, let the sound fill the empty space, and dance out the stress collected from the day. But tonight was different.

Tonight, I was meeting Boone and his parents at Cassidy Ranch to discuss a new job opportunity–one I knew shockingly little about. I hadn't asked a single question, which wasn't like me at all. Normally, I was the type to weigh my options and think everything through. But this? This felt like it came at just the right time.

When I found out The Coffee Cup was closing, I'd spent hours scrolling through job listings, trying to find something that felt right. Every option was either outdoors (a hard no) or involved cleaning elementary school bathrooms (absolutely not). Nothing clicked.

Then Boone walked in last night.

His offer caught me completely off guard, but the relief I felt when he mentioned the farm stand was almost euphoric. It was something I could see myself doing—baking, chatting with customers, managing a little shop. All the things I loved about my job at the coffee shop. Plus, maybe a freshers start could mean a fresh beginning.

That's why tonight felt... significant. It wasn't just about the job. It was a step toward something new, something that might shake me out of the rut I'd been in.

My ultimate dream was to be an author. Whether that meant writing full-time or juggling it alongside another job didn't matter much to me. The Coffee Cup had given me that freedom. But I'd been struggling to find my spark—my reason to sit down and pour my heart into words. My love life certainly wasn't helping.

So far, it had been a series of mediocre hookups and fizzling relationships. In a town like mine, dating options weren't exactly plentiful. I hadn't been with anyone for six months, mostly because the last guy was my breaking point. A night full of huffs and puffs, clumsy high school-level foreplay, and a grand finale that lasted all of thirty seconds. Sure, he was hot, but that only got him so far.

To me, romance should be electric. It should hit you in the chest, make your cheeks warm, and send your heart racing. It should be more than just physical, you should crave someone emotionally, too.

Instead of my usual end-of-day routine, I decided to leave the cleaning for *future* Aspen. It was Sunday, and the shop would be closed for the next two days. Wednesday-morning Aspen could play catch-up. Locking the door behind me, I headed down the side alley to my car. My old Jeep wasn't much, but it got me where I needed to go.

Cassidy Ranch was on the outskirts of town, a fifteen-minute drive from the shop. I figured I'd use the time to call Penny, my best friend and lifelong listener.

Penny and I had been inseparable since first grade. While other kids were playing on the monkey bars, we'd skip recess to sit inside and read in silence. Despite our mutual love of fashion and books, we were opposites in so many ways—me, the homebody who loved calm and quiet, and her, the fiery spark of energy that lit up every room.

Regardless of our differences, we balanced each other perfectly. She was the yin to my yang, the universe's hand-picked partner for my life. She was also my go-to whenever I needed to talk something through. Penny had been my cheerleader through thick and thin, always ready to remind me of my worth or stand up to anyone who doubted it.

As I dialed her number, I couldn't help but feel grateful. Whatever tonight brought, I knew Penny would help me make sense of it all.

Our other friend, Theo, short for Theodora, moved to Faircloud late in middle school. Where Penny and I loved dresses and everything light and airy, Theo was what I liked to call "punchy." She rocked overalls and cowboy boots, her split-dyed blonde-and-black hair always braided. Theo had this effortless presence and a no-shits-to-give attitude that made her magnetic. She channeled that carefree energy into her career as a professional photographer, traveling the world to capture stunning wildlife and landscapes. The three of us made the perfect trio: different pieces that fit together into the prettiest jigsaw puzzle.

On the second ring, Penny picked up. "Hello, my sweet girl! How have you been?"

I hadn't called her after the news about The Coffee Cup. I'd only sent a quick text saying I was okay and that I'd call in a few days. I needed time to figure things out on my own. I hadn't even called my parents, leaving their texts unanswered. My dad's "What's next, kiddo?" felt like a loaded question, and my mom's offer to move home wasn't something I wanted to consider. I loved my family, but personal space wasn't in their vocabulary, and their version of "acceptance" didn't exactly include my current life choices.

"I'm doing better. I had a mini existential crisis—you know, the kind where you question the meaning of life and wonder if Earth is real or if we're all in a simulation," I replied, trying to sound lighthearted. The truth was, I'd been drowning in anxiety: *I'll never climb out of this hole. I'll never be successful.* It's hard to fight back those thoughts, but Penny had a way of pulling me out of my spirals.

"Oh, Aspen," she muttered softly, her tone full of empathy. "This is just a bump, babe. You'll find something that works for you. The Coffee Cup wasn't the end."

She was right, of course. Even though it felt overwhelming now, I knew I'd get through it. I just needed to take the next step.

"I actually have a job interview, or maybe it's more like a job discussion, on my way there now," I said, finishing the sentence like a question. I wasn't even sure what to call it. Should I have brought a résumé? Did I have coffee on my dress? I glanced down to check for stains, momentarily taking my eyes off the road.

"Oh, good!" Penny's voice lit up with excitement. "Let's hear it. Where is it? What is it?"

"Well..." I hesitated, cringing a little at the confession. "Boone Cassidy came into the shop last night. He said they need someone to run the farm stand at the ranch."

"Oooh, I heard about Buck and Ellie. How awful for her. Buck's such a piece of work, cheating on her and then dumping her for the new chick after what, five years?"

Ellie was Boone's younger sister, and her breakup with Buck had been the talk of the town. They were high school sweethearts, everyone thought they'd last forever. But now she was off traveling, leaving the farm stand without anyone to manage it.

"Yeah, she's left Faircloud and no one knows when she's coming back. Honestly, it's the best option I've got right now. Unless I want to scrub toilets or do landscaping."

The more I thought about the job, the more excited I became. The idea of making the farm stand my own—bringing some of the locals from The Coffee Cup down to Cassidy Ranch and creating a cozy space—was starting to feel like the fresh start I needed.

"Why you, though?" Penny asked. "Not that you can't do it, because obviously you can, but it's not like you and Boone were ever friends. We actively avoided that guy in high school."

I laughed, she wasn't wrong. Boone had always been a little intimidating—chaotic in a way that made my quiet, careful personality nervous.

"I have no idea," I admitted, turning down the dirt road that led to the ranch. "He just showed up at The Coffee Cup yesterday, and next thing I know, I'm saying 'okay.'"

Rocks crunched under my tires filled the silence as I neared the turn-off.

"Keep me posted. And if he's shirtless when you get there, please take a picture and send it to me immediately. That man is *delicious*." Penny teased.

I rolled my eyes, but a grin tugged at my lips.

"Noted," I said, pulling into the driveway of Cassidy Ranch.

We promised to catch up later in the week, saying our farewells before the line went dead. Penny had started a new job as the librarian at Faircloud's public library, a role that suited her perfectly. Like me, she loved to plan, and her days were packed with organizing events and hunting for extra funding. With the annual town block party coming up at the end of summer, a big event for all the local businesses, Penny was working overtime, trying to secure sponsors to support the library and raise money.

As I drove, I took a deep breath, savoring the rare moment of silence and collecting my thoughts. "I got this," I muttered, inhaling the fresh country air. If I kept telling myself it was true, maybe it would be.

The long driveway to Cassidy Ranch stretched ahead, lined with sturdy brown wooden fences. To my left, rolling hills of lush pasture dotted with grazing cattle unfolded like a postcard. On my right, neat rows of farmland stretched into the distance, wheat, or maybe corn? Honestly, I couldn't tell. Farming wasn't exactly my forte, but I made a mental note to brush up on it later.

As I reached the end of the drive, the Cassidy house came into view, and I couldn't help but admire it. The two-story farmhouse exuded charm, with its wrap-around porch and rich, dark brown wood offset by sleek black metal accents. Rocking chairs flanked the front door, inviting anyone to sit and soak up the peace. Above them, flowerpots brimming with vibrant pink blooms hung gracefully from the porch overhang, adding a cheerful touch.

I parked my Jeep and stepped out, smoothing my pink sundress. Its capped sleeves and flowing skirt gave me a confidence boost I desperately needed. My short hair was half-up, held back with a scrunchie, and I told myself I looked put together enough for whatever lay ahead.

Movement to my left caught my eye, and I turned—completely unprepared for what I saw.

Boone was shirtless.

For the love of—well, everything.

The mid-May Texas sun was high, and his tanned skin gleamed with sweat, muscles taut and on full display. My stomach flipped as he wiped his brow with a crumpled shirt, his khaki cowboy hat perched lazily atop his head. The jeans slung low on his hips didn't help my already frazzled state.

If I could snap a picture of this for Penny, she'd lose her mind.

Get it together, Aspen. Eyes up. Not on his chest. Definitely not on his hips.

"Hey, Aspen!" Boone called out, waving his shirt like a flag. I managed a weak wave back, forcing a friendly smile.

"Come on in." He gestured toward the porch stairs. "Just finishing up feeding. Mom and Dad are inside."

I walked toward the porch, my legs trembling slightly. Boone followed, maybe a little too close for my nerves. I could feel the heat radiating from him, or was that just me blushing?

Just as I approached the door, he quickly side stepped around me to hold the door open. His shirtless chest nearly brushed against me as I stepped inside. "Ma! Dad! Aspen's here!" he hollered, letting the screen door slam shut behind him.

The inside of the house was as charming as the outside. Worn hardwood floors gleamed under the light streaming in through large windows. Family photos adorned white walls, and antique furniture gave the space a cozy, lived-in feel.

Boone led me into the kitchen, where his parents sat at the island.

"Hi, sweetie!" His mom greeted me warmly as she slid off her stool. She extended her hand, and I quickly wiped mine on my dress before shaking hers.

"Your house is lovely, Mrs. Cassidy." I was in awe as I glanced around the kitchen.

The space was stunning. Sage green cabinets paired with white marble countertops, and gold hardware added a touch of elegance. A beautiful backsplash tied everything together, it was my dream kitchen come to life.

"Oh please." She waved at me. "Call me Jill and this is Dan."

Dan, Boone's dad, stepped forward with a kind smile, shaking my hand next. "It's a shame about The Coffee Cup," he sighed sympathetically. "That place has been a part of the town forever, but I get it. Family comes first."

I nodded. "It's the right move for them. They've been kind enough to let me stay in the apartment above the shop until the end of the month. The doors close next week."

"I didn't realize you lived there," Jill said, ushering us toward the dining table. "Why don't we sit and talk about the stand? See if it's a good fit for you."

Boone detoured to wash his hands as Jill set the table. "Dinner's ready. Do you like meatloaf, Aspen?"

"Yes!" I replied, a little too enthusiastically, which made Jill laugh as she served up steaming plates.

We settled around the table—Boone to my left and his parents across from us. Out of the corner of my eye, I noticed Boone watching me, his gaze warm and steady. Since coming inside, he'd finally put his shirt back on. Blessing or curse? I hadn't decided.

"So, Aspen," Dan asked, leaning back in his chair with an easy smile. "What made you say yes to helping with the farm stand?"

I needed a job. I didn't want to end up homeless. I didn't want to clean up vomit. And outdoor labor? Not for me. I ran through all the reasons in my head before finally blurting out, "I love interacting with customers. I have an eye for detail, and I'm great at coming up with new ideas. Oh, and I'm really organized!"

I took a bite of the meatloaf, and it practically melted in my mouth. It was so delicious, so comforting. I had to bite my tongue to stop myself from moaning. The taste reminded me so much of my Mom-Mom's recipe. It was the closest I'd had to it since she passed away.

Jill smiled as she spoke. "We've got a vision for the store. We want to expand, bring in more locally sourced products. We heard from Boone that you make a mean blueberry muffin."

I shot Boone a quick glance. He was casually chewing, his mouth full. He shrugged.

"It's true." He glanced at me with a grin. "I don't even like blueberries, but that muffin was damn good."

I felt a spark between us when he locked his eyes on mine. The feeling mimicked that of touching a livewire, hot and immediate, as it spread down my spine. It was brief, but it was there.

"If you're willing, we'd love for you to bake your muffins and sell them at the stand," Jill continued. "We've got our own blueberry bushes you could use. Ellie built the business up really well, and we want to keep it going."

Jill did most of the talking, her voice calm and inviting. She was the heart of the family, warm and easy to talk to.

The idea of baking and selling at the stand made my heart race in a good way. It was exactly what I was looking for: small-town charm, steady foot traffic, and endless opportunities for growth. I could sell honey from locals, handmade crafts... there were so many possibilities.

"That sounds perfect." I took a sip of freshly squeezed lemonade to wash down my meatloaf.

"We'd be willing to pay you more than The Coffee Cup was," Boone's dad added, his voice low but kind. "We know this job will take more work and want to acknowledge that."

The raise was enough to cover rent for an apartment. I wasn't going to get the deal I had with the Wilders, but it was a step in the right direction.

Jill, who had been nodding, added, "We also want to offer you housing. No charge. The cabin's just sitting there, and it'll be easier than you having to drive in from town."

I nearly choked on my food. I started coughing, desperate for my drink to wash down the unexpected offer. Boone's eyes were on me as I tried to recover.

"Oh, that's... so generous," I sputtered, wiping my mouth with my napkin. "I don't know if I could take it for free." Was she reading my mind? They were practically solving all my problems.

"It's part of the job," Dan said, his voice steady. "We need the help. We've invested a lot in this place, and we're hoping to see a return. If we don't get something moving soon, we'll be in a pretty deep hole."

It was incredibly generous of them, almost too generous. I couldn't help wondering—why me? I didn't know these people, and yet they were trusting me to keep the farm stand running. Knowing how much they were depending on its success made everything feel more real, more meaningful.

We spent the next hour discussing the logistics: the day-to-day of running the stand, the products they currently offered, and their vision for the future. We even talked about me—my family, my goals, where I saw myself in the future.

By the time we finished, I felt more confident about my decision than ever. Jill's warm presence made me feel like I belonged, like I had a place here. Dan stayed quiet most of the time, chiming in only when it was about business, which I appreciated.

Throughout dinner, I kept catching Boone's gaze. Every time I looked his way, he was looking at me, not even trying to hide it. My stomach fluttered each time our eyes met. I wanted to bottle up this feeling, keep it with me forever.

After dinner, I offered to help with the dishes, but Jill insisted that Boone show me the store and the cabin. Deep down, I knew I was going to accept, but I needed to see it for myself.

We stepped outside, and the sight that greeted me took my breath away. The sun was dipping behind a mountain range, painting the sky with shades of orange and purple. It felt like a dream, like something straight out of a movie. The job, the housing, the view—it all seemed too perfect to be real.

I felt like I should pinch myself, just to make sure I wasn't dreaming.

CHAPTER 4

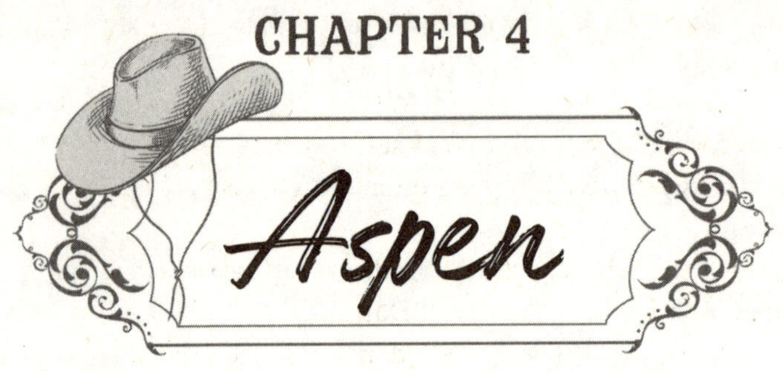

"Did you want to walk? Or we could go on horseback? Maybe take the ATV? I've got it all." Boone's smile was easy, his tone light, as we walked toward the barn. The barn loomed large ahead, its faded red paint peeling from years of weathering. Despite its wear, it stood proud.

"How far is the farmstand?" I asked, shading my eyes as I glanced over the pastures, hoping to catch a glimpse of our destination.

"It's out by the cabins, just off the main road. They've got a gravel driveway, so it's easier to ride an ATV from here."

I glanced down at my outfit, suddenly self-conscious. A dress wasn't exactly ATV-ready, though at least I'd had the sense to wear Converse instead of sandals. *Way to think ahead, Aspen.*

"The dress might be an issue, but..." I trailed off, unsure.

Boone's eyes slowly traveled the length of me, taking in every detail from the tousled strands of my hair to the scuffed toes of my shoes. His gaze was warm but thorough, and it sent a flutter through my chest. Self-conscious at his scrutiny, I tucked a loose strand of hair behind my ear.

I guess he approved of my outfit because he nodded before saying, "Hang tight. I'll back it out, and you can hop on."

He disappeared into the barn, and moments later, the roar of an engine echoed through the open doors. Boone maneuvered the

ATV out with practiced ease.

"Climb on the back. And make sure to hold on tight," he instructed with a teasing grin.

I hesitated for a second. Where was I supposed to *hold on tight*? Swinging one leg over, I settled onto the seat behind him, my hands awkwardly resting on my thighs as I waited for him to drive.

Boone glanced over his shoulder, his dark eyes locking onto mine. "Arms around my waist, Darling."

Darling. The word melted me instantly, sending warmth flooding through me. My cheeks flushed as my stomach fluttered. Heart racing, I slipped my arms around his waist, leaning closer.

"Like this?" I asked, my voice a soft murmur meant to carry over the engine. It came out lower, more intimate than I intended.

Boone's shoulders stiffened almost instantly under my touch. I could've sworn he shivered as I pressed closer.

"Yeah," he murmured, his voice barely audible over the engine. "Just like that."

Without another word, he set off, the ATV rumbling steadily beneath us. The sound left little room for conversation, which was fine, my thoughts were a swirl of sensations. The warmth of Boone's back pressed against me, the tautness of his muscles shifting with every turn, every bump. The clean, woodsy scent of him lingered in the air, mingling with the faint tang of sweat and something rugged and masculine, like teakwood.

By the time we arrived, I was almost disappointed to let go. But when I looked up, the farm stand stole my breath, and those intimate thoughts were replaced by awe.

It was charming in every way—a large shed-like structure with double doors, a small porch with an overhang to shield it from the rain. String lights hung like stars across the beams, casting a soft golden glow.

Boone swung off the ATV and turned back, offering his hand. "Come on."

I slid my hand into his, the rough texture of his calloused

fingers brushing against my softer palms. The contrast sent a spark of awareness through me.

"This is unbelievable," I whispered as I stepped closer, taking it all in.

The inside was simple but lovely—tables lined each wall, ready for goods, though most were empty for now. One was filled with buckets of wildflowers in every hue, practically begging to be arranged into bouquets. At the back stood a counter with a deli-style case, likely used to display meats and other fresh goods during market hours.

"Yes," I sighed without thinking. "I accept."

Boone's laughter filled the air. When I turned, he was leaning against the doorframe, arms crossed, a smirk playing on his lips. Faint crinkles at the corners of his eyes hinted at a genuine smile.

"You haven't even seen the cabin yet. What if it's infested with bugs? Or the roof's caved in?"

"I don't care." I smiled back. "I'll put up a tarp and call an exterminator."

Boone pushed off the frame and strode toward me, his hands stuffed casually in his pockets. He glanced around the stand, his expression softening, though a flicker of something, sadness maybe, crossed his face.

"Ellie did a great job, didn't she?" His voice was quieter now. "This was her dream. Her project."

"I'm sorry to hear about her and Buck." The words slipped out before I could stop them, bypassing my usually intact filter. It wasn't my place to comment on Boone's sister or her situation, much less bring it up unprompted.

"Yeah," Boone whispered, his voice heavy. "She hasn't been the same since. If she's willing to take a step back from all this, you know she's struggling." His eyes finally met mine, and a sad smile tugged at his lips. It lacked the easy warmth I'd seen before, the fine lines that crinkled when he smiled for real. "I know you'll take care of it. Make it into what she wanted for when, or if, she comes back."

"When?" I asked softly, my stomach twisting.

Boone didn't respond, and the air grew heavy between us. I needed to escape this tension, so I did what I always did in uncomfortable situations: I changed the subject from an awkward topic to something adjacent. "You seem pretty confident in me."

Boone let the silence linger for a moment before answering. "I watched you run that coffee shop like a pro."

I blinked, confused. He'd only been there once, for maybe five minutes. How could he know that?

Before I could voice my skepticism, Boone cut me off, his expression unreadable. "I went by every day after that first visit. I watched through the window. I knew you'd be perfect."

My mouth opened to respond, but Boone didn't give me the chance. He turned toward the door, gesturing for me to follow. "Come on. Let's check out your piece of paradise."

I glanced back at the charming farm stand one last time before following him outside.

We walked side by side to the cabins, a short distance from the stand. Boone hadn't been exaggerating when he called it my *piece of paradise*. Two cabins sat nestled among the trees, far enough apart to feel private but close enough to be considered neighbors. A gravel path led the way, winding between them like something out of a movie.

The cabin on the left showed signs of life—minimal decorations, a few personal touches, and a tidy flower bed. The one on the right was a different story. Its curtains were drawn, its porch dark, and weeds had overtaken the flower beds. But what caught my attention was the porch swing—hung invitingly, worn just enough to give it character.

"The one on the right would be yours. The left one's mine."

I froze mid-step, his words sinking in. "Yours?" I echoed, almost choking on the word.

Boone turned to me with a grin that was both mischievous and charming. "Yes, Darling. Mine."

Darling. That word again. It sent a rush of warmth through

me that I couldn't deny.

"We'll be neighbors," he continued. "Forewarning: I sometimes have friends over, and I'm up early most days. Oh, and I've never had a neighbor out here before. Sometimes I drink my coffee on the porch in my underwear. Hope you don't mind."

He winked, and I nearly forgot how to breathe.

Boone being my neighbor was...unexpected. I'd assumed I'd see him now and then in passing, this was his family's ranch, after all, but living next door? That was something else entirely. Not that I minded.

Boone reached the door to my cabin first, opening it wide and gesturing for me to step inside. The space was dark, but as I moved through it, my imagination began filling it with light.

The cabin was empty of furniture, but that didn't bother me. I already pictured my favorite pieces fitting perfectly here. The layout was cozy as a one-bedroom, one-bathroom retreat with an open floor plan. A small living room with a fireplace opened into the kitchen and dining area. Down a short hallway, I found the bedroom, its windows framing a view of the willow trees...and Boone's cabin.

It was perfect. More than perfect.

In my mind, I was already arranging furniture—a reading chair in the corner, a desk along the wall for writing. For the first time in a long time, I felt hope. Real hope. Losing my job, rediscovering my love for writing, and taking a leap of faith, it all felt like it was happening for a reason.

But the optimism didn't last. A single thought clouded my excitement: How long would this last? Ellie was coming back eventually—weeks, months, maybe a year. I couldn't dwell on it, though. I shoved the thought aside, determined to savor the moment.

"No hole in the roof. Bugs are still to be determined," Boone stepped further inside.

"I can manage." I turned to him, unable to hide my grin. "Thank you, Boone. You have no idea how much stress this takes off my shoulders."

His eyes met mine, a serious warmth in their bluish-green depths. "No need. You're doing us the favor."

I felt the weight of his words. We both had a lot riding on this arrangement, and I was determined to make it work.

Boone and I didn't linger long. Back at the main house, his parents sat on the porch, their welcoming smiles mirroring the warmth of their home.

"What did you think?" Jill asked, rising from her rocking chair.

"I'm speechless. I'd love to accept the offer, as long as you didn't change your mind while we were gone," I joked.

Jill's laugh was kind, and she pulled me into a warm hug. "We'd love to have you! You can start whenever you're ready."

I couldn't believe it. The job. The cabin. I felt excited, ready to take on what life had in store. I'd said my goodbyes with promises to call them soon. I was eager to start, eager to finally make a move in the direction I'd wanted for a long time.

Boone walked me to my car like a perfect gentleman. Before I opened the door, he held out his hand. "Give me your phone."

I hesitated but handed it over. He tapped the screen before handing it back with a smirk.

"Let me know if you need help moving,"

I glanced at the screen, and my heart skipped. His contact read *Hot Neighbor.* I mean, he wasn't wrong, a heavy emphasis on the *hot* part.

Hiding my smile, I sent him a quick text so he'd have my number. As I drove home, excitement bubbled over. I made a call to the Wilders, ready to start this new chapter. With Boone's help, I'd move into the cabin as soon as possible.

This leap of faith felt like the start of something big—and for the first time in a long time, I was ready for it.

CHAPTER 5

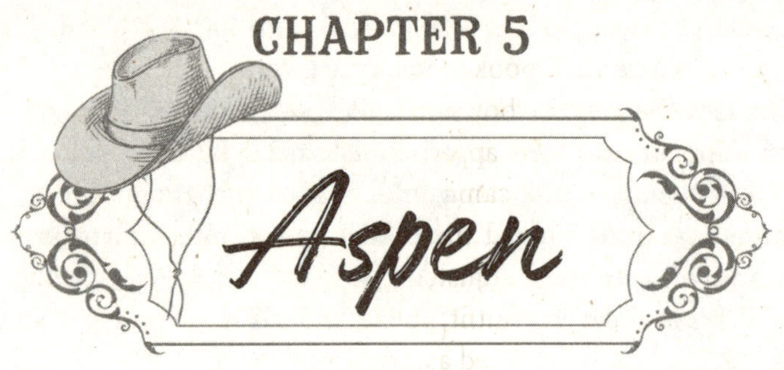

Aspen

The week following dinner at Cassidy Ranch had been a whirlwind. Between closing up the shop and moving my things into the cabin, I barely had time to catch my breath. Boone had been a lifesaver. Without him, I'd probably still be stuck on the stairs, wrestling with the last box of books.

I'd even managed to work up the courage to call my parents and tell them about the move and the new job. Predictably, the questions started pouring in, confirming exactly why I hadn't told them sooner. Their doubts and critiques had a way of making even my most confident decisions feel like mistakes. At twenty-five, I still struggled to stand up for myself when it came to them. It was easier to keep the peace than defend my happiness.

When my world fell apart, moving back in with them wasn't even an option. I'd have slept on Penny's couch forever before I dragged my sorry self back home. Still, I loved my parents. They'd given me a stable, comfortable childhood, but their need to protect had always veered into control. That control shaped me into an adult who second-guessed herself and needed constant validation. I understood their concern came from love, but that didn't make their intrusion any less exhausting.

Now, though, I was here, sitting on my porch swing, enjoying a glass of red wine while reading my favorite cowboy romance. The sunset painted the horizon in soft pinks and golds, and a cool breeze tempered the lingering heat of the Texas day. It was my kind of perfect.

I glanced at the book in my lap, a grin tugging at my lips. Wes Ryder, the rugged cowboy, could respectfully get it.

The sound of an approaching engine pulled me from the pages. Boone's truck came into view, rumbling up the access road that forked toward the cabins and the stand. I tucked my legs beneath me and adjusted the blanket draped over my lap, suddenly aware of my outfit, an old, oversized T-shirt, no bra, and shorts that barely qualified as clothing.

Boone climbed out of the truck, his boots dusty and his hat in hand. My pulse quickened as he strode toward me. It turned out I'd been wrong earlier when I thought nothing could make this night better—seeing Boone like this, rugged and a little worn from the day, definitely made it better.

"Hey," I greeted him with a small wave.

He smiled, his eyes crinkling in that heart-melting way of his, and plopped down beside me on the swing. The seat swayed gently under his weight as he leaned back, resting an arm along the top rail. His other hand held his hat, which he balanced on his knee.

"How're you settling in?" he asked, his deep voice as relaxed as his posture.

I shifted under his gaze, tugging the blanket higher. "It's going well," I replied, setting my book face down on my lap to hold my place. "It's peaceful out here. Quiet."

Boone nodded, his eyes drifting to my T-shirt for a brief moment before meeting mine again. My cheeks burned under his attention. I wasn't used to this, being looked at like that, like I was even worth noticing.

As I raised my glass to my lips, Boone moved. The pressure on my leg disappeared, and I realized too late that he'd grabbed my book. My heart skipped as he opened it to the page I'd left off on.

"Boone," I started, but his focus was on the words.

I froze, unsure what to do as he read a few lines. Luckily, I wasn't in the middle of a steamy scene or a declaration of love. That would've been too much.

When he was done, he placed it back on my leg, exactly as he'd taken it.

"What was that for?" I asked, breaking the silence.

Boone leaned back again, a lazy smile tugging at the corner of his lips. "Just curious. I wanted to see what had you so focused. It seems like you always got your nose in a book."

I rolled my eyes, though my lips twitched with a smile. "And?"

"And," he said, his grin growing, "now I know why you've been smiling all week. Smutty cowboy romance, huh?"

I gasped, scandalized, though my cheeks gave me away. "It's not smut!"

Boone chuckled, the sound deep and warm. "Darling, I read two paragraphs. It's definitely smut."

"How do you even know what smut is?" I asked, sipping my wine, looking at him over the rim of the glass.

"I have a sister. *And* a mom who always has a book in her hand."

I hid my face behind my wine glass, trying to play it cool. Boone just laughed again, the swing moving gently as we sat there, side by side, with the fading sunlight painting the evening sky.

"That was the book you were reading when I came into The Coffee Cup." Boone sounded curious. "The guy on the cover looks a little like me, minus my mustache, of course."

A loud laugh escaped me, my head tipping back in genuine amusement. I held up the book, angling it toward his face. "Wow, you're kind of right."

"What's it about?" he asked, leaning in slightly. "Besides cowboys and some sex. The few paragraphs I skimmed didn't give much away."

Whenever someone asked about the kind of books I read, I always felt a little shy.

"She's a city girl, he's from a small town. They end up working together on a project and, well, fall in love. Hence, romance book," I said casually, though I could feel the heat creeping up my cheeks.

I snapped the book closed, trying to appear nonchalant. It felt silly to be so self-conscious about something I loved. Romance novels were exquisite, no matter what anyone said. It took real talent to write about love and desire in ways that felt raw and real. I was amazed at the countless ways writers could describe a cock or vagina and still make it sound sensual.

"So, are you looking for your own small-town romance? Maybe with a cowboy of your own?"

I smiled, unable to resist the playful spark in his voice. "Maybe."

"Is that what kept you here after high school?" he asked, his gaze steady. "I always thought you'd leave, make a life for yourself far away from Faircloud."

His words caught me off guard. "I didn't know you paid that much attention to me, Boone Cassidy."

The flirty tone in my voice surprised even me. Boone, however, didn't miss a beat. He scoffed lightly, shaking his head with that signature smirk playing on his lips.

"You'd be surprised, Aspen Westgrove."

In school, I'd kept to myself. It was always Penny, Theo, and me against the world. We didn't need anyone else. Most kids were nice enough, and when they weren't, I let it slide. I didn't feel the need to connect with anyone else. My girls were my safe place, and back then, safety was all I craved.

Looking back, I suppose I did dream of leaving at some point. But the truth was, I loved this town. Faircloud, with its quaint charm, felt like home. Main Street was lined with locally run shops housed in historic buildings, their cobblestones telling the town's story. I'd always envisioned a future here, living in one of the old homes, raising a family, and soaking in the familiar comfort of it all.

"I love the familiarity," I admitted. "It's safe here. Cozy. I've never been one to take risks or do crazy things. I'm content being comfortable."

It was the truth, though it didn't mean I wasn't open to change. Sometimes, deep down, I wanted to be a little reckless. To let go of the image I'd carefully fallen into—the sweet girl who made all the "right" choices. I often wondered what it would feel like to live freely, without worrying about disappointing anyone. That's probably why I loved books so much. Through them, I could live a thousand lives. I could be a fearless adventurer, a bold lover, or even a dragon-riding warrior. Books gave me the courage to dream, even if only for a moment.

Boone had been quiet, his gaze steady on me as I spoke. There was something about the way he looked at me that made me want to throw caution to the wind.

He must have sensed the shift in my thoughts because he stood abruptly, patting my leg. "Get dressed in something more presentable. You're coming to the bonfire."

Before I could respond, he was already halfway down the porch steps, hat in hand. He paused at the railing, glancing back at me.

"Oh, and Aspen?"

I tilted my head, curious.

"I'm what you read in those books, Darling."

With a wink and a cocky smile, he placed his hat back on his head and sauntered off, leaving me stunned, my mouth slightly agape, and my body ablaze.

I'M WHAT YOU read in those books, Darling.

The only words that replayed in my head as I got ready for the bonfire. I should've declined the invitation. I didn't even know what to wear, let alone how to handle Boone's friends. But something about Boone made me say yes.

Rifling through my drawers, I pulled out a pair of straight-cut jeans with small rips at the knees and a green halter top. It was a change from my usual sundress and sandals, but who wears a dress to a ranch bonfire?

I hesitated, then grabbed my phone for support, texting the group chat.

Please tell me why I said yes to a Boone Cassidy gathering.

Penny

Because it's the only answer?

Theo

Ditto Penny!

I'm completely out of my element. Are jeans and a halter top okay?

Theo

ABSOLUTELY. Also, it's about time you live a little, A.

Penny

RETWEET! Don't overthink it, just relax.

Theo

You got this. 👍

Theo renamed the group chat: WWTD?

Rolling my eyes with a smile, I set my phone down and focused on finishing my look. My hair was curled, a soft tint of pink on my lips. I grabbed my Yeti mug, filled it with wine, and took a long sip.

Tonight, I'd take a small step toward the life I wanted—a little reckless, a little bold, starting with a bonfire under the Texas stars.

When I was younger, my parties were legendary. Wild, chaotic, and often teetering on the edge of disaster. Friends brought friends, who brought more friends, until my house was packed with people I barely knew. I didn't mind back then. The unpredictability kept life exciting, and the more girls, the better the party. I'd hop from one to another over the course of a night, earning my reputation as the town's bad-boy player. I wore that badge with pride, even when it came at the cost of broken hearts. I was in it for the thrill, nothing more.

But now, in my mid-twenties, things had shifted. Impressing people or maintaining a wide social circle wasn't a priority anymore. I cared less about counting conquests and more about keeping the people who truly mattered close. A grown-up Cassidy get-together looked a lot different with chill bonfires, good drinks, loud music, and stories shared with the same group of guys.

"Boone!" Rhodes shouted from inside my cabin. "Where the hell did you put the tequila?"

Rhodes was my best friend from school and one of the ranch hands I worked with. Outside, Logan was tending the fire, carefully stoking it to life. A few years younger than the rest of us, Logan was like my ranch apprentice, a kid I'd taken under my wing. Mac, another buddy from school, stood beside him, cracking jokes as usual.

"It's in the same place it's always been! Cabinet above the fridge!" I called back, jogging toward the front door.

I stepped inside, heading to the cabinet where I kept my shot glasses. Pulling down four, I lined them up on the counter. Rhodes appeared, tequila bottle in hand, and started pouring. Once each glass was full, we grabbed two apiece and made our way back outside.

Handing the shots around, I raised mine high, and the others followed suit.

"To friendship and a good time!" I declared.

The tequila burned its way down my throat, its warmth spreading through my chest. I placed the shot glass on the table next to my chair, knowing I'd be reaching for it again soon.

Around the fire, five chairs were set up, one more than our usual four.

"Is your new neighbor coming?" Logan asked, settling into his seat between Mac and Rhodes.

"I invited her," I said with a shrug, leaning back in my chair. My eyes drifted toward Aspen's cabin, clearly visible from where I was positioned.

Aspen Westgrove had been living rent-free in my head all week. I couldn't shake the memory of her climbing onto the ATV, the way her dress had ridden up her legs, or how her body had pressed against my back as we rode. If I let myself dwell on it too long, I'd end up sporting a hard-on in front of all my friends.

She smelled like blueberries, a scent that had stubbornly lingered in my mind. And I couldn't help but wonder—if I'd gotten just a little closer, would her skin have tasted like blueberries too?

"When does she start working the stand?" Mac asked, taking a swig of his beer.

"Monday morning," I replied.

"She's a sweet girl," Rhodes added. "My mom used to go to The Coffee Cup every morning. Always tried to convince me to go in and ask her on a date."

My chest tightened, and a rush of heat spread through me.

The thought of Rhodes taking Aspen on a date made my blood pressure spike. It wasn't like I had any claim over her, but still, the possessiveness surprised me.

Spending time with Aspen over the past week had been... nice. I'd helped her move out of her apartment and into the cabin, checking in regularly to make sure she had everything she needed. It was more than just neighborly—it was about making her feel welcome, a part of this place.

The Aspen I remembered from our school days was quiet and reserved, always with a book in her hand. But talking to her earlier today, I'd gotten the sense there was more to her than she let on. Layers waiting to be uncovered.

As if the universe had been eavesdropping on my thoughts, her cabin door opened, and time seemed to slow.

Aspen stepped out, and I nearly did a double take. She'd swapped her usual sundress for a pair of worn jeans that hugged her hips and a green top tied around her neck. My mouth went dry at the sight.

This was new. Different. And I couldn't stop staring.

The jeans, the way they fit her curves, were enough to make me forget my own name. My mind flashed to the image of her in those short shorts—a memory I clearly hadn't shaken. That image, paired with a few tequila shots tonight, might be all I needed to keep myself entertained.

"Speak of the devil," I muttered, mostly to myself.

Aspen approached, her nervous energy visible in the way she clutched a pink Yeti cup. She slid into the empty chair beside me, tucking her feet under herself.

"Hi, everyone," she said softly, her eyes darting around the circle as the guys introduced themselves.

They smiled warmly, and Aspen returned the gesture, taking a quick sip from her cup. My money was on red wine.

As the fire crackled, conversation flowed easily. At first, Aspen seemed hesitant, like she didn't quite belong, but as the night went on, and the wine worked its magic, she began to relax.

Her laugh came easier, her words more unfiltered. I learned she loved animals, farmers markets, and stargazing. Every detail she shared felt like a little treasure, and I tucked each one away for later.

Before long, she was holding her own, volleying jokes with the guys and making everyone laugh. It was like she was meant to be here all along.

After about an hour, Rhodes stood up and nodded towards Aspen. "I'm grabbing the tequila. We need a glass for our new friend."

Her cheeks were rosy from the wine, and her smile was breathtaking.

"I've never had tequila straight before," she confessed, turning to me.

"It's not that bad," I said with a grin, leaning in slightly. Lowering my voice, I added, "It burns at first, but you'll get used to it."

Our faces were inches apart, and I felt it—a pull, like static electricity in the air. Her gaze dropped to my mouth, and mine to hers. My pulse quickened, the world around us fading into the background.

The spell was broken when Rhodes reappeared, bottle in hand and an extra shot glass for Aspen. We both straightened in our chairs like guilty teenagers caught sneaking out past curfew.

Rhodes poured tequila for everyone, and Aspen stared at the clear liquid in her glass with a furrowed brow.

"On the count of three," I instructed, holding my glass out.

Aspen hesitated but knocked her glass against mine.

Logan ran the count. "One... two... three!"

We threw back the shots, and I turned to Aspen—just in time to see her cheeks puffed out, still holding the tequila in her mouth. It took a moment for her to swallow, and when she did, her face twisted into a grimace.

"Is it supposed to taste that bad?" she asked, incredulous.

The entire group burst into laughter, Aspen's wide-eyed

expression the highlight of the night.

ASPEN WAS THREE shots deep and clearly feeling it. I was tipsy myself. Logan, Rhodes, and Mac had all called it a night. After five shots of tequila and a couple of beers each, they stumbled into my cabin to sleep it off. Ranch duty waited for them tomorrow. Lucky for me, I had the day off.

"This was fun. Your friends are actually nice," Aspen confessed, leaning back in her chair. Her glassy eyes locked onto mine. "Thank you for inviting me."

"'Actually nice?'" I repeated, teasing.

"Well, I always thought you and your friends were intimidating. Penny, Theo, and I even made a pact to avoid you all."

"A pact?" I repeated her again, clutching my chest dramatically, feigning offense.

Aspen giggled, a soft, musical sound that tugged at something deep in my chest.

"Yes! You know, the bad boy in high school, the womanizer. I wasn't about to risk getting sucked into your whirlpool of sexy." She made a circular motion with her hand in my direction.

"All I heard was that you think I'm sexy," I shot back, grinning before taking another sip of my drink.

She smirked. "Well, you *are* saved in my phone as Hot Neighbor."

"Who on earth did that?" I asked in mock disbelief. "But I notice you're not denying it."

Aspen shook her head and looked up at the sky, a playful smile on her lips. "Your head's getting too big for your hat, Cowboy."

The way she said *Cowboy*, all flirty and sweet, made my pulse quicken. Every fantasy I'd had about her over the past week simmered just below the surface. I tipped my head back to join her in gazing at the stars, though the most breathtaking view was sitting just to my right.

"Let's play twenty-one Questions," Aspen declared, her gaze still fixed on the sky. "I'll go first. What does Boone Cassidy do for fun?"

"I like to tinker with things," I replied. "Anything with an engine. I love taking them apart and putting them back together."

"That sounds mildly psychotic. Should I feel safe sitting out here in the middle of nowhere with you?" she joked, a teasing smile playing on her lips.

"I guess we'll see." I smirked. "My turn. If you could travel anywhere in the world, where would you go?"

Aspen didn't even hesitate. "Easy. Ireland."

"Why Ireland?" I asked instinctively.

She wagged her finger at me. "Nope. One question at a time. It's my turn."

She paused, clearly thinking. "What's the riskiest thing you did as a kid?"

Riskiest? That was a tough one. If she'd asked for the most reckless or destructive, I'd have had my answer right away. After a moment of contemplation, I grinned and countered, "Do you want me to show you instead?"

Aspen raised an eyebrow, studying me as if trying to read my intentions.

"I'd love that."

I stood up, wobbling slightly, and extended a hand to her. When she placed her hand in mine, I pulled her to her feet. She swayed a little and giggled.

"I'm definitely feeling that last shot," she admitted with a smile. "I think I like it."

"Tequila has that effect," I teased, unable to stop myself from grinning back.

I led her past the cabins and into the woods, our hands still intertwined. I didn't tell her where we were going, and she didn't ask, trusting me—or maybe just the tequila.

"This feels a bit...dangerous. You're taking your new neighbor into the dark woods while no one is around," she said in a tone that dripped with fake apprehension. Her feet didn't slow to come to a stop, which showed me she was happy to continue walking into dangerous territory with me.

"Do you like being a bit reckless, Darling?"

Aspen's steps faltered, and I spun around, looking to see if she had tripped, but she hadn't.

We reached a clearing by a swimming hole. The moonlight danced on the water, casting a soft glow over everything. This was my favorite spot growing up, a place where my friends and I spent countless summer nights after parties.

"What are we doing here?" Aspen asked as I let her hand slip from mine. She took in the space around us, eyeing every tree, the open night sky, and finally looking back at me.

I stepped closer to the water, turning to face her. The moonlight lit up her face, making her look almost ethereal.

"Have you ever been skinny-dipping?" I asked, a mischievous grin spreading across my face.

Her wide-eyed expression told me everything I needed to know–definitely not. A surge of pride swelled in me at the thought of being the first person to share this moment with her. Behaving myself was going to be a challenge.

CHAPTER 7

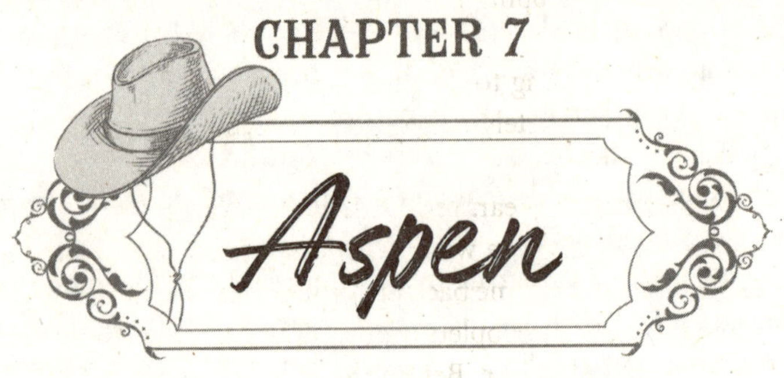

Was it the tequila, or had Boone really just asked if I'd ever been skinny-dipping? I tilted my head, studying his rugged features. Boone was clearly feeling the effects of the liquor, too. His hat was back at the cabin, which I didn't mind one bit. Without it, his tousled light-brown hair caught my attention, and I had to fight the sudden urge to run my fingers through it.

His eyes, glossy under the moonlight, locked onto mine. That infuriatingly perfect grin spread across his face as he reached behind his head and peeled off his black T-shirt.

I swallowed hard, my voice barely audible as I whispered, "No."

Boone smirked, tossing his shirt aside. "You asked me about the riskiest thing I did as a kid. This was it. My parents were usually home during my parties, so there was always the chance they'd come out to shut us down. Imagine being caught skinny-dipping with a bunch of drunk idiots by your mom and dad."

Boone toed off one boot, then the other, and tossed them to the side with his shirt. Watching as he undid his belt buckle, my body warmed, and the same tingly feeling from the other day came back. Boone finally turned away from me, discarding the last article of clothing, which happened to be his underwear. He was a boxer guy, I liked that. I couldn't complain when I got an uninterrupted view of his perfectly round ass. Boone's hands covered his cock, cupping it as he moved toward the swimming hole.

Was I really going to do this? Was I about to follow Boone into the water, completely naked? Strip down in front of a man I barely knew?

The answer was clear. Yes. Without hesitation.

Boone dove into the water with ease, disappearing beneath the surface. When he came back up, his hair was slicked back as he ran a hand through it, droplets trailing down his chiseled features.

It was now or never. Before the sliver of confidence I had could vanish, I slipped off my sandals and set them aside, my eyes never leaving Boone as he floated effortlessly. Taking a deep breath, I unbuttoned my pants, slid them off, and added them to the pile next to his.

Standing there in nothing but a hot-pink thong and halter top, I felt oddly powerful. Vulnerable, yes, but somehow stronger—like I was stepping into uncharted territory with bold determination. Boone's gaze flickered toward me, and even in the dim light, I swore I saw his eyes darken.

Turning away from him, I untied my top and let it fall, the cool air grazing my bare skin and sending a thrill of adrenaline through me. Glancing over my shoulder as I slipped off my thong, I caught Boone staring. He quickly turned away when our eyes met, feigning innocence.

With an arm crossed over my chest, I jogged toward the water, feeling both exhilarated and utterly exposed. Unlike Boone, I eased in slowly, letting the water inch up my body and adjust to its cool temperature. Boone turned back to face me, and I couldn't help but laugh.

"This is crazy!" I said, the laughter bubbling out of me.

"Is it?" Boone tilted his head, his playful expression making him look like a curious puppy.

"For me, yes," I admitted, wading further out to put a bit of distance between us. "I don't do things like this."

"Then why'd you get in?" His tone was teasing, but his

question carried weight.

I shrugged, feeling both self-conscious and liberated. "Maybe it was the tequila."

Boone chuckled, the deep sound rumbling through the night as he tilted his head back into the water. I followed his lead, letting my body float, the tension in my shoulders melting away.

"I'm guessing this isn't how you imagined tonight going," Boone said, his voice low and amused.

"Not even close." I smiled, glancing up at the stars. "But I can't say I hate it."

Our bodies drifted closer, the distance I'd created shrinking with each passing second. I told myself it was the nonexistent current.

The gap between us was nearly nonexistent as his fingers brushed against my hip, sending a shiver through me. The light touch encouraged me to shift upright, and Boone mirrored the movement. We floated just inches apart.

Boone's hand found the small of my back, pulling me closer until our bodies touched. The warmth of his skin ignited something in me, and I ached to know what was going through his mind. His gaze locked on me, and for a moment, the world felt still.

God, his body pressed against mine set both my mind and body ablaze. In this swimming hole, lost in the effects of tequila with Boone Cassidy, was the last place I thought I'd ever be. High school Aspen would be quaking. Hell, adult Aspen could barely keep it together.

On instinct, I looped my arms around Boone's neck like it was the most natural thing, acting as if my body had done it before. He moved slowly, his forehead lowering until it rested lightly against mine. His breath was warm against my skin, and our lips hovered just centimeters apart.

What were we doing? That was the question. Tequila was the answer.

I thought back to the pep talk I'd given myself in the mirror earlier, telling myself to take risks, to let go for once. This was my chance. I could blame everything on the wine and tequila humming through my veins, on the reckless courage they gave me.

I tilted my chin up, closing the gap between us. The faint brush of our lips was electric, sparking a chain reaction that shattered any restraint we might have had. What started as a soft, tentative kiss quickly unraveled into something wild and consuming.

The cool water turned into a hot tub, my body temperature rising with no way to bring it down. That was, as long as he kept touching me.

Boone kissed me with a raw hunger, one I met with equal passion. My hands found their way into his hair, fingers tangling in the thick strands as I pulled him closer. His lips were firm, intoxicating, and the taste of him only made me crave more.

I wrapped my legs around his torso, locking us together as our bodies melted into each other. My bare chest pressed against his, the friction sending waves of pleasure rippling through me. Boone groaned softly, the sound vibrating against my lips and stoking the fire burning in my core.

With effortless strength, he swam us to the edge of the swimming hole. The moment was heady, overwhelming, until my back suddenly collided with the cool surface of a rock. The jarring impact snapped us out of the haze, leaving me breathless and tingling from head to toe.

"Fuck, sorry," he muttered, panting against my lips.

"Don't worry, I can take it," I whispered back.

Boone's pupils dilated, and he wasted no time coming back to me. My core throbbed as arousal rushed through my body. I'd never experienced *want* like this.

Our tongues mixed together, hot and sloppy as we moved against each other. A moan escaped my lips as Boone pressed against my front. I'd never wanted someone as much as I wanted him. I was a goner. All the self-control I had dissipated.

Sitting up higher, I placed both my hands on his face and gently bit down on his bottom lip, pulling away slightly.

The swimming hole was my protector. In here, I didn't have expectations to maintain, I could be raw and real. What went on tonight, stayed here. If I stepped foot out of this space, I was afraid I would wake up from this dream.

My breathing turned to heaving, and our kisses lost their form. I was desperate for him in ways I'd never been before.

Boone pulled away unexpectedly, and I groaned in protest. "We can't," he confessed, pushing away from me.

Embarrassment flooded in, but the desire didn't go away.

Now on his feet, Boone towered over me, solid man and muscle. He ran his hand down his face, stopping to cover his mouth and mustache when he muttered, "Dammit, Aspen."

I pushed Boone's chest slightly to create more space between us. I needed him to get away from me.

"Look, it wasn't me who stopped." I scoffed.

"Aspen, I—" Boone began, but I wasn't having it. He wasn't about to give me some sob story or stupid apology.

"Nope. Spare me the pity party for one. I don't need you to justify it for my sake." I made my way to the edge of the hole to sit down, using my arm to cover my breasts now that I was slightly above water.

Boone exhaled, running his hands through his wet hair, clearly torn up about his decision. There was a shift in the air. Unwanted tensions built, and not the sexual kind. Boone got out of the water, using his shirt to dry himself enough to get dressed again.

When Boone pulled on his boxers and left his jeans unbuttoned, hanging low on his hips, he held out his shirt, offering it to me so I could dry off enough to get dressed, too.

I didn't want to let myself drown in anxious thoughts or let regret take over, but it was hard to ignore. The confident woman I had briefly glimpsed within me seemed to vanish, retreating into her shell. I'd let my guard down, and now here I was—sexually frustrated and rejected by the one man I'd avoided most of my life.

We walked back to the cabins in silence, the tension between us thick in the air. My mind raced. What had started as a carefree night had ended with me feeling guilty, aroused, and more attracted to Boone Cassidy than I'd ever thought possible. How was I supposed to keep coexisting with him when we were both so close to crossing that line? Now I wasn't just fighting my mind; I was battling my own desires.

When we finally reached the cabins, neither of us said goodnight. I crawled into bed, my body still tingling with the memory of him, replaying every moment over and over in my mind until exhaustion finally claimed me.

CHAPTER 8

Sleep was hard to come by after last night with Aspen. I rolled over in bed and squinted at the clock on my nightstand—nine in the morning. I couldn't remember the last time I slept this late, even on a day off.

My mind had been racing until the early hours, replaying every detail of the swimming hole. What the hell was I thinking? Hooking up wasn't new to me, but usually, the person didn't live next door *and* work at the ranch. I counted my blessings that nothing went further. As much as I'd wanted to bring her back to my place and discover the sounds she'd make while taking all of me, she was living next door, working on the ranch, and that sounded far too complicated than I needed.

Stopping when we did was the right call, but knowing it upset her gnawed at me. I didn't want to hurt her, didn't want to make her think I stopped for any other reason than the fact things could get tricky, and I didn't know how to handle it if they did.

But despite the alarm bells that were currently going off, telling me to stay away, the thought made my skin crawl. Aspen was sunshine, pure and addictive, and I couldn't seem to get enough.

I blamed the tequila—I always did stupid things when drinking. I didn't regret kissing her, swimming naked, or feeling her body pressed against mine. I just wished the circumstances were different, less complicated. She was an employee. My neighbor. At eighteen, I would've thrown caution to the wind and used every cheesy pickup line in the book to get her to come home with me. But I wasn't that kid anymore.

Yawning, I wandered to the kitchen in pajama pants hanging low on my hips and started the coffee maker. The rich aroma filled the air as I brewed enough to flush out the fog of the night before. Rhodes, Mac, and Logan were gone when I woke up, leaving the house quiet—a luxury that let me sort through my chaotic thoughts.

Should I bring up last night when I see her, or let her decide if she wants to talk? Would she even be interested in a repeat, this time with both of us sober? I needed to play it cool when I saw her again. If I acted on all the thoughts running wild in my head, I'd scare her off for sure.

I smiled to myself, remembering the way she laughed with my friends, her eyes sparkling with a dangerous mix of tequila and pure joy. If I were an artist, I'd paint her like that and frame it for the world to see.

The ding of the coffeepot pulled me back to the present. I poured a cup, adding cream and sugar, then stepped outside for some fresh air before the Texas heat became unbearable. As I opened the door, I noticed a Tupperware container on the porch. A piece of yellow-lined paper was folded neatly on top, held down with a strip of scotch tape. My name was written in elegant cursive.

Boone,

I hope these blueberry muffins help with your hangover. They sure as hell helped with mine.

With love, Aspen

I exhaled a breath I didn't realize I'd been holding. Relief washed over me. Maybe things weren't going to be awkward after all. Overthinking wasn't usually my style, but Aspen had a way of throwing me off balance. It'd only been a little over a week since I'd seen her in the coffee shop. Letting out a long sigh, I knew I was in trouble.

Wanting to do the neighborly thing and thank her, I stepped toward her cabin, but she wasn't curled up on her porch swing with a book as usual. Since moving in, the swing had practically been her home.

"Oh, come on!" A frustrated voice snapped me out of my thoughts. I followed the sound around the side of the cabin. Aspen stood in front of her Jeep, the hood propped open. She was back in another sundress—this one a soft, buttery yellow. Her hair was half up, pinned with a delicate butterfly clip that glinted in the sun.

"Everything okay?" I asked, coming up to the front of the car.

"No," she huffed, blowing a stray strand of hair out of her face. Her hands settled on her hips as she glared at the engine. "It won't start. She's never given me trouble before, but of course, now's the time. I was planning to head into town to grab supplies for the stand. I found a beekeeper selling fresh honey, but I guess that's not happening."

"Let me take a look," I offered, stepping closer. Gently, I placed my hands on her shoulders to guide her out of the way. I leaned under the hood, scanning for anything obviously wrong. The belt was tight, the fluids were fine, but I'd need to check the battery or crawl underneath to be sure. Wiping my hands on my pajama pants, I turned back to face Aspen and caught her red handed, staring directly at me.

Smirking, I asked, "You like what you see?"

Aspen froze, her cheeks dusting pink as she glanced up at me. If I had a dollar for every time this woman looked at me like I was a five-course meal, I'd be a few dollars richer by now.

Ignoring my teasing, she sighed. "The car started up fine last time. Now, when I put the key in, it just sputters." She mimicked the sound—an exaggerated sputtering noise that wasn't remotely helpful.

"Could be the battery," I suggested, crossing my arms. "If you left a light on, it might've drained. When was the last time you changed it?"

She stared at me with a blank expression, which was enough of an answer. "Let's go get you a new battery," I said, already heading toward my cabin.

"Wait!" she called, hurrying after me. "You don't have to use your day off chauffeuring me around."

"It's no problem. I need to head into town anyway. Gotta pick up some fencing for the pasture. I'll even take you to the beekeeper," I added with a soft smile.

Aspen followed me up to my front door, stopping at the threshold as I stepped inside. I spun and stared at her for a moment with one eyebrow raised. She looked apprehensive, like she'd catch on fire if she walked through the door. "You can come in, you know. I don't bite."

Nodding, she hesitated before stepping into the living room. "Thanks," she muttered, her gaze flitting around.

"There's coffee in the pot, cream in the fridge. Make yourself at home. I'll just be a minute." As I headed to my bedroom, I heard her rummaging through the cabinets and then the fridge, the clinking of a mug soon following.

"Your place is nice!" she called out.

I left my bedroom door open, catching a glimpse of her wandering the living room. Pulling on a pair of jeans and a worn T-shirt, I yelled back, "Thanks! About as nice as a single guy can manage."

After fixing my hair in the bathroom, I grabbed my favorite hat—a light khaki color that had seen better days but fit like a second skin.

When I returned to the kitchen, Aspen was leaning against the counter near the container of muffins she'd left on my porch.

"Ah, so you got my muffins." Aspen pointed at the container in my hands.

I grabbed one, taking a bite, and replied through a mouthful, "I did."

Aspen scoffed, rolling her eyes. "Doesn't look like you even have a hangover."

"Alcohol doesn't really get to me," I said, wiping crumbs off my mouth with the back of my hand. "Thanks for dropping them off. You must've been up early."

She waved it off. "I can make them blindfolded. I've been baking at The Coffee Cup for years. But you'll have to tell me what you think about the fresh blueberries." There was pride in her voice, and I knew I'd tell her I loved them, even if I didn't, just to keep that smile on her face.

"You really love to bake, don't you?" I asked, leaning my hip against the counter. I took her in, watched her drink from my mug, stand in my kitchen. I swallowed hard, my heart fluttering at the thought of everything before me.

Aspen nodded, taking another sip. "My Mom-Mom had taught me. "She was the one who got me the job at The Coffee Cup." She smiled to herself, reliving memories I wished I could see inside that pretty head.

"Is it just muffins? Or do your skills also happen to involve cookies? Maybe cake?"

She giggled, a soft airy sound that made my spine tingle. "I can make cookies, cake, not so much. It's the icing part that gets me. Plus, I suck at drawing, so having to decorate something is a huge pass for me."

It was my turn to nod, like I could relate to what she was saying. There was a silence that passed between us as she finished the last sip of her coffee.

"You really don't have to do this," she said as she discarded the empty coffee cup into my sink.

"I know. I want to. It's the neighborly thing to do. Plus, what are friends for?"

She turned back toward me as I ushered her to the door. "Friends?" Aspen asked.

"I'd say so," I replied with a smirk. I had to classify us as something after last night. The way she made me feel. I felt connected in a way I'd never felt before.

When we headed outside, I walked her to the passenger door

of my truck and opened it for her.

"What a gentleman," she teased, climbing in and settling into the seat.

I tipped my hat. "Always."

CHAPTER 9

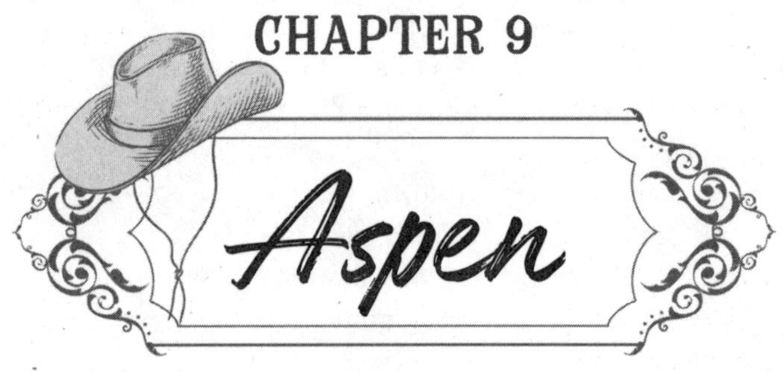

Sitting in Boone's truck wasn't something I'd expected after last night. Sobering up, I'd braced myself for regret or awkwardness, but none of that came. Instead, I felt calm. Comfortable, even.

Last night, I'd been a nervous wreck, but after some sleep and a quiet morning, I realized I had nothing to be embarrassed about. We were adults, it was normal. That's what I'd told myself, and then Boone offering to drive me into town—acting like nothing was off—validated my thoughts.

There was something different about me, like whatever happened last night flipped a switch. For the first time in a long while, I felt free. Boone had brought out a side of me that felt youthful, almost reckless, and I didn't hate it.

"Want to put some music on?" Boone asked, pulling me from my thoughts.

He fiddled with the radio until a clear station came through, Zach Bryan's "Revival" filled the cab at a low hum.

"This is perfect," I said, smiling as I reached over to turn it up.

The sun was shining, and the late-morning air was crisp. I rolled the window down, letting the wind tousle my hair. Singing quietly to myself, I put my hand out the window, letting the air stream through my fingers. Boone started humming, his deep voice blending into the melody.

Humming turned into singing, and soon we were belting out the lyrics together, our voices bouncing off the backroads as we drove into town. I stole glances at him, memorizing the way he looked—hat tipped low, hands steady on the wheel, a contented smile on his face.

This was every small-town girl's dream. Sitting in the passenger seat of a hot cowboy's truck, singing a pretty melody together. It felt like the scene of a movie or the words written in a book. There was a spark that ignited in me, a creative warmth flowing in my veins.

When the song ended, I took a deep breath and decided to bring up what had been on my mind all morning, clearly fueled by the adrenaline that presented itself in the form of confidence. "About last night..."

Boone glanced at me, his expression calm. "What about it?"

"I just... I don't want it to make things weird between us," I admitted, my voice softer than I intended.

Boone laughed, the sound warm and reassuring. "Am I making it weird, Aspen?"

No, he wasn't. Not even a little. If anything, he made me feel safer, more comfortable. Before last night, I'd been nervous around him—quiet, shy. Now, I felt freer, like I could finally breathe.

Flashbacks of last night flickered in my mind, and I fought the urge to beg him to do it all over again. I was chasing that high, the way I'd felt with him. Shaking my head to clear my thoughts, I said, "I just needed to make sure."

Boone raised a brow. "Why?"

"I...I haven't really done anything like that before," I admitted, my eyes widening as the words spilled out. "I mean, I'm pretty inexperienced."

The second the words left my mouth, I wanted to crawl under the seat. Why on earth did I say that?

Boone nodded, making a *hmm* sound.

"That came out wrong," I blurted, panic creeping into my voice. "I'm not a virgin or anything! I've had sex before. It just...

hasn't been very good. Like, mediocre. Sad foreplay and a couple seconds of action. Honestly, I don't think I've ever truly come. I've faked it. A lot."

Oh my God. What the hell was I saying? Word vomit. Pure, unfiltered word vomit.

Boone's jaw tightened, and an uncomfortable silence filled the truck, broken only by the low hum of the radio. If last night hadn't made things awkward, my big mouth definitely just did. I fought the urge to dig myself deeper, but Boone beat me to it.

"I don't regret last night," he said flatly, his voice calm but firm. "I enjoyed myself, and I hope you did too, Darling."

Something flickered in his eyes—hesitation, maybe? I could tell he had more to say, but whatever it was, he kept it locked behind his stoic expression. I nodded, avoiding his gaze, and turned to the window, watching the last of the trees blur past as we approached town. Foot, meet mouth.

When Boone parked in front of the hardware store, which happened to be my brother's store, I swallowed hard. I hadn't fully thought this through. Showing up here with Boone Cassidy in tow was bound to spark conversation. I'd have to play it cool, which was not exactly my strong suit.

Boone held the door open, and I stepped under his arm into the store's conditioned air. The place smelled like old wood and a hint of mustiness, as it always had. Generations of locals had passed through these doors.

The store, Nailed It, had once belonged to another family, but they'd sold it to Parker, my brother, at a discounted rate after he'd worked here for years. Parker was fifteen years older than me, and we hadn't grown up close. He was practically an adult when I was born, so by the time I could form sentences, he was off living his life.

But things had changed. Now, as adults, we'd rekindled a relationship that I wouldn't trade for the world.

The store was tidy and well-organized—classic Parker. He had a knack for perfection and no patience for anyone who didn't meet his standards, which explained why most employees didn't last a month. The only exception was Harry, a sixty-five-year-old retiree who worked here to keep busy.

No one was at the counter, so I rang the service bell. Over and over, doing my duty as the annoying younger sister.

"I'm coming!" Parker's voice boomed from the back. I didn't stop until he appeared, glaring at me as he laid a hand over mine to silence the relentless dinging.

"Of course," he added dryly. "Who else would be this annoying right after opening?"

I grinned sweetly and batted my eyelashes. "Who else? Your favorite little sister. It's my duty to annoy you until the end of time." I raised two fingers in a Scout's salute.

Parker shook his head, his blond hair falling into his eyes. "My only sister," he grumbled.

He looked like a cross between a surfer and a country boy, with tattoos crawling up his arms and muscles that could probably crush watermelons. "To what do I owe the pleasure?" he asked, tossing a rag over his shoulder.

"Well..." I started, turning to gesture at Boone—only to find he wasn't there. My hand froze midair as I turned back to Parker, who raised a skeptical eyebrow.

"All right, I swear Boone was right—"

"Here." Boone's voice interrupted me as he stepped out from one of the aisles.

"See!" I exclaimed, pointing at him. "Not crazy!"

Boone walked over and extended a hand to Parker. "Hey, Park."

Parker shook his hand, his sharp eyes darting between us, clearly piecing something together.

I rushed to explain. "I went to start my car this morning, and it wouldn't turn over. Boone heard me complaining and offered to drive me to get a new battery." I tried to sound casual, but my words came out too fast. The last thing I needed was for Parker to think Boone and I were...a thing?

Parker didn't say a word. He just nodded, turned on his heel, and disappeared into the back.

I let out a breath I hadn't realized I was holding and shot Boone a scowl. He shrugged, a half-smirk tugging at the corner of his mouth.

When Parker returned, he had a car battery in hand. He rang it up with the usual family discount but didn't hand it over. Instead, he leaned against the counter, his gaze sharp and probing.

"I heard from Mom and Dad that you're working the farm stand at Cassidy Ranch," he said, his tone casual but clearly fishing for information.

I groaned inwardly. I was stoked to start at the ranch, but I couldn't fangirl and show my excitement right now. How did I say that this was the best opportunity I'd had in a long time, that the Cassidys gave me the chance to make all my dreams come true? How was I supposed to sound normal and not desperate about the new job with Boone right behind me?

"Yup. I start tomorrow." My voice came out overly casual.

"I'll have to come by one of these days once you get settled. Gotta see my baby sister at work." Parker slid the battery across the counter. Then, with a pointed look at Boone, he added, "Keep your hands to yourself, Cassidy."

"Ew!" I squealed, grabbing the battery and making a quick escape. "We're leaving. Goodbye!" I snagged Boone's arm with my free hand and dragged him toward the door.

"Nice seeing you, Parker!" Boone called over his shoulder, clearly unfazed.

I groaned as we stepped outside. "I can't believe he said that out loud. In front of you. Ugh!"

Boone's laughter rumbled behind me.

"You think this is funny?" I spun around, narrowing my eyes. "I'm mortified. He *knew*! He could probably smell it on me!"

"Aspen..." Boone stepped closer, his hands finding my upper arms. His touch was steady, grounding. "It's okay. He doesn't know about last night. And so what if he did? We're adults. My hands can be wherever they want to."

His words sent an unwelcome shiver down my spine, images of his hands all over me flashing in my mind. I shook my head quickly to clear it. "Still, I don't need my brother thinking I'm hooking up with you."

Boone's expression shifted—just a flicker, but I caught it. He recoiled slightly, like I'd slapped him. Regret was instant, my body flooding with embarrassed warmth.

"That's not what I meant!" I rushed, panicking. "What I meant was—"

"I get it," Boone interrupted, his voice colder now. "You don't want your brother or your family thinking you're sleeping around with someone like me." He turned toward the truck, his jaw tight. "Let's just get going."

"Wait," I said, hurrying to follow him. "Didn't you need stuff to fix the fence?"

His change in demeanor told me how badly I'd messed up. My inability to filter myself got the best of me *again*. I desperately needed a *gag*.

"Nah. I'll check the barn later," he replied without looking back.

The drive was quieter than I'd hoped. I kept sneaking glances at Boone, trying to gauge his mood, but his focus was fixed on the road.

When we pulled up to the beekeeper's stand, my excitement bubbled back. The smile that spread on my face was undeniable. The little mason jars of honey with ribbons and dippers were adorable—perfect for the "locally sourced" table I was setting up at the farm stand. I could already picture them displayed next to the soy candles made by another local artisan.

The thought of supporting small businesses warmed me. Growing up in Faircloud, with the nearest big-box store an hour away, I'd come to know and admire the people who poured their hearts into their work. If I could use the stand to help them grow, I'd do it in a heartbeat.

Back in the truck, my stomach growled loud enough to break the silence. I froze as Boone's grin spread across his face. Whatever mood he'd been in a moment ago seemed to have vanished after picking up the mason jars.

"You hungry?" he asked, his tone teasing as he lounged an arm on the center console.

"I guess I can't deny it now," I muttered, trying to ignore the heat rising to my cheeks.

"Want to grab some pizza?" Boone offered.

"Pizza sounds amazing," I admitted, relieved to have something to focus on besides the tension floating in this truck's cab.

We arrived at the pizzeria a few minutes later. Boone held the door open for me, and I stepped inside, greeted by the cheerful hostess.

"Hi, Aspen!" Emily greeted us with a bright smile. She was one of my regulars from The Coffee Cup, always ordered an iced caramel latte and a scone before her shifts.

"Hi, Emily," I replied, smiling back.

Her eyes shifted past me to Boone, who had just stepped inside. Her smile widened, a blush taking over her cheeks. "Table for two?"

Boone nodded, and Emily led us to a booth by the window. I slid into one side while Boone took the other, his broad frame making the space feel smaller.

As Emily left, I glanced around. Why did it feel like everyone was staring at us? Peering to my right, I caught an older lady I recognized from the shop giving Boone and me daggers.

"You okay?" Boone asked after a moment, his gaze steady.

I lowered the menu I'd been hiding behind. "Does it feel like everyone's staring?" I whispered.

"Oh, they totally are," Boone replied, completely unfazed.

I dropped the menu onto the table with a frustrated sigh. "That's not helping!"

"Darling, relax. They're staring at me, not you. I don't take women out. Ever."

His words made me pause. "What do you mean?"

"I don't do relationships," he said simply, his tone matter-of-fact. "If I wanted to, I would. I just haven't found the right woman yet. So, people seeing you and me out together is odd and everyone is nosy."

His honesty caught me off guard. He sounded so sure of himself, so content. So okay with people staring at him like he was a zoo animal. "Does it bother you?" I asked softly.

"It used to. Not anymore. *Their* opinion of me don't matter." He met my eyes, his voice softer now. "Does it bother you? We can leave if you'd be more comfortable."

The sincerity in his offer was palpable, and for a moment, I considered it. But I didn't want to run away, not from him.

"No. I'm okay. Thanks for asking."

Boone's smirk returned as he glanced back at his menu, and I couldn't help but smile, too. His confidence was contagious, and I found myself relaxing.

I was beginning to think I was wrong about Boone Cassidy. The chaos and bad decisions I'd once associated with his name had given way to something steadier, something *real*. He'd taken all my assumptions and proved them wrong in the little time we'd been in each other's orbit. Boone Cassidy wasn't what I'd expected—and maybe that wasn't such a bad thing.

CHAPTER 10

Monday marked the start of another week on the ranch. Today's task: fixing a fence in the pasture. One of the steers had tried to barrel through the barbed wire during the storm, which had hit far too close for comfort.

Rhodes and I were working together, which, as usual, meant he wouldn't shut up. He'd been pestering me all morning about Saturday night, determined to squeeze the details out of me. As if I'd spill. He was delusional if he thought it'd be that easy.

That night was mine to keep. The last thing I needed was for Rhodes or any of the boys to find out and start running their mouths, especially around Aspen. She'd just started opening up to me, finally seemed comfortable enough to hold a real conversation. I wasn't about to let Rhodes—or anyone else—ruin that.

Truth was, I liked her. I liked hearing her laugh, seeing her curled up on the porch swing every night, a book in one hand and a glass of Sweet Red in the other. I'd found out it was her favorite—a locally curated wine from Faircloud—and made a mental note for later.

I wasn't usually the kind of guy to remember stuff like that. Hell, I didn't make it a habit to pay attention to what women liked or disliked in general. But Aspen? She'd always been different.

It started in high school. I'd watch her from afar, her nose buried in a book, completely content in her own little world. She was quiet, happy with the simple things, and that intrigued me. A part of me always wanted to shoot my shot back then, but what would a girl like her want with someone like me?

Now, I'd gotten to know her better—and she was a pleasant surprise.

"Come on, Boone, don't be shy," Rhodes teased, lining up the post in the hole we'd just dug.

"I'm not shy, dumbass," I shot back, crouching to shovel dirt around the post. "I'm just not telling you anything because I know you. You can't keep your mouth shut."

"Why's it a secret? I think we all know what happened. I just want to hear you say it," Rhodes pressed, his grin way too smug for my liking.

"I don't need you running your mouth and making Aspen regret it," I said, looking up at him. His grin widened, and I straightened, wiping my hands on my jeans. "Wipe that look off your face," I added, narrowing my eyes.

The details of what had happened between Aspen and me weren't for him—or anyone else. Whatever this feeling was, I needed time to figure it out without Rhodes stirring the pot.

"You like her." Rhodes smirked like he caught me red handed.

"And?" I took the post digger from him and moved to the next spray-painted mark. "I like spending time with her. She's a nice girl."

"That she is," Rhodes agreed, watching me work. "But come on, Boone. It's not like you to spend time with a woman during daylight hours. Fixing her car? Lunch? What's next, baking cookies?"

I grunted, driving the post digger into the ground. The handles groaned as I worked the tool, the hole slowly taking shape.

"She paid for lunch, for your information," I huffed, tossing the tool to the side once I was done. "And I'm done talking about this."

But Rhodes wasn't done. He grabbed the next pole and set it in the hole, waiting for me to fill it. The heat—or maybe his persistence—was starting to wear me down.

I decided to turn the tables. "How about you? Got any ladies you wanna talk about?"

Rhodes went red instantly, his cheeks matching the dusty hue of the dirt we were working with. He avoided my gaze, muttering something I couldn't quite catch.

"Thought so," I said, smirking as I packed the dirt in around the post.

Maybe he'd finally let the subject drop.

Rhodes had been single for over a year now, maybe longer. Mac, Logan, and I weren't even sure he'd been with anyone since Jess.

Jess and Rhodes had been high school sweethearts, the kind of couple everyone assumed would end up married. They started dating at fifteen, and nine years was a lot of history to share with someone. But Jess had wanted change, so she moved to the city, fully aware Rhodes would never follow. That change, apparently, included letting him go.

Since then, Rhodes hadn't been the same. He didn't talk much about love anymore and had sworn off dating altogether—not in those exact words, but we all got the message. Around here, most people marry their high school sweetheart. It's practically a rule, and breaking it feels taboo. Personally, I've always thought that mindset was outdated. Two of the people closest to me had followed that so-called rule and ended up heartbroken for it.

"Nope. I see what you're doing, and I'll let it slide today." Rhodes pointed the post at me like it was some kind of weapon. "But you can't deny it forever. It's not like you to see a woman outside of the bedroom."

"That sounds awful," I replied, scoffing. People had this idea about me—that I used women and tossed them aside. That couldn't be further from the truth. My mom raised me better than that. I'd always been upfront with my intentions, making sure no one got hurt.

"You know what I mean, man." Rhodes paused, giving me a

serious look.

Whatever was happening between Aspen and me? It was new territory. These feelings—this instant pull to be near her—scared me more than I wanted to admit.

"Right now, we're friends. That's all," I said, more to myself than to him.

Rhodes nodded and got back to work, though I could tell he wasn't convinced. He'd struck a nerve, and he knew it.

The truth was, I didn't care what people thought of me—usually. But Aspen was different. The last thing I wanted was for anyone to think she was just another name on some imaginary list.

That's why yesterday, after she'd made that comment on the sidewalk, it hurt. When I'd heard what people in town thought about me, I was usually able to brush it off. But with her, knowing she saw me the same as the rest, it felt like a knife to the chest. My mood had soured, my mind clogged. The one thing that pulled me out was seeing her radiant smile.

Every thought disappeared in that moment, replaced by thoughts of how I could make her do it again.

Rhodes and I worked in silence for the rest of the afternoon, finishing the fence before heading back to the main house. It was late, the sun sinking low over the ranch. When you start your day as early as we do, any excuse to quit while it's still light out feels like a win.

"Mom!" I called, letting the screen door slam shut behind me.

Rhodes was moving to the kitchen, helping himself to a bottle of water. Mom was there too, wearing her apron and humming as she worked.

"What's for dinner, Mrs. Cassidy?" Rhodes asked, leaning against the counter.

"Pizza in a round," she replied, grinning as she rolled up croissant dough stuffed with pepperoni, sausage, mozzarella, and sauce, shaping it into a ring on her pizza stone.

"Looks great." I leaned in, kissing her on the top of her head. My mom was a fantastic cook. Over the years, she had curated a variety of recipes that were tailored to our family. When you had as many differing opinions as we did, you had to find something everyone liked.

"Staying for dinner, Rhodes?" Mom offered.

"No, ma'am," Rhodes said with a polite shake of his head. "Got leftovers at home—and the rodeo's calling my name."

Our town's mock rodeos were a big deal in the summer, and tonight was the season opener. Very little came between a small-town man and his beloved rodeo, not even a homemade meal.

Rhodes shared his goodbyes and headed out the front door to his truck.

As I stayed back to chat with Mom, she handed me a box of mason jars. "Before you wash up, can you drop these by the farm stand? Mrs. McFry didn't need them, and I thought Aspen might like them for her muffin mix."

My chest tightened at the mention of Aspen. I hadn't seen her all day, and it was already late afternoon.

"Sure thing, Mama," I said, eagerly grabbing the box and heading out the door.

I used the time it took to walk to the stand to think about the ways I'd greet her. Maybe even try to convince her to come to dinner to steal a little more time with her.

When I got there, Aspen's back was to me. She was packing something away, bobbing her head and swaying her hips to some rhythm only she could hear.

For a moment, I just stood there, watching her. She had this way about her, this lightness that made the air around her feel softer. Her body danced around, a slight hum filling the space.

Finally, I stepped forward and set the box down on the counter. Aspen spun around with a little yelp.

"Shit!" she exclaimed, clutching her chest. "You scared me!"

I laughed. "Sorry. Didn't mean to sneak up on you."

"How long were you standing there, creep?" she asked, her

lips curving into a playful smile.

"Like twenty minutes," I teased.

"Bull," she shot back, laughing.

I walked around the counter and hopped up to sit on the edge. She turned to face me, her hand resting on the surface as her eyes roamed over me, head to toe.

And just like that, the world outside faded away.

"These are from my mom—something about muffin mix?" I said, nodding toward the box and shrugging. Taking off my cowboy hat, I ran a hand through my damp hair before settling the hat back on my head. My clothes were filthy from a day on the ranch, but Aspen didn't seem to mind. I caught the subtle way her throat moved as she swallowed hard, her eyes lingering a little too long.

"She came by earlier and mentioned you'd be dropping these off before closing. Look at you, right on time," she teased, closing the box with an easy smile.

She tossed a rag over her shoulder, leaning on one hip. Now level with my leg, her proximity sent a jolt of awareness through me. Her doe eyes locked with mine, hypnotic and unreadable.

"Wanna have dinner at the main house tonight?" The question tumbled out before I could think it through. All I knew was that I wasn't ready to leave yet.

"Can't," she said, her voice soft and a little breathy. "I'm meeting Penny for dinner. Raincheck?"

I nodded, trying to mask my disappointment. It was probably for the best. The last thing I needed was to explain to my mom why I'd invited our new employee to dinner.

"How was your first day?" I asked, reaching for the safest question I could muster. Anything to keep her talking.

"Great!" Her enthusiasm lit up the space between us. She stepped away from the counter, creating some distance, and I immediately missed the warmth of her presence. "We had a steady stream of customers all day. People seem excited about the stand and some of the new ideas I'm working on. These jars, for instance—they're going to be perfect for pre-packaged muffin mixes. Customers can just add the wet ingredients and bake. They make a great gift or an easy option for baking at home."

She beamed as she spoke, her passion spilling over with every word. The apples of her cheeks flushed pink, her energy infectious. Watching her light up like that stirred something in my chest—a tightness I'd been experiencing way too often lately.

She could've been talking about blueberry muffins, taxes, or the weather; it didn't matter. I could've listened for hours. Hell, I'd never felt like this before—like I couldn't get enough of someone, couldn't stand the thought of walking away. Her laugh, her voice, the way she brushed her hair out of her face—all of it had me completely hooked.

I was totally and utterly screwed.

CHAPTER 11

There's nothing quite like sitting across from your best friend, margaritas in hand, finally spilling the thoughts that have been looping in your head for days. A lot had happened since I'd moved to Cassidy Ranch, and I was dying to share every detail with Penny.

I took another sip—okay, more like a gulp—of my margarita as she watched me closely. Tacos and margaritas were a tradition for us, penciled into our schedules at least once a month. Life had a way of getting in the way, but we always made time for each other.

"All right, spill," Penny said, waving her hand dramatically in a circle. "I can tell you've got something juicy. Your face is doing that thing."

I laughed. "What thing?"

"You know, your eyebrows pinch together, and you get that gleam in your eyes. Out with it."

I squealed, leaning forward conspiratorially. "Okay. I kinda... maybe... I'm not sure what to call it... made out with Boone Cassidy while skinny-dipping in a swimming hole."

Penny's eyes widened, her mouth dropping open. I paused, waiting for her to gasp or yell, but she just stared at me, completely floored.

"Well," I continued, filling the silence, "we'd both had a little to drink—*tequila and wine.* Anyway, one thing led to another, and suddenly, we were taking our clothes off under the moonlight."

"Shut the *fuck* up." Penny's voice was sharp with disbelief.

I bit my lip, waiting for her to say more. But her expression was priceless—a mix of shock and giddy excitement.

When Penny didn't immediately respond, I kept going. "We were just talking after everyone went to bed. Playing twenty-one Questions. It was...actually really nice."

"How weird have you been around him since?" Penny asked, her tone accusatory but amused.

My mouth dropped open in mock offense. "*Me*? What do you mean, how weird have *I* been? Why does it have to be me? Maybe Boone is the one being weird!"

She just stared at me with that knowing, penetrating look she had. The kind that said, *Really, Aspen?*

I took a long sip of my margarita to buy myself time, then stuffed a chip loaded with salsa into my mouth for good measure. After chewing, I finally admitted, "Okay, fine! You're right! I *do* have a track record of making things weird. But this time, I think I did the opposite. I actually feel *more* relaxed around him. Like, whatever he did with his tongue in my mouth flipped a switch, and now I'm a changed woman."

Penny snorted so hard she nearly lost her margarita through her nose. "That's one hell of a way to put it! But hey, that's a good thing. You wouldn't want it to be awkward, especially since you both work and live on the ranch. Has he said anything about it? Like...maybe doing it again?" She raised her eyebrows suggestively, tilting her head.

"No." I shook my head. "He just said he doesn't regret it, which was nice to hear. Especially since my brain immediately went into full panic mode. But honestly, everything's been fine. I never thought I'd say this, but I think Boone Cassidy and I are... friends?"

"Friends?" Penny's brows shot up. "Did I miss a chapter? Besides the kissing, which, by the way, I expect a full, MLA-formatted report on in my inbox by tonight, what else has happened?"

I shrugged, trying to play it cool. "Well, he took me into town for lunch. Helped me change my car battery. And most nights, he comes over and sits with me on the porch swing. We just...talk."

"Details, woman! *Details!* What do you talk about?" Penny pressed, narrowing her eyes like she didn't trust me to be thorough.

"Just... normal stuff. Our likes and dislikes, family, hobbies, you know, friendly things. Sometimes he flirts a little. At least, I *think* it's flirting. But it's all harmless fun," I added quickly, not wanting her to get the wrong idea.

Penny grinned, eyes gleaming with mischief. "Oh, I *need* to know what Boone Cassidy considers flirting. I bet it's cheesy one-liners he finds online. But knowing him, they probably work. That man could hit me with an 'Is your dad a baker? Because you've got nice buns,' and I'd still blush."

I rolled my eyes but couldn't help laughing. "The other night, before the swimming hole, I was reading on the porch. He picked up my book and read a little. When he left, he said—" I hesitated, cheeks heating at the memory.

"What? What did he say?" Penny leaned forward like her life depended on this piece of information.

I sighed, bracing myself. "'*I'm what you read about in those books, Darling.*'"

"He *what?*" she yelled, drawing the attention of half the restaurant.

"Shh!" I hissed, waving my arms frantically to quiet her down. "What is *wrong* with you?" I whisper-yelled, trying to salvage what was left of our dignity.

"No problems here, sweetie. If a man said that to me, I'd climb him so fast his head would spin. That's some top-tier book boyfriend shit." Penny's eyes sparkled as she leaned back in her chair, clearly enjoying herself. "Boone laid it on thick. There's no way that's a line he reuses. That was all for *you*."

I blinked at her, stunned. "I guess I hadn't thought about it like that."

As much as I was attracted to Boone, I didn't want things to get weird. What happened at the swimming hole was a *one-time* thing. The attraction I had toward Boone had started way back in grade school—even little-kid Aspen had known he was cute. But I'd been fine all these years not acting on it, and I could keep it that way now. Right?

Of course, when Penny pointed out things like that, it made it that much harder.

I'd never been burned by a boy, and I wasn't about to start now. I had a knack for convincing myself things were less than they really were, just to protect my peace. I didn't let myself feel something unless I was absolutely sure it was safe. And deep down, I knew I needed to protect my feelings from Boone Cassidy. He used to be all red flags and tight Wranglers. Well, okay—he still wore the tight Wranglers.

But there was nothing wrong with being *just friends* with someone you were insanely attracted to, right?

"You know," I said, steering the conversation away from dangerous territory, "Theo is back in town this weekend. What if we hit The Tequila Cowboy for drinks and dancing? I think they've got a cover band. It could be fun."

Penny gave me a mock-concerned look. "Are you okay? I'm usually the one *begging* you to go out." She reached across the table and pressed the back of her hand to my forehead.

I rolled my eyes. "I just miss you two, and I really need a girls' night out."

"How could I say no to that?" Penny grinned, pulling her phone from her purse. "I'll clear my calendar."

A wave of warmth washed over me, and I reached across the table to squeeze her hand. "I'm really proud of you."

Penny fluttered her lashes dramatically and put a hand to her chest. "*Moi?*" she asked with a smirk. "I'm more proud of *you*. I mean, you made out with Boone Cassidy and lived to tell the tale."

I gasped, pulling my hand away. "That's the *last* time I'm nice to you!"

"No!" she squealed, lunging to grab my hand back. "I'm

sorry! Not really," she mumbled with a sly grin. "But seriously, you seem *happier* since taking the job at the ranch. There's something different about you, and I'm excited for you."

Her smile was sweet, genuine, and it tugged at my heart. Talking to Penny always brought me back down to earth. She was my rock—always had been. Whenever I needed her, she was just a phone call away. But seeing her tonight made me miss the free time we used to have to spend together.

The waiter dropped the bill on the table, and Penny slapped her card down before I could get mine.

"Let me."

"Just buy me a couple of drinks at the bar, and we'll call it even," she replied with a wink.

CHAPTER 12

Aspen

I sat with my wine and a book, indulging in a little self-care. Lately, I'd been building a routine that brought me joy, a way to ground myself when life got chaotic. It was a tip from my therapist—finding small, consistent ways to keep my mental balance. Therapy had been a game-changer, helping me combat the negative self-talk and impossible standards I used to hold myself to.

For years, I'd struggled to see myself the way others did, which made meeting new people or dipping my toes into the dating world feel insurmountable. Confidence didn't come easily, but I'd learned how to separate perception from reality, understanding that the two didn't always align. Books became a lifeline, a way to escape into someone else's story when my own felt overwhelming. Through structure and little joys like this, I'd found a way to stay afloat.

Flipping to the next page, I took a slow sip of my wine. Boone and I had closed up the stand earlier, and while he went back to his cabin to shower, I curled up outside in my comfiest clothes. Secretly, I was waiting for him to come over, though I didn't want to admit it—even to myself. He was taking longer than I'd expected, and the anticipation was starting to gnaw at me.

The sound of his front door opening pulled me out of my book. I glanced up to see Boone walking toward me, dressed in plaid pajama pants and a plain black T-shirt. His slippers shuffled softly against the ground—yes, *slippers,* not boots. Why was that just as attractive?

"What's up, Darling?" he asked, dropping onto the porch swing next to me, a beer in hand.

His hair was still damp from his shower, and the ends of his brown, tapered mullet curled at his neck. That casual, effortless look suited him so well it was almost criminal. My stomach did a little flip. How could this man just *exist* and still make me feel like a hormonal teenager?

I snapped my book shut and set it on the ground beside me. "Not much. Just reading, same old, same old."

Boone tipped his beer toward me, nodding. "Figured as much. You don't seem like the TV-binge type."

I narrowed my eyes at him, unsure if that was a compliment or teasing. Probably both.

He leaned back, resting one arm along the swing. "All right, I've got a question that could make or break our friendship."

"Oh boy," I muttered, shifting to face him. One leg was tucked beneath me while the other hung off the edge of the swing. "Hit me, Cowboy."

Boone smirked, the corner of his mouth tugging up in that way that made my cheeks heat. "I like when you call me that."

I felt my face flush and hoped the dim light masked it.

"I need to know," he continued, holding his beer like a gavel. "How do you feel about cold pizza?"

"Um, excuse me?" I blinked at him, caught off guard.

"Don't dodge the question, Darling. How do you feel about it?" His tone was playful, his lips twitching as if he were trying not to laugh.

"I love cold pizza," I said slowly, still skeptical about where this was going.

Boone grinned, leaning forward like I'd passed some kind of test. "Good. You might just be the perfect woman after all."

I rolled my eyes, laughing despite my body feeling on fire. Did Boone Cassidy just call me the *perfect woman*? How was this man turning *cold pizza* into flirting? Boone Cassidy was a problem—and one I wasn't sure I wanted to solve.

Boone pressed his lips together as if deep in thought. "Okay, how about this one: do you wet your toothbrush before the toothpaste or after?"

That made me pause. Mentally, I walked through my routine. "I wet it both times."

"You animal." Boone shook his head with mock disapproval. "The only right answer is *before* the paste."

"What?" I gasped, sitting up straighter. "Why is there a right answer?"

"Have you never discussed hot takes before? You're supposed to defend your opinion no matter what," Boone explained, leaning back casually and taking a sip of his drink.

"All right, give me another one," I challenged, setting my glass aside.

He tapped his chin, pretending to think deeply. "Crocs aren't acceptable footwear."

"Bullshit!" I yelled, pointing at him as if he'd just committed a crime. "Crocs are an absolute *must-have* item. They're versatile. Need to take the trash out? Crocs. Left something in your car? Crocs. Got a long flight? Crocs. That's a hill I'll die on."

Boone burst out laughing, the sound rich and warm in the evening air. "Okay, okay, I actually agree with you. I just wanted to see you fight back. I like it."

He took another sip of his beer, his eyes locking on mine. The intensity in his gaze made my stomach flip. I felt like melting under it, but instead of giving in to the timid girl inside me, I channeled the woman who had kissed him the other night. She wasn't about to back down.

"All right, my turn," I said with a smirk. "Toilet paper roll: does it go over or under?"

Boone didn't miss a beat. "It doesn't matter."

"It *absolutely* matters!" I exclaimed, gesturing dramatically. "Over. Always over. It's the only way to live."

"I can't agree with you there," Boone replied with a shrug. "It doesn't change how I use it, so why would I care?"

"Unbelievable," I muttered, taking a long sip of my wine to recover from the betrayal.

We spent the next hour diving into hot takes and pet peeves. Boone confessed he couldn't stand the sound of someone scraping a fork or spoon against their teeth—a stance I could respect. I shared my obsession with punctuality, explaining how I was always early to everything, no matter what.

As we talked, I felt my walls lowering bit by bit. Every time we were together, Boone revealed a side of himself I never knew existed. He was funny, thoughtful, and surprisingly charming. And as much as I tried to keep my guard up, I couldn't deny that spending time with him felt natural, even inevitable.

I hadn't seen this coming, not even close. But maybe—just maybe—I didn't mind at all.

CHAPTER 13

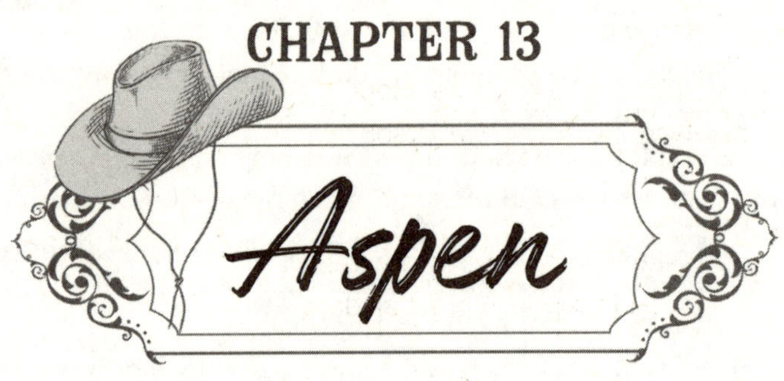

Every night since I'd started my new job, Boone showed up to help me close. He'd arrive sweaty and exhausted, the weight of the day still clinging to him. No matter how much I insisted he go home and rest, he'd stay until the job was done. As a thank-you, I'd set aside a blueberry muffin for him first thing every morning so he'd have something to eat. It felt like the least I could do.

Saving that muffin for Boone wasn't always easy—it sometimes meant bending the truth with customers. Today, Faircloud's resident grouchy old lady, Mrs. Clint, shuffled in, walker and all, ready to stock up for the week. She asked for six muffins, but I only had five to sell. If I gave up Boone's muffin, I could make her happy. But that wasn't a choice I was willing to make. When I told Mrs. Clint I didn't have enough, she stared at me like she could see right through my soul. I almost caved. *Almost.* But Boone would get his muffin, old lady be damned.

Somehow, this little routine—his nightly visits, the muffin-saving—was starting to mean something more. Our friendship was sparking into something I hadn't seen coming. Hell, I was lying to old ladies just to keep him happy.

After we'd cleaned up each night, we'd sit outside, talking over our favorite drinks—his was always a Coors Light. When the conversation ran dry, we'd let the silence stretch, staring at the stars. By morning, he was always gone before I woke up, but that didn't stop the texts from coming.

Boone

It's hot as balls out here. Hope you're enjoying the AC, kinda jealous.

Boone

You better be saving me my muffin. I've been thinking about it all day.

Boone

Which dress did you pick today?

I couldn't help but reply, keeping our banter alive. On Wednesday, we went grocery shopping together and grabbed dinner out. People were definitely talking, I heard the whispers, but I pretended not to notice. The first time we went out in public, I was shaken, but I couldn't let it ruin the bubble of happiness I'd found with Boone.

The Boone I knew now wasn't the womanizing, arrogant cowboy I'd pegged him as. He was kind, funny, and somehow managed to put me at ease, even when he caught me off guard with his lingering stares. Those moments left me blushing and flustered, my mind drifting into dangerous territory. It was a problem I wasn't ready to confront.

A week had passed since the swimming hole, and we both avoided the topic. I thought about that evening more often than I cared to admit. Boone was still a shameless flirt, calling me *Darling* and commenting on my dresses, and I'd be lying if I said it didn't make me smile. The attraction was undeniable, but I couldn't let it ruin what I'd started to build here. Cassidy Ranch was starting to feel real, and I wasn't about to let Boone Cassidy be the reason I lost that.

I was wiping down one of the tables when I heard the familiar crunch of gravel. Right on time. Boone walked up the ramp and through the door, his heavy cowboy boots thudding against the floor. His hat was in his hands, and the sweat glistening on his skin made him look...well, delicious. His hair was tousled, like he'd been running his fingers through it, and that smile—God help me, that smile—had me undone.

"Please tell me you saved me a muffin," he said, pulling out a chair at the table next to the one I'd been cleaning and sinking into it with a sigh. One leg stretched out lazily, the other bent to cradle his worn, khaki cowboy hat.

And just like that, my resolve melted a little more.

"Who do you think I am?" I teased, tossing my rag onto the table. "I swear Mrs. Clint was ready to fight me for it. I think she could *sense* I was lying when I told her we were sold out. That woman has powers, I swear."

I walked around the counter and squatted down to pull out the last muffin of the day. Grabbing a paper bag, I headed back toward Boone. My strawberry-pattern sundress swayed with every step, and I couldn't help the little grin on my face. "But I held my ground." I handed him the bag triumphantly.

Boone chuckled low, a sound that sent warmth buzzing through me, as he ripped into the bag like a man starving. His first bite earned a groan of satisfaction, and my body reacted as if that noise were meant just for me. If I had pearls, I'd be clutching them. Clearing my throat, I smoothed my hands down the front of my dress in a weak attempt to compose myself.

"Just as good as I imagined." He set half the muffin on the paper bag while casually licking blueberry from his fingers. For the love of everything holy, I couldn't look away. The way his tongue moved, the slow sweep over each fingertip...it was like something out of an erotica scene. I swear time slowed down.

"So," Boone said, breaking the spell, "once we're done here, I'll head home and shower. Should I meet you on your porch? I've got some leftovers my mom gave me—I'd be willing to share." He stood, popping the rest of the muffin into his mouth and brushing the crumbs off on his jeans.

"I, uh..." I scrambled to find my voice, taking a deep breath to regain my composure. "I won't be able to tonight. I'm meeting Penny and Theo at The Tequila Cowboy." Guilt pricked at me when Boone remained unfazed.

"Oh, no worries," he said casually, grabbing a broom. "Let's get this place cleaned up so you can head out." He flashed me a smile that made me want to cancel my plans right then and there. But I needed this night out. I needed to see Theo and Penny, to laugh, let loose, and feel like myself again.

Boone and I worked side by side, chatting like usual as we finished the closing tasks. When we were done, I locked up, and we walked to our cabins together. Boone wished me a good night and added with a teasing smile, "Don't get into too much trouble."

"I won't. Trust me," I replied, laughing lightly. "I usually just sit on the sidelines and watch Theo and Penny go wild."

As I reached for my doorknob, I felt Boone lingering behind me. Turning to face him, I caught his serious expression.

"If anyone lays a hand on you, unwanted, of course, give me a call," he said, like it was nothing, before turning and heading toward his cabin without another word.

"Thanks!" I called after him, surprised I managed to get even one word out.

Before I went inside to get ready, I watched him walk away. For whatever reason, thinking about getting with a guy at the bar tonight had zero appeal to me. I was too focused on the ass filling the Wrangler jeans of my next-door neighbor.

THE TEQUILA COWBOY was exactly how I remembered it: loud, lively, and full of memories. Being here with Penny and Theo felt like stepping back into a part of my life I'd let slip away—good memories of carefree nights and laughter that echoed long after last call.

It'd been too long since the three of us had a night like this. Over the past few months, we'd drifted. Penny's new job at the library and Theo's constant traveling for work made it hard to keep in touch. At some point, I'd stopped trying as much. I told myself I was okay with the scattered visits and occasional phone calls, but being here now, I realized how much I'd missed them.

The truth was, I wasn't okay. Watching my friends thrive while I felt stuck left a knot of jealousy tangled with guilt. I wasn't unhappy for them—I wanted nothing more than their success. But I couldn't ignore the ache that came from knowing I wasn't where I wanted to be. It was a "me" problem, and it was eating me alive.

"To us," I said, raising my tequila shot.

"To us," Penny and Theo echoed, their smiles bright and warm.

As the tequila burned its way down, I made a silent promise to myself: life was short, and regret wasn't something I wanted to carry when I woke up one day, gray-haired and alone, wondering where the time had gone.

I closed my eyes, tipped back the tequila shot like a pro, and slammed the empty glass on the bar with a satisfying clink.

The Tequila Cowboy was Faircloud's one and only bar, and it embraced every bit of its divey charm. Bright neon lights buzzed overhead, ancient beer signs hung crookedly on the walls, and the bar tops had that sticky sheen you only get from decades of spilled drinks. It wasn't fancy, but it had character. My favorite part was the black-and-white checkered dance floor, its scuffed surface telling countless stories of late-night boots and two-steps.

Penny finished her shot and set her glass down, her gaze drifting across the bar like she was searching for someone. I followed her line of sight but came up empty. When she caught me watching, she cleared her throat and turned her focus back to our little group.

"Umm..." I began, raising an eyebrow. "Were we looking for someone?" My tone made it clear she wasn't getting out of this one without spilling.

Penny huffed, planting her hands on the bar. "Okay, fine. I'm coming clean," she said with a dramatic sigh. "Mac has been coming into the library a lot, and I kinda think he's super hot. I was hoping he'd be here tonight."

"Wait—Mac Ridley? As in Boone's friend Mac?" Theo asked, her tone tinged with disbelief.

"Yup," Penny replied, popping the "p" as she took a long sip of her martini. "Look, I just wanted to have a few drinks and maybe work up the courage to hook up with him. That's all." She threw her hands up in mock surrender.

I couldn't help it, I burst out laughing. Penny needing liquid courage was almost comical. Back in high school, Penny could have had any guy she wanted. Hell, even now, she could still pull any guy that walked through the door. She wasn't just stunning; she had this magnetic personality that made people want to be around her. At five foot two, with long chestnut hair and a figure that turned heads, Penny was pure dynamite.

Meanwhile, I'd always felt like her sidekick, wishing I could borrow just an ounce of her confidence. My curves didn't make me feel "sexy," which was why I gravitated toward dresses. The flowy fabric made me feel feminine without the self-consciousness tight jeans or tank tops brought.

"I haven't seen him yet tonight," I said with a grin. "But if I do, you'll be the first to know."

Penny picked at her nails, clearly trying to dodge further interrogation. "So, Theo, what's been new with you?" Clearly, she was wanting the conversation to go in another direction.

"Ugh, you know," Theo replied with a casual shrug, "traveling and working. I've seen some amazing places. Here, look!" She pulled out her phone and started flipping through photos.

Every time Theo talked about her photography, her face lit up. No wonder she didn't come back to Faircloud much—her life on the road looked like a dream. Stunning landscapes, bustling cities, moments frozen in time that most people would never get to see.

As I admired her photos, I couldn't help feeling a little awed by her. Theo had always been fiercely independent, the type of person who seemed untouchable. People in town often described her as cold or aloof, but Penny and I knew the truth. Beneath her tough exterior was a fiercely loyal and kindhearted friend.

"Speaking of traveling..." Theo trailed off, taking a sip of her drink. "I think I'm done for a while. I'm planning to stick around and settle down back home."

The shock must have been plain on my face because Theo raised an eyebrow at me. When I glanced at Penny, she looked just as stunned. Theo, the wanderer, wanting to settle down? There had to be more to the story.

"Okay..." I said slowly, unsure how to phrase the million questions swirling in my head. "Did you want to talk about it?"

"Soon." Theo took another sip of her drink and smiled faintly. "I'm just happy we're doing this. I needed to see you two."

Penny reached over and placed her hand over Theo's, and I did the same. For a moment, we sat there in silence, our hands stacked in solidarity.

I couldn't shake the feeling that something heavy was weighing on Theo, and from the look in Penny's eyes, I knew she felt the same. Whatever it was, Theo would tell us when she was ready. Until then, we'd pretend everything was normal, just like old times.

THE COVER BAND was incredible. Every song they played seemed handpicked to get us on the dance floor. Penny, Theo, and I spent most of the night dancing, arms wrapped around each other, laughing like we didn't have a single care in the world. I lost track of how many drinks I'd had—not that I was counting.

Eventually, we all needed a break. My feet were sore, and my body craved water like it was life itself. We claimed barstools at the far end of the bar, conveniently close to the bathroom. That's when

I realized my bladder was on the verge of exploding.

"I'll be right back," I said, sliding off my stool and weaving my way toward the restroom. The world swayed slightly as I walked, but I wasn't completely drunk. I was riding that perfect buzz where everything felt amazing, and I was still fully in control of myself.

The bathroom was small, with two stalls and sinks that looked like they'd seen better days. I ducked into the first stall, took care of business, and made my way to the sink.

I paused, gripping the edge of the counter, and stared at my reflection in the mirror. My hair, once styled into soft waves, was now pulled into a low ponytail, slick with sweat. My cheeks were flushed a rosy pink, a mix of heat and alcohol working their magic. Despite my disheveled state, I smiled at myself.

I felt happy. Carefree. Alive.

It had been a while since I'd felt this good. Usually, I was great at putting on a brave face, but deep down, I'd been feeling stuck—like my life was missing something. Excitement. Purpose. Connection. Sure, my job at The Coffee Cup was nice. It gave me the freedom I craved, but it wasn't enough.

I wanted more.

I wanted to own the shop. I wanted to be a business owner, a girl boss who called the shots. Instead, I was working at the farm stand, treading water until Ellie came back. Then what? Where did I go from there?

And writing... Writing had been my dream for as long as I could remember. It was something I rarely talked about—it felt too personal, too fragile. But maybe it was time to stop dreaming and start doing.

I sighed and let my head hang for a moment, taking a deep breath. This wasn't the time for a soul-searching pep talk. Not here, not now, not with tequila sunrises and countless shots still buzzing in my veins. I straightened, shook off the heavy thoughts, and decided to focus on the fun.

When I returned to the bar, Penny was sitting alone with two fresh drinks and a pair of shots waiting for us.

"Where's Theo?" I asked, sliding onto my stool.

"She left." Penny took a sip of her drink. "Said she wasn't feeling well. Told me to tell you goodnight and that she loves you."

I nodded, picking up my shot as Penny grabbed hers. I didn't ask any questions, I knew Penny didn't have the answers. Knowing Theo, she was vague upon leaving, and I wasn't in the mind frame to try to figure out what was going on.

We clinked glasses and downed them in unison. Before I could even set my glass down, Penny grabbed my hand, dragging me back to the dance floor, our drinks in tow.

CHAPTER 14

The country cover band played hit after hit, and we belted out every lyric at the top of our lungs. The dance floor was packed with locals, mostly older men, but we didn't care. We danced and swayed and laughed until time seemed to blur.

I'd danced so much that my feet were beginning to ache, and so were my cheeks from the smile I'd been wearing. This was the first time in a while I'd felt this connected to the town I loved and its people.

At some point, I realized my vision had gone fuzzy, and there was no way I could drive. Penny wasn't in much better shape, which meant we needed to find a ride home.

"What time is it?" Penny shouted over the music, swaying to the beat with her drink held high.

I fished my phone out of my bag for the first time since we'd arrived. A text from Boone lit up my screen:

Boone

I hope you're having a good time. I also hope those boys are keeping their hands to themselves.

I couldn't stop the smile that spread across my face. Butterflies, those persistent things that Boone seemed to command effortlessly, fluttered wildly in my stomach. The fact that he was thinking about me, even now, made my chest ache in the best way.

If he were here, I knew I wouldn't be able to keep my hands to myself.

The downright indecent thought I was having, like what it would feel like to be this intoxicated while I danced with Boone instead. How our bodies would feel pressed against each other as I brushed myself along his... Boone wasn't here, and I needed to focus.

For now, it was just me, Penny, and the dance floor—and that was enough.

"11:45!" I shouted back to Penny, my voice cutting through the music. "I'm in no shape to drive."

Penny burst into giggles, and soon we were both laughing uncontrollably, the kind of deep, belly laughter that made our sides hurt.

"I can call Boone," I managed to say through my laughter.

Penny raised an eyebrow, smirking. "Boone? You think he'll actually drive out here at midnight to pick up our drunk asses?"

I nodded with absolute certainty, holding up a finger. "Stay here. I'm calling him."

I stumbled my way out of the bar's front door and leaned against the cool brick wall. The fresh air felt amazing on my flushed skin. Pulling out my phone, I scrolled until I found his contact: "Hot Neighbor." With a grin, I pressed call and tilted my head back to gaze at the stars.

Two rings later, Boone's gravelly voice filled my ear. "What's up, Darling?"

The way he said that name sent a pleasant shiver down my spine. I couldn't help but giggle. "Darling," I echoed playfully, mostly to myself.

"Boone, I can't drive," I admitted, skipping any preamble.

"Mm-hmm..." he hummed, not with disapproval, but in that way that said, *Yeah, I figured.*

"It's a problem because I drove to the bar, and I'm usually the responsible one. I don't drink when we go out. I'm always on my best behavior!" I laughed, the tequila making me babble. "Except tonight."

"Mm-hmm..." he hummed again, like he was thoroughly amused.

"And Theo left, so it's just me and Penny now. We've been dancing and singing all night. I'm having fun! I like fun Aspen."

Boone's voice was warm, teasing. "Is this your way of asking me for a ride home?"

The giggles took over again, and I could barely answer. "Maybe," I said, drawing it out dramatically.

"I'll be there in a few. You two better drink some water before getting in my truck."

"Yes, sir." I gave a mock saluting to absolutely no one.

"Sir?" Boone asked, his voice laced with amusement. I heard rustling on his end, like he was getting up and moving around.

"What are you doing?" I asked, biting my lip as I leaned back against the wall.

"I'm putting on a shirt to come get your drunk ass," he replied casually, a humorous tone on the edge of his words.

My face heated, and I couldn't help but picture Boone shirtless, lounging on his couch. The thought made my stomach flip in a way I couldn't quite ignore.

"Why bother putting one on, Cowboy?" I teased, the liquor giving me a boldness I wouldn't have otherwise dared.

"Aspen..." he said, his tone a low warning, though not unkind.

I grinned mischievously, deciding to keep him on his toes. "I'll be waiting inside with Penny. Just look for the youngest girls on the dance floor when you get here." Before he could respond, I hung up, tucking my phone back into my clutch with a satisfied smile.

It was my sad attempt to be mysterious—maybe even a little sexy. Like, *Hey, come and get me.*

When I stepped back inside, the crowd had thinned. I spotted Penny on the dance floor, pressed against some guy who looked old enough to be her dad. He had a western Sam Elliott vibe—silver mustache and all. Kinda hot, honestly.

I made my way over and leaned in to whisper in her ear. "Boone's on his way. We need to drink some water before we," I used air quotes, "get in his truck."

Penny laughed, then turned to her dance partner, murmuring something to him. The man nodded, tipping his hat before retreating into the crowd.

I gave a puzzled look before looking at the guy who sauntered away, and then back to her.

"I told him my dad was coming to get us, so he'd better get stepping," Penny said with a shrug, taking my hand in hers.

I laughed, and together we swayed to the music, letting it carry us. The dance floor was clearing out as the older crowd trickled toward the exit, but Penny and I didn't care. We danced, laughing and spinning, holding on to the last moments of the night before reality came knocking in the form of Boone Cassidy and his pickup truck.

I wasn't sure how much time had passed as I sipped the last of my tequila sunrise. A cool breeze swept in from the front of the bar, and my head instinctively turned toward the door.

A dimly lit figure stepped inside—a white T-shirt, cowboy hat, and perfectly worn jeans. Even in the low light, I knew it was Boone.

Without thinking, I bolted toward him, excitement and tequila fueling my steps. When I reached him, I jumped, wrapping my arms and legs around him like some giddy main lead in a rom-com. The melted ice in my drink sloshed over the rim, dripping down his back.

"Whoa there," Boone laughed, steadying me with his hands on my hips as I slid down. My feet hit the floor, but I wobbled, and he caught me before I could embarrass myself further.

"Boone!" I shouted, grinning like a fool. "You came!"

"You called," he replied, his voice low, just for me.

The room seemed to pause. I was vaguely aware of people

watching, but I didn't care. Adrenaline and giddiness took over, and before I could think better of it, I snatched Boone's hat off his head and plopped it onto mine.

The bar erupted with cheers and whistles.

"Well?" I teased, tilting the hat just enough and flashing a playful grin. "Does it look as good on me as it does on you?"

I looked up into his ocean-blue eyes, my heart skipping a beat. Boone had this rugged, magnetic charm that made it impossible to look away.

But instead of smiling, his expression turned serious, his lips pressed into a thin line. My heart sank. His hands were still on my hips, but the confidence I'd been riding all night crumbled like a house of cards.

Boone leaned in close, his voice barely above a whisper. "Aspen, don't do that again unless you mean it. Restraint isn't one of my strengths, Darling."

He took the hat back, settling it onto his own head with maddening ease.

Embarrassment flooded me, hot and sharp. I stepped back from his hold, avoiding his gaze as I turned away. My boldness felt foolish now, stupid. Did I push the flirting too far?

I found Penny on the dance floor, grabbed her arm, and steered her toward the door without a word. The fun meter was officially empty. My mood had plummeted, and I felt like a complete idiot. Was he embarrassed by me? Worried about how it looked in public? Maybe he didn't want his reputation tarnished by being seen with *me*.

Penny seemed oblivious as she looped her arm through Boone's and thanked him for coming. He escorted her out, but I moved ahead, tossing my empty cup in the trash outside. I made a beeline for Boone's truck and planted myself at the back passenger door. No way was I sitting up front.

The last five minutes replayed in my head, each memory a dagger to my pride. I could still hear his voice telling me not to do it again unless I *meant it*. The humiliation clung to me, heavy and unshakable.

"I'm sitting in the back too!" Penny shouted, jogging to the other rear door. She grinned. "It's like he's our chauffeur!"

Boone unlocked the truck, and we climbed in. Penny chattered away, peppering Boone with questions about the ranch, his family, and his sister. He answered in his usual calm, unbothered way, but I stayed quiet, too lost in my own head to join in.

When we pulled up to Penny's apartment, she gave me a tight hug in the back seat. "I had a blast tonight!" she said, laughing as she kissed my cheek. "Call me in the morning!"

"I will," I promised with a faint smile, soaking in her warmth before letting her go.

Now it was just Boone and me. The silence in the truck was deafening. Not even the radio played to fill the void. I stared out the window, watching the dark trees blur by, wishing I could disappear.

My thoughts spiraled. My anxiety latched onto every mistake, every misstep, and wouldn't let go.

I closed my eyes, trying to focus on my breathing. Inhale. Exhale. But even as I tried to calm my racing heart, Boone's words lingered, heavy and confusing.

Don't do that again unless you mean it.

Boone's truck rumbled to a stop in front of our little cabins. Before he could even shift into park, I was already out, walking briskly toward my door and fumbling with my key.

"Aspen, wait!" Boone called, his boots crunching on the gravel as he jogged after me.

"Come on," I muttered under my breath, jamming the key into the lock. "Stupid old hunk of metal." It refused to budge. With a frustrated sigh, I yanked the key out and tried again.

Warm hands wrapped over mine, steadying them. Boone's voice was low, almost gentle. "Let me."

He slid the key into the lock, turning it with ease. The door creaked open, and I rushed inside, needing the space to breathe.

"Aspen," he said, his tone firmer now as he shut the door

behind him.

"What, Boone?" I asked, still refusing to look at him. I made my way toward the kitchen, bracing myself against the sink like it might hold me together. "I get it. Your reputation was on the line. I shouldn't have thrown myself all over you like that."

He let out a short, humorless laugh. "What the hell are you talking about?"

I rolled my head back, staring up at the ceiling. "Me, running into your arms tonight. Me, putting on your hat. It all looked too... cozy. I wouldn't want the whole town thinking I'm tying you down or something." Turning to face him, I crossed my arms, my dress swishing with the motion. "I know what it looked like, Boone. And for the record, it's not the first hat I've put on my head."

That last part was a lie, and the tick in Boone's jaw told me he wanted to believe me.

His eyes locked onto mine, and for a moment, neither of us spoke. I thought I could hold my ground, but his next words shattered that illusion.

"You wanna ride me, then, huh?"

My stomach dropped. Heat rushed up my neck, spreading like wildfire across my skin. Boone's words hung in the air, thick and electric. My body reacted instinctively, a traitorous warmth pooling in my core.

My mind betrayed me. What would happen if I let this tension boil over? The idea of him, of us, sent my heart racing.

I let out a huff, needing to escape. Without answering, I brushed past him, heading down the short hall to my bedroom. My heels were killing me, and I needed them off.

The heavy thud of Boone's boots followed.

I barely had time to sit on the bed before his deep voice filled the doorway.

"I didn't say what I said back there because of my reputation," he began, his tone sharp, cutting. "I said it because it's not like you to throw yourself at some guy while drunk in a bar. When you put my hat on, Aspen, you were telling everyone in that room you wanted me. Do you even realize what that means?"

His words hit like a slap, and yet...I couldn't stop imagining what it would feel like to scream his name, to have his hands exploring every inch of me.

"And wasn't it you," he continued, "who didn't want your brother finding out about the swimming hole?"

I shot to my feet, anger bubbling up to meet my confusion. "Don't you dare throw that back in my face. You know I didn't mean it like that." My fists clenched at my sides, my voice rising. "You don't know me, Boone. What gives you the right to assume anything about me? Maybe I *do* want everyone to know I'm attracted to you. Maybe I *do* want the whole damn town to know how badly I want to scream your name."

Boone's jaw tightened, his eyes burning into mine.

He shook his head, stepping back. "We're not having this conversation right now. You're drunk."

"Oh, so now you're dodging?" I fired back, my boldness fueled by tequila. "What's the matter, Cowboy? Don't want to talk about me riding you?"

Boone let out a long breath, pinching the bridge of his nose. "Goodnight, Aspen." His voice was steady again, maddeningly calm. "I'll see you in the morning. I'll bring the coffee."

Without giving me a chance to respond, he turned and left, the door clicking shut behind him.

I collapsed back onto the bed, groaning into the pillows. Why couldn't I have just let it go? The entire night replayed in my head, every flirtation, every misstep. Who even was I tonight?

Later, as I stood in front of the bathroom mirror, half-heartedly wiping off my makeup, I mumbled all the things I *should* have said.

You don't control me. Drunk or not, I'd still want you. Just take advantage of me already.

I groaned, shaking my head. I needed to stop before I drove myself insane. Tomorrow was a new day, a chance to fix things—or make them even more complicated.

For now, I climbed into bed, willing sleep to take me before my thoughts could wander back to Boone Cassidy and the way his hands felt on my hips.

CHAPTER 15

I woke up with a pounding headache. For someone who claimed drinking wasn't her thing, I'd been hungover more times this week than in my entire life.

Groaning, I swung my legs out of bed and shoved my feet into my cow slippers. Every step toward the bathroom felt like a test of survival. The room spun, and my brain throbbed like it was trying to escape my skull.

Splashing cold water on my face, I prayed for a miracle. Instead, I got a good look at myself in the mirror—red eyes, puffy bags, and a complexion that screamed *you made bad choices.* At least I'd had the foresight to halfheartedly attempt my skincare routine before collapsing into bed.

I tried not to think about last night. It was the kind of memory that made your stomach churn and not just because of the tequila. The shame crept in anyway. I had thrown myself at Boone Cassidy like a moth to a flame—or, more accurately, like a drunk woman to a very sexy cowboy. Taking his hat and putting it on my head? What was I thinking?

Actually, I knew exactly what I was thinking. A small part of me had hoped for something straight out of a romance novel—Boone storming across the bar, picking me up, and tossing me into the back of his truck. Instead, I got a stern look and a cryptic warning.

When Boone walked into that bar, his white T-shirt clinging to him in all the right places, cowboy hat perfectly tilted, and those damn jeans—well, my sex drive had hit overdrive. And when he showed up just because I'd called him for a ride, it was game over. Acts of service? Be still, my heart.

Still, regret weighed heavy on me this morning. I needed someone to help me sort through the mess I'd made. On the second ring, Penny's face filled my phone screen, her wild hair sticking up in every direction.

"My brain is a raisin!" she yelled, pulling her blanket tighter around her.

"Shhh," I groaned, pressing my fingers to my temples. "Penny, I messed up last night."

"I'm glad you said it first," she replied, sitting up in bed and propping the phone against something. "What the hell was that?"

"I don't know!" I wailed, rubbing my face with both hands. "I saw him walk in, looking like *that*, and it's like my libido hijacked my body."

"Oh, people are definitely talking about this." Penny grinned like she was a gossip columnist gathering information for her next piece. "Aspen Westgrove, the town's sweetheart, throws herself at Boone Cassidy, the resident bad boy. They probably think you two had a full-on bar hookup."

"That is *not* true!" I exclaimed, but her words only made my headache worse.

"Sure, we know that." She shrugged. "But you know how this town works. Rumors here spread faster than wildfire."

I groaned dramatically, tossing my head back.

"So." Penny's tone switched to something wickedly curious. "What happened when you got home? Did he throw you around like a rag doll? Please tell me it was hot." She was practically panting for details.

I let out a miserable sigh. "The opposite."

Her eyes widened. "Oh, so he made sweet, sweet love to you? That's...not what I expected from Boone, but okay, I'm intrigued."

I rolled my eyes. "No, Penny. We didn't sleep together. We argued. Well, I argued. He kind of just stood there being all calm and frustrating."

"What did he say in the bar? He had this stern look on his face."

"Ugh, yeah. He took the hat back and said something like, 'Don't do that again unless you mean it,' because next time he wouldn't hold back." I threw up air quotes, the words still echoing in my mind.

Penny gasped dramatically, clutching her blanket. "Oh, that's good. Like, *really good*. He clearly wants you."

"Well, it didn't feel good at the time," I muttered, slumping further into my shame spiral.

Penny smirked. "Sweetheart, you've got a live wire on your hands. Now the real question is, what are you going to do about it? Because that man wants you in his bed but doesn't want to make the first move."

"If that were true, he would've taken me up on the offer last night," I groaned, pacing my bathroom. "I basically announced to the whole bar that I wanted to ride the cowboy, and he rejected me."

"Come on!" Penny shrieked, only to wince at her own volume. She quickly adjusted, lowering her voice. "You cannot be serious. He didn't sleep with you because you were clearly drunk and he wasn't. That's not rejection—it's decency!"

I wasn't convinced. Boone Cassidy wasn't just any guy. He had a reputation as the town's unattainable bachelor. A man like him wasn't about to let anyone, let alone me, mess with his image.

If he wanted to shed it, he would've done it years ago.

"No way," I muttered, wetting my toothbrush and smearing toothpaste on it. Before I could say more, a knock at my front door startled me.

My eyes darted to Penny, who mouthed, *Who is that?*

I shrugged. *I don't know,* I mouthed back.

"Let me call you back," I whispered, setting the toothbrush

on the sink.

"If it's trouble, send an SOS text. I'll come running...as fast as I can in this condition," she whispered dramatically. "Love you!"

"Love you too." I ended the FaceTime call, set my phone on the counter, and padded toward the door. Peering through the crack as I slowly turned the knob, I froze.

Standing on my porch, Boone Cassidy held two steaming cups of coffee, looking maddeningly casual in plaid pajama pants and a black V-neck T-shirt. His hair was mussed like he'd just rolled out of bed, and my mouth watered—and not at the coffee.

"Are you going to let me in or just stare?" he drawled, one corner of his mouth lifting.

I cleared my throat, swinging the door open wider. Boone's gaze swept over me, lingering a little too long on my tank top and shorts—neither of which left much to the imagination. As if on cue, the morning chill tightened things that shouldn't have been noticeable.

"Uh, yeah, come in," I stammered, crossing one arm over my chest. "I'll...grab a sweatshirt."

Boone stepped inside, the scent of coffee and something distinctly him trailing behind. I bolted to my bedroom, yanking on an oversized sweatshirt that covered everything—and I mean everything. When I returned, Boone was leaning against the kitchen counter, one coffee cup in his hand, the other waiting beside him.

"I brought you coffee," he said, nodding toward the plain white mug.

"Thanks." I approached cautiously, wrapping my hands around the cup. The scent hit me first: freshly brewed coffee with a hint of cinnamon. When I took a sip, the warmth spread through me, bringing a small, involuntary smile to my lips. Cream, no sugar—just the way I liked it.

Boone watched me, his expression unreadable, before breaking the silence. "We need to talk about last night."

"Nope." I shook my head, retreating to the couch. "Absolutely not. It's way too early, and I need this coffee to start working before we even *think* about going there."

Boone followed, sitting on the coffee table directly in front of me. His knees brushed mine, boxing me in. "Just hear me out."

I stared at him warily, but he pressed on.

"Please don't take what I did as rejection," he began, his voice low and sincere. "It wasn't that I didn't want to hook up with you. Hell, I would've loved to take you to the bed of my truck and...well, you get the idea."

My cheeks burned as his lips twitched into a smirk, but I refused to give him the satisfaction of reacting.

"But," he continued, the humor fading, "you had enough alcohol in your system to knock out an elephant. That's not how I want things to go down between us."

His words caught me off guard, and my confusion must've shown because he leaned closer, softening his tone.

"What I'm trying to say is... I like having you around, Aspen. I like spending time with you. And if we take this thing between us further, past the kissing and touching from the other night, I don't want to screw it up. I don't want you to think all I care about is sex. I like our friendship. I like your muffins."

He sighed, running a hand through his messy hair. "If we cross that line, I don't want you to feel like just another name on a list. Because you're not."

Whatever this was between us, this budding friendship, felt worth more than just one steamy night.

"I feel the same way," I murmured, staring into my coffee cup. "I'm attracted to you. I think that's pretty obvious. Last night, I don't know what came over me to act like that." I refused to meet his eyes, my cheeks burning with embarrassment.

"I meant what I said," Boone replied, his voice steady and sure. "I want to get to know you."

I wanted that too. If it meant taming my libido, I'd figure it out. Somehow. I'd never been this drawn to someone before, and it would take some serious self-control. My next-door neighbor: the town's notorious "bad boy," a rancher, and now...my friend.

"Me too," I confessed softly, finally looking up at him. Our eyes met, and something unspoken passed between us. Boone smiled, and I couldn't help but grin back.

"Why don't we head up to the main house and grab some breakfast?" Boone suggested as he stood, tapping my knee lightly. The small touch sent a jolt of electricity straight through me, a stark reminder of just how much trouble I was in. How was I supposed to be *friends* with Boone if every glance and touch sent my brain spiraling?

"Oh, please," I groaned, tipping my head back dramatically. "Bacon sounds like heaven right now."

Boone chuckled, plucking the coffee cup from my hands. "I'll run next door and throw on some clothes. Be back in ten minutes. That enough time?"

"Plenty!" I called out, already darting toward my bedroom to find something to wear.

"NO WAY! I can't believe you just said that out loud," I exclaimed, laughing as Boone and I strolled up the gravel path to the main house.

"Root beer is, in fact, better than Dr. Pepper," Boone declared with an unapologetic shrug. "You can't change my mind."

This morning, I'd ditched the dress in favor of black biker shorts and an oversized T-shirt. My hair was messily piled into a bun with loose strands framing my face. No makeup—there was absolutely no energy for that. Greasy breakfast at Boone's parents' house didn't exactly warrant a full glam routine.

Before we met back up, I'd given myself a stern pep talk. I needed to pull it together. If I wanted to keep hanging out with Boone without completely unraveling, I had to lock up my feelings and toss away the key. Scout's honor.

Because as much as I wanted him—and, wow, did I want

him—I knew pushing boundaries would only make things messier. The attention Boone gave me was intoxicating, but I couldn't let it cloud my judgment. I'd manage. Somehow.

We stepped into the Cassidy family kitchen, where the smell of breakfast hit me like a warm hug. Boone's mom, Jill, was putting the finishing touches on a casserole at the counter. I hadn't been to the house since that first dinner when they asked me to work at the farm stand. It was just as charming as I remembered—full of life, love, and about a million family photos.

Boone walked over to Jill and kissed the top of her head. The simple gesture tugged at something in my chest. Watching the easy affection between Boone and his mom made me ache for the kind of family closeness I'd never really had.

"Hi, Mrs. Cassidy," I said, giving her a little wave. I lingered awkwardly near the edge of the kitchen island, resting my hands on the cool marble surface because I never knew what to do with them in situations like this.

"Aspen, call me Jill," she insisted with a warm smile, motioning toward the big wooden farm table in the dining room. Boone picked up two plates and gestured for me to follow.

"I made breakfast casserole," Jill announced proudly as she set a dish on the table. "All of the family favorites crammed into one pan. Do you know how hard it is to make breakfast when everyone wants something different?"

"No," I admitted with a small laugh.

Truthfully, I didn't. My family wasn't like this. My brother and I were so far apart in age that we'd barely grown up together. By the time I was old enough to want his attention, he was already off doing his own thing. Life had always felt lonely, like navigating the world as an only child. It wasn't until much later that I realized my brother had my back all along.

But seeing this—Boone, Jill, and this warm, inviting home—I couldn't help but feel like I was catching a glimpse of something I didn't even know I'd been missing.

"This looks amazing." I inhaled the mouthwatering aroma of

bacon, eggs, and a medley of spices. Was that sausage in there too? Jill began dishing out four servings, making me wonder if Boone's dad would be joining us.

I took my plate and set it in front of me. Jill sat across the table, with the mysterious fourth plate next to her, while Boone settled to my left.

"The farm stand has been doing amazing," Jill said, her pride evident as she took a bite of her casserole.

"That's wonderful!" I exclaimed, scooping a forkful into my mouth. She wasn't kidding, it was a little bit of everything, perfectly combined. The salty meat paired with a fluffy, slightly sweet layer of pancakes—or was it French toast?—created a flavor explosion. I swallowed, savoring the deliciousness. "I love working there. I know it's only been a short time, but it feels so rewarding."

"I haven't seen the stand this busy," Boone added, setting down his fork and wiping his mouth with a napkin.

"How's everything working out? Those jars you made have been such a hit. The teachers at school are raving about them!" Jill replied.

Her praise warmed me from the inside out, and I couldn't help but grin. "It's going really well! I've got a few ideas lined up for this week: local handmade jewelry, candles, and other cute gift items. I think they'll be a great addition."

"Sorry I'm late," a deep voice called out from around the corner. I twisted in my chair just as Boone's dad walked into the room. He looked like an older version of Boone—rugged, with kind eyes. Taking the seat next to Jill, he didn't waste time digging into his plate.

"Nice to see you, son," he said, giving Boone a nod before turning his attention to me. "And you, Aspen. Always a pleasure."

We spent the rest of breakfast chatting, the conversation flowing easily. Boone's parents asked about me—my interests, my work—and I reciprocated with questions about the ranch. The Cassidy family was warm, welcoming, and refreshingly free of judgment. It was easy to see why Boone was so grounded.

That comforting feeling dissolved when my phone buzzed under my thigh. I discreetly slid it out to check the notification.

A text from my mom. Of course. It was like she had radar for my moments of peace. Guilt prickled at my chest as I read her message.

Mom

Hi sweetie! Are you free today? Your dad and I miss you and would love to see you.

I missed them too. But our relationship was... complicated. My parents' love came with a side of constant critique. If something wasn't done their way, it was wrong. My dream of becoming a romance author? Absolutely laughable to them. Ever since The Coffee Cup closed, my dad had been urging me to "get a real job."

Working at the farm stand felt like a fresh start, but it didn't seem like enough in their eyes. They couldn't see that I was content, even happy. My dad only saw that I was barely making ends meet. Deep down, I knew I needed to start writing, to really give my dream a shot. But the fear of failing—or worse, proving them right—kept me paralyzed.

I quickly typed a reply before my mom's patience ran out and she called instead.

I have some free time today. I'll come over this afternoon. Love you.

Tucking my phone back under my leg, I rejoined the conversation. After we finished eating, I helped clear the dishes and carried them to the kitchen. Turning on the faucet, I began rinsing plates and adding soap.

"Oh, honey, don't worry about that!" Jill's voice floated in from behind me. "Dan can toss it all in the dishwasher later."

"Are you sure?" I asked, letting the water run to warm up.

Jill smiled and turned off the faucet before I could protest further. "Yes! Let that man handle a chore for once," she said, her soft voice carrying a playful tone. "I think Boone's waiting for you in the foyer." She nodded toward the hallway, and I followed her gaze.

Boone stood there, staring down at his phone, texting someone. That gave me a moment to take him in. He looked so good—effortlessly handsome. The slope of his nose, the chiseled jaw, the rounded biceps stretching the fabric of his shirt. Was I sweating?

After saying my goodbyes, I joined him at the front door. When I came into view, he tucked his phone into his pocket and flashed me a smile that made my stomach flutter. Holding the door open, he gestured for me to step through.

The walk back to the cabins was quiet, but not in an awkward way. The silence felt comforting, like a space we both understood didn't need filling. My thoughts, however, weren't as calm. I couldn't stop rehearsing the conversation I'd inevitably have with my parents. What would I say when they asked about my plans? Would I finally tell them the truth—that I wanted to be an author? Or would I spin some story about going back to school? Just the thought of their reactions turned my stomach into knots.

"Hey, what's wrong?" Boone's voice pulled me from my spiral.

"Nothing!" I replied quickly, forcing a cheerful tone. "I was just thinking about how good your mom's casserole was. Where did she learn the recipe?"

It seemed to satisfy Boone, because he didn't push further. "One morning, she got fed up with everyone asking for different things and just threw it all in a pan. It stuck, and now it's been her signature dish since I was a kid. She hasn't shared the recipe with anyone. I think it's her way of keeping us coming around as we get older."

It sounded like something straight out of a movie. I didn't even know how to respond, so I just smiled, hoping he didn't notice the lump in my throat.

Before facing my parents, I knew I needed a moment to breathe. It felt like gearing up for a big exam. I'd have to memorize my answers to all their questions just to make it through without starting a fight.

When we reached the cabins, I trudged inside to reluctantly get ready. For them, I'd put in the effort—dress nicely, slap on some makeup, and look the part of a daughter who had her life together. At least the coffee and breakfast had done their job; I felt more human and less like a hungover mess.

Once I was ready, I grabbed my purse and headed to my car, my steps heavy with dread. With a deep breath, I braced myself for what was sure to be the performance of a lifetime.

MY PARENTS STILL lived in my childhood home, a cozy white rancher nestled on an acre of wooded land. The house hadn't changed a bit. Its long driveway, winding through tall trees. When I pulled in and parked, it felt like stepping into a time capsule.

I didn't bother knocking—I never did. Letting myself in, I was greeted by the familiar sounds of the TV blaring a mid-day soap. My mom was likely perched on the couch, glued to the drama, while my dad sat nearby with his Sudoku book. They were, and always had been, homebodies.

"Oh! Our beautiful daughter!" Mom exclaimed, pausing her show and rising to meet me.

"That's me," I said, grinning as I hugged her tight. She smelled like she always did—jasmine, orange blossom, and just a hint of sandalwood. It was her signature perfume, something she never went a day without.

"What about me?" my dad teased, standing and pulling me into a suffocating bear hug before kissing my temple.

"Why don't we go sit out back?" Mom suggested as she

ushered us toward the patio. "I've got lemonade and snacks in the fridge. You two go ahead, I'll bring everything out."

The backyard had always been my haven growing up. Even now, its peacefulness drew me in. The yard stretched out, surrounded by dense trees, with no neighbors in sight. The only sounds were the rustling leaves and birds chirping their melodies. I settled into the head of the patio table, soaking in the nostalgia, while Dad took the seat next to me, quiet but content as we waited for Mom.

She didn't take long to appear with a tray of snacks and lemonade. As she set the spread on the table, I couldn't help but notice how my brother, Parker, and I both favored her blond hair but had inherited Dad's striking blue eyes. Dad's black hair was now streaked with gray, and Parker's towering six-foot-something height always made people wonder where it came from, given our parents' petite frames.

"So, tell us how the farm stand is going," Mom said, pouring herself a glass of lemonade. "The ladies I play dominos with won't stop raving about you and all the changes you've made!"

"It's going great!" I replied, my excitement slipping out before I could tone it down. "I've been adding lots of new products and ideas. The hours are nice, and the Cassidys have given me so much freedom to make it my own."

"That's wonderful, sweetie." A smile tugging at his lips. But then came the inevitable. "It sounds like a great stepping stone for you to transition into something bigger."

There it was. The not-so-subtle hint. Mom nodded in agreement, and I braced myself.

"Yeah, well, I'm happy there," I said evenly, taking a sip of lemonade. "The cabin feels more like home than my apartment ever did."

"That's great," Mom added, taking a bite of cheese and cracker. "But maybe it's time to start exploring options for a real job."

If only they knew what I wanted my "real job" to be. My

parents had always envisioned me in tech or medicine—stable careers in the city, complete with a house, a steady income, and a perfect husband. They'd never understand my dream of being an author, of writing stories that might one day matter to someone.

I was twenty-five, stuck in that in-between phase where friends were either getting married, starting families, or still figuring life out. I fell firmly into the latter, though I at least knew what I wanted. My problem was self-doubt and fear of failure.

"Right," I said flatly. "I have a plan. You don't need to worry about me. Ellie will be back soon, and when she is, I'll be onto bigger things."

A bald-faced lie. Ellie's return date was as uncertain as my future.

The conversation meandered through updates on my friends, books I'd recommended to Mom, and Dad's concerns over how long it'd been since Parker visited. Things were going smoothly until Dad blindsided me with a question that made me choke on my lemonade.

"What's going on with you and that Cassidy boy?"

"Jack!" Mom hissed, glaring at him.

"What do you mean?" I managed, trying to keep my composure.

"The guys I golf with mentioned some rumors in town about you two dating. If it's true, I'd like to know. And I need to meet him first, of course. Can't have people knowing before your old man."

"Dad, we're just friends," I insisted, my voice steady despite the flush creeping up my neck. "I work for his family! Of course, I'm seen with him. You know how this town loves to gossip."

Nice save, Aspen. I prayed he didn't know about the bar incident and the cowboy hat. That would've been a whole other level of awkward.

"Well." Dad set his glass down, "if there is someone, I want to meet him. And for the record, I don't think that Cassidy boy is good enough for you. You're better than this town, and one day, you'll realize it."

No wonder I never dated in high school. Introducing someone to Dad would've been a nightmare.

"Speaking of dating," Mom interjected with a sly grin, "I'd love some grandchildren."

"Look at the time!" I said, glancing at my wrist as if wearing a watch. "I have things to do at home. Love you both!"

After kissing them on the cheek and dodging their questions about my next visit, I made a hasty exit. Once in the car, I let out a sigh, sinking into the seat. The guilt weighed heavy, knowing I hadn't told them the truth—about Boone, about my dreams, about anything that really mattered.

CHAPTER 16

Boone

Spending my afternoon coaxing chickens into their new coop wasn't exactly on my agenda for the day. Chickens weren't so bad, I'd thought—until I had them chirping and flapping all over the box in my truck, leaving their mark in ways I'd rather not describe. Relief flooded me when I finally pulled into the driveway and set them outside where they belonged.

The chaos helped distract me from thinking about Aspen. After she'd called me drunk last night, I couldn't shake the feeling I should've been there from the start. I should've roped the guys into a night out, disguised as some casual fun, just to keep an eye on her.

When I arrived at the bar, her reaction had been...unexpected. The way her face lit up, the sheer joy in her smile as she ran toward me—it sparked something I hadn't felt in a long time. But the moment she'd placed my hat on her head stuck with me, and not for the reasons it should have.

I'd taken the hat back, guilt swirling in my chest. I didn't want the gesture to be fake or fueled by alcohol. I'd had plenty of girls toss my hat on their heads, acting like it was some kind of trophy. But Aspen? She was different. I wanted her to wear it longer, more than just one night.

Truth be told, I wouldn't have minded letting the entire bar witness me claiming her, staking my territory so no one else would get any ideas. But with Aspen, I wanted more. More than one night, more than a fleeting moment. I wasn't ready to dive into all that, though, so I pushed the feelings aside, pretending that being "just friends" was enough.

When I stepped outside for some air, movement from Aspen's porch caught my attention. Like clockwork, she was curled up on her swing, a glass of wine in one hand and a book in the other. My legs moved before my brain could stop them, and I jogged down the steps, heading toward her.

She looked up as I approached, her face breaking into that smile—the one I'd already committed to memory. "Right on time," she teased, scooting over to make room for me. She tucked her blanket tighter around her legs, taking a sip of wine.

"What are we reading tonight?" I asked, settling beside her and draping my arm along the back of the swing. My hand itched to touch her shoulder, to pull her closer, but I held back.

"It's a second-chance romance," she said, closing the book and setting it on the railing in front of us. "Winn and Harriet were engaged, but now they're not. None of their friends know, and they're stuck on vacation together, pretending to still be in love." She leaned back against the swing, her eyes sparkling. "They obviously still love each other."

"Sounds... entertaining?" I ventured, unsure how else to respond.

She let out a short laugh. "I guess you could say that."

I pushed gently against the floor, setting the swing in motion. "How was the rest of your day?" I asked, our gazes fixed on the horizon.

Aspen scoffed. "As good as it can be after visiting my parents."

I turned to look at her, catching the soft curve of her nose in profile. It swooped down to a delicate button that suited her perfectly. "Want to talk about it?"

She sighed, taking another sip of her wine. "Actually, yeah. I love my parents, but they've always wanted a different life for me. They had this vision, me as a nurse or working in tech. Something stable. They don't get that those things just...aren't me. It doesn't matter how many times I tell them I'm happy, that I liked working at The Coffee Cup. To them, a real job is what defines you. They don't understand that I want time to read and enjoy life."

She paused, her voice turning softer. "My dream is to be an author."

Hearing her say that didn't surprise me. In the short time I'd really known Aspen, it was clear that writing was her calling. She always had her nose in a book, would light up when talking about stories.

"Then do it," I said simply, meeting her gaze. Her eyes shimmered like my words were something she hadn't heard before.

She blinked, her cheeks tinged pink. "If I ever told my parents that, they'd laugh. Or worse, tell me it's unrealistic. But I love books, imagining the stories I could create. Still, every time they ask about my future, I lie. I tell them I've got it all figured out, but the truth is...I'm scared. What if I can't do it? What if I'm not good enough?"

Her vulnerability tugged at something deep inside me. I leaned closer, catching the faint scent of blueberries clinging to her skin. I'd never cared much for the fruit before, but now? It was my new favorite.

"Why let them have that kind of control over you?" I asked, my voice softer now, but firm.

"I don't know. I don't think I could write about something I haven't experienced or don't understand," she said thoughtfully, her eyes fixed on the horizon.

"What do you want to write about?" I asked, genuinely curious.

"Love. Romance." She smiled softly, looking out into the distance. "I love when a story pulls me in, makes me feel like I'm living it. The emotions, the euphoria that comes with finding a truly great book, it's indescribable. I want to create stories that make people feel that way, that they can relate to."

She took another sip of her drink and leaned her head back

against the edge of the swing. Her head rested lightly on my forearm, an unintentional touch that sent my heart racing. I held my breath, grateful when she didn't pull away.

"What if I helped you?" The words tumbled out before I could stop them. It was a terrible idea, but her reaction—bursting into laughter, her body shaking as she covered her mouth—almost made it worth it.

"You?" she asked between giggles. "You want to help me write a romance novel?"

"Well, I'm not going to *write* it," I clarified, cheeks heating. "But what if I helped in another way?" My idea sounded ridiculous even in my own head, but I pressed on. "What if I took you on dates? Brought you flowers? You know, all the things guys do to impress a girl. As friends, of course. Maybe it'll give you the inspiration you need to write and prove your parents wrong."

I held my breath, hoping she'd go along with it. Deep down, I knew this was a terrible plan. I told myself it was purely to help Aspen, nothing more. But a tiny voice in the back of my mind whispered that maybe, just maybe, this could be something more.

Aspen was quiet for what felt like an eternity, mumbling to herself as she considered it. Finally, she nodded. "Okay. But we need ground rules."

"Agreed."

"First, no touching. After yesterday, that's definitely off the table." Her tone was firm, but I nodded, even though I hated the idea.

"Second, this stays between us. People in town might see us, but we'll remind everyone we're just friends." Another smart rule. The last thing I needed was the guys giving me grief over this.

"And third," she said, her voice serious, "we only go on three dates. No more. That keeps it strictly platonic."

"Is that it?" I asked, trying to keep my tone neutral.

"For now." Aspen added a smirk for good measure. "If I think of anything else, I'll let you know. Should I draft a contract?"

I chuckled and took her outstretched hand, giving it a firm

shake. "I don't think a contract is necessary, but if it makes you feel better, go ahead."

"What do you want in return?" she asked, tilting her head.

I pretended to think, but the answer was obvious. "Just keep baking me those muffins, Darling."

Her face turned bright red as she groaned and buried it in her hands. "Oh God! This sounds like something straight out of a romance novel."

"So, we're off to a good start," I teased, letting my hand rest briefly on her knee before realizing what I'd done. I jerked it back quickly. "I already screwed up, didn't I?"

She peeked at me from behind her hands, her lips curving into a small smile. "I think it's okay. Just...don't let it linger."

Contract or not, I knew I'd just signed myself up for trouble. What had I been thinking, offering to take Aspen on dates? Life was about to get a whole lot more interesting.

CHAPTER 17

I won't be able to swing by the stand after work today...

Aspen

😯 you mean I have to clean up all by myself... rude 🙄

Meet me at the barn after you close up, I'll make it up to you I promise.

Aspen

...

And don't forget my muffin.

Logan texted me this morning to say he had to go out of town for a bit, leaving Rhodes and me to cover for him. It wasn't like Logan to leave on short notice, which made the text unusual, but I didn't have time to dwell on it. Between the extra work and everything on my list today, I barely had a moment to spare. Still, I wasn't going to let it stop me from keeping my promise to Aspen.

Tonight was our first "date," and I was determined to make it special.

Thinking about Aspen and her family's lack of support stirred something in me. I couldn't imagine living with the weight of knowing my dreams weren't enough for the people who were supposed to believe in me the most. My family was the opposite. If I'd decided not to stay on the ranch, my dad wouldn't have batted an eye. He never pressured me into taking on the family business—it was something I chose.

From a young age, I knew this life was meant for me. The work was hard, but it was rewarding, and there was pride in carrying on what generations before me had built. If I'd told my parents I wanted to go to college instead, they'd have been the first ones to help me figure it out. Hell, with all the trouble I caused as a kid, I don't know how they didn't pack up my things and ship me off somewhere. I'd been suspended more times than I'd like to admit, drank too much, slept around, and spent way too many nights in the back of a cop car. Just a stupid teenage boy running wild with his stupid friends.

But my family never turned their backs on me. They gave me space to figure out my shit and grow from it. I wouldn't be the man I am today without them.

I was adjusting the stirrups on Marty, one of our six horses, when I heard a rustling behind me. Turning, I saw Aspen walking toward the barn, a brown paper bag in her hand and a beaming smile on her face.

"I got your request, Cowboy," she called, waving the bag playfully.

As she handed it over, the sweet scent of her filled the air, and I felt an odd sense of comfort.

"My mouth's already watering," I said, grinning as I tucked the bag into Marty's saddlebag.

Aspen glanced at the horse and then back at me, her brows raised skeptically. "Are we doing what I think we're doing?"

I leaned against Marty, smirking. "If you think we're going

horseback riding, then yeah."

Her gaze shifted to the horse, then back to me. "You're serious?"

I held out my hand. "Come on, it'll be fun."

Without hesitation, she placed her hand in mine. The instant our skin touched, a jolt of energy shot through me, like I'd grabbed a live wire. I glanced at her to see if she felt it too, but her expression was calm, collected—completely unaffected. Maybe I was imagining things.

I led her into the barn, where Louise was ready and waiting. Louise was an old hand, gentle and patient—the perfect horse for a beginner. "This is Louise," I said, patting the mare's neck. "She'll take good care of you."

Aspen ran a hand down Louise's mane, her hesitation melting into a soft smile. "She's beautiful."

"She is," I agreed, though I wasn't sure if I was talking about Louise or the way Aspen looked, standing there with the barn light catching her hair.

As I helped Aspen get acquainted with Louise, I couldn't help but feel a mix of excitement and nerves. Tonight was about giving her an experience worth writing about, but a small part of me hoped it would be worth remembering too.

"I've never been horseback riding before," Aspen murmured, her voice barely above a whisper.

"Here, put your hand out."

We approached Louise from the front but slightly off to the side, making sure to avoid her blind spot. As we got closer, she let out a gentle whinny, and Aspen instinctively pulled her hand back.

"It's okay," I assured her. "Just keep your hand outstretched. She'll come to you."

Right on cue, Louise nudged her nose against Aspen's hand, a soft reassurance. Aspen's face lit up with a smile as she turned her hand slightly, letting the horse nuzzle the back of it.

"She's a gentle girl." I watched the connection form between them, a smile blooming on Aspen's face. "I thought we could practice a bit here, then ride up to my favorite overlook for the sunset."

"That sounds lovely," Aspen replied, stroking Louise's nose with growing confidence.

I slid the mounting mourning block closer. "Step up here," I instructed, tapping the stirrup. "Put your foot in and swing your back leg over. I'll hold her steady."

Aspen hesitated for only a moment before stepping onto the stool. She placed her foot in the stirrup and swung her leg over, her dress shifting slightly in the process. I quickly took off my hat and held it to shield her until she was situated. When I was sure she was comfortable, I placed my hat back on my head.

"You're a natural," I said with a grin, grabbing the reins.

"I feel so tall up here!" Aspen exclaimed, her voice tinged with delight.

She looked beautiful up there—radiant, even.

I guided Louise out of the barn at a gentle pace, and Aspen bent forward slightly to pet her mane, letting her fingers trail down the horse's neck. As we emerged into the open, the golden hues of dusk bathed everything in a warm glow.

We started in a wide circle, and I talked Aspen through the basics—how to guide, the dos and don'ts of riding, and how to stay balanced. She listened intently, nodding along as she took in every word.

"How's it feeling?" I asked, watching her carefully.

"Fun!" she replied with a cheerful laugh. "I think I'm getting the hang of it. She's so sweet."

Louise let out a soft huff as if to say, *That's me you're talking about.*

I chuckled. "Hold these for a second," I said, handing Aspen the reins and leading rope.

She took them tentatively, watching as I jogged over to Marty. In one fluid motion, I stepped into the stirrups and swung onto his back. Adjusting my hat, I guided Marty closer to her and held out my hand.

"I can take those back. Not so scary, huh?"

Aspen handed them over, her shoulders more relaxed now. "How long have you been riding?" she asked as we headed toward a break in the trees.

Her voice was casual, but her appearance was anything but. She looked stunning, her ankle boots paired perfectly with a black-and-red floral dress that rode up slightly on her thighs as she sat in the saddle. The glimpse of her bare skin sent my thoughts spiraling.

Most of the time, Aspen wore flowing dresses that accentuated her curves without revealing much, but this—this was something else entirely. I forced myself to look away, my jaw tightening as I fought to redirect my focus.

Friends, Boone. She's your friend.

I tried to distract myself by adjusting the reins, but my eyes betrayed me, drawn back to the way her body moved with the horse's gentle rhythm. It wasn't just her skin now—it was everything about her—how natural she looked up there, like she belonged. My thoughts turned dangerously vivid, and I cursed silently, willing myself to think of anything else. Baseball. Golf. Ice cream. Anything.

Shifting in the saddle, I readjusted myself and forced my attention back to the conversation. She'd asked me something.

"How long have I been riding?" I repeated, making sure I'd heard her correctly.

She nodded, her eyes full of curiosity.

"All my life," I answered, exhaling slowly. "I've been riding since I was old enough to hold myself up on a horse."

Her gaze lifted to the sky as she took in the scenery around us. "That's impressive. Who taught you?"

"My dad," I replied. "It's in our blood. My grandpa taught him, and his dad before that."

"That's really sweet. Your family sounds special." Aspen's voice carried a note of sadness, though I knew she'd never admit it outright.

"It's okay to want more from your family," I said, probably pushing the boundaries of our conversation. "Growing up, I sometimes wished my parents had stepped in more—guided me away from bad decisions. They had this hands-off approach to parenting. They let me make my choices and supported me, even when they knew the outcome wouldn't be great."

I paused, realizing this might be the first time I'd ever voiced this.

"I used to get so angry as a kid. I wondered if I kept screwing up just to get their attention, to make them more involved. But now, as an adult, I see it differently. Their approach made me who I am. I learned by doing and messing up, and now I know that whatever happens, I can handle it. I can fix it."

Aspen stayed quiet for a moment, the soft sounds of the horses' steps filling the silence. Finally, she sighed.

"I just wish my parents were less...judgmental," she admitted. "I want to feel like I can tell them things, but instead, I just accommodate them. I want to express myself, to share what I want and who I am, without fearing their disapproval."

She paused, her voice thick with emotion, then continued.

"I think that's why I never took risks or made any wild choices growing up. My parents made all the decisions for me. I've always played it safe, but I'm resentful. I want to live, to feel free. And these past few weeks...I've felt that freedom. I think I owe that to you."

Her words hit me hard, stirring something deep in my chest.

"That's all you," I said gently. "You made those choices. You're the one who decided to let go, to have fun. I just happened to be there."

She shook her head slightly. "It's different with you. I feel like I can be myself, like I can tell you things or do things, and you won't judge me."

"It's not my place to judge anyone," I replied.

"That's a beautiful thing." She smiled softly.

Her smile made my chest tighten, and I found myself opening

up more than I ever had with anyone.

"I'd never shared this stuff with anyone," I admitted. "Not about my frustrations as a kid or how I felt growing up. But it feels...good, letting someone in."

The trees opened up, revealing a flat section of land that overlooked the valley where Faircloud was nestled. The view was stunning—my second-favorite spot after the swimming hole. It was a place where my mind felt the clearest, and now, I knew I'd brought the right person here.

The timing was perfect. The sun was setting, painting the sky in brilliant hues of orange and pink. My favorite kind of sunset.

I dismounted Marty, tying him to a nearby tree. Then I approached Aspen and Louise, taking the reins.

"Sliding down is the easiest way," I explained. "Lie on your belly and glide down toward me. I'll catch you."

Aspen did as instructed, her movements graceful. As her feet touched the ground, I placed my hands on her hips to steady her. She spun around, her back pressing lightly against Louise, but my hands stayed on her hips.

I didn't want to let go.

Our eyes locked, and for a moment, everything else faded. Her blue-green eyes drew me in, and my breath caught. My gaze fell to her lips, and I fought the urge to close the gap between us.

But Aspen moved first, stepping out of my grasp and heading toward the cliff's edge. I let out a slow breath, trying to regain my composure. I'd almost crossed a line—date one, and I'd nearly messed it all up.

She perched on a large rock near the edge, scooting over to make room. I joined her, close enough that our thighs brushed against each other.

"This is amazing." Her voice was full of awe. Her gaze swept across the valley, where the town's lights twinkled like stars against the dusky backdrop.

"This is my second-favorite place to come," I said, my voice low.

She tilted her head, a curious smile playing on her lips.

"The swimming hole is the first," I clarified.

Her cheeks turned a soft shade of pink, and I couldn't help but smile. I loved when she blushed. It started in her cheeks and spread to the tips of her ears, sometimes even her neck. It was adorable—and maddening.

"I can see why. This is a great first date."

Her teasing pulled me from my thoughts, and I laughed, the sound echoing into the open air.

She had no idea what else I had planned.

"Oh, just you wait," I said, standing and jogging over to the saddlebag. I pulled out the brown paper bag I'd stashed there earlier. When I returned to sit next to Aspen, her eyes widened, and she let out an exaggerated gasp.

"Are you seriously going to eat that right in front of me?" she demanded, bumping her shoulder against mine.

I smirked and pulled out the muffin, breaking it neatly in half. "Nope. We're going to share it while watching the sunset." I handed her half.

"Wow!"

"That's boyfriend material, right?" I teased, winking at her. "If this doesn't inspire you for that book you're writing, I don't know what will."

Aspen giggled, taking a bite. I followed suit.

God, I loved these muffins. Before Aspen, I couldn't stand blueberries. Now, I didn't think I could live without them.

We sat in easy silence, the kind that felt like a warm hug. The quiet stretched between us, but it wasn't uncomfortable. Aspen had this way of making everything feel effortless. There was no pressure to fill the gaps with mindless chatter. She listened, truly listened, and seemed interested in knowing me for more than just surface-level stuff.

That was rare.

Most women I'd been with had clear expectations—usually revolving around one thing. But Aspen? She seemed content just to *be* with me. The thought made my chest tighten, like I couldn't quite catch my breath.

"I've been thinking," I started, brushing muffin crumbs off my fingers. "I want to have another bonfire Friday night. The ranch hands are covering for me Saturday, so I've got the day off. You wanna come? I promise to keep my hands to myself this time."

Aspen nodded, crossing her legs as she traced shapes in the dirt with her finger. "Of course. I'll be there. But I have a request." She wiped her hands together, dusting off any crumbs.

"Go on," I said, trying to keep my tone casual while bracing for whatever she might say.

"Can Penny and Theo come?"

"Sure. Why would I say no?"

She shrugged. "I didn't think you would. I just wanted to be considerate and ask first."

Of course, she'd ask—Aspen was thoughtful like that. It was one of the many things I admired about her.

"I also have a secret," she added, a mischievous glint in her eye. "And I need your help."

I raised an eyebrow. "You need my help again? I'm starting to think I should charge you."

Aspen scoffed, leaning her head against my shoulder. "Excuse me? You were the one who offered to help with my story, remember? I never asked."

I chuckled, knowing she was right. "Fine, fine. Spill your secret."

She lifted her head to meet my gaze. "Okay, so Penny has a crush on Mac. Well, more than a crush—she wants to, uh, *you know,* with Mac."

I laughed, but she kept going.

"When we were at the bar the other night, she was looking for him, but he never showed up. I thought the bonfire might be the perfect chance for them to hang out. You know, give Penny a shot at getting some action."

Aspen's expression was priceless—wide-eyed and biting her

bottom lip, clearly gauging my reaction.

I let out a loud laugh, throwing my head back so far my hat nearly fell off. "Oh, hell yeah, I can help with that. I'm always down to play wingman." I lifted my hand for a high five, and she smacked her palm against mine.

"Apparently, he's been coming into the library a lot." Her voice lowered conspiratorially. "And Penny can't keep her eyes off him."

I shook my head, smiling to myself. "Mac? The guy who's never stepped foot in a library unless he had to? Oh, I *know* why he's been going."

Her eyes widened in realization. "Oh *shit!*" she said, laughing as everything clicked. "He's into her too, isn't he? Project *Get Penny and Mac Together* is officially a go!"

Her excitement was contagious, and I couldn't help but grin. Aspen leaned into me, her laughter lighting up the quiet evening. In that moment, with the sun dipping below the horizon and her by my side, I realized I didn't want this feeling to end.

CHAPTER 18

Aspen

A few days had passed since my date with Boone, leaving me plenty of time to sit with my thoughts—maybe too much time. Whether that was a good or bad thing, only time would tell.

That night had been perfect in every sense of the word. It left me feeling things I hadn't experienced in a long time, maybe ever. When Boone helped me off the horse and we froze for a moment, my heart thundered in my chest, even though I did my best to look calm. My whole body was on high alert, wanting to lean into the moment and see if his lips felt the same sober as they had the first time. I felt genuinely happy. Excited.

The stand was doing well, the Cassidys appreciated my help, I was reconnecting with friends, and I'd even felt inspired to start writing. That night with Boone lingered in my thoughts, not just because of what we did but because of how he made me feel. He was a complete gentleman—not that he wasn't usually—but during that date, he was on another level. Gentle, patient, attentive. He listened to me, never dismissing my questions or making me feel like a burden while teaching me something new.

And then there was the muffin. Who saves the last muffin just to share it at sunset? The more I got to know Boone Cassidy, the more he left me in awe. He wasn't just the boy I'd once known; he was so much more. He'd opened up to me, shared a vulnerable side I doubted many people ever saw.

Thinking about it, I wanted to write the whole night down. From the moment I saw him tacking up the horse to the way his smile looked at sunset. Capture every detail, every feeling, so I could savor it forever.

Luckily, Theo and Penny had agreed to come to the bonfire, so I sent them a quick reminder.

Don't forget. Cassidy Ranch, 8 p.m.

Penny

🫡 Yes ma'am!

Theo

Will do!

Penny

What should I wear?

Penny

Better yet, will Mac be there?

Last I heard, Rhodes and Mac will be there.

Theo

Penny, I'll pick you up at 7:30! You better be ready!!

A smile formed while reading their texts. Having Penny and Theo at the ranch tonight felt exciting, like two parts of my life were coming together. The idea of hanging out with Boone and his friends, along with my own, was something I never would've imagined. If someone had told me years ago I'd be at a bonfire with Boone, Penny, Theo, Rhodes, and Mac, I'd have called them crazy.

But here I was, getting ready in my little cabin to spend the evening with the "hot neighbor" and his crew. Life had a funny way of keeping you on your toes.

BOONE AND I were outside, setting up for the night. I loaded drinks into the cooler while Boone poked at the fire. He squatted by the flames, using a metal poker to adjust the logs. That signature hat sat low on his head, and his mustache was on full display.

I reminded myself to keep my thoughts in check. Alcohol and I hadn't been on the best terms lately, especially where Boone was concerned. Tonight, I'd made a sworn oath to keep things platonic.

Not that it was easy. Boone looked good—like, *really* good—in his usual uniform: straight-cut jeans, plain T-shirt, and that hat. The man had one style, but damn, did it work for him.

I'd opted for something a little more casual. My favorite--and only—pair of flare jeans, a black tank top, cowboy boots, and my hair half-up, half-down, held in place with a claw clip.

"Hell yeah!" Mac hollered, striding out from the trees with Rhodes in tow.

Mac was tall and lean, with an unmistakable energy that filled the space around him. Most people would describe him as a grungy bartender, which, to be honest, is pretty accurate. His wickedly curly brown hair was tucked under a backward cap, and tattoos covered his arms in a patchwork style that told a dozen little stories. He was wearing a cut-off T-shirt, clearly a DIY job, and old, scuffed boots.

Mac had a personality you couldn't ignore: electric, over-the-top, and larger than life. As he approached, I couldn't help but picture him with Penny. The thought made me grin. What a pair they'd make—fire and brimstone, loud and unapologetically chaotic.

Rhodes was about the same height as Boone, but he gave off

the energy of a grizzly bear—rugged and formidable. His jet-black hair was an unruly mop on his head, a testament to the fact that haircuts were clearly not a priority for Boone's crew. His sharp green eyes, the color of summer grass, stood out against his darker features. Like the others, Rhodes kept his style simple: a plain T-shirt, jeans, and cowboy boots. Though he was quieter than Mac, he had an easy, approachable energy. You'd have to, I figured, to keep up with Boone's circle.

Rhodes and Mac approached, each carrying a six-pack of beer, which I assumed was their drink of choice for the evening. Along with the beers in the cooler, we had the ever-reliable tequila, and I'd brought my favorite red wine—not that I expected anyone but Penny to drink it. Theo, I knew, was more of a beer girl.

"I've got a cooler set up by the steps!" I called, pointing toward Boone's cabin, where I'd left the ice-filled cooler.

"Atta girl," Mac replied, flashing me a wink.

I poured myself a glass of wine and claimed one of the chairs around the fire. Boone had abandoned his spot tending to the flames and was now over by Mac, greeting him. The sun had almost set, leaving the sky painted in deep hues of purple and orange, the firelight flickering warmly against the encroaching dark. I took a sip of my wine, the fire's heat on my skin.

"How have you been?" Rhodes asked as he settled into the chair on my left. He popped open a can of beer, foam spilling over the edge as he took a quick sip.

"I've been good," I replied, smiling. "How about you? How's ranch life treating you?"

Rhodes and I hadn't talked much outside of the last bonfire, so I wasn't sure how to keep the conversation going.

"Working with Boone is easy. Can't say I have much to complain about," he said, taking another drink. Then he hesitated before adding, "I, uh, saw Theo was back in town."

That caught me off guard. "Yeah! She is. I think she's staying for a while. She and Penny are coming tonight."

"Nice," Rhodes replied, clearing his throat. "People love the farm stand since you took it over. My mama's one of them. She swears by her weekly trips just to see if you've got anything new."

Hearing that made my heart swell. Positive feedback like that gave me the confidence to believe I was doing something right.

"I think I'm loving it too," I confessed. "I enjoyed working at The Coffee Cup, but something about the stand just feels...right."

We chatted easily for a while, Rhodes asking about my plans for the stand. I dodged his questions where secrets were involved, but I enjoyed the steady flow of our conversation. Meanwhile, Boone and Mac stood on the other side of the fire, talking amongst themselves.

The crunch of gravel signaled Theo and Penny's arrival. I glanced at my phone: eight fifteen. Classic Penny, not ready on time. Standing, I set my wineglass on the arm of my chair and walked to meet them halfway. Penny carried a box of wine because, of course, she loved anything cheap and convenient.

"It's about time!" I teased, pulling them in for side hugs.

"Yeah, well, Penny wasn't ready," Theo said, rolling her eyes with mock exasperation. "You'd think after all these years of friendship, I'd know better by now."

"I *had* to look good!" Penny whispered conspiratorially, grinning as we neared the fire. Then, with a little finger wave to the guys, she called out, "Well, hello!"

I glanced at Mac, searching for any kind of reaction—interest, intrigue, anything—but his face betrayed nothing. Undeterred, I turned my attention to Boone. He was watching me, and I gave him a look I hoped screamed, *We need to get to work*. Whether he picked up on it or not, I'd find out soon enough.

Back at the fire, I reclaimed my seat. Penny plopped down next to me, conveniently placing herself beside Mac. Theo, meanwhile, wedged herself between Rhodes and Boone. I was grateful that Boone was seated across from me. It gave me the perfect excuse to keep my distance from the man I was trying—and failing—to stay away from.

AS THE NIGHT wore on, I couldn't shake the feeling that someone was watching me. Finally, I glanced up from the conversation I was having—and caught him. Boone reclined in his chair, staring at me over the flickering flames. A slow, teasing grin spread across his face as he raised his beer to his lips, taking a deliberate sip. The way his Adam's apple bobbed when he swallowed felt more intimate than it should have.

Once? Sure, I could chalk it up to coincidence. But this had become a pattern. I forced myself to look away, determined to resist the temptation. We were friends. Boone was my neighbor, my writing muse, my...nothing else. That one date had been enough to spark something, but I wasn't going to let it go further than what we'd agreed upon.

"Boone, you're never going to guess who I ran into in town the other day," Mac said, breaking my train of thought.

Boone took another sip of beer and sighed. "I don't think I want to know."

"Miranda Yert." Mac wiggled his eyebrows in a way that immediately made my stomach churn.

"Miranda Yert!" Rhodes exclaimed, his shock evident. "Man, I haven't heard that name in a long damn time."

That name was like nails on a chalkboard. She'd been the prom queen in high school, the quintessential Southern belle with her blond hair, perfectly curled, and her syrupy-sweet accent. She had the boys in school lining up to take her out.

Miranda also happened to be one of the meanest girls I'd ever met. She didn't just gossip behind your back; she made sure you heard it. I cringed at the memories of her snide comments and cruel pranks, the worst being when she convinced Justin Bullock, my eighth-grade crush, to pretend to ask me to the school dance. I didn't need a therapist to tell me how much that had messed with my confidence.

I sipped my wine, silently praying the conversation would shift.

"Boone, you were one of the lucky ones to get in her bed," Mac said, shaking his head like it was a badge of honor.

My chest tightened, a sharp heat spreading through me. Jealousy. There it was—raw and unbidden. Boone and Miranda? Of course, they'd been a thing. Why wouldn't they? She was gorgeous, and he was... well, Boone. But knowing didn't make it any easier to hear.

"Meh," Boone replied with a shrug, his tone dismissive. "I don't even remember it."

"Come on," Rhodes pressed. "She was all over you until we graduated. It must've been something."

Boone's smile dropped, his voice firm. "Once was enough."

When I dared to glance up, Boone's gaze had found me again, steady and unreadable across the fire.

"Yuck," Penny cut in, her nose scrunching with distaste. "Miranda was vile. The shit she put Aspen through? She deserves every bit of bad karma coming her way."

I flushed, this time with embarrassment. I needed to steer the conversation away from Miranda—and fast.

"All right!" I clapped my hands, forcing a bright tone. "Why don't we play a game or something?"

Penny jumped on the idea. "How about *Cheers to the Governor*?"

Simple and chaotic, it was the perfect choice. Everyone nodded, and I breathed a sigh of relief as the group shifted focus.

"I'll go first!" Penny announced. "Then Mac, Boone, and so on."

We made it through the first round easily, cheering, "Cheers to the governor!" before taking a collective drink. Boone landed on twenty-one, which meant he got to make the first rule.

"No one can say my name. You have to call me Daddy," he declared, smugness radiating off him.

I groaned, rolling my eyes. Naturally, Boone noticed.

"What, Aspen?" he asked, his grin widening. "You don't want to call me *Daddy*?"

The firelight danced in his eyes as he raised his beer, taking another long, deliberate sip. When he lowered the can, his tongue darted out to catch the moisture on his top lip.

Play it cool, Aspen.

I didn't flinch. Instead, I smiled, lowering my lashes as I met his gaze. "I bet you'd like that, Cowboy."

The air between us crackled with tension. I felt it, thick and undeniable, and I knew the others did too. Penny cleared her throat, but I didn't break my stare. Neither did Boone.

It was a game of wills now, and I wasn't about to lose.

Being the sneak he was, Boone blew me a kiss from across the circle. I raised my hand, pretended to catch it, and tucked it into my pocket with an exaggerated smirk.

"Theo, you start this round," Mac said, steering the game along.

The second round flowed just as smoothly as the first, the group buzzing with alcohol and laughter. No one stumbled over the rules, which only seemed to prove that drunken coordination was its own skill. When my turn came, I hit twenty-one. That meant I got to set the next rule, and I was determined to make it count.

I took a moment, pretending to deliberate. "You can't make eye contact with another player. If you do, you drink."

As I scanned the group, my gaze landed on Boone, who was already looking straight at me, his expression daring me to react. Without hesitation, he lifted his drink, his lips curling into a slow, satisfied smile as he took a sip. The circle cheered, and I grudgingly took a drink too.

What had I expected? Of course, Boone wouldn't play by the spirit of the rule. Instead of avoiding eye contact, he seemed to relish breaking it, each deliberate glance in my direction followed by another sip. It wasn't just defiance; it was a statement. He knew the rule was for him, and he wasn't about to let me win.

My heart pounded every time our eyes locked, his steady gaze making it impossible for me to look away. I wanted to feel triumphant, but Boone's persistence flipped the script. His quiet confidence, the way he turned my own rule against me, left me feeling like he'd won this round.

Eventually, the group grew tired of the game. Conversations splintered into smaller clusters, and I noted with satisfaction that Penny and Mac were deep in their own private bubble. Penny's fingers twirled through her hair, her telltale sign of interest. For someone who was usually so bold, her newfound shyness around Mac was almost comical.

I glanced at my phone. It was late, and fatigue was starting to settle in. Stretching my arms over my head, I stood, shaking out the stiffness from sitting too long.

Theo noticed and rose as well. "I think I'm going to head out," she said, shooting a glance at Penny.

Penny wasn't ready to leave—that much was obvious from her reluctant sigh. She leaned toward Mac, murmuring something that made him chuckle before turning back to us.

I hugged Theo, wrapping my arms around her shoulders. She hesitated before relaxing, her hand settling lightly at my waist.

"I'm here if you want to talk," I whispered into her ear. She didn't reply, just nodded subtly as we pulled apart. Whatever she was holding in, I hoped she'd share it.

"Mind if we crash at your place?" Mac asked Boone as he stood and stretched.

"Nah, go on in," Boone replied, his tone easy. "I'm going to stay out with the fire for a bit."

Rhodes began collecting bottles and cans, tidying up the space before heading inside. The fire crackled softly, its flames still strong, a quiet beacon in the darkness. Boone settled back in his chair, his silhouette relaxed but commanding in the glow of the firelight.

I hesitated, my feet shifting on the dirt. I should've gone inside, called it a night. It had been a good evening, one where I hadn't let the wine or Boone get the better of me. But something held me back.

"I can wait with you," I offered, my voice softer than I intended.

Boone's gaze lifted, his expression unreadable as he nodded. He leaned back farther in his chair, his posture effortlessly casual, while my heart raced in the quiet between us.

I knew I should've walked away, but the pull of his presence—steady, warm, and impossible to ignore—kept me rooted in place.

I walked Penny and Theo to the car, giving them a hug goodbye. As they pulled away, I blew them an exaggerated kiss and waved obnoxiously, just to make them laugh. When I turned back, Boone was the only one left around the fire. The trash had been picked up, the alcohol put away, and all that remained was the soft crackle of the flames, slowly dying down. I dropped down next to Boone, where Theo had been sitting. A yawn overtook me, and I quickly covered my mouth, trying to be at least a little graceful.

"You can go inside if you want," Boone said, glancing my way. "I'm a big boy."

I smiled and shook my head, not ready to leave just yet. Before I could respond, he spoke again. "Do I still need to drink if I want to look at you?"

My heart skipped. The heat in my cheeks was instant, and my stomach fluttered—of course, he wasn't going to make it easy. "I'm surprised you aren't already sloppy."

Boone chuckled, that deep, rumbling sound that made my pulse quicken. I took a moment to really look at him—the low flames casting an amber glow across his face, making the stubble on his jawline and the curve of his mustache stand out. The way his lips tugged into a smile made my breath catch.

He was casually reclined in the chair, his curly brown hair curling just enough at the back to form a perfect, slightly unkempt mullet. His hat was tipped forward, hiding part of his expression, but there was no mistaking the confident tilt to his lips.

"I couldn't help myself," he said, and I was both relieved

and...slightly frustrated by how at ease he was.

He shifted the conversation, thankfully. "Was it just me, or did it feel like Mac and Penny were hitting it off?"

"Oh, definitely." I was happy to focus on anything other than the way my heart was still racing from our previous exchange. "Even Theo and Rhodes were talking."

I didn't see Theo and Rhodes starting anything romantic, but I liked the idea of her connecting with more people. She was always the loner, especially after all the traveling she'd done. Now that she wasn't off exploring new places, I didn't want her to feel like she was lost here, stuck. I wanted her to be happy.

"Yeah, it was like I was stuck in the middle of their little date," Boone teased, and a laugh bubbled out of me. Then, his expression shifted. "Speaking of dates... I've got ours planned."

"Already?" I sat cross-legged, my legs tucked underneath me. I finished my drink earlier but had decided not to get another one. "Where are we going this time?"

Boone leaned forward, placing his elbows on his knees, his posture suddenly serious. "Farmers market in town, Sunday. I'll knock on your door at nine a.m. sharp. So, you better be ready."

His spontaneous plans made me smile. I was usually a "plan it out" kind of girl, but there was something about Boone taking charge that felt...right. The farmers market was one of the things I loved most about this town. It covered blocks, and even the streets were shut down for it. Locals and travelers alike came to browse the stands of produce, flowers, and handmade goods. I could easily lose hours walking through it all.

"I love the farmers market!" I squealed, my excitement bubbling over. The smile that spread across my face was unstoppable. I'd already started mentally listing what I wanted to buy—candles, soaps, maybe some flowers for my dining room table.

"I know," Boone said softly, his voice low, almost like a secret.

"Lucky guess?" I teased.

Boone's eyes met mine, his expression almost unreadable. "I

pay attention to you, Darling," he whispered, his gaze intense, like he was savoring the moment. The fire flickered lower, its warmth fading. His smile softened, and for a second, everything around us seemed to quiet.

The moment stretched, and I realized I was holding my breath. Our eyes locked, and I couldn't look away, even though it felt like we were on the edge of something I wasn't sure I was ready for.

Finally, I broke the silence. I didn't know what to say, so I stood up quickly, my legs stiff from sitting too long. "The fire's dying down. We should head in."

Boone stood as well, following me in silence. We walked toward my cabin, the weight of the moment still hanging between us.

"Goodnight, Boone," I said, my voice quieter than I intended.

"Goodnight, Aspen," he replied, his voice low and warm, as though the night was far from over in his mind.

CHAPTER 19

Boone

By midmorning, Rhodes and Mac had left, giving me the chance to prepare for my day off. With the other ranch hands stepping in, I finally had some time to myself—and I planned to spend it with Mom. It felt like ages since I'd given her the attention she deserved.

As I was getting ready in the bathroom, the sound of my phone ringing from the living room broke through my thoughts. No one ever called me unless it was important, so I jogged down the hall, grabbing it just before it stopped. I didn't even glance at the caller ID.

"Hello?" I said, voice probably a little breathless and anxious.

"Hey, big brother." Ellie. My sister. It had been over a month since anyone had heard from her. Even when she was in Faircloud, I'd worried about her every single day.

"Ellie." I exhaled her name with relief, a smile tugging at my lips. "It's good to hear your voice." The relief was short-lived, though. Why was she calling me and not Mom? Was everything okay?

"Yours too. I just wanted to let you know I'm alive. I'm in Maine right now."

Maine? That was about as far from Texas as she could get without crossing an ocean.

"At least I know you're safe," I said, the knot in my chest tightening again. "It's been too long, El. Mom's worried sick about you. Dad too. Hell, I'm always worried about you. Please, tell me you're okay."

She let out a heavy sigh. "I'm okay, Boone. I just... I needed to get away from that town. After everything that happened, I can't show my face there."

"When are you coming back?" I tried to sound hopeful, even though I wasn't sure I believed she'd give me the answer I wanted. When she left, I refused to accept the idea that it might be forever. She couldn't stay away—not Ellie.

"I don't know if I can." Her voice cracked, and I knew she was crying. Ellie never cried. She was the tough one, like Dad, letting nothing and no one get to her. But now, she sounded broken, hollow. "The scrutiny is too much. I'm embarrassed, Boone. I needed to hear your voice."

I swallowed hard, my own emotions threatening to spill over. "None of this is your fault, Ellie. You hear me? None of it. That asshole's actions are on him. If anyone shouldn't show their face, it's him. And trust me, I'll make sure he regrets ever crossing you."

She let out a small, shaky laugh, but it quickly faded. "I don't know when I'll be ready to come back. Just know I love you, Boone. I really do."

"I love you too, El. You've got us—me, Mom, Dad. We're all here, waiting for you when you're ready."

"Tell Mom I called, okay?" she said quietly. "I can't handle talking to her yet. Texting's all I can manage for now."

"Of course. Anytime you need to talk, I'm here."

Ellie murmured her thanks, then hung up. I stared at the screen for a moment, feeling the weight of our conversation settle in. Hearing her voice should have been a comfort, but instead, it left me even more on edge.

Not many people knew what really happened with Buck—just our family and his. To the rest of the town, it was a simple case of infidelity, but it went deeper than that. Much deeper.

I needed to talk to someone, but the only person I could think of was Aspen. And this wasn't my story to tell. It wasn't my secret to share.

I turned on my go-to playlist, hoping music would help me clear my head as I finished getting ready. By the end of the second song, I was out the door.

I walked past the farm stand on my way to see Mom. Normally, I'd stop to chat with Aspen, but today, I couldn't. She'd see right through me, and I wasn't sure I could hold back. Still, I couldn't resist slowing down just enough to catch a glimpse of her.

Aspen moved gracefully around the stand, collecting empty mugs and plates. She was a natural—laughing and chatting with the customers as though they were old friends, her movements smooth and effortless, like a figure skater gliding across ice.

As I continued toward the main house, my thoughts shifted to what I'd tell Mom. Ellie's call weighed on me. I knew sharing the news would hurt her. She and Ellie were always close, but I understood my sister's choice to keep her distance. Mom would try to convince her to come home—and knowing Ellie, she probably would've caved—but that wasn't what she needed right now.

When I reached the house, my internal monologue faded, and I veered around to the backyard. If I knew Mom, she'd already be out in the garden, tending to her flower beds.

Sure enough, there she was, crouched in front of her flowers, focused and in her element. I approached quietly, crouching beside her. She startled, letting out a gasp.

"Oh!" she exclaimed, her hand flying to her chest. "You scared me! What are you doing here?"

"I wanted to spend my day off with the most amazing mom in the world," I teased, reaching for a clump of weeds in the mulch.

Mom rolled her eyes playfully and pulled off her gloves. Sitting back on the grass, she wiped her brow, beads of sweat glistening on her forehead. I joined her, stretching my legs out in front of me.

"How's my son this morning?" she asked, taking a sip of water.

"I'm good," I said, fiddling with a clover in the grass. I

hesitated, then decided to rip the bandage off. "I, uh, heard from Ellie this morning."

Her face paled slightly, the flush from working in the sun disappearing. "She's in Maine," I added.

The look on her face wasn't unexpected, but it still hit me. She quickly masked her emotions, putting on a brave face. "I'm glad someone's heard from her beyond texts. How did she sound?"

"Not like herself," I admitted.

Mom sighed and shifted back into a crouch, sliding her gloves on. I picked up the bin and held it steady as she tossed weeds into it. "I'm really worried about her, Boone. It's not like her to run like this or avoid her family."

"She just needs time, Ma. She's hurting. We have to give her space. She knows we're here for her, and that's what matters." I believed it as much as I said it. Ellie would find her way home. She just needed to know we had her back when she was ready.

"I know," Mom murmured, her voice soft with worry. She rested a gloved hand on my arm, giving me a faint smile. "But she's my baby. I worry about both of you—about you finding your way and being happy."

"I know," I replied, swallowing the lump in my throat.

"Since we're having a moment, I have to ask you something." Her tone shifted, and I knew this wasn't going to be fun. "What's going on with you and Aspen?"

"What's going on?" I repeated, stalling. I put the bin down and busied my hands with more weeds. "Nothing's going on. We're friends."

"Don't think I don't notice—or hear the gossip around town." She ticked off her fingers as she spoke. "Lunch dates. Picking her up from The Tequila Cowboy. Meeting her at the stand at night. Bringing her over for breakfast the other morning." Her eyebrow quirked. I was caught.

"I don't know," I admitted truthfully. "We're friends. I like spending time with her."

Mom gave me a look that screamed she wasn't buying it.

She could read me like a book. I wanted to tell her everything—how Aspen made me happy, how I couldn't stop thinking about her, how I was helping her find inspiration for her writing. But I chickened out.

"Don't play me for a fool," Mom said, narrowing her eyes. "It's more than that for you, Boone. I see it. I don't know how she feels, but I've never seen you spend this kind of time with a *friend*."

She had me. Backed into a corner, I sighed, giving in. "She's different. There's no pressure with her. It's easy. I like how she makes me feel." I shrugged, tossing another weed into the bin. "I don't know what's happening between us, whether it's just the excitement of something new or if I'm catching feelings for her, but I'm taking it day by day. For now, we're friends, and that's enough for me."

"Just know, she's welcome anytime. She's sweet, and as long as you're happy, I approve." Mom flashed me a warm smile.

It felt good to hear her reassurance—not that I doubted it. But having her blessing made the uncertainty a little less daunting.

By the time we finished in the garden, my stomach was growling for dinner. I decided to stay and spend some time with both my parents before heading back to the cabin. I told Dad about Ellie, but his response was exactly what I expected: not much. Emotions weren't his thing. Like Ellie, he kept everything bottled up.

When I finally left, it was well after dark. Exhausted in every way, I made my way back home, looking forward to collapsing into bed. As I got closer to the cabin, I spotted Aspen in her usual spot on the porch swing. She noticed me too, waving me over.

There was no way I could say no. I needed to see her.

"What's up, Cowboy?" she asked, closing her book—the same one I'd seen her reading the other night. She held a glass of red wine in her hand, her go-to. Aspen was a creature of habit, and I liked that about her.

"I like it when you call me that," I said as I sank down beside her on the swing, my arm naturally draping over the back.

"Oh yeah?" she teased, her tone playful and inviting. "Well, I like it when you call me Darling."

The power shifted between us in an instant. Her voice softened, dropping an octave, and it hit me like a lightning bolt. I wanted to pull her closer, to taste the wine on her lips. My heart raced, and my pulse thudded in my ears. Instead, I swallowed hard, reining myself in and steering the conversation back to safer territory.

"How was your day?" I asked, desperate to reset the moment.

Her gaze lingered on me for a heartbeat too long before she blinked and smiled. "The stand was busy, which I was happy to see! You should've been there. I was everywhere—cleaning, restocking, ringing people up. If it keeps up like this, I might need reinforcements. How about you?"

I almost told her I'd seen her earlier, how effortlessly she managed everything, but I held back. "My day was kind of draining, not gonna lie," I admitted, rubbing my hand against my knee.

"Do you want to talk about it?"

God, I loved how gentle she was. She didn't pry or push—just offered me the space to share what I wanted when I was ready. Was it always supposed to feel this easy with someone?

After spending the afternoon with my mom and hearing her approval of Aspen, I knew I could trust her. And I needed someone to talk to.

"I talked to Ellie today," I began. "She hasn't called us since she left after the whole Buck thing. I told Mom, and that was tough."

Aspen didn't say a word, just nodded, letting me continue.

"Most people don't know what really happened between her and Buck. It was ugly. I wanted to wring that bastard's neck for what he did to her." I paused, taking a deep breath. "He didn't just cheat on her once—he'd been doing it for years. She caught him this last time, and to make it worse, the girl he was messing around with is pregnant with his baby."

Aspen's eyes widened, her hand flying to her mouth. "Oh my God, Boone. That's awful."

"She left because she couldn't take what people were saying about her. She didn't want anyone finding out the truth. She's embarrassed and being here felt like a constant reminder of everything she went through." My voice was tight with frustration. "The thought of her running from the place she loved, her home, because of that asshole makes me want to kick his teeth in."

"I don't blame her, or you, for feeling the way you do. I can't even imagine what you're all going through. Boone, I'm so sorry." Aspen's hand rested on my thigh, her thumb tracing soft, soothing circles. The gesture was grounding, a reminder that she was here. With my free hand, I placed it on top of hers, anchoring myself to the moment.

"It's been eating at me for a while," I admitted. "We've been keeping it a secret, like I said. No one knows. I can't really talk about it with my parents. Mom gets upset, and Dad shuts down. I miss Ellie, and I worry about her every single day."

A tightness formed in my chest, the sting of emotion threatening to break free. There was no way I was going to cry in front of Aspen. She flipped her hand over, lacing her fingers with mine. Then, she leaned her head on my shoulder, her presence a balm to my frayed nerves.

"You have me, Boone," she whispered. "I'm not going anywhere."

Her words were like a lifeline, pulling me out of the storm. Knowing I had someone to confide in, someone who truly cared, eased the weight pressing on me. For the first time in a while, I felt lighter. "You don't need to navigate it alone," she added softly.

That last sentence nearly undid me. The truth in her voice hit me hard, loosening the tight grip I had on my emotions. But I managed to hold it together, swallowing the lump in my throat.

"Thank you," I murmured, pressing a kiss to the top of her head. We sat in silence, hand in hand, her head resting on my shoulder. I traced gentle circles on the back of her hand with my thumb, the small connection grounding me. I could've stayed like that forever, unwilling to break the quiet comfort of the moment until she did.

After some time, Aspen spoke. "Can I help in any way?"

"Nah," I replied. "Just letting me vent helped more than you know. Is it okay if we change the subject?"

"Of course, Cowboy. What's next?" she asked, still nestled close.

"Have you started writing yet?"

"Eh, I've plotted some stuff out, but no words on paper yet," she said, her tone light but honest.

"Do you have a storyline? Any details you want to share?"

"It's a secret!" She turned her head to face me, her eyes sparkling with mischief. "Maybe when I've written something, you can be the first to read it."

I chuckled, leaning my head back against the swing. "You want me to read your romance novel? I don't know how much help I'll be, but I'll do it for you."

"Well, you're helping me find inspiration, so it's only fair," Aspen replied, grinning.

She had a point. I was curious to see what her writing would reveal, to learn what parts of our time together might spark her creativity. "Speaking of inspiration," she added, "are you sure you still want to go to the farmer's market? I'd understand if you needed some space."

"I'm not canceling a date with you to mope," I said firmly. "If anything, I need the distraction—and I'd much rather spend the day with you than sit alone in my cabin."

Aspen smiled, sitting up and untangling her fingers from mine. "If that's the case, I'd better head to bed. Nine a.m. sharp, remember?" She tapped my leg before standing from the swing.

I rose too, now toe to toe with her. Pulling her into a hug, I felt her melt into my chest. My chin rested perfectly atop her head as I whispered, "Thank you again," and squeezed her tight.

"That's what friends are for," she replied before stepping back.

Friends. The word stung more than it should have. Being just friends with Aspen was harder than I ever imagined. But for now, I'd take whatever piece of her she was willing to give.

CHAPTER 20

Waking up at the crack of dawn wasn't just a choice—it was necessary. My alarm barely buzzed before I swung my legs out of bed and slid my feet into my cow slippers. Today was the farmers market with Boone, and I was determined to be ready before nine a.m. Not just physically ready—mentally *ready*.

When Boone hugged me goodnight, I didn't want to let go. The warmth of his chest and that intoxicating teakwood scent wrapped around me like a security blanket. His hard-earned muscles weren't just nice to look at; they were a comfort.

And then there was his vulnerability. Boone had opened up about Ellie, and it made my heart ache. The weight he and his family carried was unimaginable. Poor Ellie had every right to escape and rebuild herself after everything she'd been through. I was glad I could be there for Boone, offering him a space to unburden.

I took extra care with my makeup today. It was going to be hot, so I kept it light—just a touch of concealer, some contour and bronzer, a dab of blush, and a swipe of mascara. Natural, but enough to feel put together.

Next came the dress. This was *the* dress, reserved for special occasions because it made my boobs look amazing. A white milkmaid style with tiny baby blue flowers, paired with light brown sandals and my cowhide purse. I felt confident and a little dangerous. To top it off, I grabbed some reusable bags—I was prepared to splurge. How much could one person spend at a farmers market? Unlimited. Show me fresh flowers or handmade candles, and I'm a goner.

At exactly nine a.m., not a minute early, not a second late, there was a knock at my door. Boone's timing was uncanny. I rushed to open it and had to stop myself from outright gawking. There he stood, devastatingly handsome in a short-sleeved button-up and light jeans. His hair was brushed, though mostly hidden under his cowboy hat. He was a sight to behold, and I had to take a moment to compose myself because—*wow.*

Boone gave me a once-over, lingering just a second too long at my chest. I couldn't blame him; the dress was doing its job.

"Eyes up here, Cowboy," I teased, a grin spreading across my face.

He laughed, bringing his gaze to mine. "You look nice," he said, his voice warm.

I curtsied dramatically. "Why, thank you."

Ever the gentleman, Boone extended his arm for me to take. I looped mine through his and closed the door behind me. He opened the passenger door of his truck, and I climbed in with a smirk.

"I don't think I've ever seen you in anything but a T-shirt or, well, nothing at all I guess," I joked as he slid into the driver's seat.

"Ha, so funny." He tilted his head toward me with a mock glare. "I *can* clean up when I want to."

"Well, you clean up pretty good," I admitted, and his smirk turned into a full-blown grin.

The drive to town flew by, and Boone parked a few blocks away from the market. My excitement bubbled over as we walked toward the main street. The air was alive with music from a live band on the corner, mingling with the hum of voices and the scent of fresh bread and flowers.

"What's your budget for the market?" Boone asked, his tone teasing as we reached the edge of the bustling street.

"Budget? Never heard of her." I grinned, pulling a small collection of reusable bags from my purse. "I'm thinking candles, soaps, maybe some jewelry. And I definitely need flowers for my table." I could have kept going, but I didn't want to scare Boone with the full list of my farmers market dreams.

"Challenge accepted." Boone smirked, taking my hand and weaving us through the bustling crowd. His touch was warm, steady, and sent a tiny thrill up my arm. I noticed a few people starting to glance our way. News of us being here together would spread like wildfire, and I wasn't looking forward to the inevitable chatter from my parents—especially my dad.

I tried to shake off the memory of his last comment about Boone, claiming he wasn't good enough for me. It still made my blood boil. Who was he to decide that? Boone treated me with more respect and kindness than any of the polished city boys my dad seemed to prefer.

Flashing back to the day outside the hardware store, I internally cringed. Replaying what I said, more so how I said it made me want to go back in time and apologize, maybe even stop myself from saying it altogether. In the moment, I wasn't any better than my father.

We stopped at a candle stand, the table covered with colorful jars and enticing labels. I picked up one labeled "Warm Vanilla" and took a sniff. It was nice, but screamed fall, not summer. Holding it out to Boone, I asked, "What do you think?"

He wrinkled his nose. "Nope."

Laughing, I reached for another—this one was lilac-scented. The delicate, floral notes made me smile, reminding me of fresh spring mornings. I passed it to Boone, who gave a thoughtful nod, leaning in for a second whiff.

"I think we have a contender."

We worked our way through the entire table, sniffing every candle, but nothing spoke to me quite like the lilac one—until I found a jar labeled "Lavender and Vanilla." The scent was perfect: soothing lavender with a warm, cozy undercurrent of vanilla.

Boone leaned closer to get a good sniff, his face inches from mine. "That one's nice," he said, grabbing the lilac and lavender candles. "We're getting both."

"We?" I raised an eyebrow, pulling out my wallet as I followed him to the cashier.

"Morning, ma'am," Boone greeted the older woman behind the table, handing over the candles.

"Boone, you are *not* paying for those!" I protested, fumbling to pull the right amount of cash from my wallet.

But Boone was faster. He handed the woman a crisp hundred-dollar bill, collected his change, and slipped it into his wallet before I even finished counting.

"Too late, Darling," he teased, holding up the bag. "Where to next?"

"We're not just going to blow past the fact that you paid for these." I narrowed my eyes, clutching my wallet. "How much was it? I'll pay you back."

Boone ignored me entirely, his attention conveniently drawn to another stand. "Ooh, jerky! Let's check it out."

Groaning, I trailed after him, resigned to my defeat—for now. Maybe I could buy him some jerky instead. But Boone must have been one step ahead, because after sampling nearly every flavor, he left empty-handed.

For what felt like hours, we wandered through the market, sampling snacks, listening to live music, and picking up more treasures than I planned. Boone insisted on paying for my bouquet of flowers despite my protests, though I did manage to win the battle for my soap.

Finally, we reached a jewelry stand near the edge of the market. The table was small, but the pieces were stunning—delicate silver and turquoise creations that gleamed in the sunlight.

I took my time trying things on, savoring the way each piece sparkled against my skin. Slipping on a silver ring adorned with a small turquoise stone, I held my hand up to Boone.

"What do we think?"

Boone nodded with a soft smile, his male stamp of approval making me grin. As much as I loved the ring, my eyes drifted to a bracelet hanging in the background. Thin silver links accented with tiny turquoise stones.

Curious, I swapped the ring for the bracelet, sliding it onto my wrist. It fit perfectly—snug but not tight, like it was made just for me. My heart skipped as I admired it, but the feeling was short-lived when I flipped over the price tag.

The gasp escaped before I could stop it. Real silver, real turquoise—of course, it cost a fortune. Quietly, I unhooked the bracelet, setting it back on the table with a wistful sigh.

"What's wrong?" Boone asked, picking up the bracelet.

"I know I said I didn't have a limit, but I think I just found it," I said, clearing my throat. I loved the bracelet, but I wasn't willing to spend that much on myself.

Boone turned the bracelet over in his fingers, examining the craftsmanship.

"Good thing I don't have a budget." A playful grin tugging at his lips as he held the bracelet out of my reach.

"No, Boone. The flowers and candles are more than enough. I can't let you buy this for me. It's way too much." I reached to grab it, but he pulled away, his free hand gently cradling my cheek.

I froze, the sudden warmth of his hand stilling my protests. His fingers tipped my chin upward until my gaze locked with his.

"Let me do this," he said softly, his eyes searching mine.

I swallowed hard, my cheeks flushing as I nodded, unable to argue anymore. Boone lingered for a moment, then pulled away, walking over to the vendor. I stood back, watching as he handed the girl the money and leaned in to murmur something. She smiled, snipping off the tag before handing him the bracelet without bagging it.

Boone turned back to me, his free hand resting lightly on my forearm as he guided me away from the bustling crowd. We stopped at a nearby bench, and he motioned for me to sit first. I perched on the edge of the seat, still clutching my flowers like a lifeline.

"Boone—" I began, ready to protest again, but he cut me off.

"You should've seen your face when you put it on," he said, holding out the bracelet. "I couldn't let you walk away without it."

He took my hand, gently slipping the bracelet onto my wrist. I couldn't stop staring at it. The delicate chain and turquoise stones gleamed in the sunlight, as if they were meant to be there.

"Thank you," I murmured, my voice barely above a whisper. I leaned in impulsively, brushing a quick kiss on his cheek. "It's perfect."

Boone grinned, his fingers lingering on mine as he admired the bracelet.

"You do have great taste," he said with a wink before finally letting go.

I let out a breath I didn't realize I was holding, feeling a little steadier now.

"I had an amazing time." My grin spread as wide as my heart felt. The day had been perfect—the weather, the company, everything.

"It's not over yet."

I raised an eyebrow. "What else could you possibly have planned?"

His devilish grin widened as he stood and extended a hand to me. I took it, letting him pull me up. He carried my bags while I held onto my bouquet, and we walked back to his truck. Boone placed everything inside, then reached into the bed and pulled out a large woven basket.

"Are we having a picnic?" I asked, my voice brimming with disbelief.

"Would that be a good thing?" Boone asked, suddenly looking a bit uncertain.

"Oh, hell yes!" I laughed, my excitement bubbling over.

He chuckled, tucking me under his arm as we crossed the street to a nearby park. Finding a quiet spot, Boone spread out a red blanket and set the basket down at the edge.

"After you." He gestured for me to sit.

I settled onto the blanket, watching as he opened the basket to reveal a bottle of wine and two glasses. My eyes lit up as I recognized the label—it was my favorite. Boone poured us each a glass, handing one to me.

"Cheers to a fun date," he said, clinking his glass against mine.

I took a sip, marveling at how thoughtful he'd been.

"This might just be the best date I've ever been on," I admitted, unable to stop smiling.

"I had to pull out all the stops." Boone leaned back on one hand. "But just wait."

"Oh no," I teased. "What's next?"

He smirked. "I've already planned our next date. It's the grand finale."

A pang of sadness tugged at my chest. One more date. Just one more, and then... what? I hadn't even *really* started writing yet, and our time together was slipping through my fingers.

Boone reached into the basket again, pulling out a brown paper bag. The familiar smell hit me instantly.

"Is that a blueberry muffin?" I asked, laughing as I took the bag.

"One of your muffins," he confirmed, his grin as warm as the sunshine spilling over us.

We spent the next hour lounging on the blanket, watching people pass by and making up silly stories about their lives. Of course, most of them were people we already knew, which made it even funnier. By the time Boone drove me home, my heart felt light, though a part of me was already aching for the next date.

It wasn't just the bracelet, the picnic, or the flowers. It was him—his thoughtfulness, his laughter, his everything. And I couldn't stop replaying every detail of the day over and over again.

CHAPTER 21

Aspen

I need to meet with you, ASAP please tell me you are available tonight. I'm about to explode.

Theo

SAME.

Penny

I'm scared 😨 I can make time.

Please and thank you!

Penny

How about the Tequila Cowboy 😉

Theo

Tacos?

Penny

SAY LESS.

My mind had been nothing but chaos since spending the day with Boone at the farmers market. Normal functioning? Out the window. I hadn't told anyone about the date, and I flat-out refused to take this bracelet off. Being trapped in my head with all these new and confusing emotions wasn't exactly a party. My only hope was to lay it all out for Penny and Theo and get their take on the situation.

Writing had been coming in spurts lately, but at least I was making progress. Right now, I was feeling pretty good about how things were flowing. I'd set the scene for my story in a small town out west, one inspired by Faircloud but with its own quirks. Pinterest had become my sanctuary, helping me create a mood board that brought my vision to life. It was therapeutic, a creative outlet that kept my mind busy. This was the farthest I'd ever gotten in writing a novel, and I was riding a wave of cautious optimism.

But whenever I thought about my story, Boone's face popped into my head. My main male character was basically Boone with a different name. He was every Zach Bryan love song come to life—the last great American cowboy, full of charm and a touch of gentleness.

I pulled into the parking lot of the restaurant where I was meeting Penny and Theo. I desperately needed this last-minute girl time because I hadn't had a single coherent thought outside of Boone Cassidy in days. Our nighttime chats hadn't stopped, and we were definitely more touchy-feely than before. I found myself sneaking small touches—my hand on his knee, tapping him when he made me laugh, leaning into the crook of his arm on the swing. And it wasn't just me. Boone had started sitting closer, brushing by me when he helped clean up at the stand. Every time he got near me, I felt like my skin was buzzing.

Penny and Theo were already waiting for me at a booth in the far back corner, tucked away exactly how I liked it. I slid in next to Penny and let out a dramatic sigh, plopping my purse onto the window ledge.

"You two aren't ready for this," I said, exhaling like I'd been holding my breath all day.

"Well, hello to you, too," Theo teased, raising an eyebrow.

"Spill it now," Penny urged, leaning in. "Your text sounded urgent."

"I think I'm falling for Boone *fucking* Cassidy," I blurted, finally releasing the whirlwind of thoughts in my head. Before they could jump in with questions, I kept talking, needing to get it all out. "These past few weeks have been a lot of self-discovery, okay? I love books, I love reading romance, as you both know, and I've always wanted to be a romance author. But I never felt like I'd had enough experience with love to write about it. Boone and I made a deal, three dates to inspire me to start writing. I thought I could handle it, that we'd stay friends. But now... I don't know. I think I've caught feelings."

"Hi, ladies!" Carmen, our waitress, appeared at the table, cutting off the flow of my confession. I clamped my mouth shut, not wanting anyone else to overhear.

"Can I get you anything to drink?" she asked cheerfully.

"A margarita for me, please!" Penny raised her finger.

"Make that two—extra salt, extra tequila," I added with a tired smile.

"I'll take a Coke with lemon, please," Theo said. Carmen jotted down our orders and headed to the bar.

Theo was the first to break the silence. Penny, for once, was quiet, her expression unreadable.

"Oh, wow. Okay," Theo said slowly. "What changed for you?"

"Yesterday was our second *date*. We went to the farmers market. It was honestly the best day I've had in ages. He even set up a picnic at the end. And then..." I held out my wrist, showing them the bracelet. "He bought me this."

Penny grabbed my hand, inspecting the silver and turquoise

stones like she'd just discovered a hidden treasure.

"Shut up!" Penny squealed.

"I know!" I said, my voice rising to match hers. "He got me candles and flowers, too. I don't know what to think. Does he have feelings for me, or is he just being ridiculously generous to help me out?"

"Couldn't it be both?" Theo asked, ever the rational one.

"I mean, I guess?" I sighed, slumping back against the booth. "But it's Boone. I don't think I could handle another rejection from him without my ego taking a massive hit."

"Another?" Theo pressed, narrowing her eyes.

Crap. I'd never told them about The Tequila Cowboy or the way things had ended in the swimming hole. The humiliation was still too fresh, so I'd locked it away in a mental vault and thrown away the key.

"He definitely has feelings for you, A," Penny said confidently. "No man buys a woman a bracelet like that just to help her write a book."

"Or takes her on public dates for fun," Theo added. "Real dates, out where everyone can see you two together."

Either they were right, or Boone was a saint walking among us mortals. By taking me out in public, he'd pretty much staked his claim, whether intentionally or not. People would assume things, no matter what we told them.

"I don't know what to do," I groaned, burying my face in my hands.

"Tell him you need more dates," Penny suggested, pulling my hands away from my face and laying them on the table. "Say the writing isn't going well. Use it to your advantage. If he agrees, I think you've got your answer."

"Flirt with him. Let yourself explore whatever it is you're feeling. Live a little, A. Don't let yourself stay content, take the leap and let yourself fall." Theo's words struck a chord deep inside me. She knew me too well, knew I tended to shy away from risk. Her encouragement reminded me that the people who loved me the most also wanted to see me grow.

Over the past few weeks with Boone, I'd felt more like myself than I ever had. I was shedding the layers of self-doubt and letting the Aspen I wanted to be break free.

"If things go south, you'll always have us." Penny pulled me into a warm hug. Theo reached across the table and took my hand in hers, her steady grip a silent promise. These two women meant everything to me. Having their friendship made me feel like the luckiest girl alive.

"I feel better," I admitted, feeling the tension in my shoulders ease.

"I have an idea!" Penny squealed, clapping her hands together like she'd just won the lottery. "Let's all go to the rodeo tomorrow night! You can invite Boone and his friends, like a triple date!"

"Whoa, whoa, whoa!" Theo held up her hands. "I am not going on a date with any of those boys."

"Oh, come on!" Penny huffed, crossing her arms. "It'll be fun."

I took a moment to consider it. Honestly, it wasn't a bad idea. It gave me more time with Boone, and having my girls there would make it feel less intimidating.

"Penny, it'd give you more time with Mac," I pointed out.

"Yes!" she exclaimed, pointing at Theo. "You need to do this, for me."

"Fine!" Theo relented, rolling her neck like she was bracing for battle. "But who's going to be my *date*?"

That left two options: Rhodes or Logan. Thinking back to the night of the bonfire, the answer was clear.

"Rhodes," Penny and I said in unison, exchanging a knowing look.

Carmen arrived to take our food orders. I went with my usual: two tacos and rice. After Penny and Theo ordered, I turned to Theo.

"You said you needed to debrief, too. What's going on?" I asked.

Theo tensed, and a sinking feeling settled in my stomach. Whatever it was, it wasn't going to be easy to hear.

"I'm just going to rip the Band-Aid off." Theo took a deep breath. "I'm pregnant."

Holy. Shit. Goosebumps prickled along my arms.

In my head, I'd braced for something far worse. I'd assumed Theo had come home because her mom, her only remaining family, was sick.

A baby? That was something I could handle.

"Okay," Penny said, voice measured. "Good thing or bad thing?"

It was always tricky figuring out how to react when someone dropped pregnancy news.

"At first? Very bad," Theo admitted. "Mental-breakdown bad. But now that I've had time to process, I feel good about it." She placed a hand gently over her belly, a small smile tugging at her lips.

"How long have you known?" I asked, replaying all the times we'd been together since she came back.

"Since the weekend I got back to Faircloud. I'm six weeks along now." Theo's smile grew a little wider. She looked happy, and I smiled along with her.

"Do we know the father?" Penny asked, tackling the question I wasn't brave enough to voice.

"No," Theo said simply. "He was a random guy I met while traveling. I don't even know where he's originally from. He doesn't know about the baby, and I don't plan to tell him. I don't need the drama. I can do this on my own."

That was so Theo. She didn't need saving, didn't need anyone else to step in when life got tough. She was fiercely independent, and I admired her strength, even when it meant she carried her burdens alone.

"You're not alone, Theo. You've got us," I said, voice steady despite the tears prickling in my eyes. "And I'm going to spoil this baby rotten. Aunt Aspen can't wait to meet them."

Theo smiled, her eyes glistening. She was going to be an amazing mom—a badass woman raising a badass kid.

Next to me, Penny sniffled and dabbed at her eyes with a napkin. "Wow, I'm so happy."

Even Theo was getting emotional, her usually sharp gaze lined with red. My mind raced, replaying moments from The Tequila Cowboy, the bonfire, even tonight. How had I missed it? Not once had she actually ordered alcohol. Sure, we'd all gotten a shot at the bar, but now I realized she must have ditched hers when no one was looking.

Carmen arrived with our food mid-cry, setting our plates down with practiced grace. She didn't bat an eye at the emotional mess we must've looked like. I bet she'd seen plenty of women cry over tacos and margaritas.

Once she walked away, I jumped back into the conversation. "When do you find out the gender? I know nothing about pregnancy, so I'm completely clueless here."

Penny leaned in. "What about an ultrasound? Did you go yet? Can we see it?"

Theo chuckled, shaking her head. She must've known what she was getting into by telling us. The questions wouldn't stop. "I have my first ultrasound next week. I won't find out the gender until around eighteen to twenty weeks, though, so there's still a long way to go."

"Oh my gosh, I hope it's a little girl!" Penny squealed, clapping her hands. "We can play dress-up and have tea parties. And when she's older, we'll all go for manicures together."

Theo's face lit up, her smile brighter than I'd seen in a long time. This baby was going to be so good for her. On the surface, Theo could come across as tough, her style and attitude a bit rough around the edges. But beneath all that, she loved fiercely and wholeheartedly. Once someone earned her trust, they had a friend for life.

This baby was already breaking through her walls, little by little. I couldn't help but think how proud her dad would've been.

We ate and let ourselves daydream about the newest addition to our little group. Names and nursery colors flew around the table, the ideas fueled by tacos and margaritas. I demanded a copy of the ultrasound to hang on my fridge. Penny begged to go with Theo to the appointment, but Theo gently declined. She needed to do this part on her own.

As we left the restaurant, a wave of peace washed over me. My earlier doubts and fears had melted away, replaced with a newfound resolve. Theo and Penny's advice stuck with me. I decided then and there that I would let myself enjoy my time with Boone without overthinking it.

If things didn't work out, I knew I had a soft place to land—with my best friends by my side.

CHAPTER 22

Aspen

When I asked Boone if he'd be down to go to the rodeo as a group, he didn't hesitate. The plan had worked perfectly—Mac and Rhodes tagged along too. We all piled into Boone's truck, the girls in the cab with Boone and the other two guys riding in the truck bed.

I loved Faircloud's amateur rodeos. Watching locals compete was thrilling, and the food? Always incredible. The grounds buzzed with food trucks lining the edges, their savory scents mixing with the crisp evening air. Overhead lights bathed the space in bright fluorescence as the sun set, casting long shadows on the dusty arena. My favorite events were barrel racing and steer wrestling. The latter always had me laughing—there was something hilarious about watching people try to wrestle down an angry steer.

Tonight, I'd dressed for the occasion: a green cap-sleeved dress, brown cowboy boots, and a cream-colored cowboy hat that, coincidentally, matched Boone's. I secretly loved that. Penny wore a star-patched pair of flared jeans and a tank top, while Theo opted for black jean overalls and a bandeau, her hair styled in twisted pigtail braids. She accessorized with her usual abundance of jewelry. Even the guys had cleaned up—Boone looked especially good in a pearl-snap shirt. I nearly passed out when I saw him.

We paired off naturally: me with Boone, Penny with Mac,

and Theo with Rhodes. I hadn't told Boone it was a "triple date," but in my head, that's exactly what it was. Boone leaned close, his warm breath tickling my ear as he whispered, "You look gorgeous, by the way."

I felt giddy, like a teenager on her first date with the high school heartthrob. "Well, thank you," I replied, bumping my shoulder against his arm playfully.

Boone raised his voice slightly so the others could hear. "Should we grab food first or find seats for the event?"

"The steer wrestling starts in, like, twenty minutes," Penny interjected. "We should probably grab seats now and eat after."

I nodded. "Agreed. Let's snag good seats before they're gone."

Leading the way, Boone and I headed toward the bleachers in the main event space. I liked sitting higher up for a better view, so we climbed several rows to find a spot in the middle-high section. Boone sat at the edge, then me, with Penny on my other side. It felt cozy and safe being between them.

As I settled into my seat, I felt a hand on my waist. Boone gently pulled me closer, his face unreadable as he stared off into the distance like nothing had happened. My heart fluttered, but I didn't question it. Instead, I shimmied up against him, resting comfortably at his side. Neither of us said a word, but the unspoken connection was clear.

"I heard Buck is competing in steer wrestling tonight," Rhodes said, leaning over to talk to Boone.

Boone's jaw clenched, his body going rigid. "Fuck that guy," he muttered.

I placed a reassuring hand on his thigh, silently letting him know I was there. His gaze dropped to mine, our faces closer than I'd expected. If I moved even an inch, I'd feel his breath on my lips. *Thank you*, he mouthed, his eyes softening.

I nodded and looked away, focusing on the arena as the announcer's voice boomed over the loudspeaker, signaling the start of the event. The first competitor was a local favorite, Henry, who never failed to entertain.

Henry rode into the arena on horseback, dressed in his usual ridiculous getup—this time, a banana costume, complete with yellow face paint. At forty-something years old, Henry had the spirit of a teenager, and the crowd adored him for it. He waved his arms dramatically, hyping the spectators as they roared with approval.

I cupped my hands around my mouth and joined the chants of his name. My voice was going to be shot by the end of the night, but I didn't care. Nights like this were worth it.

The chute doors banged open, and Henry shot out with the steer. His horse raced alongside the animal, and with a practiced lean, he grabbed the steer's horns. The crowd erupted in cheers as Henry clung on, wrestling the thrashing animal to the ground. Boone let out a sharp whistle next to me, the sound cutting through the chaos. Henry held tight, bringing the steer onto its back in a triumphant finish.

"Hell yeah!" Penny shouted, springing to her feet and clapping.

I wasn't the one wrangling the steer, but just watching made my adrenaline spike.

"Next up, Buck! Everybody make some noise!" the announcer called over the speakers.

The six of us stayed silent, pointedly ignoring the plea for applause. Seeing Buck tonight was clearly bothering Boone, and for good reason. Knowing that guy got to live his life unbothered while Boone's sister had felt forced to leave her hometown made my blood boil. I wasn't typically a violent person, but if Buck tripped and fell flat on his face tonight, I wouldn't be upset.

Buck entered the arena atop a stunning white horse, waving and clapping for himself as he paraded in a wide circle. His showboating only fueled my irritation. I narrowed my eyes, silently willing him to fail. Who knows? Maybe tonight was the night I'd discover latent witchy powers.

"I'm hexing him," I whispered to Boone, leaning close.

"Are you a witch? Will it work?" he whispered back, a hint of humor in his voice.

"Maybe if I think hard enough," I replied with a shrug.

The chute opened, releasing Buck and the steer. As Buck leaned forward to grab the horns, he slipped clean off the saddle and hit the dirt face-first.

"Shut up!" I yelled, jumping to my feet and pointing at the fallen cowboy.

Buck stood, brushing himself off and revealing a fresh smear of something unpleasant on his shirt.

"He fell in shit!" I doubled over, laughing so hard tears blurred my vision. Boone joined in, his deep laughter ringing out as he wiped at his eyes.

"You *are* a witch," he said, high-fiving me before pulling me into a hug.

When we separated, the rest of the group stared at us, their expressions a mix of amusement and disbelief.

"What?" I asked, feigning innocence.

Mac and Rhodes raised their hands in mock surrender. Penny and Theo exchanged a knowing glance before shaking their heads with smirks.

By the end of the event, most of the riders hadn't managed to wrestle their steers to the ground. Buck didn't even bother returning to bow with the other participants. Sore loser.

We left the arena with the crowd, making our way toward the food trucks. To get there, we passed the games and activities booths, including a large inflatable ring housing a mechanical bull.

"Boone, you should show that bull who's boss," Mac teased, pointing at the ring.

"No fucking way," Boone said, shaking his head and walking backward to address Mac.

"You should totally do it," I chimed in, grinning. "Unless you're scared." I wiggled my fingers at him in mock challenge.

Boone scoffed, stopping to glance at the bull. "I'm not scared. I'm just not dressed for it."

"Oh, boohoo!" Penny teased. "Just take off the hat and unbutton the shirt. You'll be fine."

"Yeah, Cowboy," I added, winking. "Live up to your nickname."

Boone rolled his neck and grabbed my arm, pulling me toward the ring. "If I'm doing this, you have to be front and center for motivation."

"Motivation?" I asked, laughing as he dragged me along.

"Yeah, Darling. I'm doing this for you."

At the entrance, Boone handed the unimpressed attendant a five-dollar bill, then turned to me. Removing his hat, he passed it over and unbuttoned his pearl-snap shirt to reveal a white undershirt.

Lord help me, he looked devastatingly good—his messy hair and lazy smile nearly did me in.

The attendant opened the gate and gave Boone a quick rundown of the rules. With one hand on the bull and the other for balance, Boone nodded and climbed aboard. As he prepared, I fidgeted with the hem of my dress, nerves bubbling up for reasons I couldn't explain.

Boone glanced at me one last time, a smirk tugging at his lips. Then, with a firm grip, he gave the signal, and the bull came to life.

It started slow, but as the speed picked up, Boone's hips moved with the rhythm, his body rocking back and forth with the mechanical beast. My jaw nearly dropped—there was something insanely attractive about watching him ride.

"Come on, Boone!" I shouted, jumping up and down as the big red timer on the far wall ticked away.

Boone held on valiantly, but at nine seconds, the bull bucked hard, sending him flying. He landed flat on his back with a loud thud.

I rushed to the edge of the ring, peering over. "How'd I do?" he asked, still sprawled on the floor, catching his breath.

Giving him a thumbs up, I grinned. "You looked damn good doing it."

Boone laughed, standing and dusting himself off. Taking his hat from my hands, he adjusted it on his head before wrapping an arm around my shoulder.

"Funnel cake," Theo declared as we rejoined the group.

"Then funnel cake it is!" I said proudly. If my pregnant best friend wanted funnel cake, she was getting funnel cake.

CHAPTER 23

Boone

I hadn't eaten this much funnel cake and fried Oreos since I was a teenager. Theo kept the orders coming like the world was about to run out of powdered sugar and batter, and she'd never see another funnel cake again. When Aspen told me Theo was pregnant, she made me swear, with the consequence of death, not to tell a soul. I'd been shocked at first, but Aspen said Theo was happy—and that was all that mattered. It took a strong woman to do what Theo was about to do, and I admired her for it.

I silently thanked fate for not letting me wait until after eating to ride that mechanical bull. One spin and I'd have lost myself in front of everyone. I still didn't know what had possessed me to hop on in the first place. Maybe it was seeing Aspen on the sidelines, cheering me on. The way her face lit up made my heart leap. I wanted her as my permanent cheerleader.

Having her there when Buck made his rodeo appearance dulled the usual ache of anger and betrayal. Seeing him live his life so carefree turned my stomach, but Aspen's soft voice whispering that she was "hexing him" had made me laugh. And damn if her witchy powers didn't work—him falling face-first into horse shit was exactly the petty justice I didn't know I needed.

Being at the rodeo tonight, watching Aspen's eyes sparkle as she cheered for the riders, made me realize just how beautiful and vibrant she was. She had this way of softening the rough edges of life, turning bitterness into something almost sweet. If it weren't for her, I probably would've walked out the second I heard the announcer say Buck's name.

We strolled in pairs through the grounds, me with Aspen, Mac with Penny, and Rhodes trailing in the back with Theo. My hand itched to reach out and hold hers. Instead, I glanced down at her, drinking in the sight of her green dress, which hugged every dip and curve. Under the rodeo lights, her blond hair shimmered like silk, catching the glow and making her look ethereal. I couldn't help stealing glances, especially when she wasn't looking.

Suddenly, Aspen stopped short, her cheeks flushing pink under the brim of her hat—the hat that happened to match mine. Penny let out a surprised squeal, throwing her hands up to avoid bumping into her, and took a quick step back. My eyes followed Aspen's, and that's when I saw her.

Miranda Yert.

She was strutting through the crowd, holding hands with two girls I didn't recognize. Aspen's shoulders stiffened, and I knew she was in her head, just like at the bonfire when Miranda's name came up. I didn't know the details of their history, but I knew enough to see that Miranda was her sore spot.

Reaching out, I rested my hand on Aspen's elbow, giving it a gentle squeeze.

"Look at me," I murmured, low enough that only she could hear.

Reluctantly, Aspen tore her gaze away from Miranda and met mine. Her wide eyes locked on to me, and for a moment, everything else faded. She had my back earlier tonight—I'd have hers now. I offered her a small, reassuring smile, my thumb brushing against her arm in silent comfort.

Something shifted in her. Her face softened, and the tension in her eyes melted away. It was like she felt safe with me, and I'd be damned if I let anyone take that from her.

But Miranda had noticed us. Her gaze landed on Aspen, flicked down to my hand on her arm, and then snapped back to my face. An all-too-familiar, smug grin spread across her lips as she lifted a hand to wave at me with two mocking fingers.

I didn't care. My focus stayed on Aspen.

Leaning down, I whispered in her ear, "Don't let her win."

Aspen swallowed, her lips curving into a small, determined smile.

"Oh, hell no," Penny barked from behind us. "Someone hold me back."

She tried to push her way between Aspen and me, breaking our contact, but Mac was quicker. He grabbed her by the biceps before she could make good on whatever dramatic scene she had planned.

Instead of entertaining Miranda, I steered the group toward the carnival games. Rows of colorful booths stretched out before us, each lit up in neon glory beneath the dark sky. The lights twinkled, drawing crowds in with the promise of a prize. I was about to be another sucker—everyone knew the games were rigged, but that didn't make them any less fun.

At the ring toss, brightly colored rings clattered into rows of glass bottles. Kids cheered as their parents did their best to win them a prize. I had to be strategic about what game I chose—there was no way I was winning the ring toss.

A little farther down, the balloon darts were calling my name. Brightly colored balloons were pinned to a board, just waiting to be popped. This was more my speed: throwing a dart at something stationary. Should be a breeze.

"What should I aim for?" I asked Aspen. The rest of our friends dispersed, heading to other games, leaving us standing together. Aspen paused for a moment, her eyes scanning the stuffed animals hanging from the booth.

"I think one of those big bears suits you well," she teased, nudging me with her shoulder.

I wanted to pull her out of whatever headspace she was in after seeing Miranda. But I wasn't about to pry. I'd ask her about it later, when the time was right.

A bear? Maybe for me, but it definitely didn't match *her.* I stood, tapping my chin as I considered the prizes. There were so many stuffed toys to choose from, but as soon as I saw it, I knew exactly what I wanted.

I pulled out my wallet and handed the guy enough money to pop every balloon if I needed to. The skinny teenager manning the booth handed me a bucket of darts and muttered some half-hearted instructions. He looked like he'd rather be anywhere else.

One after another, I aimed for the highest-value targets. Aspen stood beside me, cheering me on.

"Aim up top! Get the green!" she encouraged.

I followed her lead. Green was the highest value, and to win what I had in mind, I needed every single one. After I popped all the greens and a few blues for good measure, I looked up at the kid, waiting for my total.

"Do I have enough for that?" I asked with a grin, pointing to the biggest stuffed bunny I'd ever seen. It was light pink, with a white chest. It reminded me of Aspen—playful, kind, and gentle.

The kid glanced at the tiles and punched the numbers into his phone's calculator.

"Yeah, sure," he said, stepping up on a ladder to grab my prize.

"You definitely aren't the bunny type," Aspen joked.

"Well," I said, taking the bunny from the kid before he could even come down the ladder. "This isn't for me. It's for you." I handed the massive stuffed animal to her, and she took it hesitantly. The bunny was almost as big as she was, and she had to hold it with both arms to keep it from dragging on the ground.

"Me?" she asked, peering around the enormous animal. "You won this for me?" I couldn't help laughing as I watched her try to manage the oversized bunny. It engulfed her; she was completely hidden behind it.

Shrugging, I replied, "You remind me of a bunny. I saw it and couldn't resist."

Aspen laughed, her head tipping back, and the carnival lights bathed her face in a warm glow. Damn, she was captivating. I held out my hand to take the rabbit from her—there was no way she'd be able to carry it all the way back to the truck.

"Let's go find the rest of the crew," I said, tucking the bunny under my arm. Stealing another glance at her, I saw her smiling to herself. My plan to pull her out of whatever funk she'd been in seemed to have worked.

The only question now was: where in the world would she put this huge bunny?

CHAPTER 24

Life at the farm stand had been a whirlwind. Traffic was picking up, leaving me with less time to tackle all the extra tasks on my to-do list. I rarely worked this hard, not even during my shifts at The Coffee Cup. On top of being the face of the stand, I managed inventory, prepping, and all the operational logistics entirely on my own. But I wasn't complaining. I'd much rather stay busy and let the days fly by.

The night after the rodeo, I started sketching out my story. Boone—and his ridiculous bunny—had sparked something inside me. When I got home, I plotted so much my brain felt like mush, but the ideas flowed easily. The hard part, I knew, would be connecting the dots. Still, I chipped away at it every night before bed. I'd read online that writing five hundred words a day could produce a full-length novel in about five and a half months. That thought comforted me—I didn't have to rush. Letting the story flow naturally was working so far.

Around mid-afternoon, there was usually a lull in traffic. I used the downtime to prep for closing or make the next day's work easier. But today, I had an unexpected visitor.

Parker strolled through the open doors, his eyes roaming the stand as if taking in every detail. I looked up from counting jars of honey and broke into a smile.

"Hey, Park!" I exclaimed, setting my clipboard down on one

of the empty round tables. I walked over and hugged him tight, the familiar warmth of my brother making me grin.

"I had to come see what my little sister's done with the place," he said, pulling back and giving me a lopsided smile. "I'll admit, I'm a little jealous I didn't rope you into working for me instead."

I motioned to the table. "Sit down, big brother. Can I get you something? A drink? A muffin?"

Parker loved my muffins—almost as much as Boone. When I worked in town, he used to visit and grab one for the road.

"A muffin sounds perfect," he replied, settling into the chair.

I made my way to the baked goods cabinet, pulling out the second-to-last muffin. Boone had already claimed one this morning, so I didn't have to worry about him going without. I sliced Parker's muffin in half and ran it through the toaster, knowing he liked it warm with a bit of butter. Bringing the plate to the table, I sat down with my coffee, savoring the caffeine boost I'd need to power through the rest of the day.

"How's life on the ranch treating you?" Parker asked, biting into the muffin.

"It's amazing. Hard work, but I love it."

"I'm glad to see you happy," Parker said, his tone warm. "Despite what Mom and Dad think, I'm proud of you for sticking to your guns and living life on your terms."

His words made me pause. I bit my lip, feeling a wave of guilt. If only he knew how wrong he was. I was a pushover when it came to our parents. I hadn't told them about my dream of being a writer. Instead, I let them believe I was still planning to follow *their* dreams for me.

"Well, I don't really know about that," I admitted softly.

Parker raised an eyebrow. "What do you mean?"

I traced the rim of my coffee mug with my finger, hesitating. "I haven't been honest with them—or myself. They keep telling me I have *more potential* than staying in Faircloud, that I could do so much more. I've never told them I love it here. I always fall into their trap, making excuses to keep their hopes up. The truth is, I have no intention of leaving or going back to school."

Parker leaned back, studying me thoughtfully. "I never thought you did. So why not just tell them? Rip off the Band-Aid. I did."

"I know you did. That's why they're focused even more on me," I said, my voice rising slightly. "I don't want to disappoint them, Parker. I can't stand the idea of seeing Dad's face when he finds out his baby girl doesn't want to be a doctor or some high-powered tech genius."

Parker's expression softened. "What does Aspen want to be?" he asked, his voice steady and calm.

I took a deep breath. "A writer," I whispered. "I want to publish my book."

I braced myself, expecting criticism or doubt. But Parker just nodded, his face unreadable for a moment before he smiled.

"Then do it." He made it sound so simple. "Start writing. And when you're ready, show it to Mom and Dad. They'll come around. Trust me."

He made it sound so easy. But looking at my brother, calm and sure, I couldn't help but feel a flicker of hope. Maybe, just maybe, he was right.

"I am. Writing, I mean, I started a little while ago. It's still in the early stages, but I'm enjoying it so far."

I felt like a rookie in the world of writing, but from what I'd read online and heard from others in the community, I was doing pretty well for a beginner.

Parker leaned back in his chair, his gaze steady and thoughtful. "Don't let them bully you into resentment." Parker's voice was firm. "Giving in might make them happy for a while, but what about you? Over time, it'll eat at you, the fact that you never got a say, never took a chance to do what you truly want with your life."

His words hit me like a lightning bolt. He was right. This was *my* life to live, and no amount of pleasing others could outweigh the regret I'd feel if I didn't try to follow my dreams.

"Thanks, Parker," I said, voice full of gratitude. Hearing support from someone outside of Mom and Dad was a much-needed boost. It reminded me why I was chasing this dream in the first place. I had goals, plans, and ambitions—and I wasn't going to let anyone dictate or control my actions anymore.

"You're going to do great things, whether you believe it or not." Parker gave a small smile. "And just know, I'm here for you. Whenever you're ready to tell Mom and Dad, I'll have your back."

"Please don't say anything to them," I said quickly, putting my hands together like I was begging. The last thing I needed was for my parents to hear about this from Parker and start blowing up my phone.

"I promise. Scout's honor." He held up *The Hunger Games* salute.

I laughed. "That's not even the right reference."

"Close enough."

Parker stuck around a little longer, chatting while I checked on customers and offered him more snacks and drinks. Before he left, I gave him another hug, telling him he could stop by anytime. Now that he'd hired a new employee for his shop, he had more free time to get out of that stuffy store.

After he left, I got to work filling the wildflower displays, organizing the soaps and candles, and sweeping the floor in preparation for closing. Tonight, after my date with Boone, I planned to sit down and write. My conversation with Parker had left me buzzing with motivation. He was right—if I wrote enough and could show my parents the progress I'd made, maybe they'd finally get on board with my dreams.

Boone

IT WAS A SCORCHER today—the kind of heat that made you want to dive headfirst into a cold lake and stay there. The sun beat down relentlessly, not a single cloud in the sky to break its intensity.

I'd ditched my shirt hours ago, but my skin was starting to redden under the sun's wrath.

Rhodes and Logan were with me today, helping clear out the unused pasture to make space for more livestock. We were expecting a new herd of cattle soon, and the extra room was a must. It was rare to have both of them working alongside me on the same project, but I wasn't complaining. This was a big task, and I needed all the muscle I could get to finish it.

"Have you heard from your sister?" Logan asked, taking a swig of tea from his oversized jug.

"Yeah," I said, wiping sweat from my brow. "She called me last weekend—for the first time since she left."

Logan raised an eyebrow. "And you didn't tell us?"

"Didn't think it was a big deal," I replied, shrugging.

"Not a big deal?" Logan scoffed, looking genuinely offended.

Rhodes chuckled from where he was stacking some old fencing. "Come on, Boone. You can't just drop something like that and expect us not to be curious."

Neither of them knew the whole story—just the bare minimum. The truth was something only my parents and Aspen knew. And that was fine by me. Some things were better left unsaid.

"It slipped my mind to tell you. What's the deal?" I asked, trying to figure out Logan's tone. It was throwing me for a loop. He rolled his eyes and looked away like a kid mid-temper tantrum. I glanced at Rhodes, hoping he'd back me up.

"I bet he told Aspen," Rhodes mocked, smirking.

That wasn't much help—it made things worse. My so-called friends were ganging up on me, throwing punches I didn't see coming.

"Whoa, okay. Let's take a step back," I said, holding my hands up in mock surrender. "What the hell is going on with you two?"

Logan scoffed again, clearly pissed off, so Rhodes took the lead. "I want you to come clean about your relationship with her. I've been getting grilled with questions I can't answer, man. Do you know how it feels to have random people in town know more about your life than I do?"

That one hit like a sucker punch. The last time Rhodes and I talked about Aspen, I thought we were good. But now, I realized things had escalated—probably because word had spread about our *very* public date and, well, the equally public affection. And yeah, I knew I'd gotten a little handsy at the rodeo.

The truth was, I hadn't thought about anyone but her. I was straight-up infatuated with Aspen. I'd do just about anything to spend more time with her, even if it meant sticking to our so-called "fake dates."

"I'm sorry. I didn't even think about that," I said honestly, trying to tread carefully. "But it's not what you think."

I didn't want to spill the whole story—especially the part about her parents—but I had to say something to get them off my back. "I'm helping her with a project. We're going on fake dates so she can use it as inspiration for her writing."

Logan stayed quiet, which only made me more anxious. I leaned back, stretching my legs out and propping myself up with my arms, trying to seem relaxed even though I wasn't.

"Come on, Boone." Rhodes' eyes narrowed. "You gotta be honest with yourself."

"What are you talking about?" I asked, genuinely confused.

"It's more than just 'fake dates. I've seen you two together. There's something there, and I just hope you're too blind to see it, not holding back for *my* sake."

Wait, what? Did he think I was hiding my feelings for Aspen to spare him because of what happened with Jess?

"No, not at all," I said quickly, letting out a heavy sigh. "I do like her, a lot."

That was the truth. They were going to figure it out eventually, so I might as well admit it.

"But we haven't talked about being more than friends," I added. "I don't even know how to start that conversation, so I'm just... going with the flow for now."

Rhodes's expression softened. "Coming from someone who's

been in that position and lost it—don't let it slip away. When you feel something real, it's special. Not acting on it because you don't know how? That's just stupid."

I blinked at him. Rhodes never talked about Jess, let alone shared his feelings like this with us. It wasn't his style. Hearing this kind of honesty from him was...unexpected.

"I don't even know how she feels about me," I admitted, pulling off my hat and running a hand through my hair. "I know there's attraction, but beyond that? It's a big fucking question mark."

Talking about my feelings for Aspen made them feel even bigger—like they were towering over me, waiting for me to deal with them. And honestly? It stressed me out.

"It doesn't have to be hard. Just go for it and do what feels right in the moment. Life's too short to let it eat you alive," Rhodes' voice was steady but laced with something deeper.

I could tell he was thinking back on his own experiences. The change in his face said it all—his jaw tightened, and his gaze dropped to the ground as he absentmindedly pulled at the grass. He was shutting down, retreating back into himself. I'd tried to broach the subject with him before, but he'd never been open to sharing. I hoped that one day, he'd find someone he could really confide in.

Logan stayed silent through the whole conversation, his face unreadable. Who would've thought a day on the ranch between three men would turn into an impromptu therapy session?

BREAK TIME ENDED, but Rhodes's words stuck with me. Maybe it *wasn't* supposed to be so complicated. If I wanted something real with Aspen, I needed to step up and talk to her about it. The thought of being with someone else hadn't even crossed my mind since she'd come into my life—and, honestly, I was fine with that.

"Hey, Logan. Wait up!" I called, jogging to catch him before he climbed into his truck at the end of the day. The sun had been brutal, and we were all worn out, but I couldn't let him leave without figuring out what had been eating at him all day.

"What's going on with you?" I asked, stepping in front of him as he stood by the open door of his pickup.

"Nothing, man. I'm good," he said, brushing me off, but his tone betrayed him.

"Bullshit. Something's got you fired up. If it's about Aspen, I'm sorry if I made you feel—"

Logan cut me off with a sharp laugh, one that sounded more bitter than amused.

"You think this is about you and Aspen? If anything, I'm happy for you."

"Then just spill it," I snapped. "You've been acting like a prick, leaving town without warning and walking around with a chip on your shoulder. Don't think I haven't noticed."

Logan's expression darkened, but he kept his voice even. "It's nothing that concerns you."

"You're my best friend." I took a deep breath, forcing myself to calm down. Matching anger with anger never ended well. "Of course, it concerns me."

He let out a long breath, his frustration simmering just beneath the surface. "I'm just worried about Ellie. I've been trying to reach her, and she hasn't been responding."

"You're all worked up over my sister?" I asked, narrowing my eyes to make sure I hadn't misheard.

"She—" He hesitated, stumbling over his words. "I mean, it's Ellie. She's like a sister to me too."

We'd all grown up together, and Logan and Rhodes had practically lived on the ranch with us. Still, I felt a pang of guilt for not keeping them in the loop. Ellie was family to them too, and they deserved to know she was okay.

"You're right," I admitted. "I should've told you about her call. I'm sorry."

Logan sighed, some of the tension easing out of his shoulders.

"It's okay. I shouldn't have reacted the way I did."

I clapped him on the shoulder, offering a small grin. "Can we just forget it and move on?"

Logan nodded. "Yeah. Thanks, Boone."

"Sure thing, kid," I said, giving him a mock salute as I stepped back. "See you tomorrow. We've still got work to do."

He climbed into his truck, the engine roaring to life as he backed out, a cloud of dust kicking up in his wake. I stood there watching him drive down the long driveway, already thinking about the next day—and about Aspen.

CHAPTER 25

Boone

I couldn't figure out why I was so in my head about this date with Aspen. We'd already been on two, and both were amazing. But something about tonight felt different—heavier, like there was more at stake. Maybe it was Rhodes's words lingering in my mind, pushing me to see what this could really be.

I stood in front of the mirror, smoothing out my shirt and tucking it into my dark-washed jeans. Tonight, I decided to leave the hat behind. Instead, I dressed up the outfit with my favorite belt and buckle, hoping the small change would make an impression.

Our dates had been planned with purpose. First, I taught her something new—horseback riding. Luckily, she'd never done it before, and it worked out perfectly. Then, I took her to a place she already loved, the farmers market. Another home run. Tonight, I was pulling out the stops and leaning into the romantic side I didn't even know I had.

I ran wet fingers through my hair to tame the wild strands sticking out. While shaving, I left the mustache because I knew she liked it, even if she wouldn't admit it. After giving myself a final once-over, I slipped on my favorite square-toed cowboy boots.

Aspen had no clue what I had planned tonight, except for the vague instruction to wear something comfortable. Her first question, of course, was, "Can I wear a dress?" There was no way I'd ever deny her that.

Leaving my cabin unlocked—it wasn't like anyone was coming out here—I walked up to Aspen's door. My nerves kicked in as I raised my hand to knock. Three quick taps, and a soft "Come in" drifted from the other side.

Stepping inside, I took a moment to admire the space. She'd done so much since moving in, and it showed. The shelves lining the back wall were packed tight with books, leaving no room for more. The couch sat in the center of the living room, facing the front door, cozy and inviting.

"I'll be ready in a second!" she called from down the hall, her voice carrying a mix of apology and excitement. "I lost track of time while I was writing, and now I'm behind!"

Smiling to myself, I followed the sound of her voice to the bathroom. She stood in front of the mirror, already dressed with her hair done. She leaned close to the glass, carefully applying mascara.

"This is new for me," she said, catching my eyes in the reflection. "I'll adapt, I promise."

Leaning against the doorframe, one boot crossed over the other, I replied, "Take your time, Darling. I'm in no rush."

She finished with a swipe of light pink gloss, rubbing her lips together and wiping away the excess with her finger. The simple act sent my pulse racing.

"Okay, ready!" She spun around with a bounce in her step. "What do we think?" She swayed back and forth, modeling her outfit.

"Perfect," I muttered, a grin tugging at my lips.

She brushed past me as she left the bathroom, the lightest touch of her against me making my heart race. Was I really that far gone? Following her, I watched as she grabbed her purse and tossed her phone inside.

"Can you at least give me a little hint?" she asked, holding her fingers up to emphasize just how little she meant.

"Nope." I was firm, standing my ground. As much as I wanted to give in, I wouldn't. The wait would be worth it.

WE TURNED OFF the gravel driveway onto an overgrown path. The weeds were tall, and tree branches hung low, casting eerie shadows in the truck's headlights.

"Your super epic and legit surprise is death?" Aspen asked, her tone playful but a little wary. "Because it feels like you're taking me to a remote location to make killing me easier."

"It's not death!" I laughed. "It's creepy, but trust me, it'll be worth it. Now, shh."

She didn't say another word, though I could tell she was bursting with curiosity.

When we finally reached the spot, I put the truck in park and turned to her. "Stay put," I said before hopping out and heading to the back. I opened the tailgate and pulled out a blue bin filled with everything I needed to set up.

Approaching the passenger side, I grinned. "Okay, close your eyes, no peeking!"

Aspen swung her legs over the side of the seat and covered her eyes with her hands. I grabbed her waist to help her down, guiding her toward the back of the truck.

"On the count of three, you can look," I whispered in her ear. "One...two..." I paused heavily before saying three, building suspense. Aspen wiggled impatiently, doing some kind of shimmy that made me laugh.

"Three."

Aspen removed her hands, and her jaw dropped. Before us, the truck bed was transformed into a cozy haven, layered with soft blankets and pillows. Warm, glowing lanterns cast a gentle light on the scene. In the middle sat two wine glasses and a bottle of her favorite red, chilling in an ice bucket. Nearby, a plate of chocolate-covered strawberries completed the setup, perfect for stargazing.

"Boone..." she whispered, spinning to face me, her eyes wide with wonder. The moonlight highlighted her features, and for a moment, I couldn't look away. Gently, I placed my hand on her cheek, my thumb brushing over her soft skin.

"I had to pull out the big guns for the grand finale," I said, my voice low, as if I might break the magic of the moment. Her eyes locked onto mine, and it took everything in me not to kiss her right then. But instead, I broke the tension, nudging her toward the open tailgate.

"C'mon." I gripped her hips and hoisted her up. She laughed softly, settling herself amidst the pillows.

Aspen scooted back, her movements effortless, while I kicked off my boots and climbed up after her. Once we were both settled, I reached for the wine, pouring us each a glass. Normally, I wouldn't touch the stuff—beer or tequila was more my speed. But if Aspen liked it, I figured I could, too.

"I'm honestly blown away." She shook her head in disbelief as she accepted the glass. The bracelet I'd given her glimmered in the lantern light, and seeing her wear it filled me with a quiet pride.

"It's time to get your creative juices flowing," I teased, leaning back against the truck bed. Aspen nestled close, her side pressed against mine from ankle to hip. The warmth of her presence was a comfort I didn't realize I'd been missing. "How's the writing going?"

"Honestly? Really good. I've been writing a couple hundred words a day. I haven't read through any of it yet, but I'm feeling confident."

"I love hearing that," I replied, meaning it. Knowing she was finding her groove made me feel like I was doing something right.

For a while, we sat in silence, gazing at the stars above. The quiet field was filled with the soft hum of crickets and the occasional rustle of a breeze through the trees.

"How's Logan?" Aspen asked, breaking the silence.

I'd told her about Logan's reaction when he found out Ellie had called, but I'd left out the other parts of the story—especially the bits about Rhodes and my tangled feelings. Once again, I'd chickened out.

"It's been good since. He hasn't brought it up, and I've left it alone, too."

"If you want my opinion," Aspen said, her voice thoughtful, "I think it's more than just because she's *family.*"

"You think Logan has a crush on my sister?" The idea caught me off guard. We'd all been in each other's lives for so long that Logan felt like a brother. The thought of him liking Ellie felt strange, almost unnatural.

"I mean, what do I know?" She shrugged. "But whatever got him that worked up tells me maybe there's something more."

She had a point. His reaction had been intense—out of proportion. I reached down and intertwined my pinky with hers, the small connection soothing the swirl of thoughts in my head. I wanted to be closer to her; my body craved her touch.

She leaned her head against my shoulder, cradling her wineglass close.

"Do you think just asking him straight out is a good idea?" I asked.

"It depends on how you feel. Do you think he'd be honest?" she countered.

I thought about it, weighing the possibility. I wasn't sure Logan would tell me the truth. "No," I admitted. "I don't think so."

Aspen nodded, her voice gentle. "Again, not that you asked for my opinion, but if that's how you feel, maybe just wait and see what happens."

She was right. Pushing Logan now wouldn't get me anywhere. Better to keep my distance and watch things play out naturally.

Her head shifted from my shoulder to my chest, and our fingers laced together fully. Something about tonight felt different—less friendly than before. It was as if we both knew this "just friends" thing was hanging by a thread.

Having her this close in private made my resolve crumble. I wanted to kiss her, to taste the gloss on her lips, to feel her warmth pressed against me. My heartbeat quickened, drumming in my neck.

It was now or never, Boone. Buck up.

I took my hand away from hers and placed it under her chin, tilting her head up toward me. Her eyes danced between mine like a pinball in a machine. I was captivated by her beauty. I was so fucking lucky.

I leaned in slowly, touching my lips to hers with a soft peck. I pulled away just enough so I could still feel her lips brush against mine.

I hesitated briefly before going back for more. Placing more soft kisses in bursts on her full lips, Aspen's hand came up and cupped my cheek. The feeling of her soft hands on my skin was intoxicating. I wove my fingers into her hair to support the back of her head and pulled her closer. Aspen's body moved in sync as she sat up fully and deepened the kiss.

The wine glasses were moved before I lifted her onto my lap, allowing her the room to straddle me. Her curves felt like heaven under my touch; my hands mapped out every dip and divot.

Aspen's body rocked against mine, and our kisses turned heavy and rushed. I needed more—I wanted her in every way I possibly could.

Aspen nibbled my bottom lip, pulling it down slightly before coming back in for a kiss. She opened her mouth for me, my tongue slipping in and meshing with hers. She tasted like that damn wine, which drove me even more to the brink of insanity.

We kissed as my hands explored her body, palming her ass through the thin fabric of her dress. I brought my left hand back and laid a slap on her ass cheek. The restraint I'd been holding onto snapped. What had started out as a cute final date would end up with us tangled together, our kisses rushed like if we stopped, one of us would come to our senses.

Aspen yelped and smiled, giggling when I grabbed her again.

Fuck, she was driving me mad.

The only thoughts I had consisted of how desperate I was to feel her around my aching cock. To hear the sounds she'd make as I made her unravel.

Slowly, she brought her fingers to my neck and wandered down to my chest. Her touch ended up under my shirt after pulling it free from my pants.

Aspen took her time feeling every ridge on my stomach, each ab getting the attention it deserved. I liked her teasing me. The anticipation grew inside, my heart pounding. I swore I felt her mutter a groan against my lips. She wanted me just as bad as I wanted her.

Aspen adjusted and grabbed for my belt buckle, pulling away from the kiss like she was asking for permission.

"If you do that, Darling, there's no stopping what comes next."

I'd like to think I was good at keeping myself under control, but Aspen Westgrove had been making me question everything I thought I knew about myself. Once she gave the go-ahead, I'd be unleashing a beast from deep inside me. The way I needed her was primal. There was no way I'd pass up the opportunity this time. I was dumb once, I wasn't going to let it happen twice.

She nibbled the lobe of my ear slightly before peppering kisses down my neck.

"Who said I wanted to stop?" she whispered into my skin. I let my head fall back and a whimper escaped my lips. She kissed and licked my neck as she worked to undo my belt. Her teeth left a sting in her wake—she was way too good at this teasing thing. My neck was the easiest way to get me fired up.

Aspen popped the button on my pants and the warmth of her hand reached into my boxers, her soft skin made contact with my cock, and it jolted from her touch.

With devilish intent, she played with my neck and my length at the same time. She squeezed lightly, finding the tip and brushing a finger underneath.

"Fuck, Aspen," I groaned through clenched teeth, she was going to be my undoing. I couldn't let her play any longer. I knew I wasn't going to last another second if she kept stroking me.

There was only one way this night would end, and it wasn't

going to be in my pants.

Reaching my hand up, I wrapped it around her throat and squeezed while pushing her away from me.

Her lips crashed against mine with my hand still around her throat. I laid one long kiss on her plump lips. When I flipped her onto her back, the truck bed rattled.

"Tell me how you want it." Needing to tease her, I bit at the soft skin under her ear.

I straddled her as I pinned her arms above her head, fully intent on giving her a taste of her own torture. My cock was rock hard and uncomfortable, pressing against my jeans.

"Hard," she demanded, not breaking eye contact.

"Rough," she moaned. I moved my hand from her throat and placed my thumb on her bottom lip. Her tongue darted out, licking the tip.

"Hot," she mumbled. Aspen pulled my thumb into her mouth and sucked. I whimpered like a fucking puppy. That was the hottest thing I'd ever experienced. It was total bullshit when she said she didn't know what she was doing, because this woman was going to make me finish way too quickly.

"Christ," I muttered, my eyes rolling into the back of my head. Aspen got a kick out of seeing me crumble. She smiled around my thumb, victorious at the reaction she pulled from me.

My cock was going either in her mouth or between her slick thighs. It was just a matter of where she wanted it. I took my hand back and grabbed her breast through her dress. I could see the peaks of her hard nipples under the fabric. Her breasts were barely being held in by the top of her dress, which was perfect for me. I pulled down her straps and let her breasts free. They were perfect and plump, her nipples a dusty pink.

Using the thumb she was sucking, I lightly touched her nipple, flicking and rubbing in circles. The soft skin felt like silk beneath mine.

"Lord, help me," Aspen whispered, her head falling back against the truck bed. I laughed, bending down and taking the nipple I was playing with between my teeth. I bit down lightly and pulled away, letting it pop out of my mouth. She tasted salty, sweat glistened on her bare skin. I stood up to remove my jeans all the way, which left me in just my T-shirt.

"Come on, Cowboy. You might as well just take it all off," Aspen teased, the look on her face begging for more. She bit her bottom lip and sat up, unzipping the back of her dress to shimmy out of it.

Laying down under me in nothing but her black lace thong, I admired the curves of her body, her full hips and round breasts. This, right here, was heaven on earth. I grinned at the sight before me. A woman who seemed so put together and timid was unraveling at my touch.

"Before I keep going, I need to hear you say you want this," I growled, now kneeling over her body.

"I want you, Boone. Right. Now," she proclaimed, her eyes never leaving mine. That was all I needed to hear.

"Then I need you out of this pathetic excuse for panties." I hooked my thumbs into the band and pulled down. Her pussy was on full display, she was slick with need, and it was all for me. There's no way I was ever going to share.

Aspen kicked off her underwear, and they went flying somewhere into the dried-up field. That was a problem for later. Right now, all I wanted was to focus on her. I placed a finger on the top of her clit tracing slow, soft circles—her body bucked slightly beneath me.

Growling, I used my free hand to pin her down to the truck bed as I continued to pick up speed, still playing with her clit. Darkening, her eyes flashed with need.

"Boone," she moaned. Hearing my name on her lips was music to my ears.

"I would keep teasing you, Darling, but you're already soaked for me," I said, bringing my glistening thumb to my mouth. "Look at me." Aspen did as I asked. A slow smirk grew on my face, one that told her I liked her submission, maybe a little too much.

"Good girl," I muttered and slowly sucked her wetness off my thumb.

"Fuck, I need you in me. Now," Aspen begged, her jaw clenched. I reached for my pants, digging out a condom from my wallet. I held it up, but she grabbed it from my hands, ripping it open with her teeth. I'd never had a girl rip a condom open like that before.

She sat up, my cock was in her face. Aspen pulled the condom out, but before rolling it down my length, she took almost all of me in her mouth. She gagged and looked up with tears in the corners of her eyes. Going back again, the tip hit the back of her throat. My cock sprang from her lips, making a popping sound before she placed the condom on.

Settling between her, I spread her thighs wide so I could fit. I touched my tip to her entrance and pushed slowly as she expanded around me. She took me so well. In awe, I watched as she fell apart. Her head fell back, and she bit down on her lip.

"Do you need me to stop?" I asked.

"No way." She laughed. "Keep going. I can take it." A woman of her word, she took all of me. I drove into her, adding a deep thrust at the end.

Aspen felt so fucking good. I took one leg and placed it on my shoulder to get as deep as possible.

"Yes," she moaned as I plunged into her. She felt so good around me, her walls squeezed tight, and I knew she was close. Her nails dug into my back, scraping down my skin. The pain brought me back to life, stirring up something inside me. The hair on the back of my neck was dripping with sweat, and I drove into her pretty pussy again. The release built at the bottom of my spine, blacking out my vision as I came with her.

"You are so good," I huffed, holding myself up with my hands to hover over her. Aspen's chest heaved, her breaths fast and shallow. "Please let me do that again."

"Oh, hell yeah," she replied, laughing. "That will be happening again."

I climbed off her, trying to find my boxers and pants to put them back on. I remembered I had to hunt for her underwear. Jumping from the truck bed, I worked my button shut on my pants and tried to find her thong.

Since it was so dark, I couldn't see the black fabric without lighting. Aspen decided to put her dress on, forgetting the underwear. I used one of the blankets I brought to help clean her up. She lay back down exhausted, and I knew we were both going to sleep well tonight.

CHAPTER 26

Rhodes and I decided to take the horses out for a quick ride before calling it a day. Things between us had settled. I chose not to bring up our earlier confrontation, letting it stay in the past where it belonged. He'd had every right to call me out for being a jackass, and honestly, I was glad he did. If Rhodes hadn't pushed me to face myself, last night with Aspen might not have happened.

I couldn't stop thinking about her—her touch, her voice, the way she looked at me. Every memory of her lit a fire inside me, and I knew there was no going back.

We rode through the same field I'd taken Aspen to the night before. The scene felt different now, charged with new memories. I glanced over at Rhodes, considering whether to come clean before he heard it from someone else—not that I thought Aspen would share. She wasn't that kind of person.

I cleared my throat, but before I could speak, Rhodes pointed to something on the ground.

"What's that over there?" he asked, steering his horse toward the spot.

Following his lead, I rode closer and hopped down to investigate. I crouched to pick up the item, grinning when I realized what it was. Aspen's thong dangled from my finger.

Rhodes burst into laughter, his voice echoing across the field. "You dirty bastard."

I smirked, tucking the lace into my back pocket before remounting my horse. "I was just about to tell you, but I guess karma beat me to it."

"You made your move," he said, grinning knowingly.

"I did, and I wish I'd done it sooner," I admitted. "I like her, man."

Rhodes gave me a rare, genuine smile. "It's about time. I'm happy for you."

His words hit me harder than I expected, a mix of relief and gratitude. Still, a small part of me felt guilty, knowing what he'd been through.

"We haven't talked about what it means going forward. I hope she feels the same way, but I don't want to make assumptions."

"Ask her," Rhodes said simply. "Be honest with yourself and with her."

"There's something different about this," I admitted. "I care too much about saying the wrong thing, scaring her off. With anyone else, I'd just lay it all out there and see what happens. But Aspen? She's worth more than that."

Aspen

CLOSING TIME COULDN'T come soon enough. I was grateful to have the day behind me—not because it had been bad, but because my mind wasn't on work at all. I had the writing bug, and my thoughts were consumed by plots, characters, and dialogue. Every free moment was spent jotting down notes on my phone, ideas spilling out faster than I could organize them.

Last night had done something to me. When Boone dropped me off, I couldn't sleep. Instead, I stayed up, typing my heart out well past midnight. I wrote down every detail I could remember from our date, capturing the way it made me feel. This morning, the first thing I did was read it back.

Now, as I danced around the farm stand, humming to myself,

I couldn't stop thinking about Boone. His body was the stuff of romance novels—chiseled abs, strong arms, the kind of physique that came from real, hard work. It wasn't just his looks, though. He had this way of making me feel seen, like I didn't need to hide or hold back.

I blushed at the memory of how bold I'd been, how I'd let go of my usual shyness. Boone had a way of bringing out a side of me I didn't even know existed. I'd kissed him like I was starving, whispered things I never thought I'd say. I wanted him—hot and hard, no holding back.

Thinking about it now made my cheeks burn and my heart race. I didn't know what had come over me, but I wasn't about to regret a second of it.

Reflecting on the first time we hooked up at the swimming hole, I couldn't help but smile at how differently I'd acted last night. I'd been confident, comfortable in my skin, enough to bring him to his knees—literally. Giggling at the memory, I worked through my closing tasks, my mind on priority one: getting home to write.

"You started without me?" Boone's voice came from the doorway, teasing and warm. I turned to see him standing there, hands tucked behind his back. Dropping the towel I'd been using to clean, I gave him my full attention. He was sweaty and dirty, and my first thought was that this man desperately needed a shower. My second? I'd happily volunteer to scrub every inch of him.

Butterflies swirled in my stomach as I took him in. This was the first time I'd seen Boone since our night together, and spinning to face him made me a little dizzy—or maybe it was his smile and that infuriatingly sexy mustache.

"I can't wait on you forever," I said, walking toward him with a smirk. "I've got writing to do." I pulled at my dress, feeling uncharacteristically shy under his gaze. His hands were still behind his back. I wondered if he was hiding something. Leaning slightly to the side, I tried to sneak a peek.

"Curious, are we?" Boone asked, his grin widening as he turned to block my view. He walked backward to the counter, keeping his secret hidden. "You don't get this until I get mine."

I instantly knew what he meant. Like every other day, I grabbed the paper bag holding his muffin. Holding it behind my back, I flashed him a sweet smile. "I'll show you mine if you show me yours."

"We both show when I say go," Boone countered, his tone playful and challenging.

The moment hung between us, anticipation crackling. "Go!" he shouted.

In one fluid motion, he brought his hand out from behind his back, revealing a bouquet of wildflowers—vivid and fragrant, clearly handpicked from the field behind the stand. My muffin suddenly felt very underwhelming.

I stepped closer, taking the flowers from him and handing him the brown bag in return. "These are gorgeous." I brought them to my nose. Their sweet, earthy scent was intoxicating, much like the man standing before me. Boone opened the bag, peeking inside as if to confirm the muffin's presence.

Leaning casually against the counter, he crossed one boot over the other. "I thought you could put them on your desk. For inspiration."

My heart melted into a puddle at my feet. For a moment, I was speechless, staring down at the flowers in awe. The feelings I had for Boone were growing at an alarming rate, and it was both thrilling and terrifying.

"You know how to treat a woman, Boone," I said, my voice soft. And I meant it. Any woman would be lucky to have him. Deep down, I wished I could be that woman. But I knew this was temporary. We both knew it. Boone was free to do whatever—and whoever—he wanted, and that thought left a sharp ache in my chest.

"Good?" he asked, his tone almost shy.

"Amazing," I muttered, glancing up in time to catch him smiling to himself. I wanted to know what was going through his head. Where his heart was after last night.

Curiosity won out. "How are you feeling after yesterday?" I asked, my fingers playing with a petal on one of the flowers.

Boone paused, setting the brown bag on the counter. "I wanted to talk to you about that."

My stomach flipped. That wasn't what I expected him to say. "Me too, but you go first!" I blurted, nervous energy making my voice higher than usual. I wasn't about to confess how much I'd been thinking about last night, how much I wanted to do it again, if he was about to let me down gently. Maybe the flowers were his way of softening the blow.

"Last night was amazing." Boone's voice was steady as he crossed his arms over his chest.

Shock must have been written all over my face because he smiled softly and added, "I haven't stopped thinking about it. Everything. Not just the sex."

"Me neither," I admitted, my heart thudding as I stroked a flower petal. His words filled me with a cautious sense of hope.

Boone pushed off the counter and stepped into my space, close enough that I could feel the heat radiating from him. Toe to toe, I tilted my head up to meet his blue-eyed gaze.

I was falling for this man—falling hard. The thought was both exhilarating and absurd. If you'd told me years ago that I'd be falling in love with Boone Cassidy, I would've laughed. Now? I wasn't laughing. I was hoping, praying, that this thing between us wasn't about to end.

With Boone standing here, telling me he hadn't stopped thinking about our night together, I finally found the courage to share my feelings too. "I don't know what to do about this," I admitted, my voice soft but steady. "When we made this deal, I promised myself I wouldn't let my guard down. I can't tell if it's lust or something else, but I don't want whatever this is to mess up our friendship."

Boone took the flowers from my hands and gently placed them on the counter, his eyes never leaving mine. "What if we changed our deal?" he suggested. "What if we went on another date... maybe two? We could blame it on needing inspiration."

He had a good point. Could I trick myself into believing this was just about my writing career? If I agreed, it would mean more time alone with Boone outside the porch swing. More moments to explore, more sex... for research. I wasn't a scientific girl, but for the sake of my libido, I'd definitely participate. There was nothing wrong with being friends who had sex, right? I was a grown woman, surely I could keep my emotions in check.

I put my hands on my hips, giving him a playful look. "On one condition."

Boone raised an eyebrow, his grin growing wider. "I don't think rules work well for us, Darling."

"I get to see you shirtless whenever I want," I replied with a wink.

Boone burst out laughing, his head tipping back in a way that made my stomach flutter. His neck, oh, that neck, I kissed, licked, and sucked just last night. The sudden urge to leave a mark on him flared up. "That's a rule I think I can follow," he said, wrapping his arm around my shoulder and guiding me toward the barn-style doors.

"Wait!" I squealed, pulling away from his embrace. "My flowers." I jogged over to the counter, grabbing the bouquet, Boone's muffin, and the rest of my things.

Boone sucked in through his teeth, chuckling. "Whoops, I was too focused on the *take your shirt off* part."

Of course, he was. Boone Cassidy didn't need much encouragement to show off those rock-hard abs. I smiled, rolling my eyes as I returned to my position under his arm, and together we walked back toward the cabin.

"Did you want to come over for dinner?" I asked, my heart skipping a beat. I desperately hoped he'd say yes. My fridge wasn't stocked with gourmet options, though. The best I could offer was pasta and garlic bread—if the loaf wasn't moldy. I didn't exactly market myself as the "wife" type, especially since cooking was not my strong suit.

Boone and I stopped in the middle of both our cabins. He spun to face me, placing both hands on my shoulders with a soft intensity. "Let me go get cleaned up. I doubt you want to spend any more time with me while I smell like this."

Oh, how wrong he was. That scent, the light dirt smudged on his face, the messy mullet... it only added to his appeal. I'd climb him like a tree, just the way he was. But I nodded, shooing him away. "Go. I'll be here when you're ready, Cowboy."

Spinning around, I raced up the stairs and into my cabin. I had to make the bed and clean up before Boone came over. My place was a disaster, and there was no way I was letting him see it like that.

In a frenzy, I quickly remade the bed—morning Aspen hadn't been awake enough to do it earlier. I tossed my dirty clothes into the hamper and lit a candle in the bedroom. Ironically, it was one of the candles Boone had bought me at the farmer's market.

I walked to the window and pulled back the curtain, hoping to let in a bit more light and make the room look less like a cave and more inviting. I hadn't realized why I always kept that curtain closed, but I was quickly reminded when I caught a glimpse into Boone's cabin.

To be fair, the curtain had already been closed when I moved in, and I'd never felt the urge to open it—until now. Not only could I see into his house, but his bedroom was directly in my line of sight. My gaze locked on him as he stood in his room, wearing nothing but a gray towel wrapped around his waist. My brain forgot how to blink as I stared at his damp, dripping skin. His hair was still wet, messy from being towel-dried.

There was something about a man fresh out of the shower that was as captivating as a man covered in dirt from hard work. And I wasn't about to let Boone know this little secret. He turned away from the window, dropping the towel, and I got a full view of his perfectly sculpted ass. My heart skipped a beat as he stepped into his boxers and turned toward me, adjusting himself casually.

Heat rushed to my face. I raised my hand to my throat, and

the motion instantly brought back memories of last night—when he'd pinned me down with his hands around my neck.

Before last night, I hadn't thought about sex in months. Now? I felt like I was gasping for air, drowning in desire. I needed to get away from that damn window.

I hurried into the kitchen, pulling a pot from the cabinet. Cooking would definitely get my mind off what I had just seen.

After filling the pot with water, I placed it on the stove, letting it come to a boil. As the water warmed up, I took the flowers Boone had brought me and laid them out on the table. One by one, I trimmed the stems to fit my vase, arranging the vibrant colors together in a beautiful display. I placed the vase on my little desk in the far corner of my living room, where I'd set up my writing space.

I'd bought that desk a while ago at a secondhand store, but until now, it had just collected junk I didn't know what to do with. Today, it was finally getting some use.

There was a knock on the door, and before I could answer, Boone walked right in. He'd ditched the jeans and was now wearing gym shorts and a white T-shirt. "I hope you don't mind my outfit," he said, shutting the door behind him. "I also forgot to give you something."

"Boone!" I laughed. "You've already given me enough. The candles, jewelry, flowers, and...let's not forget, that orgasm."

Boone shook his head and walked over to me in the kitchen. "This is different." He reached into his pocket and pulled out my black lace thong from last night.

"Oh my God!" I gasped, snatching it from his hand. "Please tell me you found it in the blankets!"

"Do you want me to lie?" Boone asked with a grin, making his way to the stove to check on the boiling water. He grabbed the box of pasta and poured it into the pot.

"Where was it?" I asked, still cringing.

"Rhodes and I were out riding, and he found it in the field."

I shrieked, "Rhodes found my thong in the field?!" I buried

my face in my hands. "I will never be able to look him in the eye again!"

"Well, technically, he spotted it from a distance, and I'm the one who picked it up. If that helps." Boone was trying to hold back his laughter, but his casual attitude only made me more mortified.

I groaned and stormed down the hall to the bedroom. I needed a change of clothes, so I quickly swapped out my dress for a pair of biker shorts and a tank top. As for the thong? It was going straight in the trash. I couldn't keep it as a reminder that Rhodes had seen it.

CHAPTER 27

It was another beautiful Sunday on the ranch. Texas in June was always hot, and I secretly thrived when the UV index climbed past seven. Sitting in a lounge chair behind my cabin, I decided it was time for a two-way FaceTime with Theo and Penny. I hadn't spoken to them properly since my night with Boone—aside from a few scattered texts. Theo had been riddled with morning sickness—but all day long—Penny was busy with her library work.

As I waited for them to answer, I closed my book and set it on the ground. Finally, I'd finished my latest read after chipping away at it for the past week. Between writing, work, and Boone, there hadn't been much time to relax. Reading had always been a daily ritual, but lately, my priorities had shifted in ways that surprised even me.

On the third ring, Theo's face popped up on the screen, quickly followed by Penny's. Theo lay face down on her bed, her phone propped against a pillow.

"Ugh, I feel like garbage!" Theo groaned dramatically.

"My poor Theo," Penny cooed. "How much longer does the sickness last?"

I was curious, too. Pregnancy wasn't exactly my area of expertise. With just one sibling—Parker, who was child-free—I didn't have much exposure to it.

"My doctor said it should ease up by the second trimester. I'm a little over eight weeks now, so...five more weeks of torture." Theo let out another groan. "Ugh, enough about me! You called us, so give me a distraction from this personal hell!"

Penny's eyes lit up. "Oh my God, is it a Boone update?" she squealed, clapping her hands like a kid waiting for candy.

Knowing these two, they'd have a million questions, so I cut straight to the chase. "Boone and I had sex."

Theo immediately sat up in bed, eyes wide. "First things first, was it good?"

"Good doesn't even cover it," I sighed, heat rushing to my cheeks at the memory. "I think I need to invent a new word."

Screams and expletives filled my ears as they lost their minds with excitement.

"I want every single detail!" Penny begged, practically bouncing.

"He took me stargazing," I started, my voice soft as the memory unfolded. "We were in the bed of his truck, surrounded by pillows and blankets. He even brought strawberries and wine. It was...perfect. One thing led to another, and we started kissing. And, well, things got pretty heated from there."

Recalling the butterflies I'd felt that night made me smile. Writing about romance was one thing, but living it? That was something else entirely.

Theo leaned in, eyes sparkling. "Sweet and sensual, or hot and hard?"

"Hot and hard," I admitted, biting my lip. "He pinned me by my throat and—" I hesitated for a beat, then grinned. "I sucked his thumb."

Penny gasped, covering her mouth in mock shock. "Shut up!" Theo wheezed, laughing so hard her head fell back against the bed.

"That's not even the best part," I added, grinning. "The next day, he showed up at my door with my thong. Apparently, he *and Rhodes* found it in the field where we parked the truck."

Theo howled with laughter, clutching her stomach. Penny

was giggling so hard tears streamed down her face. Even I joined in, though I'd been mortified when it happened. In hindsight, it made for a pretty great story.

"I'm so jealous," Penny sighed, resting her chin in her hand like she was lost in a daydream. "I'd let that man split me in two."

"Let who split you in two?"

The deep, familiar voice boomed behind me, making me jump. I spun around, clutching my chest, and there he was—Boone. Shirtless, sweat glistening, and towering over me enough to block out the sun. His khaki hat was tilted low, and his jeans hung just low enough on his hips to make my heart race.

He must've just come in from working the ranch, and the sight of him sent my pulse skyrocketing. My mouth went dry, and every coherent thought vanished. Boone smirked, clearly enjoying my reaction. This man might just be the death of me.

Sputtering, I tried to find words to explain the situation. "I—well, Penny—"

I made no sense.

"You!" Penny shouted from the phone.

Theo burst into giggles, clearly enjoying my torment. My head bounced between Boone and my phone, waiting for someone—anyone—to say something that would save me.

Boone crouched down, his face now in the frame next to mine. With an easy grin, he quipped, "Why thank you, Penny. But I think I've got my hands full with this one." He nodded toward me, his smirk deepening.

"Hot," Theo muttered, covering her mouth as if that could hide her amusement.

Desperate to change the subject, I asked, "What did you need, Boone?"

"I heard you talking and came by to check it out," Boone replied, his tone casual as if he hadn't just derailed my entire morning.

"I'm hanging up now," I announced to my friends, my voice sharp with exasperation. "You two are officially on my shit list."

I hit the end button before they could reply, then spun to face Boone, scowling. "And *you* are, too!"

Boone raised his hands in mock surrender. "Me? You were the one talking to your friends about us having sex. I just showed up at the wrong time."

Huffing, I grabbed my things, refusing to meet his gaze, but Boone grinned as he bent to help me gather my stuff.

"I know," I muttered, feeling my cheeks heat. "I *had* to tell someone."

My phone dinging interrupted us. Texts were firing in rapid succession. I couldn't resist peeking.

Penny

Aspen, I hope you're getting railed right now.

Theo

Boone without a shirt 🤤 Did anyone else see him dripping with sweat?

Penny

How could I not? I'm adding that to my spank bank.

Theo

Suddenly, I feel better. Who would've thought all I needed was a little dose of shirtless cowboy?

"I regret telling those two *anything*," I groaned, holding the phone out to show Boone the ridiculous thread.

Boone plucked the phone from my hand, typing out a reply before I could stop him.

This is Boone. I'd be railing her, but her phone is distracting.

My jaw dropped. "Boone!"

He just grinned, handing the phone back as if he hadn't just made my situation ten times worse.

Somewhere in the back of my mind, I knew I was falling in love with Boone Cassidy. The thought left me exhilarated—and terrified. Right now, it felt like we were avoiding the depth of it, floating on the surface while the current tugged at my feet. I knew he liked me, and he knew I liked him, but the more of myself I gave, the more I knew he'd take.

And I wasn't sure I'd survive handing over everything.

Boone

NOTHING BEATS A shower after a long day on the ranch. Summer work could be brutal, between the relentless heat and backbreaking labor. Most nights, my muscles ached, and all I wanted was a little downtime. Before Aspen, that usually meant a beer on the couch or a bonfire with friends. But now? Downtime was sitting on the front porch swing with her, talking about anything and everything until the sun dipped below the horizon.

After catching her talking to her friends earlier, I walked her back to her cabin. Hearing Aspen gush about me when she didn't know I was listening? Yeah, that inflated my ego in ways I'd never admit out loud.

She'd told me she had a lot of writing and plotting to get done tonight, which meant I was forced to find another way to occupy myself. After my shower, I decided to put my phone away for the night—mostly because I didn't trust myself not to bother her while she worked.

I crossed to my nightstand to grab my charger when movement

outside the window caught my eye. Looking up, I realized it wasn't outside, it was coming from Aspen's bedroom.

Normally, her curtain stayed closed. Tonight, though? It was wide open, and there she was, framed perfectly in the soft glow of her bedroom light.

She must've just gotten out of the shower—a fluffy green towel was wrapped around her curves. The gentleman in me whispered that I should look away, give her privacy. But the caveman in me wasn't budging.

I couldn't tear my eyes away as she moved toward her dresser, rummaging through a drawer until she found a pair of matching pajamas. Then she did it—dropped the towel.

The view of her bare ass nearly knocked the wind out of me. My fingers curled into fists at my sides, and all I could think was, *Turn around.*

What the hell was wrong with me? I was standing there, staring through her window like some kind of creep. But even as the gentleman inside me fought to take control, the dirty part was already carving plans into my brain.

Finally, I forced myself to step away, dragging a hand down my face. There was no way I'd be able to focus on anything else tonight. Since our night stargazing in my truck bed, getting her naked again had been living rent-free in my head. Hell, it wasn't just about the sex. It was *her.* I craved every piece of her—mind, body, and soul.

I paced up and down the hallway, debating. She'd said she needed to write, and I didn't want to interrupt. But then again, she'd also said she needed inspiration.

What if she knew I could see her? What if this was her way of teasing me?

"Fuck it," I muttered under my breath, grabbing my shoes.

Taking a chance had worked for me so far. Why stop now?

CHAPTER 28

Was I a bad person? Probably.

I knew exactly what I was doing when I stepped out of the shower tonight. My main goal? Drive Boone Cassidy a little crazy. I'd taken a calculated chance, leaving my bedroom curtain open just enough, hoping he'd notice.

After he dropped me off looking the way he did—shirtless, sweaty, and smug—I couldn't resist giving him a taste of his own medicine. Every move was deliberate: leaving the curtain open, standing precisely where I knew he'd have a perfect view, and bending over just enough to expose myself completely.

If my plan worked, Boone would be knocking on my door any second now, letting his desire get the better of him.

Right on cue, a heavy thud echoed from the front door. Smiling to myself, I strolled over, keeping my pace slow to build his anticipation. Time to play innocent.

I opened the door to find Boone pacing my porch like a caged animal.

"Boone? Is everything okay?" I asked, feigning confusion.

He didn't answer. Instead, he stepped inside, the door clicking shut behind him. His eyes burned into mine as he jabbed a finger toward the hallway. "Please tell me you did that on purpose."

I tried, really tried, to keep a straight face, but my grin slipped through. Smirking, I replied, "Whatever could you mean,

Cowboy?"

Boone planted his hands on his hips, shaking his head. "You dirty girl," he muttered, but there was no mistaking the heat in his voice.

The shift in his eyes was my only warning before I realized I was in trouble. I took off down the hallway, giggling like a schoolgirl. His heavy footsteps were right behind me, and before I could reach my bedroom, his strong arms wrapped around my waist.

With zero effort, Boone tossed me over his shoulder like I weighed nothing. "Boone!" I shrieked, laughing as he carried me into my bedroom.

He tossed me onto the bed, and I landed with an ungraceful bounce against the comforter. Boone loomed over me, arms braced on either side of my head, the mattress dipping beneath his weight. His face hovered so close, I could feel his breath against my skin.

"I should punish you for pulling a stunt like that, Darling," he murmured, his voice a low, dangerous rasp, sending shivers down my spine.

I bit my bottom lip, grinning up at him. My hand slipped to the waistband of his pajama pants, toying with the elastic. "I'd say I'm sorry," I teased, "but that would be a lie."

His scent—clean from his shower but still so uniquely him—wrapped around me, making my head spin. Part of me wished he'd shown up still covered in dirt and sweat, raw and rugged, but honestly? I wasn't about to complain.

Boone tsked, grabbing my wrist and moving my hands away from his pants. His smirk turned wolfish. "Not so fast," he said, voice dark and full of promise. "You don't get that yet. It's my turn."

I laid my hands flat on the comforter with my palms down. Boone dipped his head, slowly placing kisses down my jawline, my neck, and the tops of my breasts, exposed from my satin tank top. My nipples rubbed against the fabric, the sensation almost too much.

Boone moved off the bed, kneeling on the floor between my

thighs. He grabbed my hips and yanked me closer to the edge, placing kisses on my inner thigh. "I want to hear you scream my name," he said into my skin, his hot breath driving me mad. "I'm quite possessive." He dragged his facial hair against my skin, teasing me.

Boone reached for the band of my bottoms and pulled them off in one swift motion. Watching him, I swallowed hard as the saliva pooled in my mouth. My body anticipated what was coming next, and my core throbbed with need.

"Yes, sir," I breathed. Boone wasted no time pressing his mouth to my core. He licked from my entrance up to my clit with the tip of his tongue, swirling around the bud.

I moaned his name, my eyes rolling into the back of my head. I was going to black out. Boone moved his tongue up and down my center again, and at this point, I was dripping.

My hands went to the back of his head, gripping his hair. I pushed his mouth deeper into me, silently begging for more. As Boone devoured me, my clit rubbed against his mustache; shockwaves rippled through my core.

"I'm so close," I moaned, panting his name. I was going to come with Boone's face between my thighs.

Suddenly, the heat dissipated, and I was left to fall off my climax. I sat up on my elbows and stared at Boone, who was still on his knees, wearing a cocky grin. He stood up and wiped his mouth with the back of his hand.

"No way. I'm not letting you come that easily." Boone laughed, flipping me onto my stomach. He was in control tonight, and I was down for it. I inched more onto the bed, leaving space so he could climb on behind me.

My tank top bunched at my shoulders as I raised my hips into position. Boone climbed behind me, palming my ass.

"You want me from behind?" Boone growled. "That's my girl."

I shook my ass back and forth, begging him to fuck me. My cheek was pressed into the bed, but I caught a glimpse of him on his knees as he palmed his cock in his hand. I wasn't sure at what point he took his clothes off, *thank God*, because I needed him now. Boone bent over me, kissing my shoulder as he used his fingers to spread my sex. He plunged two fingers into me, and I moaned, gasping from the intensity. I was so wet that his fingers slid in and out of me easily.

Boone removed his fingers, and I groaned at the loss of him inside me.

"Open wide," he said, putting the same two fingers into my mouth. I sucked myself off him, admiring the taste. I'd never tasted myself before. It was erotic.

"I hate to do this, baby, but I don't have a condom." Boone's voice fell flat. I didn't either. I hadn't bought a box since I was a teenager. He couldn't stop now; I was on birth control and clean.

"Have you ever had sex without one?" I asked, pushing my ass back against his hard cock.

"No. Have you?"

"No, I'm also on birth control." I needed him badly, and there was no way I was letting him walk out, leaving me like this. Boone's cock was the only way to finish what we started.

"Are you sure?" Boone waited for my response, rubbing my ass with his calloused hands. The sensation sent me over the edge.

"Yes. Fuck me, Boone," I said, eager as ever. Boone didn't wait, he lined up his tip to my entrance and pushed in achingly slow.

"Oh, fuck, that's good," he groaned. The feeling of his bare skin inside me was indescribable. Every move was intensified. He started with slow thrusts, my walls stretching around him. I needed more. I liked it rough. My previous partners never took my requests seriously. Then again, I never really spoke up.

"Harder," I begged. My walls were coming down.

Boone reached for my hair and bunched it in his fist. He pulled up, my head tilted back, and he fucked me harder, his skin slipping against my ass. His deep thrusts felt so good that I moaned his name, screaming like no one else in the world existed. Our bodies rocked back and forth on the bed, the frame squeaking with each thrust. I swear I saw stars; he was hitting me so deeply. I'd never felt it like that before.

Boone pulled out as I came. His release fell in warm spurts on my lower back and seeped down my ass.

"Christ," he said, not moving from behind me. His fingers ran through the warmth and shoved inside me. He was leaving his mark. I let myself take in the moment. Boone Cassidy knew what he was doing. He was placing his claim, and I wasn't mad one bit.

"Stay here. I'll grab you a towel." Boone got off the bed, running naked to the bathroom to grab the same green towel I had used after my shower earlier; how ironic. This man was perfect. His toned back, messy hair, and still-hard length made me want to go again.

He cleaned me up, his touch gentle as he wiped away the aftermath of our time together. I reached down, fumbling for my shorts, and slipped them back on. I combed my fingers through my hair, snagging on knot after knot. I must've looked exactly how I felt—like someone who'd just had her mind completely blown.

Boone reappeared from the bathroom, freshly dressed in his pajamas, his hair still tousled and wild. He looked as wrecked as I felt, but in the most irresistible way. His easy smile tugged at my heart as he walked back to the bed, sitting on the edge.

He reached over, tucking a stray piece of hair behind my ear, and my breath caught. Damn, he was *pretty.* Those piercing blue eyes and sun-kissed skin were enough to make me melt, but it was the softness in his expression that truly undid me.

"Did you get a chance to eat yet?" he asked, his voice low and warm, his hand lingering on my cheek. I leaned into his touch, shaking my head.

"What can I make you?" he offered. His sincerity, the gentleness in his tone—it was a stark contrast to the Boone who'd just left me breathless minutes ago.

I smiled, feeling bold. "How about frozen pizza? We can eat in bed and watch a movie?"

His lips curved into a grin as he held out his hand to me. "Sounds perfect. But you're keeping that shirt off, Darling," he teased, his gaze flickering down appreciatively. "I need to enjoy those perfect tits a little while longer."

Laughing, I took his hand, and he pulled me to my feet. Together, we made our way to the kitchen. As we prepped the pizza and waited for the oven to preheat, Boone wrapped me in his arms from behind, pressing his chest against my back. His chin rested lightly on the top of my head, and for a moment, we just stood there in a comfortable, intimate silence.

When the timer broke the quiet, we assembled our pizza and carried it back to my bed. Boone picked the movie—*Talladega Nights,* of course—and we settled in.

After finishing our food, I curled up against him, resting my head on his chest. His heartbeat was steady beneath my ear, soothing and grounding. By the second movie, his breathing deepened, and his body twitched slightly as he drifted off to sleep.

I let myself relax, my eyes growing heavy. Before long, I followed him into peaceful slumber, wrapped securely in Boone Cassidy's arms.

CHAPTER 29

Stretching out, I reached across the bed, searching for warmth that was no longer there. My fingers brushed against something unfamiliar on the pillow. Rubbing my eyes, I sat up and found a piece of paper resting where Boone's head had been all night.

> *Coffee's in the pot. Sorry I couldn't be here when you woke up, work calls. I'll see you later.*
>
> *-Boone*

Pressing the note to my chest, a smile spread across my face, soft and involuntary. Boone Cassidy had effortlessly claimed a corner of my heart, and lately, it felt like my heart was entirely his. No one else could make it race the way he did.

Last night played on repeat in my mind. When Boone showed up, his usual self-control abandoned, I knew I had him exactly where I wanted him. Leaving the curtain open was a calculated move, a small gamble to lure him to me. I'd been craving him since the night in his truck bed, and honestly, I hadn't expected it to work so easily. But I was grateful it had.

Boone's "punishment" had made me want to misbehave more often. I'd gladly break every rule just to see how he'd handle me next. Falling for him was exhilarating and dangerous, like diving headfirst into the unknown. It felt like skydiving without a parachute, and I loved every second of it.

I swung my legs over the side of the bed, wincing slightly. My body was deliciously sore, a lingering reminder of Boone's intensity. My legs felt weak, and I smiled to myself, replaying the moment he took me from behind. I'd never experienced anything quite like it. If I had a favorite position before, it had officially been replaced.

Reality nudged its way back in as I glanced at the time. Work was waiting, and I needed to kick into high gear if I wanted to make it on time. Grabbing my phone for the first time since Boone had stormed in last night, I was met with a flood of missed calls and texts.

Scrolling through the notifications, I spotted one from Boone's mom. I was solely focused on Boone, so future Aspen would read the others later.

Boone

Call me before you leave.

Boone

Did you get my note?

I'll call you in a bit! I guess I slept too well last night 😴 Running late! And yes, I'm drinking the coffee now—just how I like it.

Setting the phone down, I hurried to the bathroom to pull myself together. My go-to style for mornings like this was a quick half-up, half-down bun. It required no heat and only a few seconds to perfect. Boone might have derailed my schedule, but I wouldn't have had it any other way.

I dabbed on some concealer and brushed through my

eyebrows. If there was one thing I could be grateful for, it was my naturally full brows—they always looked good with minimal effort. After finishing my quick routine, I slipped into my bright red dress, which hit just above my knees, and paired it with my trusty cowgirl boots. Living so close to work was a blessing; I could leave my front door and be there in under three minutes.

When I arrived at the farm stand, I noticed the door was propped open. My steps slowed, and I peeked cautiously around the corner. A small part of me worried—what if I was about to stumble into a robbery or, worse, a murder scene?

Thankfully, it was neither. Instead, I found Jill Cassidy bustling around inside, organizing the tables with product displays. Relief washed over me as I stepped through the doorway.

"Hi, Mrs. Cassidy!" I sang, the cheery tone in my voice masking my earlier paranoia.

She straightened up and greeted me with a warm smile. "Good morning! I know I'm early. Thought I'd come down to help. Did you get my text?"

Oh. That must have been one of the messages I'd ignored this morning. Whoops. Playing it cool, I avoided answering and set my things down behind the counter.

"No problem at all!" I said instead. "How long are you planning to stay today? I really appreciate the help."

"With school out for the summer, I thought I could spend weekends here or even take a weekday shift if you wanted a break." Jill leaned on the counter, watching as I rolled up my sleeves.

The idea piqued my interest. Having an extra hand would free up some time to work on my book.

"That's exciting!" I replied, grabbing a bowl and preparing the muffin mix for the day. "I could definitely use the help."

Jill hesitated, her expression shifting slightly. "I do have a small favor to ask." She winced, as if bracing for a no. "You've already done so much for us, so if it's too much, I understand!"

I laughed softly, pouring the wet ingredients into the mix. "Jill, after everything you and Dan have done for me, I'd be on the operating table if you needed a kidney. Just tell me what you need."

Relief and amusement flickered across her face. "Well," she started, "the annual block party is coming up in a couple of weeks. Cassidy Ranch is partnering with the local library to raise money for their fall programs. I could really use your help to make it a success. I have a few ideas, but I need someone younger to help bring them to life."

Sliding the muffin tray into the oven, I turned and raised a brow at her. "Am I allowed to know what I'm getting into?"

"All I'll say is, I think it's going to be a hit." She grinned, her excitement contagious.

Her enthusiasm made it impossible to say no, even though I wasn't entirely sure what I'd just agreed to. "After everything you've done for me, you've got my full support. Even if it involves swimming with sharks."

Jill laughed and pulled me into a hug. Her sweet, candy-like perfume lingered as I squeezed her back. Her hugs could rival anyone's.

"You have no idea how much you've helped Dan, Boone, and me," she said as she grabbed the mixing bowl and moved toward the sink. I followed, ready to help clean up. "This is the happiest I've seen Boone in a long time, whether he admits it or not."

Her words made me pause, warmth spreading through me. I busied myself drying the dishes she washed, a soft smile tugging at my lips. Boone wasn't the only one who'd found happiness here—I'd rediscovered it, too.

"It's good to see the farm stand doing well. I imagine it makes him proud to see Ellie's vision thriving."

Jill nodded, her smile filled with gratitude. "It truly does."

As we worked side by side, I couldn't help but think how much this place—and the people here—had come to mean to me. Life had a funny way of taking you where you never expected to go, and I was starting to think this was exactly where I was meant to be.

"But sweetie. Boone's happiness isn't from the farm stand." Jill chuckled, handing me a clean bowl. I took it, my brow furrowing as I dried it with the towel, feeling a little uncertain.

"I don't know how else I'd have helped his happiness." A nervous laugh escaped. "He cares so much about Ellie, and I know it means the world to him to see her dream thriving." My voice wavered as my nervous habits kicked in—tucking my hair behind my ears, avoiding eye contact, and twisting the towel in my hands like a lifeline.

Jill sighed knowingly. "He pulled the same act with me," she said, shaking her head. "But I know my boy better than he realizes. Boone hasn't exactly been a saint when it comes to relationships. He's earned a reputation around town, one that's not becoming of a Cassidy. But you're the first girl he's ever brought through the front door."

Her words sent my mind spinning. I froze, bowl in hand, unsure what to say. "I—I care about Boone," I stammered, desperately trying to form a diplomatic answer. "He's a great guy and has been such a big help while I've been settling in at the ranch." I forced a confident smile, though my heart was racing.

Jill's knowing gaze softened. "I get it, you don't want to share too much with his mom. But I wouldn't be doing my son justice if I didn't point out the obvious." She turned to face me fully, demanding my attention. "Dan and I didn't give Boone much direction growing up. We let him figure things out for himself, learn right from wrong the hard way. But after what happened with Ellie, I see how much we missed. It changed everything for us.

"I don't want him to take what happened to his sister and use it as an excuse to hide from love or relationships forever. If Boone never wanted to settle down, fine, that's his choice, and I'd support him. But I know my son, and I know this: You're good for him. Don't let him control the narrative and risk losing something important because he's afraid."

Her words resonated deeply, quieting some of the doubts I'd been carrying. Jill had peeled back a layer of my heart I wasn't ready to admit to myself, let alone Boone.

I placed the towel down and cleared my throat. "I'm going to step outside for a minute."

Jill's sly smile stopped me in my tracks. "Oh, and just so you know—I saw him leave your place this morning. So there's no use pretending otherwise."

I squeezed my eyes shut and let out a laugh, a mix of exasperation and amusement. Of course she saw. The conversation wasn't out of the blue—she'd caught us red-handed.

Boone had asked me to call him anyway. Pulling my phone from my apron pocket, I stepped onto the porch, the screen door creaking as it closed behind me. I dialed his number and took a deep breath as the line rang.

"Hey," Boone answered, his voice warm but rushed. I could hear the noise of the ranch in the background.

"Hey," I replied, suddenly feeling a bit shy. "Sorry, I forgot you were working."

"No, no. It's fine. Give me a sec." The sounds faded, and after a beat of silence, he came back. "How's your morning?"

I laughed, the tension breaking. "Well, your mom was waiting for me at the stand this morning."

Boone groaned. "Yeah, that's why I wanted you to call. She saw me leave your place."

"Oh, I know," I teased.

"Great. What'd she say?"

I hesitated. "We need to talk." My voice sounded more ominous than I intended, and I winced.

"Uh, okay," Boone said cautiously. "When I'm done here, I'll come by your porch. Same spot, keep it warm for me."

I smiled, tipping my head back to look at the sky. Please let this conversation go well, I thought. Please let him feel the same.

The rest of my shift dragged, the clock taunting me with how slowly the hours passed. Jill stayed the entire day, and luckily, the earlier conversation didn't make things awkward. If anything, she made the chaos of the busy day bearable.

We found a rhythm that worked, and customers seemed to enjoy our easy banter. Jill's presence was a blessing, and I found myself genuinely enjoying her company. She wasn't just Boone's mom—she was a kind, warm soul who saw me in ways I hadn't expected.

By the time closing rolled around, my nerves were in overdrive. Boone was coming, and I was about to lay my heart bare. The thought terrified me, but I couldn't avoid it any longer.

This wasn't just about Boone. It was about me, too. I had to be honest with myself and stop hiding from what I felt. And if Boone didn't feel the same? Well, I'd cross that bridge when I got to it.

For now, I just had to hope.

CHAPTER 30

After Aspen's call this morning, I couldn't focus on anything else. My mind was tangled in knots, replaying her words and wondering what she needed to tell me. What did Mom say to her?

When I saw Mom earlier, there'd been no avoiding the truth. She'd caught me coming from Aspen's cabin at dawn. We'd locked eyes, and though neither of us spoke, I swear I saw the corner of her mouth lift in a knowing smile.

Thinking back to our conversation, I'd downplayed my feelings for Aspen. I hadn't known how to navigate them. Relationships had never felt like a priority before, at least, not serious ones. But with Aspen, there was something undeniably different. She sparked something in me I hadn't felt before, and it scared the hell out of me. What if I ruined this? What if I lost her?

By the time I reached her cabin, the stand had already closed. I'd stayed away, knowing Mom would be there. She already suspected the truth, and showing up would've been like admitting she was right. Guilt nipped at me, but I couldn't face her yet.

Aspen sat on the porch swing, her silhouette bathed in the golden glow. There was no book in her lap this time—just a glass of red wine cradled in her hands. She didn't look at me when I approached, her eyes fixed on some distant point.

"Hi, Darling." I kissed the top of her head and plopped down beside her. Removing my hat, I placed it on my bent knee, trying to seem calm even as my thoughts raced.

Aspen cleared her throat, her voice soft but firm. "I think it's time to be real, with myself and with you."

My heart pounded, a thousand scenarios flashing through my mind. "Okay," I said, hesitant, bracing myself for whatever came next.

"When I needed someone the most, you swooped in like some kind of knight in shining armor. Without you, I'd probably be cleaning toilets at the elementary school and crashing with my parents." She took a shaky breath, her words heavy with meaning. "I like you, Boone. I look forward to seeing you, to bringing you muffins, to sitting here with you every night." Her voice wavered, and she paused, as though weighing her next words.

I stayed silent, giving her the space to continue.

"I want to date you, for real," she said finally, her voice steady but vulnerable. "I want to go out in public with you, to not care what the town thinks. I want to kiss you at The Tequila Cowboy and dance to a cheesy cover band. I want to put that hat on my head and make it clear to everyone who you belong to." She took a longer sip of wine, still avoiding my gaze, as if bracing herself for my reaction.

Her honesty disarmed me. I took a deep breath, feeling a pinch of relief as I spoke. "I think I've wanted you for a while, probably since that night at the swimming hole. These feelings are new for me too, and I've been scared to figure out what they mean."

"Me too," she admitted, her laugh breaking the tension. "When I moved in, I told myself I wouldn't let Boone Cassidy break my heart. I thought I was doing all the right things to keep my distance, but...well, I failed."

Her laugh was infectious, and I joined in.

Reaching out, I rested my hand on her thigh. "Let me prove to you that your heart will be safe with me. I want you to claim me, to hold my hand in public, to dance with me to the worst cover bands you can find." I pulled her close, wrapping my arm around her shoulder and cupping her jaw to tilt her face toward mine. Her blue eyes held me captive as I studied the delicate slope of her nose and the freckles dotting her cheeks.

"Let's try," I said softly. "Let's take things slow and see where it goes."

Aspen nodded, her forehead resting against mine as our breaths mingled. Slowly, I leaned in and kissed her, savoring the sweetness of her lips. My hat fell from my knee as I wrapped her in my arms, but I didn't care. All that mattered was her—the way she tasted faintly of wine, the way our lips moved together in perfect rhythm.

"I want to take you on a *real* date," I murmured between kisses.

She laughed against my lips, her voice playful. "Where could we go that's better than this?"

"It's not about being better," I replied, pulling back just enough to bury my face in the curve of her neck. "I want to show you off."

Her laughter turned into something softer, more intimate. She gently tugged my face back toward hers, her lips teasing mine. "Can we go inside first?" she asked, biting her bottom lip in a way that sent a rush of heat through me. "It'll be quick."

I didn't need convincing. Standing, I scooped her up, her legs wrapping around my waist as I carried her into the cabin. I was going to show her just how much she meant to me, just how lucky I felt to have a woman like Aspen take a chance on a man like me.

Aspen

BOONE AND I climbed into my Jeep and headed to Martin's drive-in movie theater. It was my idea, who doesn't love watching a good movie from the comfort of their car? As teenagers, Penny, Theo, and I practically lived here, showing up every week to watch whatever random movie was playing on the big projector.

The lot was already packed, cars squeezed into every available space. The snack stand was bustling, handing out tubs of popcorn, fountain sodas, and candy by the handful. Tonight, *The Heat* with Sandra Bullock and Melissa McCarthy was playing—one of my all-time favorite comedies. After the day I'd had, filled with emotional exhaustion and the aftermath of my conversation with Jill, I needed a distraction. A funny movie and some quiet alone time with Boone were just what the doctor ordered.

I glanced over at him as we parked. My stomach fluttered in that familiar, thrilling way it always did when he was near. Lately, we'd been stepping cautiously out of the friend zone, feeling our way into something more. And I liked it—liked him. Slow and steady was the way to go. We didn't need to dive headfirst, but it felt good to let the walls down and see where this thing could lead.

"I'm going to grab us some snacks. Any requests?" I asked, leaning over the console to steal a kiss.

"Surprise me," Boone murmured, his lips brushing mine in a way that sent a delicious shiver down my spine.

I climbed out of the Jeep and jogged toward the snack stand, the smell of popcorn and freshly cut grass filling the air. Standing in line, I bounced on the balls of my feet, taking in the sights. It had been years since I'd been here, but nothing had changed. The white paint on the snack shack was still peeling, the rusty trash cans looked like they'd weathered decades of storms, and the grass was so worn down there wasn't a green patch in sight.

I was pulled out of my thoughts by a voice calling my name.

"Aspen? Is that you?"

I turned to see Marjorie Winchester making her way toward me, her bright red hair practically glowing under the parking lot lights. My stomach sank.

"Oh! Hi, Mrs. Winchester!" I replied, pasting on a polite smile. Marjorie was infamous in our town—a one-woman rumor mill with a knack for turning the smallest tidbit into front-page gossip. If you didn't want your business spread across half the county, you didn't talk to Marjorie.

She enveloped me in a hug, then stepped back with a beaming smile. "Congratulations on the farm stand! Those muffin jars are genius!"

"Thank you!" I made my best attempt at sounding enthusiastic, yet my body gave me away as I shifted on my feet.

But Marjorie wasn't one to be easily dismissed. She glanced around theatrically, her gaze sharp as a hawk. "Who are you here with, sweetie? Surely, you're not alone?"

I froze. Lying would only feed the gossip machine, but the truth wasn't exactly stress-free either. My parents finding out about Boone through Marjorie was hardly ideal.

"Uh, no, I'm not alone." I cleared my throat.

Marjorie's grin widened. "A date then? Who's the lucky man?"

My heart pounded, but for once, the dread didn't stick. I took a deep breath and straightened my shoulders. This was my life. My choices. "I'm here with Boone Cassidy."

Her eyes widened in dramatic surprise. "Oh, my!"

Before she could press for more details, it was my turn at the counter. I glanced back at her as I stepped forward. "Have a good night, Mrs. Winchester," I said firmly, ending the conversation.

When I returned to the Jeep, my arms were overflowing with snacks. Boone took the drink from my hand and laughed as I climbed in.

"I bought one of everything," I joked, settling into my seat.

"I can see that." His grin widened as he grabbed candy boxes from my lap. "We're stocked for the next three movie nights."

"Guess who I ran into at the snack stand?" I said, popping a sour gummy worm into my mouth. Boone raised an eyebrow, waiting. "Mrs. Winchester."

He groaned. "Oh no. Did you tell her we're here together?"

"Yup," I said with a confidence that surprised even me. "By tomorrow morning, your bachelor status will be the talk of the town."

Boone studied me, his brow furrowing slightly. "What's going on up there?" he asked, tapping his finger lightly against my temple.

I sighed, setting the candy aside. "I didn't want to lie. If we're going to give this a real shot, I have to start being honest about us and with myself. I've spent my whole life walking on eggshells around my parents, worrying about what they'll think. It's exhausting, Boone. I need to own my choices, even if it means facing their disappointment."

Boone reached for my hand, his thumb brushing gently over my knuckles. "Why don't you go see them tomorrow and talk it out? I'll come with you if you want."

"No. This is something I have to do on my own. It's time I stop running from the hard conversations. I'm scared, but...I'm ready."

He brought my hand to his lips, pressing a tender kiss to the back of it. "You've got this, Darling. And no matter what happens, I'm here."

I smiled, my heart feeling a little lighter. Whatever tomorrow brought, I knew I wasn't alone anymore—and that made all the difference.

CHAPTER 31

Logan texted the group earlier, calling for a meetup. It'd been ages since we all hung out—last time was the bonfire, and even then, Logan was out of town. But tonight felt different. Big. I had news to share, and I wasn't going to chicken out.

I'm officially a taken man.

I'd thought a lot about what the guys might say. For a while, I'd kept my feelings for Aspen to myself—not because I wanted to, but because I wasn't sure how they'd react. I'm not the kind of guy who wears his heart on his sleeve, but I believe in being straight with people. Tonight, I was putting it all out there.

I got to The Tequila Cowboy first. We'd picked the place because Mac was working, and if we were all getting together, it wouldn't have been right to leave him out. The bar was quiet for a weeknight. The regulars were scattered around: the guys escaping their wives, the ones without wives who were just plain miserable, and a couple or two sharing beers and burgers.

Mac was behind the counter, wiping it down. He glanced up, cigarette dangling from his lips. "What can I get ya?"

"Just a beer, whatever's on draft." I drummed my fingers on the worn wood, glancing toward the door to see if Rhodes or Logan had shown up yet.

Mac nodded, keeping the cigarette between his lips but angling the smoke away from the glass. The Tequila Cowboy allowed smoking inside. If they hadn't, the town would've rioted years ago.

"Thanks, man," I said when he slid the beer my way. I took a sip of the cold foam, not quite as satisfying as a beer after a hot day on the ranch, but close.

The front door creaked open and slammed shut as my two friends walked in. They still had on their ranch clothes—couldn't even bother to change. Rhodes and Logan slid onto the stools on either side of me.

"What's up?" I asked, smirking at their dusty boots.

"Not much. That damn cattle kicked my ass today." Rhodes laughed as he took off his ball cap to scratch his head.

Logan grinned. "Dude, they made Rhodes look like a rookie. I've never seen a grown man run like that."

He seemed lighter tonight, more like the Logan I grew up with—the one who always found something to smile about, even when life gave him a raw deal. He's the youngest of us, and we've never let him forget it. With his messy blond hair, soft cheeks, and bright blue eyes, he's got a boyish look that tattoos and a little muscle haven't managed to toughen up. Sure, he's shorter than most of us, but the guy can toss hay like nobody's business.

"Take it easy! I didn't see your sorry ass helping me when that heifer charged. A few more pounds on her, and she'll be ready for sure," Rhodes said, shaking his head.

Mac and I laughed. Mac's the odd one out in our crew, the guy who skipped ranching to take over the family bar. Well, technically his sister's running it now, and she's as tough as they come.

I took another sip of my beer, then decided it was time. "All right, I'm about to get sappy, so buckle up. I wanted to tell y'all about Aspen and me before you heard it from someone else." I looked pointedly at Rhodes and then Logan. "We decided to try things out, taking things slow. There's something between us, and we're both ready to figure out what it means."

None of us were the overly emotional with each other type—

everyone nodded in response.

Rhodes and Logan clapped me on the back as Mac set a couple of shot glasses on the bar. “This calls for a toast.”

“To Boone,” he said, raising his glass, “who’s no longer Faircloud’s most eligible bachelor.”

We clinked glasses, and I shook my head with a grin.

“It’s about damn time,” Rhodes muttered after his shot.

“I’m serious about her.” The words spilling out before I could stop them. “She makes me feel...good. Like I always want more. More time, more words, more—”

“Sex,” Logan interrupted with a smirk. “You should’ve just said that first. We all know where your mind’s at.”

“She’s more than that,” I shot back, my tone firm.

For the first time, it wasn’t about the physical stuff. It was about the way she made me rearrange my whole day just to get a few extra minutes with her, the way my chest ached when she wasn’t around.

“Damn, Boone.” Mac leaned on the bar, both hands flat against the worn wood. “I don’t think I’ve ever seen you like this.”

“Like I said, Aspen’s different,” I admitted. “She makes me want to settle down—something I never thought I’d say out loud. I always figured my life would just be the ranch. But she’s got me thinking about a future that’s more than that.” I sighed, taking another sip of my beer.

For a moment, the four of us sat in silence. None of us really knew how to handle conversations like this—big, emotional talks. As men, we didn’t exactly grow up being told it was okay to share what we were feeling, so it always felt a little awkward when someone did. But I wasn’t about to let that stop me. The way Aspen made me feel deserved to be talked about. There was no shame in being honest with your friends.

“I’m really happy for you.” Rhodes finally broke the silence. The others nodded in agreement. “I know I’ve been closed off since Jess. It’s just...not easy to figure out what I went through, let alone explain it to you fools.” He chuckled, the sound low and self-deprecating. "But there is someone I've got my eye on."

My eyebrows shot up, Mac cleared his throat like he'd just choked on air, and I'm pretty sure Logan's jaw hit the floor.

"Well, well, well," I said, leaning back in my chair. "Do we know this lucky lady?"

Rhodes hesitated, his gaze dropping to the beer in front of him. "Yeah, you know her. But I haven't worked up the nerve to say anything yet."

I didn't push. The guy was clearly still working through his feelings, and the last thing he needed was us hounding him. Still, my mind started racing through every woman we knew, trying to figure out who could've caught Rhodes' attention.

"Look at all of you growing up," Mac teased, placing a hand dramatically over his heart. "I'm so proud."

"Watch it, Mac," I shot back. "Don't think we haven't noticed the way you've been eyeing Penny Hudson. The library? Seriously? We all know you can't read."

"Penny?" Logan asked, his voice dripping with disbelief.

Mac shrugged, grinning unapologetically. "What can I say? She's stunning. I love a sassy woman."

Rhodes chuckled, shaking his head, but then turned his attention to Logan. "What about you, man? Got anyone special? Maybe someone you had to leave town to see this weekend?"

Logan's face turned bright red, and he suddenly found his drink very interesting. "No," he stammered. "Nope. No one. Not me." He took a long sip, refusing to meet any of our eyes.

The rest of us exchanged glances but decided to let him off the hook—at least for now.

We stayed there for a while longer, catching up and trading stories. It felt good, finally telling them about Aspen. Last time, I kept my feelings bottled up, and it didn't do me any favors. But now? Now I felt different, like I'd become someone new—and I was starting to like him.

CHAPTER 32

Aspen

Turning the knob to my parents' house dissolved the confidence I'd worked so hard to build. I'd spent hours talking to Boone—well, mostly *at* Boone—practicing what I'd say. But crossing the threshold of my childhood home erased all of it. The moment I stepped inside, my hands started wringing, and my foot tapped nervously against the floor while I waited out back for my parents to join me.

When I arrived, they were ecstatic to see me. Hugs were exchanged, their smiles warm and familiar, and I knew immediately that Marjorie hadn't beaten me to the news. For once, I was ahead of the rumor mill.

My parents stepped out onto the patio together, my mom predictably carrying a plate of cookies. She placed them on the table, and they sat side by side, perfectly in sync like always.

"How's our girl doing?" Dad asked, his voice full of affection. I could only hope it would stay that way once I said what I needed to say.

His last words about Boone rang in my ears: *I don't think that Cassidy boy is good enough for you.*

"I'm good!" My voice came out brighter than I intended, almost too eager. "I've been seeing more of Theo and Penny. Theo's staying for a while, she's pregnant." The words tumbled out, unplanned, like some subconscious effort to ease the tension

I felt building.

Mom gasped, clapping a hand over her mouth. "No way! Sissy must be over the moon to be a grandmother!" Her enthusiasm was a relief. At least that part of the conversation was going well. "Is the father involved?" she whispered, leaning closer.

"No, she's doing it on her own," I said, pride swelling in my chest. Talking about Theo always reminded me of her strength. That woman could take on the world and come out on top.

"She must be scared," Mom replied, shaking her head slightly. "If she needs anything, please tell her to reach out."

"I will," I promised. "I want to throw her a gender reveal party when she's ready."

Mom's face lit up, her giving nature shining through as always. But I knew that same nature often came with a lack of understanding for perspectives that didn't align with hers.

"I actually had something I wanted to tell you both." My voice wavered as I picked apart a cookie, pulling out the chocolate chips one by one to avoid eye contact. The nerves I'd hoped to mask were showing.

I forced myself to sit up straight and look at them. It was time. "I'm seeing someone. We're taking it slow, but I wanted you to hear it from me."

Dad tilted his head slightly. "Who's the lucky guy?"

"Boone Cassidy," I said, and before either of them could react, I pressed on. "And before you say anything, let me finish. Boone and I have been friends since I moved to the ranch. He and his family have been nothing but kind and supportive. I like him, a lot. He makes me happy and pushes me to be a better person. I know you might not approve, but this is my decision."

Dad's expression darkened instantly. "Better person?" he scoffed. "That boy is a mess. His reputation doesn't suit my daughter, and I won't stand for it."

I clenched my fists, heat rising in my chest. "That *boy* has treated me with more respect and kindness than any city guy ever could. He's hardworking, thoughtful, and encourages me to chase my goals, not yours. This isn't up for discussion. I'm seeing Boone, and that's final."

"You're insane," Dad shot back, his voice calm but cutting. "My daughter won't stay here and ruin her life with a Cassidy."

"You don't even know him anymore!" I yelled, my hands flying up in frustration. "No one in this town does. You're stuck judging him for who he was as a teenager. He's grown, Dad, just like I have."

Mom cut in, her tone softer but no less disapproving. "Honey, are you sure he's what you need? What about the future you planned—school, the city? You made it sound like you were getting back on track after the coffee shop closed."

I laughed bitterly, shaking my head. "That was never *my* dream. That was yours. I want to stay here and write. I want a quiet life in a place I love, not some big city where I'll get lost. Boone supports that. He supports me."

"You want to be a writer?" Mom's voice was almost a whisper, as if the idea itself was too fragile to say out loud.

"Yes. And I want to stay in Faircloud, with Boone. Please try to understand."

Dad stood abruptly, his chair scraping against the patio. "I won't accept that. I want better for you than this damn town and these damn people." He walked inside without another word, and Mom followed after him, casting me one last sympathetic glance before disappearing into the house.

I sat there, the weight of their rejection pressing down on my shoulders. I'd stood up to them, spoken my truth, and still felt defeated. Tears stung my eyes as I left through the back gate, the flood of sadness and frustration breaking loose the moment I climbed into my car.

I'd always thought that standing up for myself would feel freeing. But right now, all I felt was heartbreak.

I was furious. Furious at my parents for refusing to listen, and even angrier at myself for letting it get to this point. If I'd just been honest about what I wanted from the start, this blowup could have been avoided. Their disappointment wouldn't feel like such a crushing weight.

But now, the damage was done, and I needed an anchor—someone who understood the madness that was our family.

The tires of my car squealed as I sped down the road, my mind too chaotic for even music to drown out the noise. Every word from our argument replayed on a loop, each memory sparking fresh waves of frustration.

"The audacity!" I yelled, gripping the steering wheel tighter. Weren't parents supposed to want their kids to be happy? Instead, mine clung to the broken shards of their unmet dreams, cutting me with every sharp edge.

I pulled up to the hardware store, slamming the car into park. Parker. He'd get it. If anyone understood the insanity of our family dynamic, it was him.

Storming inside, I let the door slam behind me. "Park!" My voice echoed through the small space as I stomped toward the counter.

Parker stood there, startled but composed, his wide blue eyes locking on mine. His blond hair was tied back in a low bun, and his broad shoulders strained against the fabric of his worn T-shirt. He looked annoyingly unbothered, as always.

"Our parents have lost their minds," I groaned, flopping onto the counter dramatically.

"You're just realizing this now?" he muttered, tinkering with a tool in his hands.

"No, but I've officially hit my breaking point."

He didn't even look up, just kept working. "Tell me what happened."

I let it all out in a chaotic stream, recounting every detail of my parents' reaction to Boone, complete with over-the-top impressions of all of us. Parker listened silently, his expression unreadable, though I caught the faintest twitch of his mouth when I got to the part about Marjorie.

"And then I left," I finished, throwing my hands in the air.

"Didn't even go back inside. I mean, you'd think I told them I joined the military or ran over the neighbor's dog!"

"To them, you might as well have," Parker said, finally looking up from his work. He sighed, resting his hands on the counter. "Look, I had fifteen years with them before you were born. I saw what staying in Faircloud did to them. Neither of them planned to stay here forever, but plans change when you have a baby at seventeen."

His words hit like a slap. I hadn't thought about it that way. I never knew the version of my parents he did—the young dreamers who had their lives derailed before they even began. It gave me perspective, sure, but it didn't make their behavior any easier to swallow.

"Maybe," I huffed, leaning against the counter. "But that doesn't make their reaction okay. And honestly? I blame myself. I should've shut this down years ago."

"You didn't," Parker said bluntly. "So here we are."

"Gee, thanks for the support," I muttered, rolling my eyes. Dropping my head onto the counter in defeat, I let myself breathe for the first time since storming out of my parents' house.

After a moment, I lifted my head and met Parker's gaze. "Please help me," I whispered. The words felt heavy, like admitting I couldn't do this alone was the hardest thing I'd ever done.

"You really like Boone?" he asked, his tone gentler now.

A laugh bubbled up, surprising even me. "Yeah, I do. I think I have for a long time, but I'm just now admitting it to myself. He makes me happy, Park. Like, *really* happy. He brings out a side of me I didn't even know existed." My chest tightened as I thought of Boone—the way his smile softened when he looked at me, the warmth of his voice when he teased me, the steady reassurance he always seemed to offer.

Parker studied me for a moment before nodding. "If you're happy, I'm happy for you. Don't let Mom and Dad take that away from you. You're old enough to make your own choices. And if you crash and burn? So be it."

A loud pop from whatever he'd been working on punctuated his words, and he grinned triumphantly. "Yes!"

I couldn't help but laugh, the tension in my chest easing just a bit. Parker was right. My parents would come around—or at least calm down enough for us to have a real conversation. I wasn't perfect in that argument, but I stood up for myself, and that was progress.

"Thanks, Park." I walked around the counter to hug him. He wrapped his arms around me, his hand rubbing soothing circles on my back.

"Just know," he said as I pulled away, "if that Cassidy boy breaks your heart, I'm coming for him."

Laughing, I shook my head. I didn't doubt it for a second. But I wasn't going to let my parents—or anyone—prove me wrong about Boone. Not today.

CHAPTER 33

Boone

Before Aspen, the ranch had been my whole life. I buried myself in work, spending every waking moment moving cattle, exercising horses, or jumping on whatever task needed doing. It was my way of staying grounded, of proving to myself—and everyone else—that I was capable of taking on the family legacy.

When I graduated, I knew it was time to grow up. Time to focus not just on the ranch, but on shaping the life I wanted. My future started the second I threw my cap in the air at Faircloud High, and I wasn't about to let anything—or anyone—distract me from that.

But then, *she* happened.

Aspen Westgrove.

Suddenly, my priorities shifted. The ranch was still my heart and soul, but now it wasn't the only thing I wanted to build my life around. I found myself thinking about her constantly, in a way I'd never thought about anyone before. She invaded every corner of my mind, sneaking in when I least expected it.

Even when I was working, I'd catch myself drifting into daydreams. Daydreams of her laughter echoing through my house, of us tangled up together with nowhere to go, no one to impress—just us. She made me feel like the man I wanted to be.

What the hell had happened to me?

I was under the farm truck, wrestling with the brakes, when

my mind wandered to her again. Aspen had come home last night after a run-in with her parents, and it was clear things hadn't gone well. She was quieter than usual, her bright energy dimmed. I'd learned a lot about her over the last few months—enough to know when she was deep in her head about something.

I tried to get her to talk, but she'd brushed me off, retreating into herself in a way that wasn't like her. So I let it go. Sometimes she just needed me to be there, to hold space for her, and I was more than willing to do it.

Physical labor usually helped me clear my head, but today it wasn't working. I was halfway through removing the back passenger-side brake when a loud knock on the barn door startled me.

Rolling out from under the truck, I wiped my hands on a towel and looked up to see Parker Westgrove stepping inside. Aspen's brother.

"Oh, hey, man," I said.

Parker wasn't exactly the friendly type, and seeing him anywhere other than the hardware store was rare. He didn't waste time with pleasantries. "I need to talk to you."

Straight to the point. Classic Parker.

"Sure." I crossed my arms over my chest. I didn't mean to look defensive, but with Parker, you never knew what was coming.

"I'm here as a concerned brother," he started, his tone sharp. "Aspen doesn't know I'm here, and I want to make sure she's not just another pawn in whatever game you're playing."

I stiffened, my jaw tightening. "Look." I began, keeping my voice steady. "I care about your sister. If you're here to convince me to leave her alone, you're wasting your time. I'm not going anywhere."

To my surprise, Parker smirked—a small crack in his usually stern demeanor. "Good answer," he said. "Aspen cares about you too. I haven't seen her stand up to our parents the way she did last night. She was furious—more passionate than I've ever seen her. That tells me enough."

"Then why are you here?" I asked, my arms still crossed.

"Because our parents think you're not good enough for her."

"And I want to know if you're willing to prove them wrong."

The words hit me square in the chest. For Aspen, I'd do anything. I didn't give a damn about anyone else in this town, but her family? If proving myself to them would make her life easier, I was all in.

"What do you have in mind?" I asked.

"She tell you how they reacted?"

I shook my head. She hadn't shared the details, just leaned against me on the porch swing while I stroked her hair, her silence speaking louder than words.

"They blew up. She left crying. They don't think you're good enough for her. They're wrong, obviously, but that's their opinion."

I laughed bitterly, running a hand through my hair. "I'd do anything for your sister," I said honestly. "She's special—one of a kind. She makes me want to be a better man. If your parents can't see that, that's on them."

Parker's expression softened, his rigid posture relaxing slightly. "I have an idea." His lips curving into a grin.

"I'm listening."

"You up for it?"

I stepped forward, holding out my hand. "Tell me what I need to do."

Parker shook my hand firmly, and in that moment, I knew I'd do whatever it took to prove my feelings for Aspen. Keeping this plan a secret from her was going to be tough, but if it was the only thing I ever hid from her, I could live with that. For her, I'd take on the world.

Aspen

IT HAD BEEN a couple of days since the blowout with my parents, and I still hadn't heard from them. The silence was deafening. I knew I needed to step away and gather my thoughts before approaching the subject again. After my conversation with Parker, I spent hours turning over what I would say—how I could express myself without sounding bitter, without letting the anger slip out. Today was the day I would finally face them, and I had a plan.

Parker had texted me to meet him at our parents' house. It felt like the right moment—having him there by my side made it a little easier. I didn't want to fight this battle alone.

I had decided I'd tell my parents that I respected their opinions, that I could understand where they were coming from—but I wasn't going to back down. I would apologize for my reaction, for how I'd shut them out. I'd own that, but I wouldn't apologize for my choices. I had a life to live, and I wanted them to see that.

Boone didn't know exactly what had happened when I last saw my parents. I hadn't told him the details because I didn't want him to be hurt by them. He'd known it hadn't gone well, but he hadn't pried, and I loved him for that. He simply held me while I cried, my head resting against his shoulder on the swing, letting me find some comfort in his presence.

When I pulled up to my parents' house, my heart was pounding in my chest. I parked and took a deep breath, gathering my courage. With Parker there, I wasn't alone in this. It wasn't two against one anymore. It was the moment to put my thoughts into action.

When I walked in, the house was quiet, too quiet. My dad's recliner was empty, the TV off. I shut the door softly behind me and tiptoed toward the kitchen, hoping they were just taking a nap or hiding away. That's when I heard the soft murmur of voices from the back porch. I froze.

The sliding glass door was just off the kitchen. I stood by the window, peering outside, and that's when I saw him. Boone.

"Thank you for letting me come over, Mr. and Mrs. Westgrove." Boone's voice rang out clearly, steady. "I hope I'm not intruding."

My heart stopped. There he was, sitting with my parents

at the patio table. I could only see the back of his head, topped with that ever-present cowboy hat. I knew it was him instantly—no mistaking it. His shirt, his boots, the way he sat with a quiet confidence. My dad was seated across from him, arms crossed tightly over his chest, face set in a hard line. My mom was beside him, blonde hair pulled back, her smile soft but guarded.

I crouched, my breath catching in my throat, not wanting to make myself known yet. I wanted to hear this conversation.

"You came over unannounced," my dad said, his voice cold. "So yeah, I'd say you're intruding."

"I'll make it quick, then," Boone replied, his voice steady, unbothered. "I like your daughter. It's clear you don't accept me or our relationship, and I'm here to address that. Man to man. I want to make sure you know who I am."

I could feel the tension in my father's silence, but Boone didn't waver. His voice softened, just enough to show respect but never backing down. "Your daughter means something to me. I'm not here to argue. I'm here to say that I care about her. More than anyone else has." His words cut through the air with a clarity I had never heard before. My chest tightened. *This* was the man I was falling for.

My mom spoke then, her voice gentler than my dad's, but laced with concern. "We just want what's best for our daughter. We don't want her to get hurt."

"I get that," Boone said. "But Aspen's happiness is my top priority, too. I know her better than you think."

The words stung me deeply. *He knew me better than they did.* Boone had seen parts of me I hadn't even shared with my own parents. We had a connection that went deeper than anything I'd ever had with them. I wanted to shout it to the world, but instead, I just pressed my hand to my chest, feeling the ache of it.

My dad scoffed, shaking his head, but my mom's voice softened again. "She's always been gentle...easily bruised."

Boone's response was calm, measured, but filled with a strength I hadn't expected. "Ma'am, your daughter is stronger than you think. You've done an amazing job raising her into the woman she is today. The way I feel about her...it's something I've never felt before. I may have been a foolish boy in the past, but today, I'm a man who cares for her deeply."

My heart felt like it was swelling inside my chest. Boone was talking about me, about *us*, and for the first time, I saw what he saw. His words hit me like a wave, and my hand instinctively pressed against my chest. He was right. This thing between us, it was more than I ever expected.

My father sat in stunned silence, and my mom, for the first time, seemed to soften. Boone had done what no one else had been able to—he had stood his ground for me, and I loved him for it.

I stood up slowly, gathering every ounce of courage. As I stepped outside, all eyes turned toward me. I didn't feel nervous, though. I didn't feel small. I felt... empowered. Boone had given me the strength to walk into that room and not apologize for who I was or who I loved.

"Hi, sweetie," my mom said, rising to meet me with a hug. I hugged her back, my gaze locked on Boone. I smiled and mouthed, *Thank you.*

He tipped his hat, his grin full of warmth, and winked at me, stirring up the butterflies in my stomach.

I sat down next to him, and he immediately took my hand under the table. His touch was reassuring, grounding. His presence gave me the confidence to be strong.

I turned to my dad, trying to break through. "I'm sorry for how I handled things the other day. I didn't mean to come off as hateful or disrespectful. I'll own that."

My mom's smile softened, and my dad remained silent, his eyes locked on Boone. He wasn't ready to listen, but that didn't matter.

"I'm not going to stop seeing Boone. I'm not going back to school. I'm writing a book, and I'm proud of it." I placed my hand on Boone's, squeezing it tight. "I'm happy. Really happy."

"That's all we want," my mom said softly, her voice filled with quiet relief.

My father didn't say anything. But I took the nod he gave me as a small victory. Over time, I'd prove to them both that Boone and I were meant for each other, that I was following the right path for me.

I didn't know how long it would take for them to see it. But I was willing to fight for it, for us. I'd keep pushing, one step at a time, until they understood that I was in control of my own future. And Boone? He was right there beside me, every step of the way.

CHAPTER 34

It had been a hell of a week since seeing my parents with Boone. I learned that Parker never had intentions of showing up that day—it was all part of a plan he and Boone had orchestrated to get me there. Boone knew he would be the first to talk to my parents, and he also knew I was listening in on everything. That night, we went back to my place, and I let him show me just how much he cared about me.

Today, I was at the farm stand by myself. Jill was busy at the library, getting everything ready for the charity event tied to the block party next weekend. I was still in the dark about what Jill needed from me, and that unease kept gnawing at me. But I'd push through, no matter what it took.

When the usual lull in traffic hit, I used the moment to restock and call Penny. After everything that had happened with Boone, I needed to tell her about him—about us.

I hadn't seen her, so I thought it'd be the perfect time to plan a celebration. A night out with our friends—and Boone's friends—at The Tequila Cowboy.

I held the phone between my ear and shoulder as it rang. The dial tone cut off, and Penny's voice filled my ear.

"Hello!" she sang, practically beaming through the phone. "Switch to FaceTime. I wanna see your beautiful face!" I put down the box of honey I'd been carrying and propped the phone up on the table. Penny's face filled the screen, her bright smile pulling a smile from me in return.

"How's the library? Are you ready for the block party?" I asked, shifting back to stocking the shelves.

Penny let out a dramatic sigh, sinking into her chair. Behind her, the library's muted walls were decorated with cheerful quotes like "libraries are for everyone" and "reality is overrated."

"I'm dying over here. I've been buried in expense reports, trying to prove what we need for the Fall. There's no way we're going to make it without the ranch's help and the block party. Everything is riding on it," she explained, her stress practically radiating through the phone. I could tell she hadn't even bothered to tame her messy bun—she was all business, and it made me smile.

"Whatever Mrs. Cassidy has planned, she's excited about it," I said, hoping to ease her stress. "I'm going to hustle everyone for donations. We'll make it happen."

Penny laughed, clearly skeptical. "You? Hustle? I can't wait to see that."

"I can be persuasive when I need to be," I shot back with a playful grin. I grabbed a handful of wildflowers I'd picked that morning to fill the display buckets. "But what I think you really need is a night out."

Penny raised her brows. "A night out?"

"Yeah! We could all go to The Tequila Cowboy. You, me, Boone, Rhodes, Logan, Mac—and we can even see if Theo's up for it."

Penny groaned, clearly already picturing the fun. "I would love that. And speaking of Mac, since that night at the bonfire, we've actually been talking every time he comes into the library. Not only is he insanely hot, he's also so funny."

"Well, use this as another chance to see him! I'll make sure he's working when we go," I said, organizing the flowers into bunches, mixing the colors to make a perfect arrangement.

"Please, and thank you." Penny was practically begging. "And

I think Theo and Rhodes hit it off too. They were non-stop talking at the bonfire. How cute would that be? It's like straight out of a romance novel."

I groaned dramatically, fanning myself with the flowers. "I love that 'not his baby' trope. Swoon-worthy."

Penny laughed. "Knox Eden could respectfully get it every time. If that man claimed my baby as his and cooked for me like that, I'd have another baby for him."

Barking out a laugh, I returned to the phone, propping it up on the counter. I leaned in to be in the frame and said, "The things I'd do to be in one of her romance novels. Those men are *chef's kiss.*"

"It sounds like you have one of those types of men already," Penny teased, waggling her eyebrows.

"I guess I kinda do," I admitted, a grin spreading across my face. Boone wasn't just my real-life boyfriend—he was a man who truly understood me, supported me, and knew how to make my heart race.

"Have you talked to your parents since... you know, since the Boone thing?" Penny asked gently, her voice quieter now, a trace of concern slipping through.

I shook my head. "Nope. I've been giving my dad some space to cool off. I texted my mom and invited them to the block party to help support the stand."

"And?" Penny pressed.

"They said they'd come, but who knows? Town events aren't really their thing," I confessed, a knot forming in my stomach.

My parents had always been distant from the community. Growing up, I had to beg them to participate in things like trunk-or-treats, block parties, or library events. While I loved Faircloud's small-town charm, my parents seemed to resent it—resented how involved everyone else was, and how detached they were from it all.

"I can't imagine they wouldn't show up to support you," Penny said, disbelief in her voice.

I rolled my eyes, unable to stop the bitterness that crept in. "I could count on one hand the number of times my parents came to The Coffee Cup. I worked there for years. My mom stopped in maybe three times, and my dad, once. Their disapproval has always been loud and clear."

Penny's face softened. "I'm sorry, babe. But they'll come around. You'll show them you're doing what's right for you."

"I think whatever Boone said to them really made a difference. That man can captivate a room with just a glance, let alone his words. The fact your dad didn't throw him out speaks volumes," Penny said, her smile soft but tinged with sadness.

She was right. My dad wouldn't have hesitated to show any man the door if he'd shown up uninvited, especially with the audacity to go against his wishes and still pursue a relationship with me. But Boone... Boone was different. The fact we'd left together meant that something Boone had said had struck a chord with my father, enough to potentially spark a change in him.

I raised my hands in mock surrender, giving her the victory. "You might be right, and I really hope you are. Anyway, I've gotta go. I'll text you and Theo the details for The Tequila Cowboy later."

Penny blew a kiss through the phone. "Talk to you soon. Love you."

I caught the kiss in the air and sent one back. "Love you too."

THE REST OF the afternoon passed slowly. There were only a handful of customers, but each one kept me moving until closing time. As I counted the day's earnings, my back to the door, I heard the familiar sound of boots that made my heart race. Spinning around, a smile instantly spread across my face as Boone walked through the door. He was sweaty and covered in dirt, just the way I liked him. There was something about the ruggedness of a man who worked hard with his hands that made me ache for him.

"Hello, Darling," he said, his voice warm and soothing as he pressed a kiss to my cheek. He wrapped an arm around my waist, pulling me closer, and I set the money down, needing to feel him, needing to touch him. My hands went to his neck, and his hot skin against mine sent a shiver down my spine.

"Hi, Cowboy," I whispered, looking up into his eyes with a sense of longing. I rose on my tiptoes, brushing my lips against his in a soft kiss. He responded with another, deeper this time, his lips lingering as if he never wanted to pull away.

Boone's hat sat carelessly on his head, his hair messy and damp at the edges. He looked like he belonged in a dream. "You ready to clean up and grab something to eat? I'm starving." His words made me smile, but I wasn't hungry for food.

"Mm-hmm," I murmured, kissing him again, unable to keep my lips from his. The taste of him, salty from the day's work, was addictive. His mustache tickled my upper lip, sending heat flooding through me, and I kissed him over and over, losing myself in the moment.

Boone pulled back slightly, a playful smirk on his lips. My body collided with the counter, and his growing arousal against my thigh. The pressure of him made my pulse race. He was ready. But so was I. I was a different woman when I was with Boone—he made it impossible to control the desires that surged within me.

"You better take it easy. If you keep it up, I'll have to take you right here. My mom may not like that," he muttered against my lips. I kissed him back, slipping my tongue into his mouth. He welcomed me, matching my energy. My hands slid around his neck and explored their way to his hips. I put a finger in the waistband of his jeans, savoring the touch of his skin, and then came around to his belt buckle.

"She doesn't have to know," I muttered against his lips, pushing him back. Boone's body hit the counter as I sank to my knees. I needed him in my mouth, craved watching him come undone in a space where someone could see.

What the hell was happening to me?

Boone groaned, tossing his head back. I saw him mouth

something, a prayer maybe, before I slid my fingers across the metal of his belt buckle and popped it open. Jean removed, his boxers clung to his muscular thighs—I licked my lips at the sight. Eager as ever, I swiftly pulled down his pants, allowing his cock to spring free.

"I'm taking my time," I said, looking up at him through my lashes. He was staring down, his pupils larger than before. The hat he always wore still perched on his head, and he held his shirt up with a look of pure lust on his face. As much as I loved a sundress, right now, it was getting caught under my knees, which simply wouldn't do.

Leaning forward slightly, I placed my hands on the backs of his thighs and opened my mouth to welcome his hard length. I started slow, circling the tip with my tongue. "Fuck," Boone growled, eyes glued on me.

I took his tip into my mouth, sucking lightly. A salty taste hit my tongue, and I savored it. I opened wider, my cheeks hollowing as I sucked. Adding to the dramatics, I pulled away, a popping sound coming from my mouth. I wanted to torture him, taking his length slowly.

"You're killing me," he said, his free hand gripping the back of my ponytail. Wearing my hair up today was proving to be a good choice, I'd pat myself on the back for that one later.

Boone pulled my head back toward his cock, not wanting me to stop. I looked up, keeping eye contact as I took him. He was so big I gagged when the tip of his length hit the back of the throat. I dug my nails into the back of his thighs, surely leaving a mark.

"Darling," he moaned. "Faster. I want to come in that pretty mouth."

Teasing him, I pulled back and ran my tongue underneath his cock, making sure to linger when I hit the tip. Boone grew frustrated, setting the pace as he fucked my mouth.

"Suck," he demanded.

I brought my hand up to my mouth and spit. Using my saliva, I played with his shaft before taking him again. He tasted salty, dirty, and the combination sent shivers down my spine. Heat bloomed in my lower belly.

"You're such a good girl," he groaned, wrapping my little ponytail around his fist. "That's right, suck me." Faster, I moved my hands along his shaft in a twisting motion. That sent Boone over the edge. He grunted and his head flew back again, that damn hat staying on his head which made me even more feral.

I hummed as I took him and Boone whimpered in response. His head snapped down to watch me on my knees, pleasuring him.

A spurt of warm liquid filled my mouth, and I swallowed, making sure I had his full attention. My tongue darted out to clean the side of my mouth where some dribbled down. I'd never swallowed before.

"You amaze me," he said, laying both his hands on either side of my face. He pulled me up to him, kissing my swollen lips.

"We forgot to shut the door." I noticed the breeze coming from the front of the stand.

"Even hotter for when I do this. Everyone can see," he muttered, placing a kiss on my cheek and down my neck. Swiftly, he scooped me up and twisted to put me down on the counter, my back facing the front door.

"Boone," I warned, but he didn't respond to my protest. He pulled up his pants and redid his belt.

"I said I was starving. I think I need a little treat before my main course." He took the hat from his head and placed it next to me on the counter. His hair was disheveled and his eyes were filled with need.

Boone sank to his knees and pulled up the skirt of my dress to slip underneath, covering himself completely. Even though I couldn't see him, I could feel him. Boone placed soft kisses on the inside of my thigh, working his way to my core. My legs trembled under his touch.

His calloused fingers brushed against my swollen clit, moving my panties to the side. Boone's warm tongue licked me in small, repetitive motions that drove me crazy. The teasing of his hot breath and soft touches was more than my body could take. My legs quaked.

Boone removed my underwear, my sex on full display centimeters from his face.

"You're so wet already," he said, kissing me again and again. "Did sucking my cock make you this needy?" If he kept teasing me like this, I wasn't sure how I'd keep my composure long enough to fully enjoy this.

The risk—the fact someone could walk in at any moment—fueled my need for him.

Groaning out an "mm-hmm," I shoved myself into his face, hoping to give him a hint. He laughed, his mustache scratching against my swollen clit.

"Ride it, Darling," Boone said before devouring me. He let all control go and began to feast on me like a man who was truly starved. A moan escaped my lips, and I couldn't stop the string of curse words that followed. My core clenched, followed by the tingly feeling. The noise coming from him between my legs sent me into a tizzy, my vision was fuzzy as I panted like a damn dog.

"Boone." I whimpered. "Yes, like that." My hand flew to the back of his head, grabbing his hair and pushing his mouth into me.

Stars formed as I closed my eyes, every sound around me muting as I focused on my release.

I came with Boone between my legs, and he continued as I rode out my climax. When it felt like too much, I had to physically shove him away so I could catch my breath.

"Fuck," I breathed, panting heavily.

"Hey, Aspen. Is Boone here? He forgot—" My head flung around so fast I swore I gave myself whiplash. Logan was standing in the doorframe, eyes wide like he just saw a ghost.

I faced back around and my head fell back. *Are you shitting me?*

Boone came out from under my skirt, standing up. He towered over me, wiping his mouth with the back of his hand with a shit-eating grin on his face as he looked at Logan over the top of my head. I couldn't turn around again, I was too embarrassed.

The only solution was to move far away and change my name.

"I'm here," Boone said, a little too friendly, that cocky son of a bitch. He grabbed his hat from next to me on the counter and placed it back on his head. Bending down he kissed my cheek and muttered, "I'm not sorry," before leaving me to recover.

"Jesus Christ," Logan scoffed. "It was, uh, nice seeing you again, Aspen."

I lifted my hand in a lazy wave, refusing to turn around. "Yup. You too, Logan." I sighed before dropping my head and letting out a laugh to myself.

CHAPTER 35

Tequila Cowboy. 9 p.m. sharp. Be there.

Theo

My pregnant ass in a bar? I can see the rumors now...

Theo

'Theo Matthews was caught dancing on the bar chugging a bottle of Jose with her belly hanging out'

Penny

I'd be the one to leak that... because honestly, sounds bad ass.

I'll let you pass this time.

What kid doesn't want to hear their mom was dancing on a bar while pregnant?

Penny

TRUE LOL

Theo

Boone and I were the first to arrive at The Tequila Cowboy, a fact that didn't surprise me. The bar was always packed, the town's only place for music, laughter, and neon lights. It had charm—nostalgia, even—with its jukebox playing classic country tunes. It was the kind of place that felt alive, like it had soaked up every story and secret whispered within its walls.

Mac was working the bar alongside Dudley, the local boy with an endless reserve of charm. Watching them was like witnessing some sort of magic. They didn't just serve drinks—they kept the place spinning, their banter and effortless rhythm captivating the crowd.

Boone and I claimed the last free spot at the bar, waiting our turn. Mac caught sight of us and raised a hand in acknowledgment, promising he'd be over soon. Boone tipped his hat, then leaned his elbows on the bar's sticky surface, the casual movement drawing my attention.

Tonight, he looked good. *Too good.* His baby-blue pearl snap shirt hugged his shoulders just right, and his dark jeans were paired with polished boots that made me want to melt. In typical Boone fashion, his hair was deliciously messy. I admired his rugged good looks.

Tonight? He looked like trouble—the kind I'd happily get into.

I'd chosen a strapless black dress that hugged my curves and paired it with knee-high cowgirl boots. It was simple but effective—Boone had already made that clear. He couldn't keep his hands off me, his touch lingering every chance he got. His hands were possessive, his kisses trailing along my neck in a way that left no room for doubt: I was his, and he wanted the whole bar to know it.

I felt his gaze on me, hot and heavy, and turned to catch him watching me. He grinned, the kind of smile that could melt steel, and stepped behind me, pulling me flush against him.

"This dress is driving me crazy," he murmured against my ear, his lips brushing the sensitive skin. He nipped lightly, and a shiver ran down my spine as I instinctively tilted my head to give him more access.

"I know. That's why I wore it," I teased, my voice low and full of mischief.

"Dirty girl," he groaned, his voice thick with need. I laughed softly, the sound swallowed by the music as we swayed together, lost in our own little world.

Mac finally made his way over, his expression amused as groans erupted from the people still waiting.

"Take it easy," Mac said with a grin. "This lovely couple is just as thirsty." He leaned in, his voice rising to carry over the music. "These people, man. They're relentless."

Boone ordered for us—a beer for him and a tequila sunrise for me. The way he always knew my drink, without needing to ask, made my chest tighten with a sweet ache.

As Mac went to grab our drinks, I glanced at my phone. Right on cue, Penny walked in, her presence like a burst of color against the dim backdrop of the bar. She was stunning, her chestnut hair in loose curls, a bandana framing her face, and a bright, body-hugging dress that showed off her every curve. She wasn't just dressed to impress—she was dressed to conquer.

"Finally," I called, waving her over. Her face lit up, and she jogged toward us, practically glowing.

Breaking free of Boone's hold, I hugged her. "You made it!"

"I had to look good," she whispered conspiratorially, tilting her head toward Mac.

I laughed. "Figured as much. Get over here and order."

But Penny had other ideas. She leaned over to the nearest man sitting at the bar and whispered something in his ear. He stood immediately, grinning as he relocated. Boone and I exchanged a look, and Penny just giggled.

"I told him that blonde over there was into him. A girl's gotta do what a girl's gotta do." Then, she shrugged.

Mac returned with our drinks, but my attention was on Boone. He spun me onto the dance floor, his hand firm on mine. The music wrapped around us, and I let go, my body moving in rhythm with his. Song after song, we danced, the world outside fading away. Boone's arms never strayed far, his touch grounding me in a way that felt safe, steady, and entirely too exhilarating.

When we finally returned to the bar, Penny was in deep conversation with Mac. She twirled her hair as she leaned closer, her determination clear. Boone chuckled, pulling me into his side as we ordered a round of shots.

"She's relentless," I said, watching her with a smile.

"So are you," Boone murmured, his lips brushing my temple.

And maybe he was right. After all, love wasn't for the faint of heart—it was for the bold, the stubborn, and the utterly captivated. And tonight, it felt like anything was possible.

"That bastard left me here alone," Mac muttered, lining up shot glasses in a perfect row. His jaw tightened, his frustration evident, but his hands remained steady as he worked. The bar had finally begun to quiet down now that most of the older crowd had filtered out, leaving the younger patrons to linger.

"We'll take a round of the dealer's choice," Boone said from behind me, his voice low and steady, with that hint of a drawl that always sent a shiver down my spine.

Mac glanced over, his expression lightening as he smirked and held up a finger. He spun to grab a bottle of Buffalo Trace, filling the glasses generously. "Fuck it, I'm taking one too," he declared, placing the shots in front of us.

I grabbed mine, raising it high, and the others followed suit. Mac counted down, and we tipped them back. The bourbon burned on its way down, a pleasant heat that settled in my chest. I shook my head, slamming the empty glass onto the bar as warmth spread through my veins.

Leaving Penny to her strategic occupation of the bar, Boone and I returned to the dance floor. He pulled me close, his large hands enveloping mine as Brooks & Dunn's "Play Something Country" started up. The twang of the music wrapped around us, and Boone led me with a confidence that left me breathless.

His movements were fluid, graceful, but still undeniably masculine, and I couldn't help the smile that spread across my face. The world blurred around us as we took over the dance floor. When he spun me and dipped me low, I barely had time to catch my breath before he leaned in, dragging his tongue teasingly from the base of my throat to my chin.

"Boone!" I squealed, laughing as he brought me back up.

He grinned, mischievous and unrepentant. "You looked so good, I had to see how you tasted."

By the time the song ended, my cheeks were flushed, my hair clinging to my damp skin. Boone's hair was matted under his hat, and his shirt clung to his broad chest. I fanned myself with my hands, feeling the heat of the room and the intensity of his presence.

"I need a drink," I said, pointing a finger at him. "Stay here. I'll grab you another beer."

Boone tipped his hat, watching me with a look that made my stomach flutter as I made my way back to the bar.

Sliding into the empty stool beside Penny, I let out an exaggerated exhale, still catching my breath. She turned to me, her head resting on my shoulder with a dreamy sigh.

"You two are adorable," she said, her voice tinged with envy.

"I'm really happy," I admitted, unable to keep the goofy smile off my face. The words felt monumental. I hadn't been able to say that about myself—or my life—in a long time.

Boone had a way of making me feel seen, cherished, and wanted. He wasn't just a man I was falling for; he was becoming *my person*. The realization should've scared me, but instead, it felt like coming home.

Mac appeared in front of us, snapping me out of my thoughts. "What can I get the lovebirds?" he teased.

I ordered a tequila sunrise for myself and a Jack and Coke for Boone, deciding to keep things interesting. Drinks in hand, I turned back toward the dance floor, ready to rejoin him.

But what I saw stopped me cold.

Boone was standing in the middle of the floor, his easy smile directed at none other than Miranda Yert. My heart thudded painfully, then settled into a slow boil as my eyes took her in.

She was dressed to kill in a white dress so short it barely covered anything, paired with cowgirl boots that screamed, *Look at me*. Her bleach-blond hair hung limp down her back, and her laugh carried obnoxiously over the music as she leaned into Boone, twirling a strand of hair around her finger.

My grip tightened on the cups in my hands, the urge to march over there nearly overwhelming. The shy, reserved girl who'd once shrunk in Miranda's presence was long gone. Tonight, I was something else entirely—angry, possessive, and done with her games.

Boone noticed me before I reached them, his eyes lighting up as he stretched out a hand and pulled me against his side.

"There she is." He pressed a kiss to the top of my head.

Miranda's expression soured, her flirty demeanor evaporating as her gaze landed on me.

"Here you go, Cowboy," I said, my tone sweet but pointed as I handed Boone his drink.

He grinned, taking a sip before turning back to Miranda. "Oh, where are my manners? Miranda, this is my girlfriend, Aspen."

The word *girlfriend* hit me like a shot of adrenaline, wiping out my earlier jealousy and replacing it with a surge of joy. Boone's declaration was as clear as a neon sign, and Miranda clearly got the message.

I couldn't resist twisting the knife. "It's nice to see you again, Miranda," I said with a sugary smile, my voice dripping with faux warmth.

Miranda's lips curled into a snarl, her hand dropping from her hair as her gaze locked onto mine. "You too, Aspen. I have to say, I'm shocked to see Boone here with a girl like you."

My stomach tightened, but I kept my face neutral. "What's that supposed to mean?" I asked, struggling to come up with a retort that didn't betray the sudden heat in my chest.

"Well," she drawled, her smirk widening, "basic and boring come to mind. Boone, don't you need a little excitement in your life? Not someone who cares more about fictional men than the real ones standing in front of her." She ran her tongue along her canine, her expression daring me to crumble.

I felt the old, familiar urge to shrink back, but this time I refused to give her the satisfaction. Instead, I stepped closer to Boone, slipping an arm around his waist, staking my claim.

Boone caught on instantly. His hand came to rest on my hip, pulling me closer. "You know, Miranda," he said, his voice low and deliberate, "jealousy isn't a good look on you." He paused, letting the words sink in before adding with a mischievous grin, "But on her? It's fucking hot."

Miranda's eyes widened, her cheeks reddening as though he'd physically slapped her.

Then Boone did something that made my breath hitch. He tilted his head down, removed his khaki cowboy hat, and placed it gently on my head. His lips captured mine in a slow, deliberate kiss, his tongue teasing its way past my lips as his hand pressed against the small of my back, pulling me closer.

For a moment, the world disappeared. It was just us, and I fed into the kiss, letting Miranda see just how "boring" I really was. When we finally came up for air, she was gone—her bleach-blond hair a ghostly memory in the crowd.

"Suck it, Miranda," Boone whispered against my lips, planting another quick kiss.

"Girlfriend, huh?" I asked, my voice teasing as I stared into his eyes.

His mustache twitched as he grinned. "You like the sound of that, Darling?"

I didn't answer. Instead, I reached up, adjusted the brim of his hat perched on my head, knowing it was a symbol as much as an accessory. Rising on tiptoes, I kissed his cheek.

The rest of the night went off without a hitch. Miranda didn't dare show her face again, likely too embarrassed by Boone's very public dismissal. Boone found a seat at the bar while Penny decided it was time to show off on the dance floor.

She dragged me out with her, a drink in one hand and her other clasped in mine as we swayed to Big & Rich's "Save a Horse, Ride a Cowboy." The irony wasn't lost on me, especially with Boone's hat still resting on my head.

From across the room, Boone watched me with a dark, heated stare, his Jack and Coke forgotten in his hand. His intensity sent a thrill through me—I knew he was barely holding himself back.

Blowing him a kiss, I let Penny spin me until my back was to him. "You're driving that man mad," she giggled in my ear.

"Isn't that the point?" I replied, laughing as I tilted my head back.

After a few more songs, Penny and I decided to call it a night. Despite the buzz of the evening, I'd kept it light—two drinks and a single shot. Boone, on the other hand, had indulged. As I approached the bar, I counted four empty shot glasses and two rocks glasses beside him.

"There they are!" Mac called out, grinning. "You two were the stars of the night. Don't think anyone had eyes on anything but that dance floor."

I turned to Boone, whose smirk was lazy, his eyes heavy-lidded from the alcohol. Before I could say a word, he swept me off my feet—literally.

"Boone!" I squealed, clutching at him to keep my dress from riding up. He took his hat, placing it strategically over my thighs as he carried me toward the door.

"I'm taking you home," he growled, his voice rough and full

of promise.

"But you can't drive!" I protested as he set me down by the driver's side door.

"You are tonight," he said, digging into his pocket for his keys. Placing them in my hand, he leaned in close, his breath warm against my ear. "How else are we getting back so I can put my hands all over you?"

I stared at the keys in disbelief, then back at him. "You want me to drive *your truck* home?"

"Trust you with my heart, don't I?" He grinned, opening the door and motioning for me to climb in. "After you, my beautiful girlfriend."

I slid into the driver's seat, unable to stop the smile spreading across my face. Boone Cassidy trusted me—not just with his truck, but with *him.*

As I gripped the wheel and started the engine, I glanced over to see him watching me with that same smoldering intensity. The night wasn't over yet—not by a long shot.

CHAPTER 36

Aspen *fucking* Westgrove was driving my truck. Hell, I never thought I'd see the day. No woman had ever taken the wheel of my Chevy before, not even my mom. That truck was my first big purchase after years of sweat and long hours on the ranch. It was my pride and joy, but tonight, seeing Aspen's hands gripping the steering wheel. It looked damn good on her.

I could tell she was nervous. Her knuckles were white, and she kept stealing glances at me like she thought I'd suddenly change my mind. But I trusted her. Trusted her to get us home safely, especially since I'd had more to drink than I should've. Funny how the tables had turned—last time at The Tequila Cowboy, I was the one driving her drunk self home. Now, she was returning the favor.

Watching her dance tonight had damn near driven me crazy. The sway of her hips, the way her hair caught the light—it was impossible not to stare. And every man in the bar felt the same, their eyes glued to her like she was the only thing worth looking at.

Normally, I wasn't the jealous type. But tonight, every time a guy looked like he might step toward the dance floor, I shut it down with a hand on his shoulder and a shake of my head. They could watch all they wanted; she was *mine*. My girl. My Aspen. And if the sight of her wearing my cowboy hat wasn't enough to make that clear, throwing her over my shoulder and walking her out of the bar definitely should've done the trick.

"I like seeing you drive my truck," I said, my voice slurring just enough to give away how far gone I was.

Aspen glanced over at me, her eyes soft with concern. "You all right?"

I nodded, letting my head fall against the cool glass of the window. "Just tired, Darling. Keep your eyes on the road." Lie. A big. Fat. Lie. I was wasted.

Her lips curved in a small smile, and my chest tightened. How could a single look from her make me feel so damn content? My eyes drifted closed, the hum of the engine and the soft scent of her perfume pulling me under.

The next thing I knew, I felt her hands on my arm, tugging gently to wake me up. I blinked, groggy, and saw her standing beside the truck, the door open and a determined look on her face.

"Come on, Boone," she said, bracing herself like she actually thought she could catch me if I stumbled.

"I can get out myself," I grumbled, sliding out of the truck with a thud. My boots hit the ground harder than I intended, but I steadied myself quickly, throwing an arm around her shoulders. "Let's get to your cabin."

At the base of her porch steps, she stopped, turning to face me. "And where do you think you're going?"

"Inside," I replied simply, cupping her face in my hands. Her skin was soft under my touch, and the moonlight made her cheeks glow. "I don't want to sleep alone. It's late, and I'm scared." I pouted, adding just enough drama to make her laugh.

"Scared, huh?" she teased, taking my hand and leading me up the steps. "Fine, but you better behave yourself."

I stumbled again, catching myself on the railing. "I always behave," I muttered, earning another laugh from her as she unlocked the door.

Inside, I wasted no time collapsing onto her couch. I heard the faucet running in the kitchen, and a moment later, she returned with a glass of water and a bag of Goldfish crackers.

"Goldfish?" I grinned, taking them eagerly. "You're spoiling me, Darling."

"Drink your water," she said, crouching in front of me. She reached for my boots, tugging them off one at a time.

"Wait—what're you doing?" I asked, startled.

"Getting you ready for bed. Eat your snack." She set my boots aside.

I couldn't take my eyes off her. Aspen Westgrove, this beautiful, kind, incredible woman, was taking care of me like no one ever had. My chest ached with something deeper than gratitude, something I couldn't quite put into words.

She sat beside me on the couch, tucking her legs up to her chest. I watched her, my heart pounding. "You amaze me," I said, the words slipping out before I could stop them.

Her cheeks turned pink, the blush creeping down her neck and onto her chest. My eyes followed the path, catching on the curve of her collarbone and the soft rise of her chest.

"Boone," she murmured, her voice shy, but she didn't look away for long.

Leaning back, I popped another handful of Goldfish into my mouth. "How did I get so lucky?" I said around the crackers, more to myself than to her.

She smiled, the kind of smile that made me feel like I'd finally done something right.

I held out the bag of Goldfish, and she took a few, popping them into her mouth one at a time.

"I used to give these to Penny and Theo whenever they drank too much," she said with a little laugh. "Soaks up the alcohol real good."

Her voice was like a melody, low and comforting, and I couldn't get enough of it. Every small detail she shared was a piece of her puzzle, a glimpse into the life she'd lived before me. The more she revealed, the more I wanted to know—wanted to hold onto every word, every moment.

"I need a bed," I mumbled, finishing my glass of water in one long gulp.

Aspen stood and held out her hands to help me up. Her touch steadied me as I pushed myself to my feet, leaving the bag and glass on the table. "Will you help me take my pants off too?" I teased, smirking as I winked at her.

"Oh, Boone," she sighed, shaking her head with a soft laugh. Her eyes sparkled with exasperation, and I loved that look on her. She led me down the hallway, my steps heavy and uneven as I followed her. Barefoot and still in her dress, she moved gracefully, her hair brushing over her shoulders.

"Lie down in bed," she said, her tone gentle but firm. "I'm going to take a quick shower. I need to wash the bar off me."

I nodded, dragging myself toward the bed. But as I sat on the edge, something nagged at me. My hat. I ran a hand through my hair and cursed under my breath—I must've left it in the truck. I couldn't let it sit out there all night.

Unbuckling my belt and pulling my shirt free from my jeans, I fumbled with the snaps. The shirt landed somewhere in the corner, but I didn't care. I stood, swaying slightly, determined to retrieve my hat. As I shuffled toward the door, I felt a pair of hands on my arms, small but firm.

"Where do you think you're going?" Aspen's voice was light, teasing, and laced with amusement.

Turning to face her, I caught my breath. Her hair was damp, and she was wrapped in that green towel again—the same one from before. God help me, that damn towel was going to be the death of me.

"My hat," I muttered, hiccupping as I pointed toward the door. "It's in my truck. I can't let someone steal it. It's... It's precious."

She laughed softly, shaking her head. "I promise you, Boone, no one is going to steal your hat." Her hands guided me back to the bedroom, her touch warm and grounding. "Let's just get you out of these clothes and into bed, okay?"

I stopped, catching her face in my hands. Her skin was

soft, her cheeks flushed from the warmth of the shower. I leaned down slowly, pressing my lips to hers. It wasn't just a kiss—it was grounding, a tether keeping me steady in the haze of drunkenness.

When Aspen pulled back, her eyes glimmered with something unspoken, but she didn't say a word. She just stepped back and let me finish undressing. I kicked off my pants, leaving my boxers on, though the fabric strained against the obvious reaction my body had to her.

"I could probably go forever right now," I murmured, my voice heavy with honesty.

She sighed, shaking her head with a small smile. "As much as I love *that* and the things it can do, you need to sleep."

I chuckled, unable to argue with her. Climbing into bed, I let the sheets wrap around me like her arms. The faint scent of her lingered on the pillow, a mix of lavender and something uniquely Aspen.

Just as I was settling in, she dropped the towel in front of the dresser, her back turned to me. My breath hitched as her bare body came into view, her skin glowing in the dim light. When she turned to step into her sleep shorts, I caught a full glimpse of her, a sight so beautiful it left me speechless.

I told myself I'd stay awake until she climbed into bed, just so I could thank her for taking care of me. But the warmth of the sheets, the soft hum of her moving around, and the lingering image of her body pulled me under.

Sleep came fast, and as I drifted off, the last thought in my mind was her—every curve, every smile, every bit of Aspen Westgrove burned into my memory.

CHAPTER 37

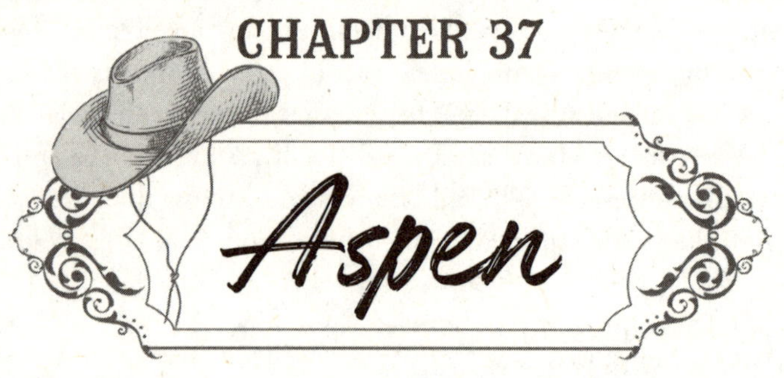

Aspen

The big day had finally arrived. The annual block party was in full swing, and the weather couldn't have been more perfect—blue skies, warm sun, and just the faintest whisper of a breeze. Main Street buzzed with life, lined with colorful vendor stalls, long tables, and game booths filled with families laughing and making memories. Folk music floated through the air from the big stage in the town square, where the first band of the day was playing.

I hadn't slept much the night before. Excitement and nerves had stolen my rest, and Mrs. Cassidy's cryptic late-night text didn't help. All she said was, "*Wear a bathing suit.*"

When I arrived early this morning to help Boone set up, I wasn't prepared for what I saw. A dunk tank. A *dunk tank*. My heart sank and my stomach twisted as I stared at it, and Boone's lopsided grin didn't do much to reassure me. He swore up and down he had no idea what his mom was planning, but the mischievous sparkle in his eyes told me otherwise.

Beside the dunk tank, the Cassidy Ranch stand was picture-perfect, complete with a long wooden table under a canopy displaying the ranch's logo. The spread was mouthwatering—jams, honey, fresh-baked goods—and it had already begun drawing in customers. Penny had outdone herself, creating a goal tracker shaped like a thermometer so we could tally donations for the library in real time.

The dunk tank, however, was *my* post for the day. Jill's brilliant idea was to let people pay for the chance to dunk me, all for charity.

The sun beat down mercilessly as I perched on the hard seat, my damp hair sticking to my neck. It was only midday, and I'd already been dunked more times than I could count. Boone, of course, had taken full advantage, delighting in every splash.

"Get ready, Darling!" he called out, winding up for yet another throw.

I glared at him, sweeping my wet hair out of my face. *Why didn't this man play baseball?* Before I could finish the thought, his ball smacked the target dead-center. With a loud *clang,* I plunged into the water again.

Resurfacing, I gasped for air, water streaming down my face. "You're going to pay for this!" I shouted, pointing a dripping finger at him.

Boone only laughed, blowing me a kiss. His easy charm sent a warmth through me that had nothing to do with the sun.

Jill appeared at the edge of the tank, her face lit with pride. "You're doing great, sweetie! We're well past the halfway mark on our goal. Between the stand and the dunk tank, the library's going to be in fantastic shape."

Her words made it all worth it, and I managed a tired smile. Penny, ever the instigator, had disappeared into the crowd to recruit more people to join the fun. She was enjoying this far too much.

Even my parents had come by earlier. My mom laughed openly at the sight of me drenched and sputtering, promising to return later to spend time at the Cassidy Ranch stand.

"Come on down, folks!" Boone hollered a few feet away, his voice carrying over the crowd. "Two dollars a ball or three for five to dunk Miss Aspen Westgrove! All proceeds go to the library!" He turned and winked at me, the kind that made my heart stutter despite my best efforts to resist.

A little boy stepped up next, clutching his three balls with nervous excitement. He missed all three throws, and when his face crumpled, my heart sank. He ran to his mom, burying his face against her legs.

Boone crouched down, speaking softly to him. Whatever he said made the boy wipe his tears and nod. Then Boone swept him up, carrying him toward the tank as they both laughed. The boy reached out a small hand and smacked the target, sending me plunging into the water yet again.

When I surfaced, I couldn't be mad. The boy's laughter was infectious, and the way he hugged Boone melted me. Watching Boone with him was a revelation—gentle, patient, and so full of joy. I couldn't help but think how natural he looked. *He's going to make an amazing dad one day,* my heart squeezed at the idea.

After the boy and his family left, Boone sauntered over to the tank, leaning against the side. His usual cowboy hat was gone today, replaced by a backward trucker cap. Somehow, it made him look even more irresistible.

"Sorry about that," he said, his smirk betraying zero remorse. "He really wanted to dunk you, and I couldn't say no."

I rolled my eyes but smiled. "No hard feelings. I'd have done the same thing."

Before Boone could reply, Penny shouted from across the crowd. "Boone! Get back to work! Quit flirting with your girlfriend and make me some money!" She stormed over and physically steered him back toward the stand, leaving me laughing despite myself.

As the day wore on, more people arrived, filling the streets with laughter and music. At the main stand, someone was giving lasso lessons, drawing a growing crowd. The sense of community was palpable—neighbors helping neighbors, everyone coming together for a shared cause.

Looking at the thermometer chart, I saw we were inching closer to our goal, and it wasn't even late afternoon yet. Despite my sore arms and waterlogged swimsuit, my heart was full. Faircloud wasn't just a town—it was a home. A place where people cared, where they rallied around each other in times of need.

And as I sat there, dripping wet and exhausted, desperately needing a water bottle, I knew this is where I was meant to be.

I climbed down the back of the dunk tank and grabbed the towel Boone had set aside for me. The fabric was rough but welcome against my damp skin as I moved toward the canopy, seeking refuge from the relentless sun. I collapsed into the lawn chair behind the table, savoring the cool shade, and closed my eyes with a sigh. The faint scent of sunscreen clung to me, a reminder that I needed to reapply soon.

"I can't believe how well we're doing!" Penny squealed from the seat beside me, her oversized sunglasses hiding her bright eyes but not the grin that stretched across her face.

"Me neither," I said, smiling back. "Though I'm pretty sure Boone's single-handedly funding half of this just to see me get dunked."

Penny laughed, the sound light and infectious. "That man's a one-man marketing team. He's been roaming around, dragging anyone he can find over here to spend money. Honestly? It's kind of amazing."

Boone had a way of throwing himself wholeheartedly into everything he did, and today was no different. The Cassidy family was like that, really—selfless, warm, and utterly devoted to the people they cared about.

I spotted my parents making their way toward our table. My breath caught in my chest. I was glad they'd come, but it was the first time I'd seen them face-to-face since Boone went to their house.

"Hey, Mr. and Mrs. Westgrove!" Penny said, standing to greet them. Her enthusiasm helped ease the tension in the air.

I stayed seated, mustering a smile as my mom beamed at me. "Hi, honey!" Her voice carried the warmth I'd missed.

Standing, I waved. "I'm glad you two could make it." I tried to keep my tone light, masking the nervous energy that knotted my stomach. My dad, stoic as ever, only nodded before turning his attention to Penny.

"I'll take a pack of the meat sticks, a jar of muffin mix, some of that honey," he said, pointing to the jars neatly arranged on the table. "And a carton of eggs."

Penny rang him up while I bagged the items, each motion grounding me. Seeing my dad actually buy something—a gesture that went beyond a casual visit—was a surprise.

As I handed him the bag, he finally spoke. "Can I steal you for a second?"

I glanced at Penny, who waved me off with a knowing smile, already engrossed in conversation with my mom. Following my dad, we walked in silence to a bench overlooking the bustling street.

He sat down, his hands resting on his knees, and I waited, unwilling to speak first.

"I want to apologize for how I reacted," he began, his voice quieter than usual. "There's a lot about your mother and me that you don't know. I wanted the best for you and Parker, but...I realize now that I was chasing what I thought was best, not what you wanted. I'm sorry for not giving you the chance to explain yourself. And I'm sorry for being so quick to judge Boone."

I stared at the towel draped over my lap, picking at its edges. His words carried a weight I hadn't expected, but they unlocked something in me.

"I appreciate that," I said softly. "And I'm sorry too. I should've listened more, tried to see where you were coming from."

He shook his head. "None of this was your fault. It was my own stubbornness. Your mom and I...we were forced to stay in Faircloud when we had Parker so young. It wasn't what we wanted, and I was afraid you'd feel trapped like we did. But I see now your love for this place runs deeper than mine ever did."

I placed a hand on his forearm, my chest tightening. "Dad, growing up here made my life amazing. It's why I want to stay. This is where I belong."

He sighed, his gaze softening. "I see that now." He rested

his hand over mine, giving it a gentle squeeze. "And as for that Cassidy boy... I've been watching him run all over today, trying to get people to help support you and your friend. Maybe he's not so bad after all."

Smiling, I leaned my head against his shoulder. The warmth of his presence filled a space in my heart I hadn't realized was empty.

"He's pretty great," I admitted, my eyes scanning the crowd until they landed on Boone. He was coming down Main Street with Rhodes, Logan, Mac, and Theo trailing behind him, all laughing like kids at recess.

"I approve," my dad said, ruffling my damp hair. "For now."

Laughing, I hugged him, the moment cementing itself into my heart. Our talk was short, but it was enough—more than enough. My dad was a man of few words, and I'd learned to treasure every one he offered.

Before I could return to my post, Boone intercepted me, scooping me up in his arms. My feet dangled as he spun me around, his laughter infectious.

"Boone!" I squealed, throwing my arms around his neck.

"I hope you're ready," he murmured in my ear, his voice laced with playful mischief.

Turning, I saw our friends lined up at the dunk tank, each armed with three balls.

One by one, they took their shots. Rhodes hit the target every time, Logan scored twice, and Mac—clearly too busy trying to impress Penny—missed entirely. Theo handed her balls to Boone, marched to the tank, and slapped the target herself, shouting, "I'm pregnant! Let me have this win!"

By the end of the day, I was completely spent. My muscles ached, my skin felt waterlogged, and I probably looked like a prune. But as I stood there, watching my parents laugh with Boone and Jill, even Parker joining in on the fun, I knew today was about more than just surpassing our fundraising goal.

It was about love. About family. About finding my place in this beautiful, messy, imperfect life.

CHAPTER 38

"What an amazing turnout!" my mom exclaimed, her smile radiant as she surveyed the emptying lot.

We stayed behind to clean up after Aspen went home, her energy completely spent. Penny had lingered for a while to help but eventually had to head back to the library to finalize the totals from the fundraiser.

Now, with the last of the supplies loaded into the back of my truck, I was ready to call it a day. The sun didn't bother me much—I was used to it—but the pavement's heat had been brutal. I shut the tailgate with a satisfying thud.

"Everyone in town showed up for the dunk tank," I said, wiping my forehead with the back of my hand. "Aspen was a real champ about it." I could still picture her smile, bright and unwavering, even though I knew by the end of the day she was worn out. When she leaned against my chest, her exhaustion was palpable, and I didn't hesitate to hold her up.

My mom nodded, falling into step beside me as we walked to the driver's side door. "I don't know what I'd do without her. Not just today, but at the stand, too."

"Me neither," I muttered, a small smile tugging at my lips.

She noticed and reached out, giving my bicep a gentle squeeze. I couldn't help but think about Aspen and her dad's earlier conversation. From where I stood, it seemed like a good talk—something long overdue. Her family had stuck around most of the day, even buying from the stand. But I needed to hear it from her, to make sure everything was really okay.

For now, though, I had to get home and clean up. My mom and I exchanged goodbyes before I climbed into the truck, the drive home silent except for the hum of the AC on full blast.

Pulling into my driveway, I noticed Aspen's lights were off. She'd probably collapsed the moment she got home, and honestly, I didn't blame her. With no perishables left in the truck, I decided the rest of the unloading could wait until tomorrow.

As I stepped inside, the cool air greeted me like an old friend. I dropped my keys on the counter, toed off my boots, and headed toward the hallway. I raked my fingers through my sweat-slicked hair as I yanked off my cap, loosening the strands.

The walk to my bedroom felt endless, my feet dragging with every step. But as I crossed the threshold, something on my bed caught my eye.

It took a moment for my vision to adjust to the dim candlelight. Aspen sat propped against the metal headboard, wrapped in my sheets, her skin kissed by the warm glow of the flickering flames. My cowboy hat rested on her head, its shadow playing across her face. The blanket draped her bottom half and barely covered her chest, leaving just enough to the imagination.

"Jesus," I muttered, my voice low and rough. I stepped closer, my body reacting instantly, the tightness in my jeans unmistakable. The sight of her like this—bare, vulnerable, and wearing *my* hat—had my thoughts spiraling. "Not that I'm not thrilled to see you naked, but... what are you doing?"

Aspen smiled, tilting the brim of my hat toward me. "You like it, Cowboy?"

All I could do was swallow hard and nod, utterly captivated by her. She was breathtaking—more than that. She was *mine*.

"I realized something today," she began, her tone soft but sure. Her hands held the edge of the blanket, keeping herself modest despite the heat radiating between us. "The feelings I have for you, Boone, they're unlike anything I've ever known. You make me feel confident, beautiful, like the best version of myself. And now that I have you, I can't imagine my life without you in it." She laughed, the sound nervous yet genuine, as she let her head fall back against the headboard. "This probably sounds so silly, and trying to say it out loud instead of writing it down feels impossible. But I had to try."

Her words hit me square in the chest, their rawness and honesty leaving me breathless.

"Say it," I urged, stepping closer, my voice barely above a whisper. "Say it all. No filters. No edits. Just...tell me."

I needed it—the unvarnished truth, straight from her heart—because I knew, deep down, I felt exactly the same.

We were so close, yet somehow, it still didn't feel like enough. Aspen's eyes locked onto mine, her gaze unwavering, her vulnerability laid bare.

"I'm so hopelessly in love with you," she whispered, her voice trembling with emotion. She sat up straighter, her confidence and raw honesty radiating in every word.

As much as I wanted to let my eyes wander over her bare body, I couldn't tear my gaze away from her face.

"When I see you, it feels like my chest is about to burst," she continued, her voice thick with passion. "Like someone planted a star inside me, and the energy is too much to contain. I think about you every minute of every day."

I sank onto the edge of the bed as she leaned forward, grabbing my face in her hands. She knelt to meet me, the blanket slipping away, forgotten, as if nothing else in the world mattered but this moment.

"I'm proud to be with you," she said, her voice steady, her emotions raw and unfiltered. "I'd stand on the highest mountain and shout to anyone who would listen how amazing you are—and how beautiful you make me feel."

My heart pounded so fiercely it felt like it might break free from my chest. The sound of it roared in my ears. Every fiber of my being screamed to close the gap between us, to feel her lips on mine, but I held back, letting her words wash over me.

"I love you," I finally said, my voice firm and certain. The words spilled out, and they felt right—so damn right. "I *fucking* love you."

Saying it out loud, giving voice to the truth I'd been holding in, filled me with a sense of completeness I hadn't known I was missing. Being with her was like finding the final piece of a puzzle I hadn't realized was incomplete.

"You are worthy of the same love you give to everyone around you," I whispered, my voice thick with emotion. I placed my hands gently on her cheeks, my thumbs brushing the soft skin there. "Thank you for giving me the privilege to cherish you, to love you the way you deserve. I can't believe I've gone so far in life without you by my side. A part of me will always belong to you, as long as you'll have me."

Her tears brimmed, pooling in the corners of her eyes before spilling down her cheeks.

"I love you too," she said, her voice breaking as the tears flowed freely.

I reached up, using the pads of my thumbs to gently wipe them away, feeling the warmth of her skin beneath my touch.

Aspen had changed everything I thought I knew about love, about myself, about life. In her, I found not just a partner, but a purpose, a home, and a future brighter than I'd ever dared to dream.

I laid her down and trapped her body underneath mine. She fell flat, my hat sliding from her head as I kissed her. I took it and tossed it across the room, not letting another minute pass where my lips weren't on hers, hat be damned.

My body was on fire, skin prickling with excitement, and my heart throbbed against my chest. My hands found her damp hair, and I intertwined my fingers in her strands. Aspen's tongue separated my lips and tangled with mine. Her hands explored my body and up my shirt, her soft touch caressing the muscles on my my hand around her throat.

My girl seemed to like that.

Aspen had this smile on her face and this devilish look in her eyes every time I squeezed down slightly. Her hands found my ass, and she clawed at my skin, shoving me back into her deeper. I let her take control, setting the pace as we moved with each other. Watching her as she came, her tight heat wrapped around me, I couldn't hold back my release.

When we were both done, I panted heavily and stayed inside her, needing a moment to catch my breath. Her body slumped against my bedding, my sweaty forehead made contact with hers. We both needed to shower desperately. I wanted to feel bad that I had made her dirty again, but I couldn't.

With a tender touch, I picked her up and carried her to the bathroom. Aspen placed sweet kisses on my neck. I was hopelessly in love with this woman. She deserved everything in life, and I was going to give it to her.

I placed Aspen down on the small counter in the bathroom and started the shower. "You amaze me," I muttered, pushing a piece of hair behind her ear.

"You said that to me the night you were drunk."

"Drunk words are sober thoughts," I replied, placing one hand on each side of her as I leaned in for another kiss. Our lips moved in sync while the water warmed the room. Steam covered the mirror by the time I broke away.

Both naked, we climbed into the small shower. It wasn't made for two, but we made it work. I washed her hair first using my shampoo, there was something erotic about knowing she was going to smell like me.

Lathering her hair, I took my time and admired her as the suds washed down her body. She moaned at my fingers massaging the soap into her scalp.

"This is nice," she mumbled, her eyes closed in bliss.

"It's even better for me." I had the perfect view of her body, so I couldn't complain.

One of her eyes popped open, and she shook her head in response. I brought her head under the water and let the shampoo rinse from her hair. Her body was next, so I squeezed the scented wash into my hands and rubbed them together to form suds.

I started with her shoulders, rubbing down each arm and over to her breasts. I was getting hard again, wanting to see how good we could fuck in the shower. My mind drifted to all the positions I could take her in such a small space.

"You wanna go again, Cowboy?" She pulled me from my thoughts, nodding her head at my cock.

"See what you do to me?" I quipped, grinning. Aspen grabbed my shaft, stroking me up and down. There was no way in hell I was going to be able to make it go away now.

Aspen pressed her body against mine, and I was a goner. Not only did we go for round two in the shower, but there was round three while we waited for dinner to cook. I was even ready for number four, but she told me she needed a break and didn't know if she could handle another. We ended the night by lying on the couch, watching old movies we'd both seen multiple times. When she fell asleep in my lap, I carried her to my bed. Nothing could top seeing Aspen Westgrove fast asleep, wrapped in my bedsheets.

CHAPTER 39

Four Weeks Later

"No!" I shouted, my voice a mix of frustration and determination, as I ran toward Boone and Rhodes, who were carrying in the backdrop. They froze, exchanging a glance before looking back at me. "It can't go there. It has to go over by the cake stand! This is where Theo's chair is going. I've got a vision, okay?" With a grunt and a nod, they shifted, trudging toward the correct spot. I had spent the entire morning coordinating every detail, and my patience was wearing thin. Boone, though, was lucky I loved him so much.

Today was Theo's gender reveal party, and I had been obsessively planning for weeks. I was the only one who knew the secret. Well, me and Boone—but Theo didn't know that, and I planned to keep it that way. I'd been strong enough to hold back from telling Penny, though, knowing her, she'd have spilled the beans to the whole town by now.

My Pinterest board had come to life—everything was teddy bear-themed. There were cupcakes shaped like little bears, and a photo backdrop split between light and dark brown hues. Theo wasn't the type for "pink for girl" or "blue for boy"—she adored neutral tones.

Instead of the typical color reveal, I had commissioned a cake with a secret layer. The top piece of paper would burn away to reveal a word beneath, and I was *so* proud of myself for finding a baker who could pull it off.

The backyard, where Theo's mom had graciously hosted, was filled with decorations—a mix of bear-shaped balloons, bouquets of brown-toned balloons, and sweet wildflowers from the farm. I'd even gone so far as to make little honey pots for goodie bags, filled with Teddy Grahams to snack on.

"This looks amazing!" Theo's voice broke through my thoughts, and I turned to find her standing beside me, soaking in the results of my hard work. She looked breathtaking in her form-fitting dark brown dress, her growing belly just beginning to show at eighteen weeks. Her skin glowed, and the morning sickness had finally eased off. She was happier than I had ever seen her, and I couldn't help but feel a swell of pride for the incredible woman she was becoming.

"I think I outdid myself," I replied, placing my hands on her belly as I crouched, my voice filled with excitement. "And I can't wait for you to find out what this little munchkin is!"

Theo laughed, placing her hands over mine with the most loving smile. "Auntie A can't wait to meet you!"

"Whatever they are, they'll be spoiled," Theo murmured softly, the warmth of the moment wrapping around us.

"Damn right!" Penny called out from behind us, juggling two glasses of wine. She handed me one and kept the other for herself, and I gratefully took a long sip, feeling the relief of a well-earned break from the chaos.

Everyone was beginning to arrive—my parents, Mac, and Logan. Boone and Rhodes were already there, and so was Theo's mom. It wasn't a huge crowd, but she was surrounded by people who loved her, and that was what mattered most.

Boone appeared behind me, his arms slipping around my shoulders in that familiar, possessive way. He kissed my cheek gently, and I couldn't stop the smile that spread across my face. "Now, what can I do?" His voice was soft but full of eagerness, and

I adored that about him. Never once a complaint, always ready to help.

"The chair for Theo is in the garage," I said, pointing toward the rug beneath the balloon arch where I had set up a special little corner. "Could you grab it and set it over there?" I had gone to a local thrift store, and they'd been so kind to let me rent some vintage pieces—an old rocking chair, a quaint coffee table, and little trinkets to complete the look.

"Anything for you, Darling," he murmured, planting another soft kiss on my neck before heading off. I couldn't help but watch him go—his rugged physique and the way his jeans hugged his form, well...let's just say I was grateful for the view. I fanned myself, trying to ignore how hot it was outside.

Alone now, I took a moment to observe. Theo was greeting guests while Penny stood in the corner, her animated conversation with Mac a stark contrast to how content the rest of the party felt. My parents were chatting with Theo's mom. And then there was Rhodes, beer in hand, eyes locked on Theo. I noticed the longing in his gaze, and a sly smile tugged at my lips. That was a look I recognized all too well. I'd have to point it out to Theo later.

The party rolled on—cornhole was being played, music blasted through the speakers, and laughter filled the air. The food was perfect, catered by the town's one and only Italian restaurant, because Theo couldn't get enough of pasta right now.

Once the meal was finished, I knew it was time. I could feel the buzz of anticipation in the air, and I quickly stopped the music. I cupped my hands around my mouth and called, "Hello, everyone! Can I have your attention?"

I tried my best to project, but my voice wasn't cutting through. My dad, ever the showman, whistled loudly, and the conversations around us immediately quieted. Once the crowd was still, I continued, my voice shaky with excitement, "I think it's time we have the beautiful mom-to-be come up here so I can finally share this secret with you all!" A few people laughed, and Theo waddled over, a gleam of excitement in her eyes.

The cake sat perched on an old whiskey barrel, looking just as perfect as I'd envisioned—white icing with a bear holding neutral-colored balloons. The piece of wax paper, delicately placed, was waiting to be burned away, revealing the gender.

"Okay, you're going to light the paper on fire," I instructed, stepping back as I pulled a chair from the table to stand on. I needed the perfect angle for the photo. "When the paper burns away, the secret will be revealed."

Theo nodded, holding the lighter carefully. Her eyes were filled with a nervous excitement, and I couldn't help but smile at her anticipation.

"On the count of three," I said, holding up my camera. "Ready?"

"Oh my God! Yes!" she squealed, jumping up and down with that infectious energy.

"One...two...three!" the crowd counted, and I watched, heart pounding in my chest as Theo clicked the lighter, the flame flickering to life. She held it steady against the cake, and in an instant, the paper began to disappear.

Within seconds, the words were revealed: *baby girl.*

A million photos snapped in an instant, and the room erupted into cheers. Theo turned to the crowd, her voice loud and full of joy. "It's a girl!" The words were barely out of her mouth before I was on her, hugging her tightly, my heart swelling with happiness.

Penny rushed over, squealing, "I'm so happy for you!" Her voice was practically in my ear, but I didn't mind. It was pure joy.

"I knew it was a girl," Theo said, her voice warm with certainty. "I don't think I'd make a good boy mom."

As I watched her, my heart swelled even more—full of pride, happiness, and so much love. I had spent years being a quiet observer, watching life happen from the sidelines, never fully allowing myself to be a part of it. But now? Now, I was *living.*

Over the past few months, I had transformed in ways I never thought possible. I had stepped out of my shell, taken risks, and allowed myself to feel things I never had before. I was writing my first novel. I was in love, and I was in control of my own destiny. I had the power to create the life I wanted—and I was never going back to the girl who was afraid to take chances.

And through it all, there was Boone. The man who had broken down my walls, who loved me without hesitation, and who I knew, without a doubt, was worth every risk.

For the first time, I felt ready to take life by the horns and let that bitch buck.

THE END

AUTHOR'S NOTE

The story you read was a rough draft of the story titled, *The Story We Wrote* by Aspen Westgrove. The plot closely reflects real life events and characters which were used as foundation for her writing.

BONUS CHAPTER

Aspen

Checkmate.

I couldn't hold back the laugh that bubbled up when I saw Boone step out of his cabin. It was one of those moments when the more I tried not to laugh, the harder it became. I'd planned to wait until he left in the morning to spring the surprise on him, but the anticipation gnawed at me like a hunger I couldn't shake.

"What's going on?" Boone asked, stepping onto my porch in nothing but pajama pants, slippers, and a sweatshirt with the hood lazily pulled over his head. He was the picture of calm, but the tension in the air was electric. I couldn't lie to save my life, and as much as I tried to play it cool, my grin betrayed me.

"Nothing!" I squealed, but the giggles escaped faster than I could choke them back. My face flushed crimson, and I couldn't meet his gaze. My embarrassment was as obvious as the grin on my face. "Well," I added quickly, "nothing bad."

Boone's expression shifted to one of playful suspicion as he stood in front of me, hands on his hips. I was trapped now—his stare was too sharp, too knowing. My instinct was to hold my ground, to maintain my innocence, but in the face of him, I folded like paper.

"Fine!" I huffed, throwing my book aside and setting down my wine glass. I stood up, feeling the weight of the moment. "But you're going to have to figure it out. I'll give you a hint."

back.

Fuck, I loved this woman.

Her exposed, beautiful breasts were begging for attention. I moved my kisses from her lips to her jaw and down her neck. Taking my time, I lightly nipped at the skin as I made my way down.

I loved the soft pants and moans she made under my touch. Any man would fall apart at the sound of her need.

"You're mine, Darling," I mumbled in her ear, biting the lobe before directing my attention to the peak of her nipples. She let out a muffled "hmmm" as I dragged my tongue over the tip, playing with her soft skin. Her scent filled my nostrils, *blueberries.*

I watched her every move and reaction as I teased and flicked. She was so responsive to me. Her eyes rolled back, and she bit her lip—Aspen was putty in my hands.

My free hand moved between her legs, going straight for her entrance, the tip of my finger feeling her slit. She was already wet and it was all for me.

"What a good girl," I purred, taking her slickness and rubbing it up and down her center. I brought the finger to my mouth as I hovered over, licking her off me.

"Fuck," she said, rubbing herself against my leg for friction.

These were officially my favorite pair of jeans.

Pulling away, Aspen groaned in protest, but I quickly filled the void with my fingers again. Rubbing her clit, I applied slight pressure with my thumb as I pumped my other finger inside her.

"If you don't take these damn clothes off now, I'm going to do it myself," she hissed through her teeth. What the woman wants, she gets.

I didn't want to rush through this. I wanted to love and cherish her body. Aspen clearly had other plans. I learned quickly that she liked it rough and fast; she was not the type you made sweet love to, and I was okay with that.

Removing my shirt, I then tossed it on the floor, pausing for a moment to take in her beauty. She had tucked the wet strands of hair behind her ears and watched me with burning intent. I took off my pants and my boxers together, desperate to minimize the time holding me back from her.

Aspen laid back on her elbows to hold herself up. She had a slight smile on her face as she bit her lip, eyes fully on my cock—the definition of perfect.

I reached down and stroked myself with my hand, pumping as I thought of all the dirty things I wanted to do to her.

"How do you want my cock?" I asked, not faltering eye contact.

"I've never done it standing up," she confessed. Aspen looked at me through those long lashes, begging me with her hypnotizing blue eyes. I'd been put on this earth to make all her dreams come true, so fucking standing up it was.

Without hesitation, I scooped her in my arms and carried her to my bedroom door. Those curvy legs wrapped around my waist like she had done this a million times as her back slammed against the wood. My hard erection sat between us, the shaft lying against her wetness.

Aspen grabbed my face and crashed her lips against mine. We kissed with enough passion to set the world on fire.

Changing the angle, I placed my shaft at her entrance. Lining it up with nothing but pure determination, I drove inside her. She gasped into the kiss as I shoved deeper in, her warmth squeezing around my cock.

"You feel so fucking good," I groaned, working my cock inside her. She wasn't kissing me anymore; her head fell back against the door while she moaned my name repeatedly as I drove into her tight heat. Her pants and gasps charged me as I latched my mouth onto her neck and nibbled on the exposed column.

"Bring me to the bed," she demanded, and I liked it.

I carried her from the door without taking myself out of her. She wiggled in my hold, rocking against me, which felt too fucking good. I tossed her down on the bed and climbed over her, not giving her a moment to rest before diving back in. I wrapped

His eyes narrowed slightly, and a small smile tugged at the corner of his mouth. "Mmmm," Boone hummed, stepping closer until we were toe to toe, his presence overwhelming in the best way.

"Rodeo," I said, my voice teasing, watching him closely.

His eyes flickered with realization. "That damn bunny," he muttered, his smile turning into a grin. "I knew it was a terrible idea. Where is it?"

I grinned back, knowing exactly how this was going to play out. The bunny he'd won for me at the rodeo had become a permanent fixture in my living room, taking up way too much space for something so ridiculously large. It was practically a mascot at this point, and I'd been waiting for the perfect moment to playfully torment him with it. When he stepped into the shower tonight, I saw my chance. I snuck into his cabin, carefully planning the best way to surprise him.

I shrugged, my smile widening as Boone dashed down the porch steps. I followed him, heart racing with excitement. We entered his cabin together, and I watched him search every room with that intense look he got when he was trying to figure something out.

"If it were in here, there's no way I'd miss it," he muttered under his breath, and I bit my lip to keep from laughing.

"You're right, you would," I called out, following him closely.

He spun around suddenly, his face inches from mine. I looked up into his eyes—those dark, deep eyes that always seemed to see right through me. His gaze softened for a moment before he narrowed it in suspicion.

"My truck," he hissed.

I didn't need any more confirmation. He was on to me.

Boone hurried outside, and I couldn't stop myself from laughing as he approached the passenger side of his truck. I followed behind, barely able to hold it together.

When he saw what I'd done, I lost it completely. There, in the passenger seat, sat the giant pink bunny, wearing Boone's cowboy hat like it was the most natural thing in the world. The sight was too much—I doubled over, laughing hysterically.

Boone stood frozen, his back to me. Slowly, he lowered his head and shook it side to side, a low chuckle escaping his throat. When he turned around, his hands were back on his hips, and that mischievous grin stretched across his face. The playful challenge in his eyes sent a thrill racing through me.

"Surprise!" I said, unable to stop the laugh that followed. "I wanted you to—"

Before I could finish, Boone picked me up effortlessly, tossing me over his shoulder like I weighed nothing. My stomach flipped in a mix of surprise and excitement, my heart racing at the sheer intensity of his action.

"You think you're funny, Darling?" Boone's voice dropped into a growl, a smile tugging at the corner of his mouth. "I'll show you just how funny I think you are."

And with that, he carried me back inside his cabin, and all I could do was hold on and wait for whatever came next.

My core clenched at his voice dropping a few octaves. Usually, the consequences scared me, but I was willing to accept whatever Boone was about to do with open arms.

The front door slammed as Boone kicked it shut. He carried me past the kitchen and down the hall to his bedroom. Adrenaline was pumping through me, anticipation lingering at the thought of where this was about to go. I craved Boone in every way.

He threw me down on the bed and grabbed both of my ankles to flip me onto my stomach. He wasn't giving me an ounce of control; he was in charge, and I liked it. Even though he couldn't see my face, I grinned. This side of Boone was one of my favorites.

I felt him touch my hips and then dip into the waistband of my sweatpants. In one swift movement, he tore off my underwear and pants leaving me in my worn T-shirt. My ass was exposed, the skin reacting to the chill in the air.

Boone's hand found my ass, leaving a smack against the skin. I yelped in surprise but yearned for more. I lifted my ass slightly, wagging it to tease him. Out of my view, he huffed. I couldn't see anything he was doing, which added to the pleasure. There was a loud smack and a stinging sensation against the same skin. If I wasn't wet before, I definitely was now.

"You like that?" Boone asked, palming where he slapped, dulling the pain.

"Mm-hmm," I hummed into the bedding. He grabbed my hips and yanked upward so my ass was in the air. With another smack, he followed the sting with kisses on the raised flesh.

Need pulsed through me, a tangible sensation of emptiness, and Boone was the only thing that could fill it. The bed dipped behind me. Boone was climbing up to get into position, the soft skin of his cock brush against my ass and down to my center. He ran the tip along me. The anticipation was too much. I was growing frustrated. The teasing was pushing me over the edge. I knew he was doing it on purpose.

"I'm taking my time with you. Consider that the punishment," Boone taunted, still playing with me. He stopped rubbing his length against me and ran two fingers in its wake. There was slight pressure against my entrance that quickly disappeared. I groaned and shoved my face into the bed. I was dripping, needy, and desperate, waiting for him to push inside.

"Boone," I begged. I didn't recognize my voice as it came out more of a whimper.

"Tell me what you want." Boone removed his fingers from me, replacing it with his tongue. In one movement, he licked me from my clit to my entrance. My toes curled in pleasure, and I was taken by surprise at the wet sensation. Forming words was not a possibility at the moment, so I groaned instead.

Boone let out a devilish laugh. "I'm gonna need words, Darling."

"You. I need you. Now."

Deciding to put me out of my misery, Boone drove inside me.

BONUS EPILOGUE

Boone

Eight months later

A dull ache spread across my chest, a rush of pride I couldn't shake, as I watched Aspen sign book after book. She was more than I ever could've imagined, and with each moment, she amazed me even more.

It had only been six months since the release of her debut novel, *The Story We Wrote*, and already she was on the bestseller list.

Her book had taken the internet by storm, and I could barely keep up with the flood of love for her work. People had fallen head over heels for her characters, and, naturally, they'd fallen hard for the male lead, too. I couldn't help but laugh at some of the unfiltered comments she'd shown me—comments that were, well, a little *too* personal. The word "daddy" had never been thrown around so much in my life, and the one that had me cracking up was about how someone would "thank me for breaking their back." I had no idea what that meant, but the wild world of social media was buzzing with excitement. And all of it, *all of it*, was about the woman I loved. The woman who had my heart.

She sat at the pink-decorated table, surrounded by stickers, art prints of the characters she'd brought to life, and even little bracelets that mirrored the one I bought her at the farmer's market. There were recipe cards for her famous blueberry muffins, and fans lined up, excited to meet her, take pictures, and get books signed.

Then her eyes met mine. I saw the slight curve of her lips as she tucked a strand of hair behind her ear, the shy motion that had always been hers. That little gesture always gave away what she was thinking: *nervous*. It struck me like a punch to the gut, because, despite everything she had achieved, she was still the same Aspen—the one I'd first noticed years ago, sitting on a park bench, lost in a book.

The sight of her brought a distant memory rushing forward, unbidden.

It was the summer after my sophomore year.

The countdown to summer had begun. I could feel the pull of freedom deep in my bones, the desire to escape the confines of the classroom where I was forced to learn about things I didn't care about. The only thing I'd learned this year was how to fill out a few extra shirts with muscle, thanks to my afternoons spent on the ranch. And I'd also learned how those muscles brought around the girls, which—honestly—wasn't the worst thing.

But it was the promise of getting my permit that had me most excited. By December, I'd have my license. I could go wherever I wanted, whenever I wanted. The world would open up for me.

I'd made it a habit to walk to the middle school every day after school to meet Ellie, my little sister. It wasn't ideal, but it was the routine until I got a truck. And once I had my wheels, I could finally pick Ellie up and bring her straight home. Until then, I was stuck playing chauffeur.

One day, as I stood under the shade of the oak trees lining the road, I scanned my surroundings, the streets mostly empty with only a few people walking the track at the park.

And then I saw her.

She was sitting on the bench, book in hand, completely lost in the pages. Her blond hair caught the light, a color that matched the sun. Aspen Westgrove. The girl who had always intrigued me. She had grown that year, no longer the quiet, withdrawn girl everyone thought her to be. She had become someone I couldn't quite figure out. Something about the way she could lose herself in a book for hours, a quietness I would never have, pulled at me.

I didn't get it. I hated reading, hated being still. I was chaos in a cowboy hat, as my parents liked to say. But Aspen? Aspen had this peace about her. She was content in a way I'd never experienced. I couldn't help but wonder what it would take to make her a little wild—maybe to get her to throw her head back and laugh under the stars, her hair tousled, carefree. I could picture it.

But the thing was, Aspen had never paid attention to me. Not even once. Even when I went out of my way to make myself noticeable—leaning against the school tree, flashing my smile, tossing out playful comments—she never noticed. She was oblivious to me, the boy everyone else seemed to fawn over.

My stomach tightened with frustration. She wasn't like the others. And maybe, just maybe, that made me want her even more.

"What are you doing, creep?" Ellie's voice pulled me from my thoughts, her laughter ringing out as she must've noticed where my gaze had been. I had been staring for too long.

"Just ask her out already," she teased with a shake of her head, walking past me toward the elementary school.

Ellie didn't get it. She didn't understand why I couldn't just go up to Aspen and ask her out. But I didn't think a girl like that would want a guy like me.

What could she possibly see in me?

I blinked, shaking myself back into the present, back to the woman who had become everything I never dared to dream of. I wasn't that boy anymore—the one who craved attention, the one who thrived on chaos. Aspen wasn't the same either. The girl who sat quietly on the bench, lost in her book, had transformed into a woman who had captured the world's attention.

But some things stayed the same. Her nose was still buried in a book. She still had that look of quiet concentration that made me want to lose myself in her.

Now, as I stood there, watching her work her magic at that book signing, I realized something. The boy who had never believed in himself, the one who thought he didn't stand a chance, would have never imagined this—standing here beside the woman he loved, supporting her.

I thanked my lucky stars every single night on that porch swing that Aspen had decided I was the one worth taking a chance on. That I was the one who had gotten the girl.

ACKNOWLEDGMENTS

I want to begin by thanking all the amazing people I met on Bookstagram. If it weren't for any of you, I'd never be writing this story today. I met so many amazing people through social media who ignited my love for reading and pushed me to write.

I want to thank my fiancé, Nate, who was with me through the whole journey. The endless nights he would listen to me go on and on about something I was writing or about the content I wanted to make. Not to mention, all the people he told about my Bookstagram or the fact I was writing this book. If it wasn't for you, I wouldn't have pushed myself to do this. Thank you for being proud of me.

Thank you to my alpha readers, beta readers, and ARC readers who helped make this debut book a reality. All of your feedback and time were never taken for granted and I love each and every one of you.

Thank you to Keona, @whatskeonareading, for taking a chance on me and being my sidekick during the process. Without you, I doubt anything would have gone out on time. Also, thank you for putting up with a million 'wait, when am I posting that?' texts. You were my saving grace when I was feeling completely overwhelmed. You stepped in, took charge, and set me straight. I needed that, desperately.

Thank you to my agent, Dani. I can't even believe this is where I am right now and I have you to thank for making it all happen!

ABOUT THE AUTHOR

M. Hartley is a hopeless romantic with a soft spot for small-town charm and fictional cowboys with big hearts (and even bigger... you know). When she's not writing love stories over a glass of sweet red wine, she's spoiling her dog, Hank, or feeding her Swedish Fish addiction. Outside of writing, M. Hartley is a mental health advocate and therapist working in the community. She believes love has the power to heal, and that books are the perfect escape. Whether you're taking a mental vacation to a cozy small town or riding on the back of a dragon into battle, the possibilities are endless. M. Hartley writes romance because she believes there's nothing better than a love story that lingers long after the last page.